# WAITING
## ON THE
# RIVER

# WAITING ON THE RIVER

## TRAVIS ERWIN

For information contact

editor@barbadumbooks.com

or visit

www.BarbadumBooks.com

Cover Design by Cover Quill

ISBN: 978-1-7323257-0-8

First Edition: August 2018

10 9 8 7 6 5 4 3 2 1

*This novel is lovingly dedicated
to my wife, Connie ...*


*... absolutely
the ace
of all river cards.*

# 1

Darkness fell early this time of year, and with it came relief and a resolute comfort not unlike the feeling of being tucked carefully into bed after a long, hard day. Nightfall meant this, her little corner of earth, was hidden away out of the spotlight.

Logic told her Eagle's Rest, Idaho, was about as far from the spotlight as she could get, be it sunny or pitch black outside, but no matter where she called home this month, Lindsay Parker struggled to relax. Even here at the Talon Cafe she scrutinized not only the faces that stopped in for a bite to eat, but also the license plates of every strange car passing through town. The latter being a new habit.

Back in Seattle she would've gone crazy trying to maintain such a vigil, but the remoteness of Eastern Idaho held advantages. Still, she couldn't get careless, because here, she couldn't fade away into the busy throng of city-life if someone came nosing around. Here, she was vulnerable in ways she'd never been. But here, she felt a burgeoning hope long absent in her travels.

In Eagle's Rest she was not a stranger, and neither was anyone else. That combination made for all kinds of terrifying possibilities. Her perch in the passenger seat of Cody's

Jeep afforded a good view of the town's whopping six blocks along Idaho State Highway 32, highway in name only. Ray Everham's blue heeler loped across the road, disappearing into the shadows beyond the glow of the town's sparse streetlights. The dog was but one of several that had the run of the town.

On this Wednesday evening, there didn't appear to be a person or vehicle, not even so much as a stray pooch, out of place.

The plastic windows on Cody's CJ-7 did a poor job holding back the November chill, but Lindsay didn't mind. She liked the cold and was glad fall had given way to winter. Yet another thing that came early here, in the shadow of the Tetons, where dates on the calendar didn't matter nearly as much as the arctic winds.

Outside the Jeep, Cody rubbed his gloved hands together and cupped them over his ears as he waited for the tank to fill. Unlike her, he often complained about the cold. Peculiar, given he was born and raised here in the Rockies, and had spent his winters outside working the ski lifts. Where Lindsay grew up, they were lucky if it snowed once or twice a year.

Gassed and ready to go, Cody cranked both the ignition and the heater before he pulled the Jeep's door closed. "Swear to God, I'm moving to California before next season."

Lindsay said nothing. She'd tried California. Southern, Northern, and in-between without finding much of anything that made her want to go back.

Cody turned left out of Ray's Service Station. The wrong direction.

"I thought we were going to the movies?"

He shook his head. "Want to show you something first."

"What?"

Cody didn't bother to answer. A few minutes later he turned off the pavement and onto the National Forest gravel road that they'd come out to back in the summer. Then they hiked or mountain biked or simply hung out together on a blanket beneath the towering trees, but this time of year snow covered most places. The twin beams of his headlights provided the only light as far as the eye could see.

"Unless we turn around we won't make it over to Driggs in time to catch the movie."

He mumbled something but kept driving down the dark gravel, and increasingly snow-packed, road. He eased off the gas pedal only after they fishtailed around an icy, uphill bend in the road.

"Where are we going?"

"I want to show you something," he repeated before adding, "but I might have to stop and lock in my hubs. Snow's deeper up here than I counted on."

"Just tell me where we're going."

"It's a surprise." He leaned forward, squinting at the spot where his headlights stabbed through the darkness. He'd slowed way down, but the Jeep still slipped its way along, losing traction in the ever-increasing powder.

"Cody, this is stupid. We're going to get stuck out here." She gripped the sissy bar, dividing her attention between his tense face and the narrow, dark road. "And I'm not dressed to dig or push."

He grinned, but only for a second. "I've never been stuck in my life, but least we'd have a good story to tell."

"All your stories suck."

"How you figure?" He grinned, apparently unaware that she was dead serious.

"You leave out vital facts, ramble off track, and usually

finish with some vague assumption that the rest of the world thinks exactly like you. Finding the point to your stories is like hunting a pine cone after a blizzard. Maybe it's buried there somewhere, but never worth the effort it takes to find it."

Still he grinned on. "Well, I think I'm a bad-ass story-teller."

"And the fact you think getting stuck in the snow—on a pitch-black night—in the middle of nowhere, is anything but an act of stupidity proves my point."

Lindsay could hear the old men now. Gathered at the counter of the Talon Cafe in the morning while she refilled their coffee mugs. *Yeah Joe, I reckon down there in Tulsa there ain't no snow to get stuck in.* She wasn't from Tulsa, but Lindsay was perfectly happy to let them think that. *But up here in God's country, He chooses to weed out the tourists and tree-huggers by making life a bit more challenging.*

Joe, or Ray, or Stuart … whoever happened to be within earshot would chime in, *Yep, ain't everybody cut out to be an Idahoan.*

They'd say it all with a smile and in a very poor imitation of her Oklahoma twang, but Lindsay wasn't dumb. The verdict on her was still out with most everybody except Cody and Janine. The Talon's regulars liked her well enough, but not enough to overlook the fact she was a foreigner in their world. Never mind the fact Cody, a lifelong resident and true-blue Idahoan, was the one currently driving them straight to Stupidville.

"Stop!"

Cody hit the brakes. The CJ-7 angled sharp right and they slid a solid twenty yards, stopping three feet shy of a massive pine.

"What the hell?" He looked at her like she'd lost her

mind.

In a way, she had, but Lindsay couldn't go along with this journey another second.

"I'm freaked out, confused, and just a little pissed off you brought me out here this time of night when I thought we were going to the movies."

Cody was back to grinning, but she wasn't through. "It's not funny. *When* we get stuck. Not if, but *when*. Because if you keep barreling blind down this stupid, dark-ass road we damn sure will. And when we do it won't be you forced to listen to every old man in town say, *'Damn Janine, these eggs are slimier than a Targhee road come November.'* No, they won't even mention your damn name. It'll be mine, the tree-hug ging, vegan, Southern girl that hears all about it."

He laughed. "Ahh hell, Linds, everybody's over that tree-hugging vegan stuff. We all figured out quick enough you weren't like that idiot who brought you here."

Jabbing her finger at Cody she plunged on. "And if they do mention your name it will be Ray Everham saying some-thing like, *'You and Cody shoulda gotta room at the Kozy-Inn. Hell, I'll set you up a little cot in the g'rage at the Fill'n Station if you need a place that bad. Got a barrel a lube sitting there and everything.'*" She was trying to be funny, but the fact Cody just kept grinning that stupid smile that displayed the small chip in his right front tooth pissed her off all the more. The chip made him look even younger than the twenty-five he'd turned last week. Four years and a few months younger than her.

"Quit staring at me, and turn this damn thing around."

He shook his head. "Can't. You're too gorgeous for me to even look away."

She rolled her eyes.

"I like when you get all stoked up and your cheeks turn red."

"It's too dark in here for you to see my cheeks."

"It's not that dark."

He was right. What with his radio display, and the Jeep's headlights reflecting off the pine's large trunk, and the snow all around, it wasn't near as dark inside the Jeep as it was down the stretch of road and surrounding forest. Still his flattery wasn't going to lead her where she didn't want to go.

"Wipe that look off your face, because if you think for a second I'm giving Ray Everham's innuendos credence out here in the middle of this frozen damn forest, you're even crazier than he is."

Cody shrugged and dropped his voice a few octaves. "I'm here. You're here. There's not another soul around for miles."

"Turn the Jeep around."

"Your loss," he grinned and shifted in reverse. The grin faded when the back wheel spun without grabbing hold. He tried a few more times. The CJ-7 rocked but didn't move. He lifted his hands at her pained expression. "Relax. I'll lock in the hubs and we'll be out of here in a minute." A wave of frigid air rushed in when he stepped out into the dark roadway.

Folding her arms across her chest, Lindsay stared beyond the big pine tree and out into the forest. Snow crystals glimmered under the headlights giving the scene a fancy Christmas card feel.

Cody crossed in front of the Jeep, blocking the light for a second and spoiling her respite from reality. If they got stuck out here he for damn sure wouldn't be singing "Winter Wonderland."

He crouched by the front wheel for a minute before coming around to her side and opening her door. "Take the wheel for a second. I wanna give a little push to make sure we get out." He stood back to let her get out of the Jeep. Using his teeth he pulled the glove off his right hand as he stepped into the glow of the headlights.

In that half-a-heartbeat it took for him to drop to a knee, Lindsay realized getting stuck in the snow was the least of her problems tonight.

Past experience should have made it easier for her to re-act. But no, she stood there—helpless, hopeless, heartless—and silently watched Cody pull that small velvet box from his pocket.

# 2

Blue Riggins studied the men gathered around the table before peeking at his own cards. Three of spades, ten of diamonds. When the bet came to him, he shoved the worthless draw forward folding without a word. Movie Boy tripled the blind. Blue pegged the actor for a high pair, most likely kings or aces. Mr. Cool called and so did Donnie, meaning he too held a decent hand. The next three gamblers folded, while the fat man at the far end of the table called. Already in for the big blind, the big guy's action gave Blue no clue if he held a decent hand, or was dumping good money after bad.

Lighting a Marlboro, he studied the other players. Movie Boy winked at Blue and smiled. His perfectly capped teeth gleamed, through the cloud of smoke hanging over the green felt. "That's your fourth smoke in a row. How about taking it easy on those of us who enjoy our health?"

Blue took a long drag and let the smoke roll from his nostrils. His eyes flickered to the pungent cigar dangling between the fat man's lips and down the table to the cup of thick-brown snuff spit in front of Donnie. "Glad to know someone taught you how to count between takes, but I reckon even Hollywood has teachers for schoolboys."

The grin vanished from the actor. "I'm twenty-three."

"My mistake." Blue stared hard at Movie Boy before cutting a quick glance over at Donnie. "I was told you're in some hotshot show about high school. Wouldn't know myself. I don't watch much television."

"Everyone in the business works down in age, though if I keep inhaling your poison, I'll be in make-up twice as long when shooting starts up."

Blue took another long drag before pinching the smoking end of his cigarette between his thumb and forefinger. Rising to his feet, he slid the half-smoked Marlboro back into the package. "I'll save this for later. Would hate to overwork the make-up department." He stepped over behind Donnie and rubbed his friend's smooth cheek. "How come you never told me my smoking was damaging your silky skin?"

"Never bothered me, 'course you didn't use to smoke all that much." Donnie kept his left hand on top of his cards the way he always did with a decent hand. "Me and Blue traveled a million miles on the circuit together."

Movie Boy curled his lip. "Weathered may be an acceptable attribute for ex rodeo stars, but lead actors have to maintain their good-looks."

"We gonna play poker, or gossip about beauty secrets?" Fat Man, to whom the suite belonged, pointed at the girl the casino had sent to deal. "Let's see the flop before pretty boy demands botox."

She turned an ace, jack, ten. Mr. Cool bet two grand. Donnie's fingers slid off his cards. He folded when the action came to him. Movie Boy and Fat Man called. Blue could almost guarantee Movie Boy had three aces by his lack of eye-contact with the fat man, who repeatedly checked his down cards telling Blue he still needed a card to make a straight. Only Mr. Cool was a mystery, as he'd been the whole two hours Blue had spent at the table. Most likely his eyes were his tell. At least he had sense enough to wear sunglasses.

People were a hell of a lot easier to read than the animals he dealt with when he worked from a saddle. Now that he made his living at felt tables, his work was easier in every way. And a lot more profitable.

"Y'all should hear some of the stuff me and Blue went through together." Donnie lifted his cap and scratched his sandy blonde hair. The dimples in his cheeks deepened with a shit-eating grin. He was all-too eager to talk, now that he was out of the hand. Blue paced around the room wishing his friend would keep quiet, but that was like asking a dog not to bark.

"We grew up back in Texas. Only twenty miles apart, but I didn't meet him until I got to Oklahoma State. He was a senior by then. And a two-time steer wrestling runner-up at the College National Finals."

"Runner-up," Movie Boy said with a shrug. "That's almost like winning."

The dealer turned over the nine of hearts. Fat Man didn't look at his cards. Now the question remained, how high was his straight. Mr. Cool checked, passing the buck to Fat Man who didn't disappoint. He shoved ten grand in chips forward. "Let's make this interesting."

Blue stopped his pacing and studied the actor. Unless another ace came on the river he was dead, but would he fold three aces? A good gambler always knew when he was beat. The kid slid an extra twenty-five hundred toward the center of the table. Mr. Cool matched the bet without hesitation. Blue pegged him for the high straight.

"He oughta unretire and come back on the road with me next spring." Donnie started back in again. "My shoulder will be ready by then." He moved his left arm in broad circles to demonstrate its fitness. "Damn bull mighta won the battle, but I'll ride the bastard yet. Can't keep a good man down." Donnie shot Blue a look. "Least not all of us."

"Drop it," Blue said.

"You can't retire. It's been four years so you can't still claim your knee as an excuse. You're long healed, and hell, you ain't but thirty-two and now you don't have nothing tying you down."

"I said drop it."

The river card came a deuce. No factor.

"What's your knee got to do with it?" Movie Boy asked. "Horses do all the work for you guys."

Mr. Cool led off the wagering with fifteen grand. The large bet wiped the smirk from Movie Boy's face. He folded in silence. Fat Man called only to see his queen-high straight topped by Mr. Cool's king.

Blue bent and scooped his chips. Pocketing them he said, "You boys are too tough for me. Reckon I'll bow out."

Fat Man frowned at Donnie. "You said he'd play all day and all night. What kind of poker pro runs from a friendly game like this?"

Blue walked out of the room as if he hadn't heard. He reached the elevators before Donnie caught up.

"Where ya going? You can't be up more than four or five grand. Those guys have deep pockets."

"I don't need their money." The doors slid open, and Blue stepped in.

Donnie followed. "But I do. And they only let me in because I said you'd play. Makes 'em feel good to be at the same table with a real pro they've seen on TV. Play for me. Play for the excitement of the chase."

"I'm sick of chasing things, tired of looking at cards. And sick and damn tired of listening to rich, cocky assholes think they know how to play poker because they've seen it on TV." The elevator began its descent.

"Don't be mad because you're getting sorry hands. Your luck'll turn. Always has. Remember that summer you didn't cash for ten straight rodeos, and then BAM, you couldn't lose?"

Blue shook his head. "It's not about the cards. Everyone up there was predictable as hell. Including you. Quit touching your cards every time you have a decent hand."

Donnie's brows pinched together. "I have a tell?"

The elevator reached the bottom. Blue cocked a don't-be-so-stupid eyebrow at his friend.

"And you're just now letting me know? After all the money you've taken from me?"

Blue surveyed the casino floor. Slot machines chimed all around. Tourists crouched before the one-armed bandits praying to hit big. "I'm leaving," he said.

"Okay, how about this? You take a break. I'll go up and tell them you'll be back in an hour."

Blue started to explain he was leaving Vegas, and not just the game, but he stopped. He'd covered thousands of miles with Donnie at his side, but there were still things he couldn't say to his friend. Things he couldn't say to anyone.

A bellhop stepped off the other elevator. Blue motioned for the young man. "Shawn, find Gloria and tell her I want to check out. I'll be in the bar." He handed Shawn a black chip to make sure he hurried.

"Yes sir, Mr. Riggins, right away."

Donnie followed along to the bar. "Checkout? Ain't you gonna stay in town for The Finals?"

"No. I'm gone soon as I find Gloria."

"Ah, hell, Blue. Stick around for the rodeo. Afterward I'll ride back home with you instead of flying. It'll be like the good ol' days. Me and you eating up asphalt all the way back to Texas."

"I'm not going home. Not for a while anyway. And you know what I've always said about the finals."

"Yeah, yeah. *You ain't gonna watch 'em until you're in 'em.* But you're retired."

Blue turned his back on Donnie and raised his hand to get the bartender's attention.

Donnie leaned both elbows down on the bar and stuck his nose up close to Blue's face. "You ain't ever gonna qualify unless you come back."

Without looking at his friend, Blue said, "Some dreams die hard."

# 3

Guilt and shame. The wicked duo had long been Lindsay's chief enemies. Old hurts and past regrets had dogged her for years, but tonight fresh wounds kept her awake deep into the night. Lindsay missed the room across the hall. She'd been stupid to think of it as her own these past months. She'd gotten entirely too comfortable here in this house. In this town.

She should've predicted Cody's proposal. Should've realized her place in this house was tenuous.

The warped plastic mini-blinds in this room did a poor job blocking the glare from the security light over in the Talon's parking lot. Her brain did an even worse job filtering the remorse she felt over treating Cody so badly.

Wednesday turned into Thursday, and still she couldn't erase that look on his face.

*No.*

The cruelest of words. Definite, and condemning. Sharp, yet blunt. Quick, but never painless.

She'd tried to avoid it, tried to cut him off.

*Put it away and stand up.*

Those had been her first words, but Cody was too determined, too naive, too certain to be swayed so easily.

Standing there in that dark road with the Jeep's head-lights illuminating him, she'd refused to look at his face. She picked out a spot just above his head and bit her lip to keep from crying while he delivered his own death sentence ... "Lindsay, will you marry me?"

*No.*

She'd said it before. To two other men. Both of whom she'd thought she loved at the time.

She'd managed to hold her tears. At least that much was easier this time. Lindsay had no delusions about being in love with Cody. That didn't mean she didn't cringe at hurting his feelings, at breaking his heart.

They'd stood there for a minute or two not saying any-thing. The vapor of their breath the only sign either was breathing. Yet, even that small sign fleeting, as the little white clouds vanished as quickly as they came.

That's what she usually did after these situations. Vanish. Quickly. Quietly.

But she was sick of leaving places because she had to. She was tired of running away. Just once she wanted to stay. But that wasn't possible. Not even on that dark, snow-cov-ered road. Cody had moved first. Standing, he nodded once before moving to the driver's door of the Jeep. She followed suit, and got in without speaking. He shifted the Jeep into re-verse and backed up without the tires slipping even the slight-est little bit.

The ride back proved icy nonetheless. Cody found his voice about the time they turned onto pavement.

"I didn't mean right now." He cut his eyes her direction, but she said nothing. "I wish you'd have at least looked at the ring."

She simply stared down the road, maintaining an expression colder than the black night air.

"I just wanted to show you I'm completely devoted to you."

A lifeline. That's all he'd wanted. A way to shrug off her rejection. But she couldn't, wouldn't, toss him one.

"With Missy coming back and all," he said, his voice dropping. The last shred of enthusiasm evaporated at the mention of his high school sweetheart.

Lindsay didn't speak until he pulled up behind The Talon, at the house where she rented a room from Janine. The very same house he used to bring Missy home to. That series of facts screwed her up. No doubt the scenario completely scrambled Cody's brain. Still, she wanted to remove any doubt from his mind before disappearing inside.

"I'm sorry, Cody. I like you, but I don't love you." He flinched as if she'd slapped him. That didn't stop her from adding, "Chances are, I never will."

That had been hours ago. Now alone in the dark, Lindsay came to the conclusion things would never quite be the same here in Eagle's Rest.

Road weary from the gypsy life, she wasn't going to run this time, even if staying meant standing face-to-face with her past. Only the recent past, which was easier to confront on so many levels than long-ago hurts. Still, walking away from flaming bridges was her thing. She'd done just that time and again, but this would be the first time she stuck around to watch the trusses burn.

Cody couldn't love her either. Not truly. This had to be some lust-driven, wild-haired decision. A reaction to news of Missy's return. Tomorrow morning he'd drive over to Jackson Hole to spend Thanksgiving with his mother, giving Lindsay a day to figure things out. Sliding out of bed, she peeked between the blinds to scan what she could see of town. A delicate lacework of frost covered the car windows.

Nothing stirred. Not even a lonesome wandering dog.

She stood there a long time and might have stayed until the sun came up, but then Lindsay heard Janine moving down the hall. Her boss, friend, and landlady would be getting ready to make the three-hour drive to reclaim her daughter and bring her back for a holiday reunion.

Lindsay wondered what her own family was doing. Sleeping probably, or her mom might be awake. It was an hour later in Oklahoma. She could be up baking or getting the turkey ready for the oven.

Lindsay sighed and shook her head to clear those images. Time to get out and breathe some fresh air.

Fumbling in the shadows, she found the necessary clothes to fight off the Idaho chill. The layers would keep her warm until her morning jog created sufficient body heat. Running in these icy conditions required more motivation than back in Seattle, and it had taken her a good while to get used to the higher altitude, but the lack of traffic lent her runs a solitude the city could never provide.

She knocked on the bathroom door and spoke loudly so Janine could hear over the running shower. "I'm going out for my run! Drive safe. I'll follow your instructions so I don't screw anything up!"

Janine's muffled reply was hard to decipher, but Lindsay didn't want to engage in a real conversation anyway, so she bound her thick, dark hair into a ponytail, walked down the hall, and took off into the predawn shadows setting out at a steady pace.

The first fifteen or twenty minutes were always the hardest. The road she liked best climbed a steady, and sometimes steep, grade nearly the entire three miles to the Targhee National Forest boundary. Not the same road Cody had driven her down, but an actual paved road that led to a big loop and half a dozen primitive campsites. It was her favorite route, but today, the cold made her teeth hurt each time she inhaled so she didn't know if she'd make the entire nine-mile loop or cut it short.

Stars glimmered overhead though the sky had begun to lighten in the east. Her feet hitting the pavement provided the only sound, until a lone pickup, emitting thick grey exhaust motored past at the edge of town.

A dozen years ago, she put in five miles every morning before school, and another ten or fifteen in the evening, regardless of the weather. That had been her sophomore year, when she still dreamt of glory. When she ran for the hope of a cross-country scholarship to Oklahoma State, OU, or at the very least Tulsa. When she still believed running was the key to her future. Everything changed when she slowed down long enough for Rusty Hawkins to catch her.

Lindsay kicked her muscles into a higher gear. A crow called out in the shadow-filled forest to her right. The bird's wings flapped amongst the branches, mostly bare this time of year. The Tetons loomed before her. Focusing her attention on the tallest white-capped peak, she pushed harder. Just her, the birds, and the Tetons. Exactly how she liked it.

Her Nikes pounded the narrow road until her ribs ached and she focused solely on the physical pain and the thump of her own heartbeat. If only she could run forever. But her muscles, like her brain, could only take so much abuse. Several miles short of the loop, she slowed to a walk, and laced her fingers behind her head. Filling her lungs with the thin, oxygen-deprived air, she counted to thirty, then turned around and jogged back toward a nice hot shower.

His shoulders ached from the all-night drive and his eyelids were heavy as silver dollars, but he was getting close. The glowing green numbers on the dashboard taunted him. A quarter after six. Daybreak would be here before he could sleep, but only a few more miles separated Blue from his bed, and what he hoped would be a dreamless slumber.

Actually his bed lay mere feet behind him, hitched to his truck. He could've found a place to pull over and park hours ago, but Blue refused to stop until he reached the exact spot his wife chose their first visit to the Tetons. Staci would never believe he'd given up tents, Coleman stoves, and rock ring fires, for the sake of comfort. She would have teased him about this RV and its king-size bed, leather couch, built-in fireplace, and shower with overhead skylight. Other than their last trip, when it rained nonstop for five straight days, the two of them always roughed it out in the woods.

The truck and RV cost Blue nearly twice what they'd spent to build their house back in Texas. These days, the pickup and thirty-seven-foot travel trailer were his home. The place back in Texas lay abandoned.

Drowsily drifting into the past, Blue recalled the good times he and Staci shared on their treks to Idaho. Up here, in these mountains, he could almost hear her laughter ... feel the warmth of her body ... smell the pine needles in her hair ...

His neck unsteady, as the legs of a newborn colt, Blue didn't resist as his head tilted forward, and his heavy lids slid closed.

The pickup lurched—shuddered.

Blue jerked his head up, and yanked the wheel.

Gravel pinged the fender wells. The travel trailer fish-tailed—pulling the truck to the side.

Headlights flashed against forest trees.

Tires squealed.

White-knuckled, Blue struggled to keep the truck pointed straight ahead. A vision flashed by in a burst of light. A woman on the side of the road. "Staci," he whispered as the big black Ford skidded past the apparition and finally came to a shuddering halt thirty yards down the road.

Out of breath and unsure what he'd seen, Blue flung open the door and peered into the darkness. The stench of singed rubber hung in the air.

He slid from the pickup and moved toward the rear of the vehicle before she again came into view. His heart pounded and he swallowed hard.

She stepped closer. The excitement left him in a rush.

A stranger. He should've known better than to believe in ghosts.

The woman paused near the rear of the trailer, where the amber running lights cast an eerie glow across her apprehensive, yet pretty face. Now that he'd gotten a good look, she didn't much resemble his wife. Maybe in height, but this woman had dark hair, not blonde. And a ponytail. Staci always kept her hair too short for a ponytail. Not that he had time to notice any of this skidding past. Hope, not logic, led to his confusion.

Blue ran his fingers across his stubbled cheek. "You okay?"

The woman nodded. "I think so." She wrapped her arms across her chest as if hugging herself. "What happened?"

"I dozed off coming 'round that corner," he answered.

"The tires slipped off the shoulder, and I yanked the wheel too hard. I'm lucky the whole damn thing didn't tip." He shivered, having forgotten how cold it got up here this time of year.

Her eyes darted nervously.

"Sorry for the scare," he said, still shook from confusing this woman for his wife.

"It happened so fast I didn't really have time to be scared," she answered. "But you did get my heart rate up. I don't usually see much traffic jogging out here."

Blue frowned. It couldn't be more than a degree or two above zero. A person would have to be crazy to take off before sunrise and jog in these temperatures. He tried to remember if there was a cabin nearby or some other reason for her to be way out here. She seemed anxious already, but he couldn't drive away and leave her stranded on the side of the road. "You need a ride somewhere?" he asked in the same calm, even tones he usually reserved for horses.

She shook her head and took a step back. "No, I'm fine."

Blue tried to look as harmless as possible, but he sensed her eagerness to escape. "You sure? I don't mind." He was reluctant to leave, because despite the physical differences between them, something about the jogger reminded him of Staci.

She nodded. "The jog back to town will do me good. I'll be fine." Turning on her heels, she took off.

Standing alone in the middle of the cold black road, he watched the woman disappear around the curve. He'd never know why she reminded him of his wife.

Not that it mattered. The biggest difference was clear.

She was alive. Staci was not.

4

Still trembling from the unexpected encounter, Lindsay kept close watch over her shoulder. Running alone, in the wee hours of predawn, was nothing new to her, and she'd never been in any real danger of being hit. Not over on the opposite shoulder. But the threat of being struck wasn't what unnerved her.

That voice. That accent.

Eager to escape both, she kicked her muscles into a higher gear and again cast a look behind her. The road was empty.

The man had been friendly and apologetic, even offered to help. There in the darkness, she hadn't been able to tell much about him other than he was tall and broad shouldered. Yet his every word sent a shiver down her spine that had nothing to do with the frigid cold. A chilly reminder that no matter how comfortable she got, how far she ran, the past would nip at her heels.

At the edge of town, she slowed to a walk and quit looking over her shoulder.

She walked past the handful of houses, the snowmobile and ski rental shop, the town's lone gas station, and the Kozy-Inn, all quiet at this early hour. But not even the sight of the Talon Cafe settled the all-too-familiar dread lodged in her bones, because her workplace and refuge in this town looked strange without the usual array of battered Jeeps and pickups out front. On a normal morning, she returned to a dozen men lined up at the counter-line waiting on Janine to fill their coffee mugs.

Cutting across the empty gravel lot, Lindsay went around back, to the house. She wished Janine were home, but her friend would not be back for hours. This morning there would be no distractions.

Blue pulled his rig into the clearing and parked. For the next half hour, he lowered the RV, leveled the frame, and chocked the wheels. As he finished, the sun rose and filtered through the bare tree limbs until the soft gray light chased away the darkness.

Inside, the trailer smelled dusty and stale from lack of use. He never slept in it while in Vegas, preferring the convenience of the suite the casino offered in exchange for him playing in their poker room. Blue opened a kitchen window to let in some cool fresh air. Later, he would stock up on supplies, but first, he needed rest.

In bed he stared up at the ceiling, still bothered by ghosts and his own unanswered questions. What would he have said had the roadside vision truly been his wife?

That answer never came.

Neither did sleep. An hour ago he'd been too tired to keep his rig on the road, now the idea of dozing off seemed as foreign as jogging in the wee hours of the morning. His drowsiness had almost caused an accident. Had that woman had been on the other side of the road, he very well could have killed her. That sober realization gave his mind more to dwell upon as he laid there wishing for the sort of peace only sleep could bring.

Light spilled into the room despite the closed blinds. Turning over, he piled a pillow on top of his head. His stomach rumbled. He needed sleep, but how long had it been since he ate? Dinner in Vegas yesterday? No, he'd bought some jerky at a truck stop in Utah.

His stomach growled again.

Blue sat up on the edge of the bed, pulled on his boots, and buttoned on a clean shirt. He was kidding himself. Hunting memories while ignoring reality. Gamblers called it chasing good money with bad. The rest of the world called it disillusionment.

First thing tomorrow, after he'd gotten a decent night's sleep he would drift away and find a new place to while away a few weeks. But he couldn't leave the area without stopping in The Talon to see Janine one last time. Her food was as close to a home cooked meal as he'd get anytime soon and a hot meal  in his belly might settle his unease.

Rounding the curve from this morning, he shook his head at the memory of that jogger and his own stubborn stupidity. Stupidity that had made him think coming back to Idaho was a good idea. And the stubbornness that had kept him driving long beyond the point of common sense.

The disappointment of realizing the jogger was a stranger lingered like a bad taste in his mouth. Yep, Blue hated to admit it, but he was, indeed, one stupidly stubborn SOB.

# 5

Even after all these months, Lindsay felt strange to be alone inside Janine's. Like a trespasser with no right to be there. Lindsay never felt like this with Janine home, but by herself, surrounded by the trinkets of another's life, Lindsay couldn't help noticing the things absent from her own.

Missing the normal routine more every second, she sat on the couch and flipped through the television channels in search of a diversion. She smiled at the sight of a giant Snoopy balloon floating by the entrance to Macy's. As a young girl, she'd get up early on Thanksgiving morning and sit on the woven rug in her family's den, taking in every second of the parade. The balloons were always her favorite. Back then she dreamed of many things, like seeing the spectacle in person.

Lindsay turned off the TV and stared at the clock on the wall. Janine had left strict instructions when to put the turkey in the oven, what time to heat the dressing, when to start the gravy. But Lindsay needed something to occupy her mind now.

The cuckoo popped out of the trap door. The little birdie sang eight times and then disappeared. Janine was proud of the clock. Her son had sent it while stationed in Germany. Lindsay moved her focus to the two pictures perched on top of the television. Janine's children were a familiar sight. Hardly a room in the house lacked the image of one or both adorning at least one wall, but these, the newest shots of her offspring, held the most visible positions of honor.

The one of Janine's son, in full military uniform was taken only last month, just before his latest deployment to the Middle East. The other photo was several years old. Until yesterday, Janine had not spoken to her daughter in over two years. Now Janine had taken off on a road-trip to bring her daughter home.

A knock startled her. Lindsay stared at the front door. A large shadow loomed on the other side of the glass. Lindsay went to confront the unexpected  visitor.

Swinging open the door, she found herself staring up at the dark, troubled eyes of the man from this morning. Surprise forced her to step back, and in that moment of shock she nearly shut the door, but for the second time, she sensed he'd expected to find someone else.

He glanced over his shoulder, back in the direction of his big black truck. Only then did he return his attention to Lindsay. "I was looking for Janine."

The familiar accent of his voice again punched her in the gut. She frowned. Her eyes drifted down to take in the worn cowboy boots on his feet, almost identical to her dad's favorite pair. Squinting past him, she stared at the license plate on his truck. Texas, not Oklahoma. She let out a pent-up breath.

"The cafe was closed," he continued. "I thought she lived here. Sorry to bother you, and sorry again about this morning." He stepped back off the porch.

"This is Janine's house, I rent a room from her. She went to pick up her daughter, but she should be back any minute." A lie, but Lindsay didn't want the stranger to know she was alone, and would be for several more hours. Though in truth, nothing about the man's mannerisms elicited concern. Except his tendency to show up unexpectedly, and the slow drawl of his all-too familiar accent.

He turned around and nodded, but kept his distance. "Knew it had to be something important for her to close up shop."

"She closed for Thanksgiving."

"Thanksgiving?" He slowly nodded before offering up a crooked grin. "Yeah, I guess it is Thursday."

Lindsay smiled at his puzzled expression. How could anyone forget Thanksgiving? "I'll tell her you came by."

He nodded. "Name is Bluc Riggins." Stepping back onto the porch, he extended his hand.

She hesitated only a second before reaching out. "Lindsay Parker."

Lindsay studied his features. A white scar dipped down from just below his right ear lobe and disappeared at the back of his hairline. A sprinkling of gray lightened the area above his temple. Short black hair covered the rest of his head. She guessed him to be in his mid-thirties, yet something in those dark eyes made him seem older. His shirtsleeves bulged and his broad forearms indicated strength. Most likely the result of hard labor, since he didn't have the polished gleam of a gym rat. Crow's feet and a dark tan gave his handsome face a slightly weathered look, adding to her indecision over his age.

"Nice to meet you, and happy Thanksgiving." He turned to go.

"Same to you." An idea came to Lindsay. "How do you know Janine?"

He faced her again. "Known her for years. No trip to Idaho is complete without a belly full of Janine's fried chicken and a slice of her blueberry pie."

"You should come back for lunch. I'm sure Janine won't mind."

He shook his head. "Thanks, but I don't want to impose. Holidays are for families."

A few minutes later Lindsay watched him drive away, but his words echoed in her ears. *Holidays are for families.*

# 6

Blue shook his head. He should've realized what day it was. That woman, Lindsay, found it amusing he'd forgotten the holiday, but he was glad to see she could actually smile. Until that point she'd only looked at him with a wide-eyed expression of fear.

Eagle's Rest's lone gas station was closed, but spying a payphone he pulled into the lot anyway. Payphones were getting damn hard to find, but Blue could still count on some truck stops, and the occasional place time seemed to have forgotten. He suspected this phone lingered on as the last stop before the treacherous mountain roads began.

He refused to break down and get a cell. Last thing he needed was an electronic leash. With a deep breath, he dialed his sister's number and prepared for battle. His sister would give him an earful, but this being a holiday he owed both Ruby and Briley a call.

"Hello, Sis."

"Where have you been? It's been six weeks since anyone has heard a word from you. We'd never know if something happened. The least you could…"

He held the phone away from his head and counted to thirty. His sister could rant for hours, but she'd quit bellering once she realized he'd stopped listening. Silence greeted him when he brought the receiver back to his ear. "Finished?"

"No, but what's the point?"

"I'm going to send some money first thing tomorrow, so call the bank and check your account."

"Which means you won't be home anytime soon. Briley's birthday is coming, then Christmas."

Blue gritted his teeth and tensed his jaw. "Don't start, Ruby. I don't need you to be my calendar. I can't come back. Not this time of year."

"Save it, Blue! Life's tough, but you have a little girl who loves you. Man up, and do what's right."

Blue swallowed his pain and whispered, "Buy her something nice. I'll be there when I can."

"She needs more than money. She needs her father."

He hung up and turned his back to the payphone. He'd meant to talk to his daughter—to wish her a happy Thanksgiving. He missed her tiny little voice, but no one understood, not even Ruby. Some things he couldn't do.

A tow truck with a snow blade pulled up next to the building. Blue recognized the vehicle as the owner of the station. He knew the man by sight only, not nearly as well as he knew Janine, but he was glad to see him nonetheless. Now he could buy a few supplies.

The driver's door groaned as it opened.

"How you doing?" Blue greeted the guy as he stepped out.

The owner of the place squinted and frowned, obviously trying to connect the face with a name.

"Blue Riggins." He extended his hand. "I come up here a few times every year."

The man nodded as they shook. "Thought I recognized

ya'. You're that poker player. Totes the fancy camper."

Blue nodded. "Surprised to see you. Didn't figure any-thing would be open, this being Thanksgiving."

"Running the station would beat spending the day with my in-laws, but I'm only here to grab a couple of bags of ice and a pack of smokes for my wife's uncle. You can get gas though, if you got a credit card. Put in new twenty-four hour pumps last spring."

"I don't need gas. Just a few things here and there to tide me over until tomorrow. I have cash." Blue opened his wallet wide, hoping the man might be persuaded. "Won't take me but a second."

The owner nodded as he unlocked the door. "Make it quick. My wife knows how I feel about her kinfolk. She'll ac-cuse me of dragging my feet on purpose."

Blue grabbed a loaf of bread, a jar of peanut butter, and several bags of jerky. Given his mood, he eyed the cooler of beer, but he knew better than to travel down that road. Instead, he grabbed a gallon of milk and a twelve-pack of Dr. Pepper.

The man scratched his head as he looked at the pur-chases. "Didn't bring the keys for the register. Let me find a pencil and I'll add 'er up."

"This ought to cover it." Blue laid a hundred on the counter.

"Can't make change."

"Don't need any. I just appreciate you letting me in." Blue reached for the items.

"Let me put this in a sack for you." The man dug be-neath the counter. Now that he'd turned a nice profit, a broad smile covered his face. "I watch a lot of poker on TV. Saw you win that tournament last month. You bluffed and went all in with absolutely nothing. Got Rhett Bachman to fold with three of a kind."

Blue nodded. "I got lucky. Rhett's tough to get a read on."

"Then the next hand you pulled a flush to finish him off. Just like they say, cool as ice. Bachman always came across as kind of an asshole to me. Is he?"

Blue shook his head. "He's just like the rest of us. Trying to make a living and get by."

"Wish I had to get by on what you fellows make, but I ain't got no luck at all. If I bluffed like that, somebody would call me for sure."

"Don't be fooled. My luck's not all good."

The man handed Blue his sack of groceries. "I play once a month with a few old boys up the road. What's your trick when it comes to bluffing?"

Blue looked him in the eye. "No trick. I just don't care whether I win or lose."

$$7$$

A car door slammed. Lindsay hurried to the front room and peeked out. "Shit." She'd hoped to have dinner finished and on the table before Janine got back, but despite following the instructions word-for-word, the food wasn't yet ready. Lindsay hurried to the kitchen and basted the turkey again. The rest of the meal could turn out crappy, but she wanted the bird to be perfect.

The heat of the oven and the aroma within brought memories of Thanksgivings past. Lindsay's taste buds longed for the brown-skinned turkeys and honey-glazed hams her mom used to cook. Her mother was probably setting a pumpkin pie out to cool right now.

The front door opened and as expected, Janine wasted no time taking her place in the kitchen. She lifted lids from the pans on the stove, gave the turkey a long stare, and reached for the pan of rolls on the counter. "Looks good," she said, dabbing butter on the unbaked dinner rolls. "What d'ya think? Fifteen more minutes for the turkey and then we pop the rolls in the oven?"

Proud she hadn't screwed anything up too badly, Lindsay shrugged and smiled. "You'd know better than me." She looked around the kitchen and even peeked into the living room. Missy, Janine's daughter was nowhere to be seen. "How'd it go?"

"Good." The older woman lifted the lid to the gravy and stirred as she talked. "Been a long time since we could ride all cramped up in a car for hours and not argue every stitch of the way." She sampled the gravy right from the spoon. "You did great. Told you it was silly to fret over something so simple." Janine smiled, revealing a set of dimples.

"I wanted everything to be ready before y'all got back."

"Missy got a bit carsick on the way up. She went to her room to lie down so it worked out for the best. Maybe she'll feel up to eating by the time it's ready."

For the last few months, Lindsay had been staying in Missy's old room, but last night she moved her meager belongings across the hall. Despite assurances from Janine that the move was unnecessary, Lindsay refused to supplant Missy from the very room she'd grown up in. Things would be awkward enough over Cody, though maybe less so now that she'd broken his heart too.

Going home again was tough enough without any added stress. Or at least Lindsay imagined it would be. She'd never actually worked up the courage to do so herself.

"I invited this guy for lunch. He came here looking for you. Well, after he almost ran me over this morning. But I don't think he's going to come. He said he's known you for years. Hope you don't mind."

Janine shook her head. "Come again?"

Lindsay was babbling, but even now, something about him unnerved her. That accent for sure, but it went beyond that. Maybe the way he looked at her with those dark, troubled eyes. Or maybe he reminded her too much of the past.

Taking a deep breath, she told Janine about her run that

morning, about the conversation in the middle of the dark road, and then her anxiety when he showed up at the house. "But he was looking for you. He was as surprised to see me as I was him. He didn't even know today was Thanksgiving, which kinda made me feel bad for him. That's why I invited him. Well, that and he said he'd known you a long time. Said his name was Blue Riggins."

Janine lifted one of her painted-on brows. "So you met Blue." She clucked her tongue. "No wonder you're rambling like a twelve-year-old on espresso. Blue's man enough to fluster any woman. Been times I wished I were twenty years younger myself."

"No. That's not why I invited him. Or why I'm babbling. He just makes me nervous. I think it's his accent."

Janine laughed. "Accent you say? Had nothing to do with how he fills out a pair of jeans? Blue Riggins has made more than one woman nervous. Ain't that right, Missy?"

Lindsay turned around.

"What's that supposed to mean?" Missy plopped down in one of the kitchen chairs. She brushed a strand of bleached-blonde hair from her forehead.

"I remember a few years back when you went out of your way to get Blue's attention."

Missy shook her head. "Whatever."

Extending her hand, Lindsay said, "Nice to finally meet you. I've heard a lot about you."

"I'll bet." Missy ignored the offered hand, and instead gave a slight nod of her head. "Heard about you too. The whole way here. Must've sucked when your boyfriend dumped you here in this hellhole."

"Missy Jane! I never said he dumped her."

"I like it here," Lindsay said. "I don't regret staying when he went back to Seattle." Missy was several years younger than her, yet the girl looked older. Maybe because of the makeup.

"Nor should you," Janine interjected. "He didn't deserve you, and you don't deserve to be put down for getting shed of him. Apologize, Missy."

"Sorry."

Despite the fake tone, Lindsay merely shrugged. "I'm sure this seems weird to you. Coming home to find some stranger living in your house. Your mother has been a life-saver for me. You should've seen the smile on her face when you called last night. We're both glad you could make it."

"Yeah," Missy scoffed. "I bet. You, mom, Cody. The three of you must have been up all night celebrating."

Now didn't seem like the best time to reveal she'd broken Cody's heart, so Lindsay merely said, "We were all glad you called."

Missy rolled her eyes.

Thanksgiving dinner followed the same pattern. Lindsay tried to be sociable, but every comment was met with disdain or sarcasm. Caught in the middle, Janine played peacemak-er, encouraging her daughter to be nice, but Missy's feelings were clear. Lindsay didn't wish to deepen the divide between mother and daughter so she excused herself before dessert and retreated to her room. Or rather Janine's son's room since Missy now occupied the space Lindsay once dared to think of as her own. In all fairness, she was the actual intruder.

Lindsay sat on the edge of the bed and stared at an Army poster on the closet door. A group of camouflaged soldiers stood above the words, AN ARMY OF ONE. The concept of an army of one seemed liked an oxymoron, but she knew all about fighting alone. Her worst troubles in life had come when she made the mistake of depending on others.

To escape her growing sense of isolation, Lindsay turned on the television and flipped through the channels until she landed on the football game. The Packers were up fourteen-zip on the Cowboys. Her father, uncles, and older cousins used to gather around and watch the games every Thanksgiving while the women congregated in the other room to chitchat. Meanwhile the younger kids ran all over the house and yard playing games like tag and hide-n-seek.

Lindsay missed those days.

The Cowboys kicked a field goal.

She could almost hear her father's disdain. He hated the Cowboys and all other Texas teams. Okie to the bone, he despised the Lone Star State. Her father would never leave his La-Z-Boy with football on. Her mother would be the one to answer if someone called right now.

When the phone in the hall rang out, Lindsay jumped. Her breath caught in her chest as if reminiscing had allowed the past to track her down. Punishment for even considering calling home.

Janine answered on the third ring and squealed with delight calling for Missy to pick up in the kitchen. It was Mark, her son calling from overseas. Feeling foolish for her unfounded fears, Lindsay sucked in a deep breath of relief. In the nine years since she left home, her parents hadn't bothered to come for her. No reason they should start now.

"Missy! Hurry up. Mark is only allowed a few minutes. It's after midnight there you know."

Blue was right. Holidays were for families. Lindsay grabbed a handful of the change she'd acquired from tips at the café and headed out the door. A few minutes later, she stared at the emergency payphone next to the gas station. Fifty yards beyond the gas station, two roadblock arms pointed straight skyward, waiting to be lowered, but for now the mountain road remained passable. Everybody told her that would soon change. They told her winter was a bitch around here, so get prepared to feel isolated. They had no idea she felt like that most every day.

Her fingertips touched the receiver, yet she couldn't quite bring herself to lift it and dial. She could never go back, but Lindsay liked to picture them the way they were when she walked away. A handful of times, she'd used a computer to check on them, so she knew her family still lived in the same house. She found a few articles in the *Norman Transcript* about her brother and his talent playing baseball. Once she used Cody's Facebook account and found her brother, but his account was private, and his picture the pointed barrel of baseball bat with his out-of-focus face behind it. She knew kind of what he looked like from fuzzy newspaper pictures. Still it was hard to not think of him as the little boy he'd been when she left.

With a deep breath, she picked up the phone and pushed in a handful of quarters. Her heart quickened, and her fingers trembled as she dialed numbers forever seared in her brain.

"Hello," a deep, masculine voice said.

Panic gripped Lindsay.

"Hello?" This time the voice sounded more like a question than a greeting.

A sense of relief stirred within her. Her father always answered with, "Parker residence." He couldn't even define informal.

"Is anybody there? I'm gonna hang up."

"No. Wait." She rubbed the tension lodged in the back of her neck. "Is this the Parker household?"

"Yeah, who do you need?"

*Yeah?* Definitely not her dad, although she detected something familiar in the voice. "Clay?"

"Do I know you?"

Her head spun. His baritone voice did not come close to matching the mental images she carried of her little brother.

"Hello? Are you still there?" He questioned.

"It's me, Lindsay." She did the math in her head as she awaited his reaction. He was a little more than six years younger than her, so that made him coming up on twenty-two.

"Don't play games. Whoever you are, this isn't funny."

"Clay, it's me. Your sister." She couldn't imagine what must be going through his mind. At least she'd had time to prepare.

Silence, and then he said, "Where are you? Where have you been? Are you in trouble?" The questions came fast and furious.

"I'm in Idaho. I'm okay. How are you?"

"Wow this is crazy. I wish Mom was here. She'd freak."

Cherishing the instantly renewed bond with her brother, Lindsay savored every word out of his mouth. She wondered where her mom could've gone on Thanksgiving, but right now, she wanted to hear more about Clay. "Tell me about yourself. What's been going on?"

"Not much. Just school and stuff. I can't believe it's really you. I always knew you would show back up. I look for you at all my games."

She smiled at his excitement. He'd always been an eager kid.

"Baseball games I mean. God, I'm a dumbass expecting you to know that. For some reason I've always had this crazy idea you knew everything going on here. Like you could tune in and watch our lives like some kind of weirded-out reality show."

To let his voice sink in, she closed her eyes.

"Are you married? What's in Idaho? What have you been doing all this time?"

She didn't detect an ounce of accusation or anger in his words, but Lindsay wasn't ready to talk about herself. "I've Googled you so I know a few things. Like you're a first baseman at Baylor. And you redshirted your freshman year."

"Yeah, I probably could have played right away at some places, but Baylor had a lot of depth."

"Oklahoma schools weren't good enough for you, huh," she said with humor in her voice. She tried hard to bridge her mind from the boy she'd known, to the tall, broad shouldered ballplayer from the newspaper articles. At least he still had that same ink-black mop of curly hair.

"Baylor offered me a full ride. Dad didn't want me to play for a Texas school, but he got over that when he found out he wouldn't have to spend a dime on college."

An icy coldness settled in Lindsay's chest at the mention of their father. The conversation with Clay had given her a brief respite from reality.

"We all miss you, ya know." His voice cracked, as if he understood the emotions affecting her over a thousand miles away.

Clay had been so young. How much of what happened did he know? Or understand? She swallowed hard. "I miss you too."

"Come home then," he blurted. "It would do Mom good. It would do us all good." Desperation hung on his every word. "We need you."

His pain filled her heart. "I can't. I don't think I could

stand to see him." Tears spilled down her cheeks.

"You wouldn't have to." Clay's voice quivered. "Dad had a stroke in May."

Lindsay gasped. She'd cursed the man for years, wished for him to taste the same pain she'd felt, yet now both fear and guilt flooded over her. "Is he ..."

"He's in a wheelchair, and he can't speak. Sometimes a sentence or two, but he's hard to understand. Mom tried to take care of him here at the house, but it was too much. That's where she's at now, visiting him at Amberwood Manor."

Lindsay could not fathom her father crippled, lying in a nursing home. She closed her eyes and shook her head. The man had always loomed so large in her mind.

"Do you think you can? Come back I mean. Even for a little while."

The operator interrupted, asking for more coins.

"I don't know. I just don't know. I'll call again later."

"No, wait."

She hung up despite the desperation in her little brother's voice.

Minutes slipped by while she stood in an unmoving daze. Lindsay had dreamed of returning one day. She'd rehearsed the speech she would deliver standing in the doorway of the family den, but her vision placed her father in his old recliner, not a wheelchair.

She wanted to stand before him and ask if he regretted what he'd done, if he felt even a shred of sorrow.

# 8

Again, Lindsay couldn't sleep. The full moon lit the area above the window where a water stain discolored the paint. A reminder of some long-ago rainstorm.

She thought about her brother and tried to think what she'd tell him when she called again, how to explain she could never go back. After their conversation, Lindsay returned to Janine's and sequestered herself here in this room. Her friend checked on her several times throughout the afternoon and evening, and each time Lindsay stuck with the story she didn't feel well. Mistaking Missy as the source of the sudden despondence, Janine apologized for her daughter's behavior. Lindsay appreciated the gesture, and knew her friend's concern was sincere, but she didn't correct her. There were things about her past she'd never told Janine. Things she'd never told anyone.

Janine hadn't been her only visitor. Just after midnight, Missy came home after borrowing Janine's car to go see friends. She slipped into the room Lindsay was using without knocking, without shame, and without pretense. Missy called Lindsay a liar, a mooch, a money-grubbing con-artist, a thief, and lastly a two-bit whore.

Lindsay didn't bother to defend herself from the accusations, instead staying silent to let Missy have her say. She didn't even blame the girl. She might feel the same if she returned to Oklahoma to find a stranger living in her place and dating her old boyfriend as if her parents and everyone else had simply moved on and replaced her.

As if her running away never meant a thing.

Lindsay had never realized it, but now she knew her motivation to flee Oklahoma had been as much about hurting her father, as escaping. Sliding out of bed, she parted the curtains and peered outside.

Same as before. Frost covered Janine's car windows. Nothing else stirred. Funny how so many things just repeated themselves over and over.

The alarm on her Timex would go off in another hour. Might as well start the day now.

Fumbling in the shadows, she again layered on clothes to run, bound her dark hair into a thick ponytail, and set off into the predawn darkness for the freedom of being outside and in control of her actions.

One foot in front of the other.

One deep breath after another.

Too bad nothing else came as easy, or as predictably, as running.

Blue was restless. He'd tried to sleep, even managed to drift off a few times, but disjointed and fragmented dreams forced him awake each time. After each he sat up in bed and lit a cigarette, inhaling the smoke deep into his lungs. Only then would his heart stop thumping wildly. This place, the Tetons, used to take him back to the good times. He'd come to depend on its therapy, but this time even the majestic scenery failed him.

At daylight he finished off the last cigarette in his pack, showered, and headed for Eagle's Rest. Halfway to town, he reached for a Marlboro and cursed when he remembered smoking his last one. He should've bought a carton yesterday, when he had the chance.

At least the gas station would be open by the time he ate breakfast and said goodbye to Janine. He wouldn't tell her it was for good so with luck, he'd be out of the café and on the road before her daughter rolled out of bed. The last thing he needed was another encounter with Missy. Her visit to his camper yesterday evening had been more than enough.

Closer to town, he spotted the jogger. He studied her long, even strides as he slowed and cut halfway across the other lane to give her plenty of room. Honking as he passed, she smiled and waved, never breaking stride.

Blue pulled into the cafe. The place was dark, but he was early yet, so he sat in the warm idling truck. Fifteen minutes later a rusted-out Chevy pickup pulled up beside him. As if on cue the lights came on inside. The gas station's snowplow rig turned in and parked as Blue reached the front door. A blast of heat hit him when he stepped inside. Before Blue could sit, Janine came over and slid an arm around him in a makeshift hug. "Howdy, stranger. Heard you were in town."

"Getting so a man can't hide anywhere." He freed himself and made his way to the counter.

"Coffee will be just a minute. Food a might longer since my cook hasn't showed yet. How's things in the Lone Star State?"

Blue shrugged. "Couldn't tell you. Haven't been."

Janine nodded, as if she understood all his statement

implied.

Several people arrived in short order including the tardy cook. Janine came over Blue's way with a mug and pot of coffee in hand "Steak, medium-rare, eggs, over-easy."

He smiled. "You should play poker."

"Not me. I know a man's gut, but I can't read 'em beyond that. Wish I could. Would've saved me two divorces and a heap of heartache along the way." She slapped the order sheet down on the counter-line between the kitchen and the front and moved on to her next customer.

"Aww, come on, Janine," said the man who drove the rusted Chevy. "You've been breaking my heart for years. I pledge my love every morning, and day after day you ignore me."

Janine rolled her eyes. "I feel the love every time I pocket your fifty-cent tip."

"You can't put a price on love," the man teased.

"That's not what your ex-wife told me," Janine fired back.

The men along the counter laughed. Blue watched Janine make her way around the cafe. She reminded him of his sister, Ruby. Besides sharing an occupation, they had the same stout build and deep dimples that only appeared when they smiled. And both women possessed an easygoing rapport, yet firm control over their customers.

To Blue's left, two flannel-shirt-clad farmers discussed the winter wheat prices over the sound of sizzling meat on the grill. An empty stool divided Blue and a young kid to the right. Noting the lit cigarettes in each of the farmer's callused hands, Blue waited for a chance to interrupt. "Breakfast is on me if I can talk one of you out of a smoke."

The nearest handed over the pack and a lighter. Blue lit

up and handed the items back while inhaling deeply. There were only a few places in the world where he could sit, relax, and feel comfortable. The Talon Cafe had always been one of them. He would miss the place.

He savored the cigarette before Janine came back to refill his mug. "Missy come see you last night?" Blue nodded and noted the young kid take interest in the question.

"That was my guess when she asked to borrow the car. Said she wanted to visit old high school friends. That girl never has been any good at lying. None of her friends stuck around after graduation, except Cody here, and I doubted she was ready to face him."

The kid shook his head at Janine's stare. "I spent Thanksgiving over at my mom's place. Didn't get home until ten-thirty."

Janine shifted her gaze to Blue. "What did she want?"

Blue took a long sip. Last thing he wanted was to tell Janine the truth. "She just stopped to say hi."

"I know better."

So did he, but he doubted Janine wanted to hear about her daughter catching Blue in a moment of loneliness. He doubted she wanted to hear about the way Missy looked at him. The way she slowly approached with her moist red lips. The way she seductively pulled her shirt up over her head and unclasped her bra. Or that Blue almost gave in and reached for her before coming to his senses and realizing the woman in front of him was not who he wanted her to be.

No, Janine did not need to hear any of that. Nor, he suspected, did the nervy kid to his right. So instead Blue said, "I met your new roommate."

"Lindsay." Janine smiled. "You left quite an impression on her, too."

He nodded. "Not hard to do when you damn near run someone over."

"It was more than that. She invited you to Thanksgiving dinner, didn't she?"

The kid stood and threw down several bills. "Gotta go. First day of the season, ya know." He hurried out.

Janine smiled. "I never did like that boy, so it's good to see him squirm."

Blue didn't care about him. He wanted to know about Lindsay. "What's her story anyway? Missy says she's after your money."

"What money? The fifty cents Tom leaves me every morning? If Missy bothered to look around she'd realize how stupid that idea is. She had a problem with Lindsay before they ever met."

"Kind of hard to trust someone that gets up at the ass crack of dawn to run halfway to Yellowstone and back."

"'bout as hard as it is to trust a man who gambles for a living," Janine countered.

He shrugged. She had him there.

After refilling a few more mugs of coffee Janine returned and leaned against the counter. "Lindsay has been through a lot. Sure she's hiding something, but who isn't? Way I figure, she'll tell me when and if it becomes my business. Far as I know, she's never straight-out lied to me so I trust her. She's made my life a lot easier helping out around here. Anything I've given her, she's returned twofold, so forget whatever my daughter said about her. One of these days, Missy will figure out her momma wasn't born yesterday."

"Missy knows you're not a fool."

Janine set her coffee pot on the counter. "She's always thought she could pull the wool over my eyes." Janine leaned in closer. "Like now. I've figured out the real reason she came back and I'm glad she's here. Hopefully we can patch things up. But sooner or later she'll have to admit she's pregnant and needs my help. And I'm not going to make it easy for her by telling her I know. She'll have to come out with it herself."

The bell on the front door clanged behind them, but Blue barely noticed. He was too busy digesting that last statement. Missy pregnant? His heart tightened. He'd come damn close to really screwing up. Last thing he needed was to get involved with a pregnant woman. Knowing Missy, she'd claim he was the father, even if she gave birth tomorrow.

Lindsay wasn't surprised to see the tall Texan at the counter. She figured he was headed here when he passed her on the way into town, but still his presence shook up her routine. Usually she took a seat at the bar and ate with Cody before going to the house for a quick shower before coming back to the Talon to help with the lunch crowd. But Cody wasn't here today, and the only empty stools were far closer to the Texan than she wanted. Especially given Janine's mischievous smirk.

"Morning," Janine said.

"Looks busy," Lindsay said grabbing an apron. "I better help."

"Nonsense." Janine yanked the cloth from her hands. "Sit down and eat. I got this."

Lindsay settled onto an empty stool that left one space between her and the stranger.

"You remember Blue." Janine poured her some coffee.

He turned and nodded hello, but didn't speak. His bore

a pained expression.

"How was your run?" Janine asked.

"Good." Lindsay took a sip of the hot beverage.

"Nobody tried to run you over this morning?" Janine cut her eyes Blue's direction.

"Nope, not today." Lindsay hoped her voice didn't convey her nerves. For some stupid reason, her heart pounded harder now than during the run.

For his part, Blue still seemed distracted. Lindsay wasn't even sure he'd heard a word of the conversation.

"Ya know, Blue, you and Lindsay have a lot in common." Janine plunged on, undeterred by his inattentiveness.

He raised one brow waiting for Janine to say more.

"Besides the obvious stuff of where you grew up, and both being athletic, and good looking, and all that."

Oh God. Lindsay cringed. Here it comes. Matchmaker mode. Subtlety was a foreign concept to Janine. She often reminded Lindsay how much better she could do than Cody.

"You also have Missy in common."

"Missy?" Blue and Lindsay voiced surprise in unison.

Janine smiled, obviously pleased now that she had their attention. "She paid both of you an unwanted visit last night, didn't she? Don't look surprised, Lindsay. You know how thin the walls are in that house, and the way voices carry through the vents. I heard every word, and don't think I won't have a little talk with my daughter today. She has no right to treat you that way."

"Don't." Lindsay shook her head. "I don't want to cause problems between y'all."

"Y'all." Janine drawled the word out. She turned around to grab a plate from the divider between the kitchen and the front. "That's another thing in common between you two.

Nobody around here says y'all." She set the steak and eggs in front of Blue.

"Really, don't say anything to Missy. I understand why she's upset. Must be odd to come home and find a stranger living in your room, dating your old boyfriend. Besides, she's only here a few days. Don't ruin your time together."

Janine shook her head. "Did you notice the three suitcases we drug into the house? Or those garbage sacks full of clothes? Then there's the stereo, and collection of shoes still in my trunk? Missy doesn't plan to go anywhere soon. Least not for eight or nine months."

"Oh." Lindsay tried not to sound disappointed, but the news deflated her just the same.

"And don't think I don't know something happened between you and Cody the other night. Way he cut out of here just before you came back, I'd guess you two aren't even on speaking terms. That's a good thing, but I doubt you've realized that yet."

Lindsay didn't deny any of it.

"Blue has a different problem," Janine said. "Missy likes him a little too much. And she'll never leave him alone now that she needs somebody to take care of her. Not that I blame her for going after you, Blue. Good looking and rich to boot. The perfect man for any woman, especially one looking for somebody to play daddy."

Blue stopped, steak knife mid-slice. Lindsay's stomach knotted as she understood the gist of Janine's words.

"Long as she thinks you're available, Missy is going to keep hounding you."

Eyes wide and jaw tensed, he looked sick. "I'm leaving this afternoon. I only came in to say goodbye."

"You just got here!"

"I have somewhere to be in a couple of days."

"Last time you stayed a full month."

He stuffed a bite of meat in his mouth and chewed instead of answering.

Lindsay pushed her nearly full mug forward and stood. "I have to take a shower."

Janine said, "Missy doesn't think I know she's pregnant. If she happens to be up, don't let on you know."

Fighting back a wave of nausea, Lindsay made it outside and around the side of the building before collapsing against the wall. The chill from the brick wormed its way through the fabric of her clothes, snaked through her damp skin, and curled up in the hollow of her bones, but it was the news of Missy's pregnancy that iced her very soul.

Lindsay didn't want to leave Janine, or Eagle's Rest, but no way could she stay and watch Missy's belly expand each day. No way could she bear witness to another woman's pregnancy while a loving mom doted on her.

The minutes ticked by, yet Lindsay didn't move. Tears streamed down her cheeks. She didn't want to run away again, or wander aimlessly around the country. But she couldn't stay here. That's when it dawned on her. There was only one thing left for her to do, one place to go.

"You okay?"

Lindsay turned to find Blue's dark eyes staring at her.

"I'm fine."

"I can tell by all those tears." He offered a kind smile before adding, "Missy can be tough to take, but she'll come around. And if not, Janine will shut her down."

"I can't stay here."

Blue frowned.

"I can't," Lindsay wiped away tears on the sleeve of her

jacket. "I just can't. I have to leave."

"Janine wants you here," Blue explained. "She told me so. Don't let Missy drive you away."

"It's not Janine, or Missy. I have to leave. I have to go home. Will you give me a ride over to Idaho Falls? They have a bus station there."

# 9

Lindsay slung the backpack over her shoulder and bent her knees to grab the two duffels at her feet. Twenty-seven years on earth, and everything she owned could be crammed into three bags. Tiptoeing down the hall, she passed Missy's closed door, and eased into Janine's room.

Quickly she scribbled, *Buy the baby something nice* on a slip of paper, wrapped the note around five twenty-dollar bills, and slid the bundle beneath Janine's pillow. Lindsay would stop in the Talon to say goodbye, but this was the only way she could leave money. Her friend would never accept it otherwise.

"What do you think you're doing?"

Lindsay spun to face Janine's daughter. "Leaving."

Missy moved to block the doorway. A smug grin twisted her face. "I knew you'd shag ass the second someone confronted you." Missy folded her arms across her chest. "Don't think I'm going to let you steal us blind on your way out."

Lindsay tossed the two packed bags toward Missy. "Go ahead, look inside. I'm not a thief, and your mom means the world to me. Maybe someday you'll figure that out too."

"Don't lecture me. Let's see the backpack."

Lindsay started to say, *Go to hell.* She could easily force her way by Missy, but she didn't want a huge scene. Dumping the contents on the bed, she lifted a pair of panties, a sports bra, her running shoes, and the round container of birth control pills "Are these your mother's? How about these?"

"Don't act so smart. I caught you before you had a chance. But I know your kind. You're guilty, or you wouldn't be sneaking away."

Lindsay stuffed her belongings in for a second time, while Missy watched. She refused to let Missy have an easy victory. "I'm leaving because Blue asked me to."

"Blue?" Shock replaced the haughty expression.

"Yeah, he asked me to go away on a trip. He's picking me up at the café in a few minutes, so I have to hurry."

"Bullshit. He just got here, and you barely know him."

"What can I say?" Lindsay shrugged. "Girls like me move fast. A rich, good-looking guy like that. There's no reason to hesitate. When I see something I want, I go after it."

"I thought you were with Cody?"

"Not anymore. Girls like me move on pretty quick."

By the time Lindsay got outside Blue had already returned from the gas station. Leaning against the big black Ford, he smoked a cigarette and watched her approach.

Slinging her bags into the truck's bed, she said, "I just want to run in and tell Janine goodbye."

He nodded, but said nothing.

Lindsay started inside, then stopped and turned around. "Just to warn you, Missy will be here in a second. I couldn't let her have the last word, so I kind of led her to believe you invited me to go away with you." She bit the corner of her lip before adding, "I kind of let on me and you … well, you know."

He flashed a smile. "Go say goodbye. I'll handle Missy."

# 10

Rubbing the back of her neck, Lindsay lingered to one side, as Blue unlocked the travel trailer. She surveyed the dense forest surrounding the small clearing. The gurgle of a distant stream echoed among the pines. There didn't appear to be another human within earshot, within miles for that matter.

The door swung open and he stepped aside allowing her to go first. She'd heard a sufficient number of horror stories to know entering the RV wasn't smart.

Alone? With a strange man? In the middle of nowhere?

Three strikes that would have her fleeing under normal conditions. These were far from normal conditions.

Convincing her friend she had to leave and that her departure had little to do with Missy hadn't been easy. Finally, Janine relented and wished Lindsay well while making Lindsay promise to stay in touch. Her final word to Lindsay had been about Blue. "A woman couldn't do any better than Blue Riggins for a travel partner."

Lindsay tried to explain he was only taking her to the bus station, yet Janine acted as if he'd be taking her all the way to Oklahoma.

Blue scratched his head. "Something wrong?"

Janine had vouched for him, and Lindsay trusted her more than anyone. "No, just admiring the scenery." She climbed the two metal steps and went inside.

Blue followed. Pushing a button on the wall, he stood in the doorway as the side of the trailer slid away, adding several feet to the living area. With the flick of another switch, a gas fireplace ignited.

"Here's the remote. You can watch TV." His hand brushed hers as he handed it to her. "The fire warms it up pretty quick. Turn down the flame with this dial if you get too hot. Make yourself at home. I have one last thing to do and then we'll head out. I should be back in about forty-five minutes. An hour tops."

Lindsay went to the window and watched Blue hike through the trees until she lost sight of him in the forest. She couldn't imagine why he was hiking off to be alone in the woods for an hour.

Sitting on the leather couch, Lindsay marveled at the camper. More elaborate than any place she'd ever lived, and bigger than most, this was no ordinary RV. She reached for the magazine rack to her left for something to help pass the time. *Outdoor Life, Field and Stream, Horse and Rider, Western Horsemen.*

Catch'em, shoot'em, or ride'em. She hoped his take on women differed from his reading material. Especially, since she was already caught.

The minutes ticked by. She puzzled over the weird scenario she'd placed herself in. What kind of man roamed the countryside by his lonesome, camping in out-of-the-way places? What kind of man could afford an RV like this?

Lindsay's curiosity got the better of her. She tiptoed to the kitchen and peeked into the refrigerator. A box of baking soda, a nearly empty gallon of milk, and half a dozen Dr Peppers its only occupants. She opened the cabinets next. Glasses and dishes in one, pans in another. They were clean and organized, but nothing told her about the man they belonged to. She appreciated how he'd taken her little fib with Missy and ran with it outside the cafe, laying it on thick for the other woman. Afterward, when Lindsay thanked him, Blue simply shrugged and said, "Missy could use a bit of humility."

Lindsay wasn't sure humility was the right word, but it had been nice to have someone stand up for her like that. Sitting back on his couch, her gaze drifted to the television. Maybe she should turn it on, if for no other reason than to keep her curiosity at bay. Her wandering eyes noticed another cabinet below the set. She rubbed the back of her neck. The kitchen cupboards were one matter. Had she been caught, Lindsay could've justified her actions by claiming she needed a glass of water, but what would she say if he found her digging through the rest of his things?

Her eyes lingered on the TV cabinet. Most likely there wasn't anything of interest in there. She went to the window and peeked out.

No sign of Blue.

She tiptoed across the trailer floor. The cabinet door opened with a small click of the latch. On the top shelf she found several fishing reels, a box of bullets, and an electric knife. Her shoulders slumped. She should've expected as much after the magazines. Her mind once again began to panic. Bullets meant a gun. She pushed away her paranoia. Men like him owned guns. That didn't make him a serial killer. Still curious, she renewed her investigation.

Bending over, she rummaged through the shelf. Books

and papers lined the small opening. She reached for an over-sized cloth-bound spine. A photo album. Now she was getting somewhere. Closing the cabinet door, she carried the scrapbook to the leather couch. Lindsay hated this compulsion to pry, but she couldn't tame the urge to know more about this stranger.

The first picture revealed a much younger Blue, clad in a tuxedo. Next to him stood a pretty blonde in a flowing white dress. Lindsay squinted at the wedding picture. His hand cradled her chin while they stared adoringly at each other.

Just once Lindsay wished somebody would gaze at her that way. She turned the page. The happy couple waved and smiled in front of a pickup adorned with shoe-polished well-wishes. If Lindsay were honest, several boyfriends had been totally devoted to her. She'd been the one to always cut and run, to avoid the kind of scenes portrayed in these pictures.

More photos showed the newlyweds in various outdoor poses. Camping, fishing, hiking. Lindsay recognized several of the peaks from this area. Where was this woman now? Janine wouldn't have been playing matchmaker had Blue's wife still been part of his life.

The next picture showed Blue in an arena, on the back of a horse. Then came a shots of the wife with an increasingly expanding belly. Turning the laminated sheets, she expected to find a cute and cuddly baby, but the nicely laid out and organized pages ended.

Lindsay flipped to the back where several newspaper clippings and loose photographs jutted out at awkward angles. The first clip read, OKLAHOMA STATE SENIOR GRABS LIFE BY THE HORNS, above an image of Blue diving off a horse onto a steer. The date at the top of the paper was ten years old. That meant Blue was probably five, maybe six years older than her.

She pulled out another clipping. Two years newer according to the date of the newspaper. RIGGINS TOPS RANKINGS. Below, in smaller print, Blue's name topped the pro steer wrestling standings.

Slowly, she went through the stack of headlines and articles detailing his prowess in the rodeo arena. She read every article, studied every photo, captivated by it all. The irony of the situation overwhelmed her senses, and the fact he'd spent a good deal of time in Oklahoma renewed her apprehension.

Before she could read the last of the stories, she heard a noise on the steps. The door opened just as she stuffed the book behind a cushion.

Blue cocked his head as he studied her. "Doing okay?"

"Just fine."

"I'll back the truck up so we can get going."

When he went back outside, she hurried to stash the album in the cabinet trying to arrange the book precisely how she'd found it. The trailer rocked as he backed under the hitch. Breathing easier with everything back in place, Lindsay moved down the steps toward his pickup. "Can I help?"

"I got it." He grunted and cranked a handle to raise the trailer's leveling jacks.

Lindsay watched as he worked. She wanted to ask questions, but she had to be careful not to let him know she'd pried. "What part of Texas are you from?"

"The Panhandle."

"I grew up in Oklahoma." She waited for him to ask where.

He said nothing.

Instead, Blue headed back inside the trailer. She followed and watched him turn off the fireplace and retract the slide-outs. He didn't act as if he even noticed her. His every move seemed calculated, controlled.

A hunch told her he was always this way. From the first moment they'd met on the highway, he'd shown the body language of a man who knew what he was doing, but as she studied Blue's face another side materialized. The deep-etched lines and troubled eyes told another story.

Afraid he might arrive at the same conclusions, she looked away when their gazes met.

"You ready?"

Still afraid to look at him, she lowered her eyes noticing a slip of paper. She squinted down at the scrap. Had it been there before? Her heart sank when she realized what it was.

A picture. From the book. Her stomach tensed as she looked at Blue, but he had his back turned, surveying the room. Swift as a hawk scooping prey, she snatched the photo and stuffed it into the pocket of her jeans.

He twisted around to face her. "Everything okay?"

Lindsay nodded.

"Let's get on the road." He held open the aluminum door and waited for her to step down to the ground before locking up.

On the way to the pickup, she slid her hand into her pocket. Her fingertips touched the glossy side of the snap-shot giving her an intense desire to see the image. She didn't dare chance bringing it out for fear Blue might see.

He paused as he stepped around to the front of the vehicle. His eyes roamed over every tree, rock, and snow-capped peak while Lindsay waited.

Blue seemed reluctant to leave, as if he were waiting on something. After a few minutes, he opened the driver's door. Again, he paused. The chilly air blowing into the cab sent a shiver across Lindsay's skin, but finally, Blue slid in. The truck cranked with a rumble, and he pulled away, having never looked her direction. They rode in silence back toward Eagle's Rest. She wanted to strike up a conversation, but sensed he preferred the quiet.

When they entered town, he turned to stare at the Kozy-Inn. "Fool," Blue said and focused his attention back to the road.

"Who?" She knew the owner of the town's only motel, and he'd always seemed okay to her.

Blue turned and studied her with a curious look. Almost as if he'd forgotten he had a passenger. "What?"

"Were you calling John from the motel a fool?"

Blue sighed. "No. I was talking to myself."

Lindsay didn't know what to say. The despair in his voice clashed with the persona she'd constructed for him. He mashed his foot down on the accelerator as they pulled out of town. To lighten the mood, she laughed. "Thanks for playing along with Missy earlier. You really had her going. When you mentioned the wedding chapels, I thought she'd faint."

She expected him to laugh or at least smile, but he offered nothing. A few miles down the road he gave her a sideways glance. "You ever waste time looking for something you know damn well you'll never find?"

Lindsay nodded, stopping short of saying, every single day.

"Maybe I'm just stubborn, but it was the same even when I rodeoed. Time would keep on ticking, but I never stopped. Even after I was already out of the money. I'd wrestle them damn steers until I pulled them to the ground. No matter what."

"You must win a lot." She already knew the answer from the news clips.

He shook his head. "Not anymore. I'm retired."

His statement deflated her. Lindsay didn't know why, but she'd become attached to the notion of him as a rodeo star. She liked thinking of him as a modern-day cowboy. "What do you do now?"

He looked at her and said, "Nothing."

She smiled. He was playing coy with her. *Nothing* hadn't paid for this monster of a pickup. *Nothing* hadn't bought that fancy trailer. *Nothing* didn't enable a man to drive all over the country.

"What's so funny?"

Lindsay shrugged. "Nothing." She giggled.

Blue's brows pinched together. "How come I get the feeling I missed the joke?"

"How come I get the feeling there's more to your story than you're willing to admit?"

He nodded. "There's always more to every story."

She waited, hoping he would elaborate, but several more miles passed in silence. "I haven't been back to Oklahoma in almost a decade," she said. Maybe he would open up if she took the lead and offered something of her own past.

He put on his blinker to pass a semi. "Hasn't changed much."

"Do you spend a lot of time there?"

"I drop by and see my horse now and then. To give the man that keeps him money for feed, or to help out on his place."

"What part of the state?"

Blue squirmed in his chair and checked the rearview mirror. "Outside of Stillwater."

She waited for him to add something. Maybe tell her he went to college there, but again the conversation died. "I grew up in Norman. Never thought I'd leave. My goal was always to get a scholarship and go to OU, or Oklahoma State."

She studied his face to see if the mention of his alma mater elicited a reaction. He remained a blank sheet of paper. "Did you go to college?" she asked.

"Yep."

She wanted to scream. What was he trying to hide? Furthermore, why did she care? In another hour, she'd be waiting in the bus station with a bunch of other lost souls, while Blue motored down the highway. She'd be stuck on a Greyhound trying to ignore the briny scent of urine roiling from the back of the bus, while he breathed the fresh air of freedom.

Janine's words echoed in her head. *A woman couldn't do better than Blue Riggins as a travel partner.* She turned to Blue. "Are you really headed to Vegas?"

"Nope. Left there day before yesterday."

"You wouldn't by chance be going to see your horse?"

His eyes widened as if he knew her next thought.

"I could pay for gas," she blurted. "And you wouldn't have to take me all the way to Norman. You could drop me off wherever. My brother would come get me." She hated the desperation in her voice, but she couldn't stand the idea of the long ride to Oklahoma in the lonesome and dismal conditions a Greyhound promised. Not with dread already hanging over her head. She could fly, but doing so seemed so sudden, too sudden.

"It wouldn't be a good idea. I travel alone. And I like to take my time."

Lindsay bit her lip. She chose her words carefully. "It's been ten years. If I was in a hurry I would've gone before now." She took a deep breath. "Earlier you asked if I'd ever wasted time looking for something I'll never find?"

Closing her eyes, Lindsay said, "I've searched every single day since I left. I'll never find what I lost." Tears choked off her speech. She took several deep breaths trying to regain her composure.

She opened her eyelids to find Blue watching her.

He studied her for several long seconds, seemingly taking her in for the first time Finally, he spoke in a hoarse whisper, "I'll take you wherever you need to go."

11

Blue stared ahead as the Ford swallowed dotted white lines. He didn't so much as cast a sidelong glance at his passenger.

Lindsay hadn't uttered more than ten words since he rashly offered to take her wherever she wanted to go, but that silver lining to his cloud of stupidity would only last so long. He'd met very few women who didn't like the sound of their own voice. Inevitably she'd grow tired of the silence and fill it with small talk. Or worse, endless questions.

The pack of Marlboros on the dash called to him. A cigarette was exactly what he needed, but he didn't want to inflict his nasty habit on her when she obviously gave a damn about her body. Only a health nut would be out running before the ass crack of dawn. Though he had to admit the effort had left her fit, trim, and curvy in all the right places.

He exhaled to clear those kinds of thoughts. Otherwise he'd never think of a way out. What the hell had he been thinking? He didn't want to drive her to Oklahoma. He didn't want to drive anybody there. Matter of fact, he didn't want to be within five hundred miles of Texas until after Christmas. Now he'd be one state over, right next door, within the week. With Lindsay along, he couldn't possibly stall more than four or five days.

The proximity of her home to his wasn't the real problem, and Blue knew it. Lindsay herself scared him. She shared too many of Staci's qualities. The two of them didn't look anything alike, yet they both possessed the same boldness and determination. The same uncanny ability to make him do things he never intended.

When Blue arrived as a fresh-faced kid at Oklahoma State, his entire focus had been on bulldogging and roping. Two months later the rodeo paled in comparison to Staci. He could still remember how she looked and smelled back then. The faint freckles that decorated her high cheekbones. The vanilla scent of her honey-colored hair. The smoothness of her tanned skin. The way her eyes spoke to him.

Girlfriends and female admirers had never been in short supply, but they always took a backseat to his pursuits on horseback. Staci changed that. By their junior year, she was his wife. Not once in their eight years of marriage did he see her as an obstacle to his goals. Nor did Blue ever regret a single minute of the time they shared. Only the moments when he should've been there— and wasn't.

He reached for the pack of smokes and lit up.

Lindsay frowned and inched closer to the passenger door, but she kept quiet. At least she wasn't a fanatic, prone to preaching to others about their unhealthy habits.

Blue cracked his window. The onrush of cool air jarred him back to the present. Staci was gone. He would never find her ghost on the side of the road, and her spirit wasn't locked inside another woman. Taking a long drag, he let the smoke churn inside his lungs. Maybe he would see his wife again, but it certainly wouldn't be in this world.

Crushing out the cigarette in the ashtray, he rolled up

the window, and turned to his passenger. "I have to stop at a bank when we hit Idaho Falls. Then we'll find a grocery store. I'm a bit short on supplies."

She nodded.

"Or I can still take you by the bus station if you prefer." He tried not to look, or sound, too hopeful.

"Are you backing out on your offer?" She leveled her gaze on him.

"No, thought maybe you'd changed your mind."

Blue cringed. What the hell was wrong with him? She'd given him the opportunity to amend his earlier lapse in judgment and he'd not taken it. Something about this woman made him feel like he needed to be her protector, when it was obvious she could take care of herself.

Lindsay stared out the window at the fields of sagebrush. "Your kindness means a lot. Going home again is going to be torture. My mind is so messed up right now. Knowing I have time to prepare makes going back to Oklahoma easier."

Blue swallowed his regret. She didn't remind him of Staci. It was himself he recognized in her words. He felt her misery. He didn't know what she was running from, or who had damaged her, but he identified with the pain in her voice. She didn't want to go home any more than he did, but for whatever reason, she felt the need to confront her past and stare it down. Blue respected that. He held out hope that one day he might make such a stand.

When they reached Idaho Falls, Blue found a bank and headed inside to transfer money to his sister. He told Lindsay he'd only be a minute so she stayed in the truck, but inside the line was longer than he would have guessed. Standing behind two gray-haired women, he listened as they discussed the weather forecast. At the mention of snow he made a mental note to fill up the truck before finding a place to park the rig.

Forty-five minutes later, he left the bank. Transferring money from Vegas was a hell of a lot easier than Idaho Falls. There all he had to do was sign a paper and one of the casino hostesses took care of everything else, whereas the teller he'd just dealt with made him jump through flaming hoops.

Getting back in the truck he said, "Sorry. That was a damn mess."

She shrugged. "I'm in no hurry."

A few blocks from the bank, Blue pulled up to the pumps of a truck stop. "Might snow tonight, so I'll fill up before we find a place to park."

Lindsay nodded and climbed out to stretch. Blue watched her bend at the waist and grab her toes. Her jeans tightened to reveal the runner's muscles in her upper thighs.

Yep, she definitely took care of her body. The realization he was going to be locked inside a tiny camper, in close proximity to those well-defined curves, launched a few lustful thoughts, which he quickly shoved aside.

Lindsay glanced up and caught him looking, so he pushed open his door and said, "My back hurts just watching you stretch like that."

She raised her arms above her head. "I'm a little sore. I ran four or five miles farther than usual this morning. I do that when I have a lot on my mind."

Blue slid a credit card through the pump. Lifting the hose, he said, "I couldn't run around the block."

"Oh, come on," she said. "You have to be in good shape to wrestle those steers."

"My horse did most of the running, and like I said, I'm retired."

"Was it your back? Did you hurt it? Is that why you

quit?"

He ignored her rapid-fire questions to avoid encouraging more. He felt her staring, waiting, but he studied the numbers on the pump until she finally said, "I'm going inside to grab some water. Can I get you anything?"

He shook his head. "I'll be there in a minute. After I top off and make a quick phone call."

Blue watched her stroll away. She had the kind of sweet innocent good looks that snuck up on a man. Different from the glamour gals in Vegas he'd grown accustomed to. Women who dazzled with their appearance, but whose beauty faded each time he woke up beside one.

Lindsay was the kind of woman a man became more enamored with each day. Not that Blue was interested in becoming such a man. Never again would he fall for a woman that way.

When the pump clicked off, Blue reseated the hose and headed inside. He hoped this place would have a payphone, but if not he'd buy one of their prepaid burners and give it to Lindsay after he called his sister.

Luckily, like a lot of truck stops, this place still had a couple of phones. He punched the numbers, first off his calling card, then to the café.

Ruby answered on the third ring. "Riggins Restway."

"Hello, Sis."

"How's Idaho?"

"I sent you some money, but who knows what time it will go through. Call your bank later and—"

"It's the day after Thanksgiving," Ruby said. "Half the world's traveling down I-27 today and everyone of 'em acts starved near death. I don't have time to do anything but fill glasses and make sure Ray flips the burgers."

He pictured the old black man rolling his eyes every time Ruby barked an order. "Just call the bank and—"

"You call the damn bank. It's your money. I'm busy dealing with life, not running away from it."

"I gotta go."

"You don't have to like what I say for it to be true," Ruby said. "Buster wants you to call him. You need the number?"

"I don't owe him a thing."

"You owe him courtesy if nothing else. Call him."

Blue gritted his teeth. He watched Lindsay leave the store and head his direction.

"Donnie is looking for you, too. You need to call them both."

"I saw Donnie a few days ago."

"He told me. But he also said he needs to talk to you real bad."

"I'll call him up when I get the chance."

"Damn it, Blue. Make the chance. Donnie is your friend, and Buster has always—"

Blue hung up and turned to face Lindsay. He smiled to mask his irritation. Ruby knew how to rile him like few others could. Of course, just the mere mention of Buster's name accomplished that. Lindsay stared at him while rubbing the back of her neck. Blue had already picked up on the fact she rubbed her neck every time she felt uncomfortable, but what he couldn't figure was why she'd turned so nervous all of a sudden.

Lindsay gazed down at her feet. "Could you do me one small favor before we head out?"

Folding his arms across his chest, he waited. He'd already learned where she was involved it was best not to volunteer too fast.

"Could you call a number for me and ask for Clay?"

He stared at her for clues as to why she couldn't do that herself. Who was this Clay? A lover? She didn't strike him as the type to have an illicit affair, but there had to be a reason she couldn't make the call.

"What's the number?"

"Four-o-five..."

An Oklahoma area code. If she truly hadn't been back in nine years then this Clay had something to do with her leaving in the first place. A married man?

Blue hated to ask personal questions. He didn't want to open the door for Lindsay to do the same, but he refused to be put in the middle of something he didn't understand. "Who's Clay?"

She took a deep breath and gazed up at the smoke-grey clouds gliding by. "My brother."

The pain and loss in her voice assured Blue this was the truth. "Give me the number again." He committed the number to his memory as he dialed.

A woman answered.

"May I speak to Clay?" Blue watched the nervous anticipation dance on Lindsay's face. "Oh, he's not."

Her chin dropped.

"A message?" Blue spoke aloud and gave Lindsay a questioning look to see what she wanted him to do.

Wide-eyed, she shook her head.

"That's all right, ma'am. I'll call back another time." Blue hung up.

"Thanks anyway." Lindsay turned away and trudged back to the truck with her shoulders slumped in obvious disappointment.

Blue didn't want to care, but he did. The woman who answered sounded older. Most likely, Lindsay and Clay's mother. What happened that was so awful Lindsay couldn't talk to her parents, didn't even want to risk one of them answering?

Understanding Lindsay needed a few minutes alone, Blue walked into the store and bought another pack of smokes even though he'd picked up a carton back in Eagle's Rest. Stepping back outside, he again stopped at the phones. A trucker was loudly arguing with someone about a dispatch on one, but it didn't seem in any way a private conversation, so Blue used the other phone to dial his friend's cell. Buster could go to hell, but Donnie had been a steady friend, and talking to him usually proved entertaining.

"Hello."

Blue smiled at the familiar slow drawl of his friend. "You answered, so I guess that means you're not behind bars."

"Get throwed in jail a couple of times, and that's all anybody wants to talk about." Donnie laughed. "Where the hell are you?"

"On the road."

"Well, get your ass back to Vegas. I got us a deal set up."

"I don't want to play cards with those assholes."

"No, this is a different deal. Screw those idiots. This is even easier money. I met some old boy at the bar last night. This guy owns Tascosa Boots. They're here for Finals week, and they want me and you for an endorsement deal."

Blue cleared his throat. "I'm not interested."

"Shit, Blue. It's easy money. And they seem like all right guys. They make hats and all kinds of shit now. That's why they want us to pitch their stuff. To get the word out."

"You're the rodeo man these days. Do it without me."

"I can't." Donnie sounded dejected. "They want a buddy kind of deal, but hell I ain't stupid. They want you to wear their hat on TV when you play cards. There are forty or fifty swinging dicks in Vegas right now could give 'em more bang for their buck than me. But you're the only real cowboy on the poker circuit."

"You know I hate this kind of shit."

"I know you do. And that's why I hate to ask. But I need the money and the exposure. One more bad injury and I could be done. The Finals don't start for nearly week. Come back and play 'til then. I'll get it all set up, and you can get out real quick."

Anxious to get off the phone, Blue looked toward his truck. He stared at Lindsay. Here was his excuse. His way out.

"You know I wouldn't ask if I didn't need this," Donnie said.

Blue looked towards his truck, at Lindsay sitting in the passenger seat. "Tell them I'm in, but I can't get there this week. I'm in the middle of something.

"Don't bullshit me, Blue. I know you. Right now you're camped out somewhere in the middle of nowhere. Chain smoking Marlboros, and avoiding people like a sinner does church. Maybe you're doing a bit of fishing, but other than that, you ain't got shit going. Not until the next big tournament. Tell me I'm wrong."

"You're wrong. I'm halfway to Oklahoma." Not quite the truth, but Blue wanted to shut his friend up, and he knew that would do the trick. He tamped out a cigarette from the pack he'd just bought.

"Oklahoma? What for?"

Lighting up, Blue said, "That's my business."

"You going to Crow's?"

"Maybe."

"That's it, ain't it? You plan to start rodeoing again.

You're gonna start working out Winder."

"I've told you. I'm done. That horse is gonna stay right where he's at. Fat, and happy, and out to pasture. I'm headed to Oklahoma, but my days in the saddle are over. End of story."

"Hell, Blue, both you and Winder belong in an arena. The only reason you never qualified was because you never made enough events. We could hit a shitload now."

Blue sucked the nicotine deep into his lungs. He held it there a moment before exhaling. "Made too many if you ask me."

"Quit dwelling on that. Staci would have wanted you to—"

"Set up your deal for January. I don't even care where. I'll do it, but only if you shut up about the way things used to be. Staci's gone, and I don't want to hear another word about my horse, or the rodeo. That part of me died the day I buried her."

# 12

Ruby held the phone to her ear long after Blue hung up. Though he'd abruptly ended their conversation, her mind and worry remained connected to her baby brother. She ached to help him, to hug him tight and mend his hardened heart. Blue had always been her child more than their mother's, and Ruby the one to share his pains. When the dead air gave way to the piercing tone of a receiver off the hook, she hung up and leaned forward resting her forehead on her palms. She was out of ideas. Patience had done nothing but break her own heart, and tough love had alienated him from her and Briley all the more.

"Should I deliver these plates before they get cold?" Ray stood in the doorway to the kitchen wringing his hands the way he tended to when nervous.

"No, I will." Ruby shot the phone a longing look, before carrying the chicken-fried steaks out front.

Ray had worked for the family better than four decades, but still hated being face-to-face with customers. He preferred to stay in the kitchen, cooking and cleaning. Ruby had been only a young girl when he showed up, but now he was part of the family. Four years ago, when she closed the motel, he moved into two of the rooms. A drunk driver plowed into the end room last summer forcing them to tear that part of the building down. The other nine remained empty dusty shells, but Ruby didn't regret closing that side of the business. By herself, she barely had time for the café.

She made sure the three occupied tables had what they needed before making her way back to the stool next to the register. Staring out the front windows, she watched the tops of the eighteen-wheelers hum along. The interstate sat lower than the access road and the restaurant, hiding the smaller vehicles as they passed, but she knew they were out there, speeding past.

"Is he coming?"

Ruby looked up, surprised to see Ray out of the kitchen and beside her. She shook her head. "Not now. I suspect he'll be here a few weeks after Christmas. Just like always."

He smacked his toothless gums together and started back toward his pots and pans. "Miss Briley gonna be mighty disappointed."

"She's not the only one," Ruby whispered. "She's not the only one."

Two of the three tables paid and left before the monitor squawked with a tiny voice. "I'm up."

Ruby hit the button and said, "Okay, Honey, I'll be right there." She glanced at the lone customer to gauge how much time she had, but the man waved her over so she turned to the kitchen. "Ray, can you go get Briley? She's up from her nap."

The spring on the back door creaked as he headed to the house behind the café.

A few minutes later, Briley burst into the kitchen just as Ruby plopped a scoop of ice cream on a steaming bowl of apple cobbler. "I want 'nilla ice cream too."

Ruby eyed the young girl with skepticism. "Did you eat a good lunch before your nap?" A ring of snow-white hair fell across the child's rosy-cheeked face when she nodded. Ruby looked to Ray for assurance.

He grinned. "She ate all her ham and mashed potatoes, but her and them peas didn't seem to get along."

"One scoop," she said on her way to deliver the desserts out front.

Hungry travelers became scarce as afternoon gave way to evening. Briley sat on the floor behind the counter torturing a horde of naked Barbies, occasionally staring up at the cartoons on the corner television. Ruby tried not to think about Blue, sitting alone somewhere. She tried to tally out the register and concentrate on the week's food order.

She tried, but failed. Looking down, Ruby watched the adorable little towhead cram Barbie into the mouth of a stuffed Barney. "I will eat you," she growled. Briley shook the plastic doll's feet for effect.

Her imagination clearly showed Buster's influence. He never played with her without one or two dolls succumbing to some beast higher on the food chain. Briley wasn't interested in tea parties and dress-up. Nevertheless, Ruby couldn't imagine anyone regretting the decision to bring such a precious child into existence.

Regardless of the cost.

# 13

Lindsay bolted upright. Her heart pounded. She'd been trapped in another one of those dreams.

Relief settled over her at the realization she was on a couch in a camper in the middle of Idaho. Not back in her old room in Oklahoma.

In reality, there never had been a crib at the foot of her bed, but in her nightmares it was always there—waiting.

Wrapping her arms around her chest she rocked back and forth to fight off the chill, both within the RV and in her veins. Darkness filled the silent travel trailer. She pushed the illumination button on her Timex. Almost ten-thirty. It had been somewhere around three in the afternoon when Blue finished getting the camper leveled, and set up. Afterward, he retired to his room and she'd leaned back on the couch to ponder her homecoming. She hadn't meant to fall asleep when she reclined on the couch, but these last two days had taken a toll.

Blue had skidded past her on that lonely stretch of road only yesterday, but it seemed more like a month. The extra four or five miles she ran this morning combined with the drive had left her muscles tight and sore.

Her quads and hammies weren't the only things complaining. Lindsay's stomach rumbled. She looked toward Blue's bedroom. The door was shut, and no light seeped from underneath. He'd looked exhausted by the time the camper was situated. He'd confessed to driving straight through from Vegas that first night, and to only getting a few hours sleep the next. No doubt he'd finally crashed. She didn't want to disturb him, so rather than turn on the overhead lights, she flicked the switch for the fireplace.

The saffron flames gave the room a soft glow, and the fire's heat soon washed over her. It was almost midnight in Oklahoma. Her mother would be asleep. Her parents had always turned in right after the local news. She didn't know about Clay. Would he be home? On a date? Out running around with buddies?

She couldn't answer any of those questions. Her family's habits were foreign as a stranger's. Lindsay tried to picture her little brother as a man, but doing so filled her eyes with tears. She'd missed so much.

Her senior year of high school. Prom. College.

Seeing Clay grow up.

Her father had stolen far more than her baby. He'd taken her sense of belonging. Robbed her of hope. She stared into the fireplace. The flames licked at the ceramic logs. What she wouldn't give to burn away the past. Her father had gotten what he deserved.

Now he couldn't speak. Couldn't walk. He'd been left with nothing except his thoughts to occupy his time. If there was a shred of justice in the world, they were guilty thoughts.

Her stomach rumbled again. Lindsay tiptoed to the kitchen. Shadows cast by the flames danced on the walls as she sorted through the food Blue purchased earlier that day. She soon regretted her decision to wait in the truck while he shopped.

Feeling sorry for herself at the time, she sulked in the parking lot and watched the world around her go on about their lives, but Blue could've used help. The canned goods she found scared her. Pork and beans. Vienna sausage. Spam. She moved on to the refrigerator and freezer. Bloody hamburger meat. Ham steaks. T-Bones. Rib-eyes. Not one healthy item. Nothing but red meat.

Not a single portion of chicken or fish. No real vegetables. Closest thing was a sack of potatoes and a couple of onions on the counter.

Picking a good-sized potato from the bag, she retrieved the butter from the refrigerator, and searched for something else to improve the taste of a baked potato. The prospects of finding sour cream and chives seemed pretty slim, but just as she'd resigned herself to a dull dinner, Lindsay spotted the bacon. She hadn't eaten pork in several years, but if she fried the fatty strips long enough, she could make her own bacon bits. Not exactly healthy, but a baked potato without frills held the appeal of a fat man in a Speedo.

A few minutes later the grease popped and sizzled as she placed the meat in the hot skillet. She tried to remember the last time she'd fried anything. Had to have been when she lived with Seth. Or maybe Jaxson.

"You forgot the eggs."

Lindsay jumped. Busy recollecting her many failed relationships, she hadn't heard Blue walk up behind her.

"I didn't mean to wake you. Sorry, I got hungry."

"You didn't. The aroma rousted my stomach." He patted his midsection. "It's to blame."

"I'll put some bacon on for you." She cocked her head and looked at the refrigerator. "I don't remember seeing any eggs though."

"I was kidding. I didn't buy any." He sat at the table and watched her cook.

She took the strips she'd prepared for herself out of the pan and wrapped them in a paper towel to absorb the grease. While the rest of the meat fried, she removed the potato from the microwave.

His eyes followed as she moved about the kitchen, but his gaze didn't make her feel uncomfortable. She didn't get the sense he was ogling her, as much as studying her. Some people were good listeners. He appeared to be a good watch-er. During her stint waiting tables, she'd discovered a lot could be learned from viewing people's mannerisms. Putting the plate on the table, she wondered what Blue had decided about her.

Blue stuffed the bacon between two slices of bread while she crumbled hers and sprinkled it on the butter ooz-ing into her potato. He chewed behind a warped grin while she prepared her meal until his amused expression began to make her self-conscious.

"What?"

"Only a woman would go to so much trouble."

"What's that supposed to mean?"

He leaned over from the table's bench seat and pulled a gallon of milk out of the fridge. Reaching back without look-ing, he pulled a couple of glasses from the cabinet behind his head. "Women always make things more complicated than they need to be." He filled a glass and pushed it across the table.

"No thanks." Blank generalizations bothered her, espe-cially those based solely upon gender. "We do not, and I only drink skim. No more so than men anyway." She stood and grabbed the empty glass. "I'll have water."

"No man would fry bacon just to put on a baked potato."

"Okay, what would a man have done if he was hungry and there wasn't a single healthy thing to eat?"

"Healthy?"

"Yes, healthy. No vegetables. No fruit. Nothing but red meat."

Blue shook his head. "See, there you go. Meat is easy. You toss it on the grill, or throw it in a pan and you're done. No man would expect a three-course meal camped out in the middle of Idaho. We can live on meat and bread."

"What's wrong with chicken or fish?"

"In case you've never been around them, chickens are nasty little suckers. They don't discriminate between their food and feces. And I never buy fish."

Lindsay clenched her teeth. Feces? Who said feces? Did he think she'd never heard the word crap? Or shit? She couldn't argue with him if he was going to be so formal with her. "I still don't see why cooking bacon for my potato makes me complicated. Some people prefer to not dine like a Neanderthal."

"Do you ever do anything that's not *healthy*?" He pronounced healthy as if it were a dirty word.

She put down her fork. "Not on purpose. Why?"

Downing the rest of his milk, he stood and wiped the white away from the thick stubble above his lip. "No reason." He grabbed a pack of cigarettes off the counter.

"Do you ever do anything that's not unhealthy?"

He stopped on his way outside and smiled. "Probably not."

"Don't you care about your body?"

He shrugged. "Dying isn't the worst thing that can happen to you." He stepped down and closed the door behind him.

Lindsay sighed. Like she needed him to tell her that.

His departure left a lingering silence. She could either worry about her problems, or wonder about his. Choosing the less stressful wasn't difficult.

On the way out of Eagle's Rest, he'd said he was looking for something he could never find. Going to the window, she stared outside, just making out the dark shape of his form and the amber glow of his cigarette. What was Blue looking for? She watched until he ground the cigarette out on his boot heel and started back for the camper. Moving away from the window, Lindsay sat back at the kitchen table.

A rush of frigid air followed him inside. "Getting cold out there. A lot of moisture in the air. There'll be snow on the ground come morning."

Lindsay only nodded.

He went to the cabinet where she'd found the photo album and rummaged around. She held her breath. What if he realized she'd gone through his things? A wave of dread swept over her as she remembered the picture still in her pocket. She'd forgotten about it until now. She prayed it wasn't what he was searching for.

She shrunk down in her chair and began preparing an explanation, but her fears vanished when he sat down with a fishing reel and a box of line. Watching him transfer the string to the reel's spool, she stuck her hand into her pocket and felt to make sure the glossy print was still safely tucked inside. "Can I ask you something?"

He stopped cranking the reel's handle, but didn't raise his eyes to meet hers. "You can ask. Doesn't mean I'll answer."

"Why did you say yes when I asked for a ride?"

"You seemed desperate to get away." Blue bit through the fishing line, leaving a couple feet dangling from the reel.

"There had to be more to it than that."

"I've been that way myself. So I knew how you felt." He walked to the pantry and pulled out a fishing pole to which he attached the newly strung reel. "And I was leaving town anyway."

"Why were you in Eagle's Rest in the first place?"

"You said a question." He turned his back as he answered. "Quota's up."

She stared at his broad shoulders. So he'd come to Idaho hoping to find what he had lost. His wife? Maybe she'd run off with another man, but they looked so devoted to one another in the photos.

Once he put the now-assembled fishing rig back in the pantry and turned around, she said, "You must think I'm some kind of crazed psycho."

"If I thought that, I'd have said no. Besides, I know Janine. She's picky when it comes to choosing friends."

"You have to admit a sane person doesn't run away from home and then recruit a stranger to call back nine years later."

Shaking his head, Blue sat across from her. "There are no sane people. Spend a few hours at any poker table and you'll learn we're all crazy in some way."

Lindsay thought about his words. They might be true, but not everyone knew what real pain and guilt felt like. Something told her Blue did. "How did she sound?"

"Who?"

"My mother." Lindsay bit her lip and closed her eyes to hold back the tears. "Did she sound okay?"

He cleared his throat and stared up at the ceiling. "She sounded fine, but I have nothing to compare against."

Lindsay choked down sorrow as memories of how her family had been before she let Rusty Hawkins sweet talk her into the backseat of his silver Trans-Am.

The way her mother insisted they celebrate each and every holiday including Groundhog Day. There weren't any real groundhogs in Oklahoma, so the family made do by packing up and going to watch for shadows among a field of prairie dogs. The pride and set of her father's jaw every time an Oklahoma college bested a Texas sports team. The admiration in Clay's eyes when he showed off one of her cross-country medals. A single tear spilled down Lindsay's cheek.

Blue reached across the table. His thick, callused hand squeezed hers. "I'm sure your mother misses you. The good thing about families is they're always willing to forgive."

She took a deep breath. The good memories faded, replaced by the bad. "Forgiveness is a two-way street."

Nodding, he pulled his hand away.

Lindsay hadn't meant to sound so harsh, but Blue didn't understand. No one did.

# 14

Light filled the travel trailer. Too much light.

Lindsay tossed back the covers and went to the window to peer outside. Snow clung to the pine branches in billowy clumps, and covered the ground in a sparkling white sheet. Lying back down, she pulled the covers higher on her chest. How long had it been since she slept past sunup instead of seeing the sun rise while out pounding the pavement?

This morning, both her body and her mind told her to linger in the nice warm bed. She couldn't hear Blue stirring, so she still had time to relax and savor the rare occasion.

She'd stayed up half the night talking with Blue. After all the stories, she wanted to meet his friend Donnie. She could picture the two of them traveling the countryside from one rodeo to another. Their adventures would make a great movie. *"The Wild Adventures of the Bulldogger and the Bull Rider."* Bull being the common denominator. She'd heard enough to know they were both full of it, but they seemed to have had a good time.

Blue wouldn't tell her why he retired, and he deftly dodged her not-so-subtle attempts to steer the conversation toward talk of his ex-wife. Lindsay never even got him to acknowledge ever being married.

Leaning out of bed, she peered down the hall. His bedroom door stood open. He'd shut it when he retired for the night. She reached for her watch on the arm of the fold-out couch. "Ten after ten," she spoke out loud. Could that possibly be right? She hadn't slept that well, or lingered in bed that long in forever.

She swung her feet to the floor and tiptoed down the hall. Halfway there, she stopped. He might sleep in the nude. She didn't know if that idea excited her or scared her, but it did add intrigue to her snooping.

Like a soldier running reconnaissance, she stuck her head around the corner and pulled it right back out. The bed was empty. Made, as a matter of fact. But where was he? Not in the bathroom. Unless he did his business with the door wide open.

Back in the living area, she sat on the edge of the fold-away bed. He could've left without her hearing, but surely she hadn't slept that hard. Lindsay went to the door and looked outside. She had to shield the snow's harsh glare with her hand, but sure enough, a rectangular patch of gravel, where his truck had been parked, contrasted against the powder-covered ground.

Fear clutched her for a brief second until she realized he hadn't left for good. He wouldn't abandon his camper. Shivering, she pulled the door shut.

Lindsay reached for her bag. With any luck, she'd be showered and dressed before he returned. Lifting a t-shirt from the duffel, she spotted the picture. Last night, after Blue turned in, she pulled the photo out of her pocket. It hadn't been hard to tell who the blonde little girl belonged to. Everything about her looked like Blue's bride, except the eyes. The child had the woman's hair, the same delicate nose, and high round cheekbones. However, those dark, troubled eyes belonged to her father. On Blue, they told of his serious and quiet demeanor, but on someone so young, they seemed sad and lonesome. Almost haunting.

Normally, Lindsay refused to study the faces of children. The innocence and purity in their expressions only intensified her guilt, but something about this little girl captivated her.

Once she knew for sure Blue was asleep last night, Lindsay got the photo album back out and went through it again. There were no other snapshots of the child. Matter of fact, the pictures ended just as his wife's belly seemed ready to burst. The one small, wallet-sized portrait she'd found on the floor had fallen out of the book, as if placed inside as an afterthought.

The slamming of a car door jolted Lindsay out of her pondering. Quickly, she stuffed the photo back in her bag and sat ramrod straight. She should've put the photo back in the book last night when she had the chance, but for some reason she kept it out. Blue knocked the snow from his boots on the steps, turned the handle and entered. Clean-shaven with a smile plastered on his face, a grocery sack was tucked beneath his arm. "Morning." He tipped his head and pulled off a battered and stained black cowboy hat.

"Been out feeding the cattle?" She pointed to the head wear.

He shook his head. "Was still snowing when I left." He sat the brown sack down on the counter and disappeared to his bedroom. A few seconds later, he reemerged minus the hat. "Want some breakfast?" He raked his fingers through his short hair.

"How'd you get that scar?" She asked to deflect attention

from herself. She felt vulnerable sitting in bed still dressed in a pair of sweats and a ratty old t-shirt.

Touching the thin arc behind his ear, he said, "Bad timing. A steer in Hutchison stopped and threw his head back just as I came down." Pulling a box of All-Bran from the sack and a half-gallon of skim milk, he said, "I picked up a few things for you." He lifted clear bags of bananas, apples, and oranges. "Even stooped to buying chicken." He held up a package of breast meat. "Somewhere down the road, I'll find a stream and catch us some trout."

"You don't have to do that."

Blue shrugged. "I don't want it said I inflicted my unhealthy habits on you."

"I appreciate everything you've done for me too much to ever say that."

"I'm not worried about you saying it."

Lindsay held her breath. Was he finally going to bring up his wife? When he said no more, she exhaled. "There's nobody else around to know you gave me a ride."

"My sister knows what I'm going to do before I've ever done it." He tossed a ham steak in a frying pan. "She'll get wind of us somehow."

"You must be close. Women always know what's going on with those they love." Lindsay remembered the way her mother figured things out before Lindsay even admitted she was pregnant to herself. Just as Janine had with Missy.

"We used to be, but not anymore. That's my fault, not hers."

Lindsay threw her reservations aside and stood. Blue had already seen her sleeping, probably with her lips open and spit gathered at the corners of her mouth. What did it matter that he saw her in baggy sleeping clothes? Maybe her appearance would soften him enough to open up. "Usually it's a man's wife who knows his every move."

He didn't react. "Want me to fry you some ham?"

Disappointed, she shook her head. "No. I'll just have a piece of fruit, but I'm going to jump in the shower first."

As the hot water washed over her body, Lindsay wondered why he refused to discuss his past. She'd given him plenty of chances to tell her he was divorced. Maybe he wasn't. Maybe Janine didn't even know the truth, but men didn't hide their marital state unless they had ulterior motives. Blue didn't come across as the philandering type. Nor had he shown much sign of being interested in her that way, though she'd twice caught him checking out her ass.

Sometime today she would just come out and ask if he was divorced. He probably wouldn't offer much more than a yes or no, but at least she could direct her next line of questioning in response to his answer. She'd never met anyone so reluctant to divulge even the most basic facts of his personal life.

Blue had to be as curious about her as well, yet he hadn't tried to find out a thing. Most men tried to impress every woman they met. At least the ones she'd dated had. Tristan had used his intellect and sense of righteousness. Blaine his guitar. Shane recited poetry. Then there had been the hang-glider, the triathlete, and Sven, the Swedish snowboarder. All of them had gone out of their way to show off their athleticism and daringness.

Blue had shared plenty of stories about the rodeo last night, but not a single one highlighted his ability. Matter of fact, most of his tales centered on something stupid he'd done, usually to bail out an even dumber stunt his friend Donnie had pulled to land them in a trouble. Blue seemed more comfortable talking about his failures than his accomplishments. All except his marriage, but then again, Lindsay still didn't know for certain which category it fell into.

The scent of Blue's soap reminded her of fresh sawdust. Woody, piney, masculine. The smell fit perfectly with her perception of him. Wood was strong and durable but had to be sanded before revealing its smooth texture and beautiful grained finish. Maybe that was the approach to take. Find a way to scrape off the outer, exposed bark and get to the underlying details of his life. To do so she'd need to be as harsh and gritty as sandpaper.

She emerged from the bathroom in a cloud of steam. Blue had folded the couch and stowed the blankets. Now he sat at the table cutting up his breakfast with a steak knife.

Lindsay took the seat opposite him. "I didn't mean for you to have to pick up after me."

He stabbed a piece of meat with his fork. "I hope you're not going to apologize every time I do something around here."

"I don't want to cause you extra trouble." She hid a blossoming smile, for trouble was exactly what she intended to cause. Maybe not trouble exactly, but at the very least, she wanted to stir things up.

An hour later, Blue had the camper hitched, and they headed east out of Idaho Falls because snowdrifts closed the road south. An eager anxiousness filled the space inside Lindsay's chest. She had to be careful. Blue might take offense to her new hard-line approach. If she didn't finagle her plan just right, she could find herself stuck on the side of the road waving her thumb. Subtlety would be key.

"Don't know how far we'll make it today. Depends what kind of shape the roads are in." He flicked his turn signal and passed an eighteen-wheeled flatbed loaded with telephone poles. "Hauling a trailer gets tricky when the weather turns."

An idea came to Lindsay as she stared at the heavy load passing by her window. Shaking her head, she clucked through her teeth like a worried hen.

"What?" Blue cast a sideways glance her direction as he pulled back in front of the trucker.

"You ever consider how many big mature trees must be cut to lay even a few miles of telephone line? First they chop down those they make the poles with, and then in most places they cut down even more so some rich capitalist on a hill can dial up his stockbroker." She repeated the speech almost verbatim the way she'd heard it from an old boyfriend.

"Most rich guys use cell phones," he stated without emotion.

Lindsay chided herself for not thinking of that back when her ex, a green peace wannabe, was railing on the subject. Strike one for her plan.

Her scheme seemed so simple in the shower. Get Blue to argue with her. Rile him up so he would reveal things about himself attempting to justify his actions. She'd come up with at least a dozen things to call him out on. The fact he drove a gas-guzzler. The carcinogens his smoking inflicted on others. The cruelties against the animals used by rodeos.

"Speaking of calls," he said. "When do you want to try your brother again?"

She shrugged. "Whenever we stop, I guess."

She couldn't antagonize him. Well, she could, but she shouldn't. Not when he'd gone out of his way to help. Not to mention the fact she couldn't effectively debate any of those issues. All she could do was boldly regurgitate someone else's beliefs. One side always sounded so logical when presented to her, but soon as she heard the other view, it held merit as well. Other people had definite opinions, but she had commitment issues. In more ways than one.

Blue struck her as someone who never wavered, never straddled the fence. Looking at him, she knew making him mad wouldn't be hard, but now, with her idea out in the open, she realized he would only turn tight-lipped. He simply wasn't the type to get emotional and speak without thinking. That was her department.

She'd be better served to ponder her arrival in Oklahoma as opposed to unearthing the secrets of a man she'd never see again once they arrived. This whole fascination with Blue stemmed from her desire to ignore her own problems.

"This morning was the first time in five years I didn't get up and run. I had the flu the last time."

Blue drove without responding. The truck's tires clicked and bounced as they passed over a canal bridge.

"I'm not even sure why I do it anymore," she said.

"Why do any of us do anything?" He reached for the pack of Marlboro's on the dash. "Least running is good for you. Unlike my habits." He rolled down his window before lighting up.

With every puff, the crow's-feet bunched around his eyes, and his cheeks became hollow craters. Getting the sense he wanted to suck the poison deep into his body, Lindsay watched, unable to look away.

She waited until he stubbed out his cigarette and rolled up the window before speaking. "How would you react if your sister showed up nine years after running away?"

"I have sisters I haven't seen more than five or six times my whole life. When I see them, it's like meeting an old acquaintance. We talk, but not about anything that matters."

Lindsay knew how those sisters felt. Blue never seemed to talk about anything that mattered.

"Were you close to your brother before you left?"

His question surprised her. "Sort of," she answered. "But he's six years younger than I am, and he was young, so we didn't have a lot in common."

Blue nodded. "It'll be awkward. More for you than him. Better get it in your head now he's not a little kid anymore."

"I already found that out. I called on Thanksgiving. He sounded so much older. He asked me to come home. I told him I didn't know if I could, but now I feel this need. To see him, if nothing else." Lindsay waited for Blue to ask why she couldn't go back, or what made her leave in the first place, but her statement died in the air between them.

Traveling Highway 26, they followed the Snake River for several miles. The silence pressed in on Lindsay. She needed to talk. "How many sisters do you have?" She waited, half-expecting him to ignore the question.

"Five," he finally replied. "But I don't really know any of them except Ruby. She was the youngest of the girls. My sudden arrival surprised the family seventeen years later."

"Your youngest sister is seventeen years older than you?"

He nodded. "I was my parent's last hurrah. Or mistake, depending how you look at it. Ruby's the one who really raised me. The others were gone, either to college or married before I came along. Our dad died while I was in grade school, and Mom was busy running the café. Ruby stayed home to take care of me."

"Is your mother still alive?"

"She died my freshman year at Oklahoma State." Blue reached to turn on the radio. "How about some music? You got a preference?"

Lindsay wasn't going to let him off that easy. "Your sister must have loved you to put her own life on hold."

Blue's hand lingered on the knob. "Ruby would walk through the gates of hell for me, but she would make dang sure I knew how hot it was." Static spilled through speakers as the radio scanned the meager selection of nearby stations.

They passed through another town she didn't catch the name of. A few miles later, they came to a dam on the river. Lindsay stared at the concrete structure.

"I wanted to go to Oklahoma State," she said as Blue hit the digital tuner yet again when the current station became more static than music.

"You should have," he said over a brief interlude of classical music.

Without thinking, Lindsay lowered her head and said, "I couldn't. I got pregnant."

The tuner stopped on Johnny Cash's voice singing "Ring of Fire." Blue hit the button to leave it there as Lindsay felt the familiar flames of guilt.

Blue's eyes flicked her direction. She could almost see the question forming in his mind. What would she say when he asked where the child was? But she didn't have to worry. He didn't ask. He never asked questions.

The music played as the miles slipped behind. Johnny Cash gave way to Merle Haggard, followed by Patsy Cline. The old songs reminded her of car rides with her father.

She drifted back nine years. To that trip home from Dallas. Just Lindsay and her father and the radio. Her sobs the only accompaniment to the music. For the first few miles, her dad tried to comfort her. Said things like, "It was for the best," and "We did what we had to." He'd said, "It will get easier." Three hours later, as they pulled into Norman, he pleaded with her, "Wipe your face. Get some control. You don't want to upset your mother."

All Lindsay wanted was for him to put his arm around her and say he was sorry. For once, he could've forgotten her mother's fragile emotions. Acted like he cared about more than erasing Lindsay's mistake. Her dad could have given her time to think; instead he rushed her off to Texas.

He never even let her tell Rusty.

Maybe things would've turned out differently had her mother gone with them to Dallas. But of course that hadn't happened.

Lindsay closed her eyes. Tears filled them anyway. If only she'd had someone to wait inside the clinic with her. If only someone would've given her a say.

If only she could go back in time.

# 15

Blue stared at the sign welcoming them to Wyoming. That much closer to Texas. One month exactly to Christmas Day. Stomaching the holiday was tough enough without the added reminder Briley's birthday brought only a week before. The seventeenth of December was the one day he needed to spend alone. Each year his daughter's disappointment added another layer to the scars, but Blue simply couldn't celebrate the anniversary of his pain. No matter whom it hurt.

To chase away the past, Blue turned to Lindsay and said, "One state down."

She only nodded.

Blue appreciated the fact she could ride in silence. At times, she asked too many questions, but to her credit, even when Lindsay pressed too much, she took his hints and fell quiet again. These quiet, reflective times gave him a real sense of who she was. The cold glaze of her hazel eyes, the set of her jaw, the stiffness in her shoulders, all betrayed the turbulence within. Lindsay's hurt became all the more evident when she talked of home and family, or most recently when she revealed her pregnancy. So far, Blue had only seen tears, but he respected her pain the same he would a wounded animal. Someone, or something, had backed her into a corner.

He knew that corner well.

The afternoon sun slipped behind the clouds as they drove. High, snow-capped peaks surrounded them. The hours passed with only snatches of conversation. Occasionally she would try to draw him out. *Do you think it will snow? Have you ever been to Wyoming before? That rock reminds me of a camel. Don't you think that stream is pretty?*

He refused to get sucked in, but Lindsay's comments reminded Blue of trips with his wife.

Staci always preferred this, the more scenic route home. In truth, so had Blue, but now he refused to acknowledge the beauty of the land. Willing himself not to be inspired by the view was his way of paying a debt.

He didn't deserve to feast upon the pine-scented air, didn't deserve to gaze upon nature's magnificence, didn't deserve enjoyment from life.

Undeserving. That one word summed up his existence.

Four hours into their travels, Blue pointed at a sign that read *Rock Springs, 49 miles.* "We'll grab supper there and gas up. It'll be our last chance before we hit Utah."

"I lived in Utah for a while," Lindsay said. "Park City. I had a boyfriend who worked there as a snowboard instructor."

"I don't linger in the state any longer than necessary. I've shed a lot of blood within its borders."

"Uh-oh." She smiled. "This sounds like another Donnie story."

"Partly. Donnie and me hit a couple of rodeos there. I never cashed at a single one. Matter of fact, my fortunes got worse each time we went. Couple of more visits and they might've had to bury me."

"Bury you?" Lindsay's eyes crinkled the way they always

did when her curiosity piqued.

"That's the way things were headed. First time we went to Saint George, a wheel-bearing locked up on my horse trailer. Damn near cut my thumb off trying to get it fixed. Then on my second trip, I separated my elbow trying to get a salty steer to the ground. That was Provo. And the third and last event I hit was even worse. Winder, my horse, cut his flank coming out of the chute and later that night I wound up with eighteen stitches in the back of my head."

"From another steer?"

Blue chuckled. "Nope, Donnie."

The dimples deepened on her cheeks. "I should've known.  After what you told me about him last night, it's a wonder he didn't get you maimed everywhere the two of you went."

"Donnie doesn't mean any harm. His mouth gets him into trouble at times, and he's a bit reckless where he sheds his pants, but he's got a weakness for pretty women. Actually, they don't even have to be all that pretty. That gal in Logan was far from a beauty queen, but in Donnie's defense, he had no idea she was married. Least not until her husband came looking for her."

Blue rubbed the back of his head. Six or seven years had passed, but a knot still rose up from the spot where the man clubbed him.

"Let me guess, the husband found you instead."

"Yep. That's Donnie for you. One step ahead of disaster."

"How did the two of you become friends? Doesn't sound like you have much in common."

"He sort of attached himself to me his freshman year. I was a senior, and to tell you the truth, he got on my nerves at first. Still can at times, but he's truer than most. People I thought were my friends have bailed on me. Donnie's hung in there through the good and the bad."

They slowed as they entered the town of Farson, Wyoming. The countryside now matched his mood. Gone were the thick timbered forest and jagged peaks. Now the land had a flat, desolate look.

"Sometimes I envy Donnie," Blue said, staring ahead at the lonesome highway.

Lindsay turned in her seat to face him. "Why?"

"He doesn't have a care in the world. He can travel a thousand miles to an event, get bucked off coming out of the gate, and still get up from the dirt wearing a smile. He's always happy."

"Trust me. No one is always happy," Lindsay said with more conviction than he'd ever heard in her voice.

The tires hummed against the pavement.

Blue took a deep breath. "Maybe not, but Donnie comes a hell of a lot closer than most."

She reached across the seat and placed her hand on Blue's arm where it bent at the elbow. The miles slid by, and still she didn't remove her hand. He kept his eyes on the blacktop and his mind on Lindsay. He wanted to speak, but didn't trust himself not to part with more than he truly wanted to share.

They rode that way until she pulled her hand away as Rock Springs came into view. Blue drove into town, content with the silence, but the quick glances she shot his way told him she was working up her nerve to unleash another barrage of questions.

"Are you married?"

The question didn't come as a surprise. She'd been fishing for that information since last night. At least she'd come out and asked this time instead of dancing around.

"I was. Once."

He spotted a truck stop up ahead.

"Was? Does that mean—"

"We'll stop here." Lifting his foot from the gas pedal, he kept talking. "Truck stops are about the only places you can depend on to have a public phones these days. We can call your brother." He turned into the station.

"Are you—"

"If you don't mind, see if they have some Tylenol in there. I have a hell of a headache coming on." He turned off the truck and opened the door to escape the cab. Behind him, Lindsay sighed and climbed down from the truck.

Blue watched her walk away with slumped shoulders, clearly disappointed he'd ended the conversation. Lindsay's questions were more than he could deal with right now, but her willingness to drop the subject comforted him.

The smell of gasoline hung in the air as he filled the Ford.

"You look familiar. Do I know you?"

Blue studied the thick-necked man standing at the front of his truck. Faded green tattoos snaked up the man's arms and disappeared beneath the sleeves of a bright orange t-shirt adorned with a NASCAR logo. Despite the fact icicles hung from the eaves of the canopy above the pumps the man wore a ratty pair of cutoffs, which hung below a huge beer belly. A twelve-pack of Keystone dangled from his grease-stained hand.

Blue knew plenty of unsavory characters, but didn't recognize this one. "I don't think so." He pulled the hose out and replaced his gas cap.

Lindsay walked up behind the man.

"Kiss my ass. You are him." The man's grin was shy several teeth.

"Look, partner. I'm not even from around here so you must be mistaken." Blue stepped closer to the man.

"I know where you're from. Texas. You're 'Ice' Riggins. This is fucking crazy." Tattoo Man wiped his palm across the front of his shirt and extended it forward. "Name's Karl with a K. Karl Stephens, but most folks call me Pinky acuz of this." He held up a grease-stained hand missing its smallest digit. "I can't believe this shit. I'm never this damn lucky."

Blue shook the man's hand.

"I saw you kick that Chinaman's ass on TV, and then the very next week you bluffed old Bachman until he choked on his own balls. Fucking ice. Just like they say. Never blinked a fucking eye. Could you sign this for me?" He lifted up the twelve pack of beer. "Me and my buddies play every Saturday night" He pulled out a cell phone. "Can I take a quick picture? Nobody will believe this shit."

"Watch your language," Blue warned. "I'll sign," he shot a look in Lindsay direction, "But you need to remember you're not sitting around a poker table with a bunch of men."

The man's eyes widened. He looked over his shoulder. "Oh hell … I mean, sorry. I'm just excited. Ain't every day you meet a celebrity. Much less a champion poker player like 'Ice' Riggins."

The man leaned in tight and snapped a selfie while Blue scribbled his name. He left out the nickname. Blue hated the title, and wished the poker craze would die down so they'd quit showing tournaments on TV. His days of signing autographs should've ended when he hung up his saddle.

Lindsay narrowed her eyes when the happy man trotted off to his vehicle. "You never told me you were a professional gambler."

"It's a hobby." Blue walked past her and headed straight to the bank of payphones. He punched in the numbers from his card and followed with those Lindsay had given him yesterday.

She looked over his shoulder. "You remembered?"

The phone rang. "I have a knack for numbers. Helps at the poker table."

"Hello," a masculine voice answered.

"Is this Clay?"

"Yeah, who's this?"

"Someone wants to talk to you." Blue handed the phone to Lindsay and strode away. He understood the importance of privacy, even if no one else did.

Ruby certainly didn't. His sister thought he could just toss aside his anguish and act as if nothing had happened. She called into question his responsibility. She didn't realize he felt responsible every single day.

He'd give anything for his heart not to shatter when he looked at his daughter. He wanted to be there for Briley. He wanted to watch her blow out birthday candles. Blue knew the hurt his absence caused. He didn't want to blame Briley. Women weren't supposed to die in childbirth. Not anymore. But Staci had.

Lindsay hung up. Head down, she headed back toward the truck. He looked only long enough to see the streaks on her cheeks and the red rims of her eyes. He didn't need to ask what was said. He knew all too well the emotions involved in going home.

They pulled away from the station with silence again riding shotgun.

When the town faded from view, she said, "Now I have

to go back. I promised Clay I would be there. Why did I promise?"

This time Blue reached for her. He placed his right hand on her shoulder. "You were already going back before you told your brother. Nothing has changed."

Lindsay nodded. "Yes, it has. Before I had a choice. Now I don't."

# 16

Lindsay's heartbeat echoed in her ears as her feet pounded the cracked pavement of Main Street. Main Street of what town, she couldn't say. Northwestern Colorado, a half hour or so from the Utah state line. She knew that much. They'd driven until almost midnight, and she'd been half-asleep when they rolled into the RV park so this was her first real look at the area.

In the purple predawn light, the settlement had a bleak, down-on-its-luck kind of feel, but that impression was probably the result of her own dour mood.

Turning south she pushed herself hard to make up for not running yesterday. A dog bounded from beneath a ramshackle porch. Lindsay never broke stride as it barked at her heels. Her mind and fears remained centered on more perilous evils. The mutt yapped and followed thirty yards or so before trotting back to its gray, unpainted shelter.

Colorado.

Lindsay shook her head. The trip was going too fast. Her father used to bring her and Clay to Colorado every winter to ski. They made the trek in one day. She kicked up her pace at the thought she could be back in Oklahoma early as tonight. She wasn't ready.

She tried to conjure a mental image of her father in a wheelchair, paralyzed on one side, unable to speak. Had his thick, dark hair turned completely gray or was it only a bit lighter at the temples the way she remembered? Did the muscles in his stern jaw still tighten when he was angry, or had they too gone weak and useless? Lindsay wanted to know what to expect when she waltzed into that nursing home. She wanted the upper hand. She wanted to own the element of surprise, but that all depended on Clay keeping his promise not to tell anyone she was on her way.

Maintaining a rigorous pace, she came to a bridge where a small creek trickled underneath. Slowing to give her quivering muscles a break, she locked her fingers behind her head, inhaled deeply, and walked a few dozen yards to catch her breath. She would go see her father first. Blue could drop her off at the nursing home. From there she would walk home or call Clay to come pick her up. But the important thing was to get the worst over with.

Allowing herself only a brief respite, Lindsay took off back in the direction she'd come. Having a hint of a plan gave her hope and a renewed energy.  Again, the dog came out barking. Her pace was slower this time so the mutt veered closer showing teeth and snapping, but one quick stutter step sent the mongrel away with its head and tail lowered. She wished the rest of her problems could be dealt with as easily. Rounding the corner, she jogged up Main Street, back toward the RV park.

Lindsay had been running her whole life. Either toward something or away. Her greatest troubles always came when she slowed down. Stayed in one place too long, fell for too many of a man's lines, or gave herself too much time to think.

That's what she'd done now. Slowed to a crawl. And not

even forward. No, she was inching backward like a crab at the bottom of the sea. Back to Oklahoma.

She couldn't pinpoint what she hoped to accomplish. Forgiving her parents was not an option. She knew that much. That possibility as unlikely as Blue revealing his innermost feelings. And Blue was an entirely different problem. She'd thought riding with him would give her time to iron out her thoughts before arriving. But being around him only compounded her troubles. Every time she tried to concentrate on what to tell her dad, Blue popped into her consciousness.

Now, when she visualized walking through the front door of her childhood home, Blue was there beside her. When she thought about the child she would never have, the dark eyes of Blue's daughter sprang to her conscience. It wasn't tired worn out pick-up lines or promises that had entangled her in his trap, but his demeanor. His calm. His stoic silences. His mysteriousness. And even though it flustered her, his aloofness.

If she was honest, his butt as well. Ever since Janine pointed it out, Lindsay had been fully aware of the way he filled out those jeans. And those arms. That chest. He might've retired, but Lindsay had no trouble believing he could still wrestle a large steer to the ground. She couldn't really afford to get distracted by Blue's physique, or the fantasy that their relationship would evolve into something more.

Not when they were a day out from Oklahoma. Not when he'd dump her off to face her past early as tonight. The sun peaked over the horizon as the campground came into view. Her breath escaped in white puffs.

Maybe they'd simply spent too much time together in the close proximity of his truck. Maybe the appeal was only the product of wishful thinking. The desire for someone to be on her side of the emotional battle. She barely knew Blue, but things about him captured her imagination and compelled her to learn more. He was attractive, but not in the same way as most of the men that drew her attention. Matter of fact, nothing about him was like the other men she'd known.

Blue's appeal came from his physical and mental strength. He possessed a confidence most men only pretended to have. His skin looked as if it had seen plenty of sun and wind rather than the fluorescent lights of a tanning bed. He talked only when he wanted to, as opposed to using words as a tool to convince everyone how much he knew.

Fifty feet from the camper, she slowed to let her muscles cool. Her heart pounded inside her chest. She stopped to stretch when she reached their campsite. Lifting her right leg on to the picnic table, Lindsay leaned over and touched her toes. She did the same with her left. To complete the routine, she rubbed the tightness from first her quads, then her calves.

"Nice run?"

Blue's voice startled her. Leaned against the camper, he took a long drag off his cigarette. The smoke curled in wisps above his head.

"It was okay. Hope I didn't wake you when I left."

He shook his head. "I'd been up a while. Sleep is never easy." He stubbed out the butt on his boot heel.

"I know the feeling." She nodded. "Let me cook breakfast this morning."

"I'm not hungry. Thought we'd head down the road soon as you're ready."

"Oh... Mind if I take a quick shower?"

Lindsay went inside feeling ambushed. If there was a connection between the two of them, it apparently was one-sided. Blue wanted rid of her as fast as possible. Leaving this early, they would easily make Oklahoma tonight. It would be late, but Blue didn't seem to care. He'd driven until nearly midnight last night, and now here they were leaving again and the sun had barely cleared the horizon.

Stripping out of her sweaty clothes, she turned on the shower. She could hear Blue tinkering outside the trailer's thin walls. It sounded as if he were already raising the camper's leveling jacks. What had she done to make him so determined to get on the road? And why did it give her a thrill to know only a thin wall separated him from her naked body?

Half an hour later, she was dressed, but Lindsay still hadn't put her finger on what she'd done to wear out her welcome. Blue brought the trailer's slide-outs in and folded up the stairs. His pickup idled at the ready.

Lindsay rubbed the back of her neck. She cleared her throat and waited while Blue made one last check around the travel trailer. When he finished, she asked, "Are we in a hurry?"

"Not really." He shrugged and brushed past her. Crossing in front of the big Ford, he slid behind the wheel.

She followed suit and climbed up into the passenger seat. "Why don't you like me?" The question floating around her mind escaped before she had a chance to think, but as it came out, Lindsay wished she'd kept it there.

Blue took his hand off the shifter and stared into her eyes. "Never said I didn't."

"You didn't have to. Your actions say plenty."

His brows angled down in the center. "What's that supposed to mean?"

"You barely talk to me, and when you do it's about something idiotic like the weather or the way women do things." Words spewed from her mouth faster than she could stop them. "And now you're trying to get rid of me fast as you can. I want us to be friends, and to be able to talk, but if that's not going to happen, tell me now and I'll shut up. Or if you really want you can dump me off in the next town with a bus station."

"Are you finished?" His dark eyes never left hers.

She nodded.

"Good. I'm not trying to get rid of you. It's these RV parks I don't like, not you. They drag me down. I rarely stay in these places, but we didn't have a choice last night. That's why we're leaving so early. Has nothing to do with you. Okay?"

Lindsay nodded again. She wanted to ask how he did feel about her, but she'd said enough for now.

Blue put the truck in gear and pulled away from the campsite, but before they could exit the park, an old man stepped into the narrow gravel road. The stoop-shouldered fellow pulled a green oxygen tank with one hand, and held a leash connected to an apricot poodle in the other. Blue watched the old man long after he cleared the road. "That's why I hate these places," he finally said.

Lindsay looked again at the man who'd shuffled off, and now stood beneath the awning of a small Airstream. A heavy-set woman with blue-tinged hair bent over and scooped the dog up into her wide lap.

"What don't you like? Old people or poodles?" Lindsay smiled and turned back to face Blue, but his face looked grim.

"The people at these parks are all like that. They've been married to each other forever. Their health is bad. Their dogs are old and about to die. On the surface, the best part of their lives is over, but you know what?"

Her smile faded as she awaited his answer.

"No matter how bad things get, they have a lifetime of

good memories to think back on." He lifted his foot from the brake and pulled onto the street.

She continued to stare at him as they turned south on Highway 139 and drove out of town. Realizing Blue had revealed more of himself in that single statement than in the past two days, a sadness settled over her.

There was no traffic on the road, and as usual Blue fell silent. Country music drifted through the speakers, but Lindsay didn't pay much attention, nor did his silence bother her the way it had before. She thought about what he said back at the RV park. He hadn't pitied those elderly campers the way she first thought. Rather he envied them, for their long lives together.

What happened with his wife? How could a woman leave a man who so obviously loved her?

"You want to hear something strange?"

He glanced over, but offered no reply.

She purposely avoided eye contact. "Sometimes I think we have more in common than either of us knows. Then sometimes, I think I'm imagining something that isn't there. I don't really know much about you. I don't even know where in Texas you're from."

"I'm from the middle of nowhere."

She rolled her eyes. "See. That's what I mean."

He raised his brows, but Lindsay kept right on talking. "Why are you so afraid to divulge even the most basic parts of your life? And what about me?"

"You?"

"Yes, me. You have to be at least a tiny bit curious about me. But do you ask any questions? No. Wouldn't you like to know why I ran away from home, or why I've stayed gone so long?" Lindsay hadn't meant to get so fired up, but she couldn't stop now that she'd started. "I don't even know where we are. For all I know we'll be in Norman tonight where you'll deposit me on my parents' porch and ride off into the sunset."

Blue laughed.

Not just a chuckle or a smile, but full-out, body-shaking laughter erupted from deep in his body.

She didn't know he was capable. "What's so damn funny?"

"It's been too long since I traveled with a woman. I'd forgotten all the crazy notions that pop into y'alls head out on the road."

"Don't you dare turn this into another of your speeches about women's habits."

"Okay, okay." He held up a hand. "You just reminded me of my wife there for a second. She came up with the damndest stuff when we drove. Her mind went for some wild rides."

Lindsay held her breath. She'd already stepped off the cliff. No reason to stop now. "What happened between the two of you? Why aren't you still married?"

Blue turned to stare out his window.

Just when Lindsay thought he wasn't going to respond, he took a deep breath, and shut off the radio. Still not facing her he said, "I lost her. She passed away. Four years ago this month."

Lindsay cringed. Why hadn't she thought of that? The woman had looked so healthy in the pictures. But what did that really mean? People lost their lives in all kinds of ways. She didn't know what to say. "I'm sorry. I shouldn't have been so nosy."

He shook his head. "I should be able to talk about it, but

I struggle. Especially this time of year."

Miles passed by before he spoke again.

"I really did grow up in the middle of nowhere. My parents owned a roadside café and motel on I-27. That's the highway that connects Amarillo and Lubbock, but our mail came from Happy, and I went to high school in Grand, Texas. The nearest hospital was in Canyon. That's where I was born. So if you need a name, take your pick."

"I've only heard of Amarillo and Lubbock. My dad hated everything and everybody from Texas. He's an Okie to the bone."

"That reminds me," Blue said. "We won't be anywhere near Oklahoma tonight. I plan to stop in Cripple Creek for the night to pick up a few things I left there."

She nodded.

"I'd say the earliest we can be there is Tuesday evening."

"We don't have to hurry," she said. "I'm not ready to go home just yet."

In Montrose, Colorado, they stopped for lunch at a place called The Red Barn. He ordered steak, medium rare, and she asked for a pasta salad. When the waitress brought their drinks Lindsay asked, "So, if your parents owned a café, how'd you get started in the rodeo? I thought all rodeo guys grew up on ranches and stuff?"

Blue emptied two packets of sugar into his tea, stirred, and took a drink before responding. "Most do I guess, but this guy named Buster Glick used to hang out in the café. He owned a big ranch, but ate every meal at our place. He took me under his wing and let me hang around and help out at his spread between meals. He's the one who taught me to rope and ride."

"That was nice."

"I suppose, but he only did it because he was in love with my sister. He was married, so Ruby wouldn't have anything to do with him. By keeping me around, he got to stay close."

"That didn't raise his wife's suspicions?"

Blue shook his head. "His wife never left their house. She fell off a horse ten or twelve years before and was completely paralyzed. Couldn't even speak."

"And this Buster guy was out chasing your sister?"

"I don't know if chasing is the right word, but he couldn't stay away from Ruby. Buster eventually bought me a horse and started hauling me all over the country to junior rodeos."

Lindsay sipped her water. "What about his wife? Who took care of her when y'all went to rodeos?"

"By that point she was in a nursing home. She died a few years back."

"Sounds like the plot of a soap opera." Lindsay shook her head. "Except I guess in a soap opera your sister would've been her nurse or something."

"Buster's wife and my oldest sister were once best friends. But that sister moved, and then his wife had the accident. Still the history of it all made Ruby run from Buster pretty hard. And he had a ranch to run. A big one. Damn near four sections, so he had a lot to juggle. Still he spent a lot of time beside his wife's bed. I don't know how he did it. I only saw her once, when we stopped on the way back from a rodeo. I'll never forget the way she laid there, staring up at nothing."

"Did he and your sister ever ..." She let her question trail off, unsure how to finish.

Blue nodded and took another drink. "Yeah, he finally wore Ruby down. My junior year of high school I walked in on them in one of the motel's spare rooms."

The waitress delivered their meals.

"They never got married?"

"Not yet. Couldn't until his wife died. But Buster's still around so I expect they will one of these days."

"The whole story sounds both sad, and I don't know, kind of messed up. What with his wife stuck in a nursing home, and him and your sister having to hide away in a hotel room. I can see both sides I guess. I know love never seems to fall between tidy straight lines, but their story seems sorta twisted."

Blue shrugged. "They fought it for years. Neither was proud how it came to be. They loved each other, but they both felt guilty. Trust me, I know. Heard it a thousand times from both sides."

Lindsay was beginning to see why Blue was so withdrawn. He'd been surrounded by tragedy his whole life. His father's death when he was so young. His sister unable to marry the man she wanted. His own wife dying. Lindsay stared across the table at Blue. Love had never resulted in anything but pain in his life.

She looked down at her untouched plate. But at least Blue knew what true love felt like.

# 17

Ruby turned the sign to CLOSED and sat on the stool behind the register. She looked at her wristwatch for the umpteenth time, even though she already knew it was five after six. At times it seemed she'd spent half her life sitting on this stool waiting—waiting for customers, waiting for something good to happen—waiting for her life to start.

A pan clattered from the kitchen where Ray, the only dependable man in Ruby's life, busily washed dishes. Buster promised to have Briley home by four, but he'd yet to show, or even call. Some things never changed. As a young girl, she sat around waiting on teenage boys to call, and now here she was fifty years old waiting on a man who'd soon be collecting social security. She checked the time again. Six after six. Reaching for the phone, she dialed him again. No answer.

"I'm finished scrubbing the grill and the pans," Ray called from the kitchen. "Need anything else?"

Ruby lifted herself from her perch and pushed open the kitchen's swinging door. "No. I'll lock up."

Ray dried his hands on a towel and nodded. Reaching for the back door, he paused with his gnarled fingers curled around the brass knob. "I left their supper in the oven. Might need some heat, they don't show up soon." He shuffled out into the fast-coming dimness.

That's what Ruby hated about this time of year. It got dark too early. In the winter, the only sunlight she saw came through the front glass of the restaurant. Come summer, she could work outside in her garden after closing. Nothing felt better than cool dirt between her fingers and the warm evening sun on her face.

Ruby bent to lift the two plates from the oven just as the back door banged open.

"We saw a baby horse!" Briley ran in wrapping skinny arms around Ruby's knees. "Uncle Butter said I can keep it!"

Buster stood in the doorway with his dusty cowboy hat clutched in his left hand. As usual, a toothpick danced between his lips. His filthy boots had already dirtied the linoleum.

Ruby shot him a look. "Where have the two of you been?"

"Melody was about ready to drop her foal. Briley wanted to stay and watch."

"You let Briley watch that horse deliver? She's only three. I don't think—"

"I'm gonna name her Sparkles."

Buster nodded. "She's a fine-looking little filly."

Ruby rolled her eyes. She couldn't win this argument. Not with the two of them in cahoots. She might be able to talk some sense into Buster tonight, after she put her niece to bed, but right now he was stupid as a lovesick teenager. Briley only needed to flash her dimples and bat her lashes to make the sentimental old fool lose all reason.

"You could've called. Or answered your phone," Ruby fired one final shot.

He touched his belt. "Shit, must've left my cell next to

the wash basin."

"Watch your language." Ruby flipped the light switch with her elbow. "She listens to everything you say."

They stepped out the back door of the café and into the cool evening air. Before they entered the house Buster kicked off his boots and said, "Better take these off. They're a mite ripe. Bart and Doc Beecher needed another hand."

"Melody pooped on him," Briley snickered.

"I'll heat this up. You two get washed up. By the time we eat, and Briley has a bath, it'll almost be bedtime."

"I don't wanna go to bed. I wanna go see Sparkles." The little girl folded her arms across her chest.

"Not tonight. I don't want to listen to you whine tomorrow when you don't get your rest."

"Listen to your Aunt Ruby."

Buster ushered Briley out of the room, but Ruby heard him whisper sympathetic encouragement just the same. Used to be the same with Blue. Buster rode in and played hero, while she played the role of mother and disciplinarian.

After supper, Ruby bathed her niece while Buster sequestered himself in the recliner. By eight-thirty, Ruby was tired and frustrated. Briley had fought sleep every step of the way, but after the third reading of Dr. Seuss's *Mr. Brown Can Moo! Can You?*, she finally lost the battle.

"I'm bushed." Ruby flopped down on the couch.

"Me too," Buster rolled the toothpick across his lips. "Bart's taking the morning off to take his wife to Amarillo so I'll have to fend for myself come breakfast and lunch. Gotta watch that foal close. Briley'd be heartbroken if something happened."

"You're not really giving her that horse."

"The hell I'm not. I gave her daddy his first and I'll—"

"She's too young."

"I've already told her she won't be able to ride her for a long time. I'll get Briley something older and calmer to bide her over until Sparkles is ready. By then Briley will be ready to compete. That filly should make a hell of a barrel horse."

"Compete!" Ruby's mouth fell open. "Who said she wants to rodeo? Briley's not her father."

"Thank God for that."

"Don't start." Ruby rubbed her temples. She and Buster had argued far too many times over Blue, and she wasn't up to another round tonight.

"Told you he wouldn't call me today."

Ruby didn't need to be told which he Buster meant. "You wouldn't know if he did. You haven't answered your phone all day."

"We both know he didn't. I'm sorry you were worried, but the doc needed help." Buster's face softened. "You should've seen Briley. None of it bothered her. Sat right there on the stall and took it all in with getting a bit squeamish. She named it Sparkles because of the way its coat shined. Briley wanted to know why it was all wet like that." He lowered his voice. "I already called Oran Pratt. They're gonna dress up a saddle for her. It'll be ready in a week or so. Nobody works leather like those Pratt brothers, even if they are Okies. Oran promised to have it ready for her birthday."

"I still say she's too young for all that," Ruby countered.

"You would, but I'm proud of her. Least somebody in your family is willing to open their eyes and take a whiff of life."

"I said not to start on Blue."

Buster looked her in the eye. "Who says I was talking about Blue?"

# 18

Lindsay wrapped her arms around her chest in an effort to conserve her fleeting body heat. She tried hard not to shiver. Blue had already spotted her shaking once and told her to go inside, but she wouldn't feel right sitting in the warm camper while he worked out in the sub-zero cold.

Normally, it didn't take this long for him to get the trailer parked and leveled, but both of  the front leveling jacks were packed with snow and ice from the winter storm they hit crossing the Continental Divide. The weather had let up before they arrived in Cripple Creek, Colorado but the air here still possessed a frigid dampness that seeped all the way to the bone. Maybe it was too cold to snow. Her dad used to claim that all the time, but she'd never believed the saying, until now.

While Blue continued his struggle, she stared up the hill at the back of the buildings that made up the old mining camp's main street. According to Blue, most of the brick structures housed casinos, but from here they reminded Lindsay of warehouses. She'd expected to see bright lights and flashing neon.

Lindsay jumped when the tire iron Blue had been using as an ice pick clanged inside the back of the pickup bed.

"Let's go in and warm up." He stood beside her, huffing hot into his cupped hands.

Twenty minutes later, they sat with two steaming cups of coffee. The tip of her nose again had feeling.

Blue closed his eyes and rotated his head in slow circles. "Seems like I drove a thousand miles today. I hate pulling this thing on slick roads."

Lindsay watched the veins and sinew bulge in his neck as he stretched.

Blue lifted an arm and looked at his watch. "It's only nine. I better look up Chris and let him know I'm in town."

"Mind if I go with you?"

Blue had told her all about his friend. The guy had graduated from MIT and had won a good deal of money gambling using the mathematical theories he learned in college. Blue claimed he could memorize an entire page of numbers from the telephone book in five minutes. Any page, from any book, Blue had said, unable to hide the awe in his voice.

"No, come on. I want you to meet him," he said.

Lindsay was eager to meet one of Blue's friends, especially one who garnered so much respect. He claimed most gamblers were rich one day and near destitute the next, depending on the ebbs of their luck, but not Chris. He kept two or three things going, and one of them always hit. The man had invested his winnings in various real estate and gambling ventures, including the casino he owned here in Cripple Creek.. The aptly named Lucky Cuss.

"Are we walking?" Lindsay asked while Blue locked the camper door.

Blue shook his head. "I've already spent too much time in this cold, and Chris's place is at the far end of the street."

He drove his truck up the hill and turned down Bennett Avenue. Even here, on the front side, the establishments and street held a sleepy feel, like that of a town the interstate had long ago forgotten. As far as she could see, nothing was modern except the tour bus parked on the corner in front of brick-fronted Gold Rush. But then again, every structure was constructed from the same red brick.

Lindsay read the names of the casinos as they passed. Bronco Billy's, Midnight Rose, The Brass Ass, The Virgin Mule. She arched a brow and turned to Blue. "Not much in common with Vegas is there?"

"Only that your money will spend."

"Where are all the lights and the glitter?"

"Colorado law says the buildings have to look the way they did during the Gold Rush."

Blue pulled up under a green awning where a valet opened Lindsay's door and helped her step down. Blue handed over the keys to his truck along with a couple of bills before joining her on the sidewalk.

A man dressed in a vintage suit greeted them. "Hello, folks. Welcome to The Lucky Cuss." He pulled open the carved glass double door and made a wide sweeping gesture with his arm.

"Thank you." She smiled and stepped inside.

She'd never actually been in a casino before. The beeps, chimes, and jangle of a thousand slot machines assaulted her ears. Unlike out on the street, lights and noise filled the room. Despite the thick cloud of cigarette smoke, the aura captured her attention. She stared as an elderly woman slapped a button to set the wheels of her machine in motion. Across the way, a black man slid bills into a slot. Above his head, a digital tote board increased its dollar value in rapid order.

Blue led her over to a security guard. He leaned close to

the man and said, "Can you ask Mr. Vanderspice to meet me in the restaurant?"

"May I ask your name?"

"Blue Riggins." He slipped the man cash before walking away.

"Yes sir, Mr. Riggins." The guard vaulted into motion.

Lindsay rushed to catch up to Blue. "How come I keep getting the sense that the mention of your name gets people to do things they're not accustomed to?"

"It only works where people want me to spend money." He started up a flight of stairs.

"Why? Are you some kind of millionaire?"

He laughed. "I've fared pretty well at a couple of tournaments this year."

Upstairs, they turned to the right and sat in a dining area. The entire level was one room. Across the way, on the opposite side of the staircase, men sat around tables holding cards. Blue's eyes cut that direction. Above the tables a huge banner read POKER PALOOZA.

"Are you lost?"

Lindsay looked up at the man who'd spoken.

Blue stood to shake his hand. "Chris, want you to meet Lindsay Parker. She's traveling with me."

Chris smiled and reached for her hand. "Nice to meet you, Miss Parker. Given his inclination to travel solo, you must be especially fine company. Blue is not known to take many travelers aboard."

She blushed. "I'm afraid I didn't give him much choice in the matter."

Chris shook his head. "Trust me. Blue Riggins always has a choice in the matter. No one has the power to make him do anything he didn't already have his mind made up to do. Not yet anyway." The man winked so only she could see.

A waitress appeared before anything else could be said. Chris addressed the woman. "Sue, have Bernard toss the two best steaks in the house on the grill. One medium-rare and mine well-done as usual." He turned to Lindsay, "And for the lady," he tapped his chin and contemplated before adding, "My guess is she would prefer our alder-planked salmon with grilled vegetables."

"Bernard already shut down the grill. He's about to leave," the waitress said.

"Tell him to stay." Chris smiled, but Lindsay detected a coldness to his voice.

Blue apparently did not. He shook his head and said, "What did I tell you? He's known you thirty seconds and already knows exactly what you like to eat."

"No great feat." Chris pulled out a heavy, wood-backed chair and sat down. "Anybody can see she takes exquisite care of her body."

Lindsay tried not to stare, but something about this guy made her uneasy. She couldn't quite say why, but it especially bothered her that the man so completely enthralled Blue.

Frankly, she'd expected more. He was nothing special to look at. Thinning short brown hair, parted a few inches above his left ear, eyes the color of dirty pennies behind wire-framed glasses. A smallish build. Nothing like Blue's powerful stature and intense eyes. She shouldn't have expected an MIT grad to exhibit the same masculinity and ruggedness as a steer wrestling cowboy, regardless of who his friends were.

"So what brings you back so soon? You said it would be after Christmas before you graced us again."

Blue shrugged and cast a quick glance Lindsay's direction. "My plans changed. What's with that?" He pointed at the banner hanging on the other side of the room in an obvious attempt to change the subject.

"A shameless gesture by myself to cash in on the public's poker frenzy. The Lucky Cuss is hosting a four-day Texas Hold 'Em clinic, exposition, and tournament this weekend. You should stick around. I could put you on the payroll giving lessons to the locals and tourists."

"I don't think so. My nerves couldn't take it."

Chris nodded with a smug look. "I assumed as much. That's why I never asked. But I am bringing in another pro."

"Who?" Blue folded his arms across his chest.

"Our old buddy."

"Don't tell me—"

"Yep. Sergio will be here tomorrow afternoon."

Blue shook his head. "I wouldn't let that . . ." He stopped and took a deep breath. "I wouldn't let him step foot in any place I owned, but it's no sweat off my back. I'll be gone before he gets here."

"That's a shame," Chris said. "I've invited a few people to a little game of freeze-out Thursday night. Invitation only, but I have a seat for you if you're interested."

"I'm not."

Lindsay looked to Blue. "What's freeze-out? I thought you only played poker?"

"Freeze-out is a one-table poker tournament," Chris explained. "Each player pays their entry and play continues until one man has all the chips. He takes home all the money."

"How much does that person win?"

"That all depends on the buy-in," Chris said. "This will be a friendly game. Buy-in is twenty." This time he spoke directly to Blue.

"Not interested."

Lindsay listened while the two of them talked about people they knew and recent tournaments. She tuned out most of it, preferring to watch the wide variety of casino goers make their way up and down the staircase until the waitress brought their food.

Chris cut into his steak and stopped with the piece of meat dangling inches from his mouth. "Guess you heard Sergio won last month at Foxwoods. He has money to burn."

"If it hasn't vanished up his nose."

"Some say he's the hottest player right now," Chris said.

"Some do." Blue chewed.

"Of course, you hit back-to-back in October."

"I'm not going to play."

Chris put his fork down and leaned forward. "The two of you have met at more final tables than anybody else the last two years."

Lindsay watched the muscles in Blue's jaw tighten.

"Sergio won't always come out on top. He can't be that much better than you. No matter what everyone says."

Lindsay listened with interest. There was more going on than she understood, but even she sensed Chris was goading Blue. Just as it was clear that Blue held nothing but contempt for this Sergio character.

"You backed him at Foxwoods," Blue said.

Chris nodded. "Purely an investment. He didn't have a stake, and I knew he could cash."

Blue lit a cigarette. "I gave him the Bellagio."

"Heard about it." Chris spread his arms out in an attempt to look nonchalant, but Lindsay could see the intensity with which the man watched Blue. "You're due to beat him. He'll be surprised to see you at the table. He won't always catch the river card. Twenty grand is nothing to you, but losing it would hurt Sergio. Especially losing it to you."

"I have to get Lindsay to Oklahoma."

"I'm in no hurry," she interjected, intrigued by the possibility of seeing Blue in an epic showdown.

"Your presence would rattle him," Chris added. "Might even render him speechless. Right now he thinks he can beat you anytime, anywhere."

Blue took a long drag before saying, "Nothing will shut that jackass up."

"Losing to you would," Chris added.

Lindsay waited. She held her breath. She could see Blue considering his options. "Really, I don't mind hanging around here a few extra days. I'm not in a hurry to get home anyway. What's the river card?"

Chris winked at her again, making her wish she'd kept quiet. The last thing she wanted was this arrogant bastard to think they were a team.

He kept his eyes trained on hers as he spoke. "The river card is the final card dealt in Hold' Em. The river can make you, or break you. Fortunes have been claimed by those with the guts to hang on and hit on the river. And lost by those unfortunate souls who finally ran out of chances. The river card can run either way, but a successful gambler knows how to play the odds."

Chris turned and looked at Blue. "How about it? I have one seat available."

Blue exhaled a cloud of smoke. "I'll think on it."

# 19

The motor churned behind Lindsay. She moved to the far left of the road to give the vehicle room to climb the hill. Soon as it passed, she'd turn around and head back down to Cripple Creek. She hadn't jogged that far, but the climb was steeper than she'd figured.

The sound of the engine got louder—closer. Finally, she glanced over her shoulder. Matching her pace, a canary yellow Hummer idled a few feet off her heels. Lindsay stopped, and tried to stare through the front glass, but here in the mountain's early morning shadow all she could make out was a lone dark figure.

The behemoth SUV pulled up until the passenger window was even with her body. The glass slid down to reveal Chris's grinning face. "Good morning, Miss Parker. I thought that was you I spied heading out of town this fine day."

"You thought right." Lindsay turned away and resumed her pace up the incline.

"Nobody around here is crazy enough, or should I say dedicated enough, to tackle this hill at such an early hour. Or anytime for that matter." He continued to drive alongside her and talk. "Do you run every morning? How many miles do you put in?"

She ignored him. Breathing at this altitude was hard enough without answering questions. In truth, she wanted to turn around and head back. Her ribs ached, her calves screamed, and her quads were on fire, but she refused to let him know any of that. Lindsay felt compelled to prove something to this guy.

"Now I know how you stay in such great shape. I have a full workout room in my place upstairs at the casino." His slow-rolling tires crunched the gravel along the road's shoulder. "In case you're interested."

"I'm not." She had the distinct feeling his offer included more than a place to lift weights.

"Is there a reason you don't like me?"

Lindsay slowed her pace. "I don't trust you."

"Fair enough, but obviously you trust Blue. And he trusts me."

"Just because he does, doesn't mean he should." Lindsay cut across the road behind him. Her legs couldn't take the climb any longer.

Chris accelerated the engine and drove up the mountain. No doubt he'd find a place to turn around and be back far too soon. If there was any place to go, she would turn off and take an alternate route to avoid him, but instead, she focused on shortening her stride for the steep hill's descent.

Quicker than she wanted, he was back. "So what makes you think Blue is wrong about me?"

"You're after his money."

Chris laughed. "I don't need Blue's money. I have my own."

"And it's not hard to see how you got it."

"Are you calling me crooked?"

Lindsay exhaled. She needed to be careful. Already she'd

said things she shouldn't. For all she knew, this guy was dangerous, and here she was alone, several miles from town.

"I acquired my fortune being smarter than the next guy. You may deem that crooked. Most view me as savvy."

Lindsay felt relieved to hear the sound of another vehicle approaching from behind. Chris sped up and disappeared around the bend. She wondered when he would be back, but Lindsay jogged all the way to town before he showed. The yellow truck waited at the edge of the city. Once again, he idled alongside as she ran.

"Even if I was crooked, I assure you there are easier targets than Blue Riggins."

Back in Cripple Creek, she felt bolder. "Then why do you want him in that poker game so bad. You were trying to persuade him for some reason."

"I'm giving up my seat so he can play. The game was full."

"So you and your partner Sergio can set him up?"

He didn't respond.

She stuck to the main thoroughfare, Bennett Street. A few people were milling around, so she thought it would be safer.

"Why did you want him to play?" Chris asked.

She kept jogging. If he didn't have to answer, neither did she.

"I'll wager we share the same response," Chris said.

Lindsay pushed herself as hard as she could, hoping he would take the hint, but her muscles were fatigued and he held the upper hand. Even with fresh legs, she couldn't outpace his horsepower-charged vehicle. The situation reminded her of high school, when Coach Bacon would drive alongside his runners in a golf cart and shout what he considered motivation.

"Come on!" Chris called out. "Where's your competitive nature? This is a gambling town. At least make one bet while you're here."

She stopped running and slowed to a fast walk. Her muscles needed to cool anyway.

"You and I share more in common than you think," Chris continued. "Write down your reason and I'll write mine. If they're not similar I'll leave you alone and tell Blue he can't play."

"And if they're the same?" She hated to think what he wanted in return.

"You come inside and have breakfast with me."

Lindsay thought about his proposition before saying, "There's only one reason why I'd want him to play, and I'm sure a savvy guy like you can figure that out easily enough."

They passed by The Lucky Cuss, and Chris continued to follow. "We both want to watch him play. Let's dig deeper and make our bet a bit more interesting. Why do you want to watch him play?"

Lindsay turned back to face her pursuer. "What do you mean why?"

The corners of Chris's mouth lifted. "Tell me in one sentence what you hope to see."

She tilted her head slightly. What did she hope to see? That was a question she hadn't even asked herself. She hadn't gotten past general curiosity. A beer delivery truck chugged past while she considered. She didn't need proof of his skill. The foul-mouthed man at the gas station provided that. And she didn't know anything about cards anyway, so she really wouldn't know if he was good or not. Only after she picked up on Blue's dislike for this Sergio did her interest pique. She wanted to know why Blue despised the other man, but that would probably tell her more about Sergio than Blue. Maybe it was the fact this other guy had beat Blue numerous times, and she knew enough about him to know he wasn't accustomed to losing.

"I see I've captured your interest."

Lindsay stared at Chris. She knew the true answer. But in order to win the bet, she would have to reveal her reason, and she didn't want Chris telling Blue. He might take offense to discover she wanted to see him lose. Not that she wanted to see bad things happen to Blue, but she did want to see how he dealt with adversity. Ideally, it would be perfect if Blue won the game, but lost his patience doing so. He seemed larger than life, so in charge all the time. Just once, she wanted to see how he behaved when things spiraled out of his control. Already, he'd shown uncharacteristic flashes of contempt talking about this Sergio.

"Who decides if our answers are close enough."

Chris shrugged. "If we don't both agree you can cast the deciding vote, but I don't think that will be a problem."

Lindsay rubbed the back of her neck. "If I win,  you stay totally way from Blue and me until we leave. You can't so much as speak a word to either of us."

"Agreed."

"And if I lose, we eat in the restaurant," Lindsay added.

"I wouldn't have it any other way."

She waited while Chris pulled a sheet of paper from his visor. He handed her a pen from his shirt pocket. Turning her back to him, she considered carefully before scribbling her answer. *To see his reaction to adversity.* She reviewed the sentence. It was as good as she could muster up. She didn't want to write to watch him lose, in case Chris didn't live up to his end of the agreement and told Blue. She turned around.

Chris handed her his sheet. His white teeth gleamed in the morning sunshine. She read his note.

*You long to see the raw emotions lurking beneath Blue's stoic façade.*

Lindsay sighed. Not only had Chris guessed her intentions, he'd been able to sum them up with a clarity and elegance she did not possess.

He reached across the seat and pushed open the passenger door. "Hope you're hungry." He never even bothered to read her slip.

With her spoon, Lindsay pushed a piece of banana floating around the inside of the bowl and waited for Chris to start with his questions. To pay her debt, she had to sit here and talk to him, but she didn't have to eat her cereal, and she sure as heck didn't have to enjoy his company.

"Sure you don't want to order something else?"

She shook her head. "I like Raisin Bran."

"I can tell." Chris leaned back and folded his arms. Steam rose from the cup of coffee in front of him. "So what castle wall did Blue scale to save you?"

"I don't know what you're talking about."

"Sure you do," he said. "I know Blue. He never attaches himself to anyone unless they need him. Blue is needier himself than he'd ever care to admit, so he gravitates to those in distress in order to feel better about himself."

Putting down her spoon, she stared Chris in the eye. "I thought he was your friend."

"He is."

"Then why do you talk about him like that? He's not a fool. Sooner or later he's going to see you're trying to con him."

"You overestimate my abilities."

Lindsay wasn't about to admit the circumstances of how she met Blue, so she decided to turn the tables. "If Blue only befriends those he can rescue, how did the two of you meet?"

The casino owner nodded with a shrewd smirk. "We've all got our little secrets, don't we?"

Several minutes ticked by with only the murmur of other diners and the occasional clang of a downstairs slot machine reverberating through the air. Lindsay slid her chair back. "I should be getting back."

Chris grabbed her wrist. Not hard, but firm enough to get her attention. "I'm not finished yet."

"Don't touch me."

He lifted his fingers. "You haven't forgotten our little agreement, have you?"

"I said I would answer your questions. You aren't asking any, so I'm leaving."

"Sit back down. Please," he added when she scowled.

She took a seat without scooting closer to the table.

"I'll get right to my point," he said. "Is he going to play?"

"How should I know?"

"Surely he gave you an indication after the two of you retired to his trailer for the night."

She shook her head.

"No, I guess he wouldn't," Chris mumbled. "That sort of thing doesn't make for very interesting pillow talk."

Lindsay stood back up. "Just because we share a camper doesn't mean we share a bed."

"Oh, I'm sorry." Chris rose from the table. "Pardon my

ignorance. I just assumed. The two of you being alone out there," he spread his hand wide to indicate a vastness. "And I know how lonely he's been since his wife's passing."

She started down the stairs.

Chris leaned over the banister. "Blue is a better man than me. If I was locked away in seclusion with such a beautiful and—"

Lindsay stopped and turned around. "I'm not interested in anything you have to offer, so if this is your perverted attempt to win me over, you can save your breath."

Chris winked. "Again you're wrong about me. I would never step on a friend's toes—even if he's yet to figure out what he wants."

"Maybe it's me who doesn't want it."

"Oh, but we both know you do!" he called to her retreating form.

Outside, Lindsay hurried down the sidewalk. At the first side street she turned and resumed running. Her joints had tightened, so she loped along at an uneven gait. She didn't care if she pulled a muscle as long as she got away from The Lucky Cuss and its arrogant bastard of an owner.

Chris Vanderspice wouldn't be nearly so hard to deal with—if he wasn't right all the damn time.

# 20

The icy morning air assaulted Blue's freshly shaven skin. Lighting another Marlboro, he moved from the shade of the trailer out into the sunshine. Expecting to see Lindsay headed his way, he stared at the ribbon of blacktop snaking away from town. Nothing appeared this side of the first bend.

Last night, Lindsay mentioned jogging the road towards the gold mine. He looked at his watch. She'd been gone almost two hours. The other mornings she'd been back in half that time. Even if she ran all the way to Victor and back. Somewhere in the neighborhood of ten miles. He shook his head—how the hell would he know how long it took to run that far?

Spitting in the dirt, Blue paced the ground between his truck and the camper. He lifted the hood on the Ford and slid out the dipstick. Wiping the oily sheen with his fingers, he slid the rod back in and checked the level. Right on the money. The thin metal rang out when he slammed the hood. Again, he glanced at his watch. Waiting on other people never had been his strong suit.

Heck of it was he didn't even know why he was so anxious. He didn't have anywhere particular to be. They weren't leaving straight away, least not before he talked to Chris some more about that game.

Sergio Ochoa. Blue hated losing to the lying son of a bitch above anyone else. Once upon a time, the two had been friends. But only for a few months there in Vegas. Those had been Blue's darkest days, when his judgment was tainted by heartache, grief, and bourbon. He and Sergio shared some deep soul-searching discussions. One drunk, the other high on nose candy.

That's why Blue felt a powerful need to best a rival who knew him a little too well.

They would meet again at some tournament. Blue needed to prove to Sergio, and to himself, that he could play through the distraction. That he could look across the table and meet the other man bluff for bluff, emotion for emotion, even when his opponent knew where to attack. Blue didn't hate Sergio for what the man had taken from him at the poker table, he hated Sergio for what he himself had given away in the barroom.

Blue preferred to keep his wounds covered, the hurt festering below the surface. Could he deal with it when the bandages were ripped away and exposed to the scrutiny of others, like Lindsay?

Hell of it was, he couldn't uncover why he cared so much what Lindsay thought.

For that matter, what made him feel compelled to sit out here in the cold morning air, waiting on her, when in a matter of days he planned to leave her behind in Oklahoma.

Blue knew damn good and well why, and he feared what it meant.

He waited to see the crimson-tinge of her flushed cheeks. He waited to see the muscles in her legs tighten and flex as she stretched her road-weary legs. He waited to be near her. To be caught up by her dimples when she smiled. He waited to forget about what might've been, to instead think about what could be.

He stared up at the cemetery on Mt. Pisgah, high above town. There were a thousand reasons why he wouldn't act upon, or even acknowledge his desire, so taking one last gaze down the road, Blue dug the truck keys from his pocket.

They'd both be better off if he left before she got back. The less time he spent with Lindsay, the easier it would be to drift away once they hit Oklahoma.

On the way to The Lucky Cuss, Blue debated his decision. She could've gotten lost, or twisted an ankle.

Shaking his head, he pulled up to the valet curb. He was thinking like an old lady. Lindsay jogged every day. She hadn't needed him to take care of her before now.

Blue lit a smoke as he entered the casino. Taking a long drag, he surveyed the room. Most of the machines stood idly by, waiting for tourists to feed them. A few players were scattered around, but he didn't see any sign of Chris, so he headed upstairs. Blue spotted the casino owner at a table in the corner of the restaurant.

"If it isn't the famed and fabled Blue 'Ice' Riggins."

A waitress cleared the table as Blue took a seat across from his fellow gambler. "Should've known I'd find you up here guzzling coffee."

"Caffeine. Every recovering addict's last surviving friend." Chris took a sip and leaned back. "You just missed Miss Parker, I'm afraid."

"Lindsay was here?"

Nodding, Chris added, "We had a nice little chat over breakfast."

"I figured she was out for her morning run."

"She was. If you ask me, other women would do to follow Miss Parker's example. Exercise is an aphrodisiac. I know I certainly enjoyed the rosy complexion of exertion that colored her face. The heaving of her chest. And those running pants. I imagine that seat is still warm from the heat of her taut little—"

"I get your point."

"Yes, sir, you are indeed a man of honor." Chris carried on, undeterred by the interruption. "Just the two of you. Riding alone. Hour after hour. Camped in the rugged wilderness with only each other for companionship."

Blue stared across the table.

"Nobody can say Blue Riggins is not a man of virtue. Took me by complete surprise when Miss Parker informed me the two of you were not intimately involved."

"She said that?"

"Volunteered the information over her bowl of Raisin Bran." Chris sipped from the coffee mug. "Must be hard to maintain such devout principles in such cramped and close quarters. Those legs would be enough to do me in. The way those firm muscles ripple and flex. The—"

Leaning forward, Blue stared hard at his friend. "I said I got your damned point."

The faintest of grins flickered across Chris's face before returning to its usual bland expression. "Sorry, but sometimes it's hard to ignore the obvious."

Blue shifted his stare away from the other man and gazed across the upper floor of the casino. At this time of morning, only one table had players gathered around. "Tell me about Thursday."

"You playing?"

"I'll let you know when I hear some details."

"Let's go up to my office." Chris lowered his voice. "The last thing I need is the gaming commission getting wind of my private games. They get rather touchy about violations of their low-stakes limit. The measly amount they allow in this state isn't even real gambling. A gamble involves life or death. Starvation versus caviar. That's gambling."

Blue followed a few steps behind. He could point out that his friend made a nice living from all those measly bets, but it wasn't worth the trouble. He came for info, not an argument.

They entered a spacious room with two huge windows overlooking Bennett Street. Blue had only been to the office once before during one of his hunting trips. The walls were littered with pictures of Chris posing with a myriad of famous and infamous faces. A former president, a multitude of congressmen, singers, actors, athletes, and a former Hollywood madam. Blue sat on an overstuffed-leather couch while Chris paced the floor, laying out details of the game.

"Ten players, twenty grand apiece with the entire two hundred thousand going to the last man at the table. No limit Texas Hold 'Em. Blinds start at fifty and a hundred and double every twenty minutes."

"Who else is in?" Blue reached over and lifted a photo from the end table. There he stood, between Chris and Sergio back when the latter was still boxing and ranked among the top-ten welterweights in the world. Blue had a drink in his hand. That first year after Staci died, he always had a drink in his hand.

"Two brothers from Aurora. That's up near Denver."

Agitated such evidence of his prior bad judgment existed, Blue put the frame down. "I know where the hell it is. I don't care where they're from, give me what I need to know."

Chris raised one brow. "You seem a tad touchy this morning."

"You want me to play or not?" Blue started to rise.

"The brothers own some kind of tractor dealership. Both play strictly by the odds, but you'll be able to read them within the first dozen hands."

Chris carried on for fifteen minutes, laying out the other players. A dealer from one of the other casinos, a big shot from one of the area gold mines, two more Colorado businessmen, and a father and son from Kansas City who owned a chain of jewelry stores. All with skills, but beatable unless Lady Luck rode on their shoulders.

"That's eight." Blue squinted to study his friend. "Sergio makes nine. I'd be ten."

"I'm giving you my seat," Chris offered already catching onto Blue's line of questioning.

"Why?"

"Lindsay wanted to know that exact thing."

Blue waited. He didn't care who else had asked. Chris Vanderspice never gave a thing away unless he stood the chance to get two back.

"At least four of those guys will bring their wives. While their husbands are busy upstairs they will perch at one of my machines downstairs."

"True, but—"

"I also need Sergio to lose. The faster he spends his winnings, the quicker he'll need me again. A man can never have too many people who need him." The casino owner strolled over and lifted the same photo Blue had looked at earlier. "I'd rather have a thousand people owe me, than for me to owe a single one."

Blue shook his head. "Damn it, Chris. I've told you. You

don't owe me. I did what any friend would do."

"No, you did what most friends wish they could."

"We're even. How many times have I come up here to go hunting? To get away? You let Donnie come with me, and I know how you feel about him. Half my elk meat is sitting in your freezer right now. We're even."

Chris walked away and stopped at the window. He stared out the glass at the street below. "What you did changed my life. Saved it. I'd be busted and out of the game if not for you. If I were even alive I'd be stuck in some dead-end accounting job. You were my river card." His voice took on a hollow sound. "I'll always owe you until I do the same for you."

Tension settled in Blue's jaws. Chris had an uneasiness about him, a lack of confidence. Blue had never seen this side, not even in the old days. "A man can have too much pride."

"You in or not?" Chris sidestepped the statement.

"I'm in, but listen to what I'm telling you. There's no shame accepting help from a friend. Ego can be a hell of a thing."

"So can running from your problems."

Blue stood, and pointed a finger across the room. "If you got something to say spit it out."

Chris held up his hands in surrender. "I'm just talking to hear myself. You're right, there's no shame accepting help from a friend, and I know we're both big enough men to realize as much."

A knock sounded on the door. "Sorry to interrupt, Mr. Vanderspice, but your vehicle is ready." A female voice drifted through the wood.

Checking his watch, Chris nodded. "I do need to get on

the road. I have business in the Springs before Sergio's plane lands."

"What time Thursday?"

"I'll see you before then." Chris opened the door.

"Not likely. Not with that idiot—"

"I heard you the first time," Chris spoke harshly to the woman still standing in the hallway.

The messenger hurried away looking like a wounded dog.

"Someday, I'll find a secretary with sense."

Blue raised a brow. "Someday, some disgruntled worker is going to shoot you for being an asshole."

Chris revealed a row of perfect white teeth. "Not if I put enough fear into them first."

They parted at the stairwell. Blue took his valet ticket outside and stood on the curb to wait on his truck. There seemed to be only one attendant on duty, but he didn't care. Even though he could still see his breath, the sun had warmed things up enough to make it a fine, bright November morning.

Lighting a cigarette, he wondered what Chris was up to. The man was good, but he liked to play games. Blue had seen it too many times. He never manipulated anyone without mocking them first. Their entire conversation served a purpose, but what? It wasn't about the twenty grand. Chris was giving up the chance at more by not playing, and numbers didn't motivate him unless they were followed by at least six zeros. It had something to do with past favors, but what?

And why had Lindsay stopped here? Last night she claimed not to trust Chris. Said he reminded her of an old boyfriend. The one that first brought her to Eagle's Rest. But women rarely took a shine to Chris, and the ones who did were only after one thing. Money.

Blue didn't want to think that way about Lindsay, but maybe Missy had been right. She'd all but asked him how much he had when they got to the casino.

"You want me to fire him?"

Blue looked up. Chris had his head hung out the window of his overgrown canary on wheels.

"Who?"

"The valet. For being too damn slow."

"I'm in no hurry." Blue took a long drag. "Got nowhere to be until Thursday."

Chris rolled his window halfway up and then reversed its direction. "Almost forgot. Tell Miss Parker jogging on these lonely roads can be dangerous. You never know what might be around the next bend."

Blue stepped down off the curb. "Whatever you've got cooking inside your head leave her out of it."

"Me? I have nothing cooking, as you say. I just want to make sure she's safe."

"Damn it, Chris. I'm serious."

"Me too. A pretty woman like her shouldn't be out alone that time of morning." Chris paused. "Sergio still likes to put in some roadwork. Though, he does tend to sleep in until at least noon most days."

Blue leaned in close. "Listen to me. I'm only going to say this once. Keep that son-of-a-bitch away from her. I don't care who he's friends with, or how many men he's knocked out in the ring, Sergio will answer to me if he tries his shit on her."

Chris turned away, but not before he revealed another slight grin. "I'll pass along your tidings of cheer."

# 21

Hot water swirled around Lindsay's feet before disappearing down the travel trailer's drain. Steam rose around her shoulders and not all if it could be attributed to the shower. If only she could rinse away the agitation rooted inside her.

Who did Chris think he was—telling her how she felt? More importantly, how had he done it? One thing for certain, she couldn't afford to linger in this town. Not with the ease he looked into her mind and pulled out whatever he wanted. She had far too much pain stored in her brain to allow just anyone access.

Drying her hair, she considered the best way to approach Blue, to convince him not to play that poker game. To let him know they should move on down the road. He needed to find out his so-called friend had a few cards up his sleeve.

Setting her dirty laundry on the counter beside the sink, she slipped into jeans and pink sweater. The rumble of Blue's truck outside sped up her actions. Having already learned he preferred directness, she wouldn't beat around the bush.

The camper door rattled.

A knock sounded.

"Lindsay! You in there?"

She'd forgotten about locking the door. After her troubling conversation with Chris, and coming back to find Blue gone, she felt uneasy showering in an unlocked camper. Something told her the casino owner would do anything to advance his cause. Whatever that cause may be.

Keys jangled against the door. Tucking her hair into a ponytail she hurried to let him in, but the knob twisted in her hand just as she reached the lock.

Blue stared at her. His brows pinched together as the lines on his forehead deepened.

"Sorry, I was trying to get here," she said. "I just stepped out of the shower."

He mumbled something she couldn't quite make out and brushed past on the way to his bedroom.

"What?" She reached for his shoulder, but he moved away.

Blue paused in the doorway. "I said you sure have been busy this morning." He closed the door to his bedroom as punctuation.

Anger singed its way into Lindsay as the words sank in. He'd been to see Chris. There was no telling what that conniving snake had said, but Blue was just as bad if he was going to believe everything the cocky, arrogant asshole had to say.

Lindsay stomped down the hall. Without stopping, or knocking, she barged into Blue's room. "Busy? What was that supposed to—" She halted mid-sentence as Blue pulled a tattered t-shirt down over his broad shoulders. "Sorry, I…uh… didn't mean…" Stammering, she hurried from the room.

Blue closed the distance between them in a matter of steps. "What were you going to say?"

"Nothing." She refused to meet his gaze, but heat rose up her neck and settled in her cheeks. She hated that her flushed face gave her away.

"Let's hear it."

Lindsay rubbed the back of her neck. "It wasn't important." She cursed herself for not knocking, but she hadn't expected the sight of his muscular body to unnerve her so.

"Don't give me that. I've spent enough time with you to know when something's on your mind."

She lifted her chin and stared into his midnight black eyes. "But apparently you haven't spent enough time with me not to jump to conclusions," she spat.

He shrugged as if conceding that point. "What conclusion is that?"

"Who knows? But you aren't the only who can see things around here. I know you're mad, and I'd be willing to guess it has something to do with your so-called friend." She pointed in the vague direction of The Lucky Cuss.

Blue nodded. "There is something on my mind."

"Then say it. I'm tired of you holding back. I'm a big girl. I can handle whatever—"

"Why did you go see Chris?"

Remembering her bet, she lowered her head. She couldn't explain her reasoning to Blue, but why should she have to? "That's none of your business."

"You're right. It's not." Blue turned his back and started for the door.

Lindsay shook her head. "There you go! Going off to hide again."

He never slowed on his way out.

She didn't have a clue what just happened. They both were angry about something she felt certain the other didn't understand.

She didn't even know why she was so mad. Because Blue

said she was busy? Because he asked her an innocent question? No, because Chris exposed her feelings to the light of day, and now she feared what he told Blue.

Going to the window, she stared out. Blue, bent over in the back of his pickup, dug for something in the truck's toolbox. He lifted a box of Pennzoil, a round plastic tub, and a tool bag. She clenched her jaws. He was going to change his oil? Now? As if nothing had happened between them? She should've told him about Chris. Warned Blue not to trust his friend, but the sight of his bare skin shook her.

The thickness of his powerful chest and firm muscles of his stomach. That thin line of dark hair running down the middle his torso and disappearing below his belt. She must've looked like an idiot. Gawking, then running away like an embarrassed schoolgirl, instead of telling him his "friend" was out to screw him over.

Blue was so unlike other men she'd known. Not so much in physical attributes. She'd dated other men with rock hard abs and muscles to spare, yet Blue was different. His muscles didn't have that polished and defined weight room look. They were like the rest of him. Rugged, powerful, hidden below a firm solid surface, slow to reveal themselves. Blue guarded his strength and his emotions, as if he were ashamed of who he was, or what he'd done.

Lindsay lowered her head. She couldn't blame him for that. Not when she'd spent her life running from herself.

The need to explain, to reach out to him, drew her out of the camper. The mountain breeze blew against her wet hair. She shivered. Blue's legs protruded from beneath the vehicle's frame.

She cleared her throat. "Can we start this conversation over?"

The ratcheting click of a wrench answered.

"Hello?" She waited. "Did you hear me?"

Nothing, not even the sound of him working. Heat spread up her neck and settled in her cheeks. "So you're just going to lie under there and ignore me while I stand in the cold?"

Not a sound drifted out from beneath the truck.

"Say something!" She stomped her foot. "Ask whatever you want. I'll answer."

"Tell me about Idaho," He finally said. "Why were you there?"

"I went with a boyfriend. He was an idiot. Claimed to be an environmentalist. We went to protest snowmobiles in Yellowstone, and ski resorts scarring the mountains, and potato farmers who use too many pesticides. I thought he was interesting, but turns out he was just a self-righteous idiot. We broke up, he got mad and left me stranded in Eagles Rest."

"And Janine just took you in. Or did you find her?"

"I'd already been there two weeks. Every morning I went to the café after my run. She'd met Tristan. She knew he was a jackass, so when I told her about our fight she offered a room and a job. What does this have to do with anything?"

"It has everything to do with who you are." His muffled voice spoke, followed by the clink of metal.

"Do you expect me to stand here and talk down to your feet?"

"I don't expect anything from anybody," he said. "I've learned that lesson."

She bent and grabbed his legs just above the tops of his leather cowboy boots. "Get out here." She pulled hard, getting angrier by the second for her lack of affect and strength. "Chris doesn't know a thing about me. No matter what he thinks." Her grip slipped sending her tumbling backward onto her butt.

With both her pride and tailbone injured, she sat there in the dirt feeling sorry for herself for nearly a minute. Finally she said, "The least you can do is tell me what he said."

Blue slid from underneath the truck and stood. "Who said anything about Chris? I was asking about your deal in Idaho."

A new surge of fury brought Lindsay to her feet. She pointed a finger at Blue. "What deal?"

"The way you latched on to Janine. Seems kind of convenient. Don't you think?"

"Idaho is three states back. Why do you suddenly care what happened there?"

Blue slowly took off his leather gloves and set them on the truck's hood. "Because I'm confused about a few things."

Lindsay crossed her arms. "You're not the only one. I have no idea what we're even talking about."

"Did Janine give you money?"

His implication struck her full in the face. "Money!" Lindsay spit the word out. "You sound like Missy."

He arched a single brow.

Wide-eyed she said, "So that's what you think?"

"I call 'em the way I see'em. And Chris does have a shit-load of money."

She raised her hand to slap him, but he grabbed her wrist inches from his face. His expression never changed.

"I'm not some money-grubbing gold digger."

"What made you pick me to give you a ride?"

"You were already leaving town." Their faces were inches apart. A faint streak of motor oil stained his cheek.

"Why did you go see Chris this morning?" The heat

from Blue's breath washed over her.

She met his intense gaze. If they weren't fighting, she would think he was going to kiss her. "I didn't go see him. I lost a bet and had to eat with him."

For the first time, surprise registered on Blue's stoic face. He released his grip on her wrist. "What bet?"

Disappointment tugged at her as he backed away. "I swore not to tell, but Chris has some kind of plan."

"Of course he has a plan. Chris always has a plan."

"He's trying to set you up." She hesitated, unsure of how Blue would take her next statement. "I don't think you should play in that game."

He laughed. "Thanks for your concern, but I've already given my word."

"What if—"

"I can take care of myself at the poker table. Besides, I want to know what he's up to." Blue lowered himself back down to the ground and started to slide under the truck.

"Tell me about Sergio," Lindsay blurted, mostly to keep Blue out in the open and talking. "Why don't you like him?"

Blue stared up at her. "I don't trust him. There's more to it than that, but above all else I don't like anyone I can't trust."

"And you trust Chris?"

"Yes."

How could he trust the man when it was obvious he had a scheme going? Lindsay bit her lip. She had to ask, but she worried what the answer would be. "Do you trust me?"

Blue stared at her. "It's myself I don't trust." And with that he slid back underneath the Ford.

She stood there waiting on him to say more—needing to hear more. "What does that even mean?"

The clicking of his wrench answered.

She bent down and peered underneath the truck just as oil began to flow into the waiting bucket. "Don't pretend you can't hear me. What did you mean?"

His gaze never left the black stream. "I meant I'm finished talking about it."

"About what?" She said louder than she meant to. "I'm not even sure what we were talking about. We just got started, and now here I am on my knees watching you change your damn oil."

His chest rose and fell, yet he said nothing.

"What are you afraid of?"

He reached up with a rag. "My engine falling apart."

"I'm not talking about the oil."

"I'm not talking about anything else," he said.

Lindsay stood. The entire exchange left her frustrated in more ways than one. She stomped back to the trailer.

*It's myself I don't trust.*

Did he really expect a line like that to satisfy her? It sounded like some kind of break-up line. It's me, not you. How many men had she said that to?

Blue had to be the most nerve-wracking…the most reticent…most mysterious…exasperating…beguiling son of a bitch she'd ever encountered.. She shook her thoughts back to his statement. Was he saying he did trust her, or he didn't? And what didn't he trust about himself?

Pacing around the camper, she stopped and stared down at her open duffel bag. Blue probably expected her to come inside, sit on the couch, and leave him alone. Then sometime later, at his convenience, he'd grace her with a few more of his ever-so-wise words. And if she were lucky, he might even go so far as to reveal his favorite color or astrological sign.

Well, piss on Mr. Blue Riggins. She was tired of playing his game. Sick of having to dig and probe for every little personal nugget he parted with. She was tired of speculating there might be a spark between them, a shred of commonality. It was high time she started worrying about herself and how to handle her homecoming, and quit compounding her problems with thoughts of Blue Riggins.

Grabbing her bag off the couch, Lindsay headed out the door. Blue had his dirty laundry and she had hers, and right now the need for clean clothes outweighed her desire to know anything else about him.

The trailer door slammed. Blue braced for another verbal assault. He waited a few seconds before daring to look. Where was she?

Sliding from beneath the truck, he spotted Lindsay marching away from the camper. An alarm sounded in his brain when he spotted the bag in her hand. She was leaving. He opened his mouth to yell, to call her back, to try and explain the tumultuous mass of emotions coursing through his mind, but before he could get the words out, she disappeared into the room next to the office.

The laundry.

Relief settled over him. For the second time in the last fifteen minutes he'd almost gone too far. He was stupid to give Missy's claims even a second thought. Janine knew better. Hell, he knew better, but maintaining control around her had suddenly gotten harder. Despite his best efforts, Lindsay had forced her way in.

Earlier, he'd almost lowered his mouth to hers. He'd

wanted to. And he would have. If she hadn't caught him off guard with that comment about a bet. What was she doing gambling with Chris when he'd told her how good he was? Blue would never think of wagering with the man on anything other than cards.

Whatever they'd bet, Lindsay was none too happy about losing. That fire in her eyes had almost been too much. And the pout of her lips…The tilt of her chin…The rise and fall of her breasts with every angry breath. And that damn pink sweater. He always had been a sucker for a woman in pink.

Blue shook his head. He couldn't afford to think of such things. Not if he wanted to maintain distance.

He looked down at the oil stain along his forearm. Today was Monday. The game wasn't until Thursday. Three more days of pretending to ignore her, of resisting temptation, of hiding. He could only find so much unnecessary work to do on the truck. Eventually, he would find himself alone with her. In the camper. At night. With frost on the windows and only the sound of their breathing to fill the air.

Blue paused on the camper steps and looked up the hill at the back of The Lucky Cuss. "Damn you, Chris. I never should've let you talk me into sticking around this town."

Inside the trailer, Blue was grateful for the chance to plan. Doing laundry should keep her busy for a while. Later, he'd head up to the casinos. Nowhere could he hide and kill time like the poker table. That same theory had served him well the past four years.

Washing oil from his arm, he noticed the bundle of clothes on the counter. Lindsay's running pants and shirt. He tried not to notice the pair of sky-blue panties peeking out, or the shiny black sports bra. He tried not to think of how she would look clad only in her underthings. How she would look without anything on.

Splashing cold water on his face, Blue stared into the mirror. If he hurried, he could be gone before she got back.

Lindsay stuffed another dollar in the change machine and waited for the quarters to drop. A heaviness weighed down her spirit, unnerving her. That same unnerving feeling that used to hit her as a child late at night when she would suddenly remember some bit of unfinished homework that was due first thing tomorrow. Or later in high school, just before a big meet when regret took hold, for those afternoons she only ran four or five miles, instead of her usual ten or twelve. The weight of impending failure.

Lindsay bought a small box of soap from a vending machine and fed three quarters into the Maytag's coin slot. Nowadays the regrets just kept piling up in the form of ex-boyfriends, poor decisions, and missed opportunities. Was that what Blue was? An opportunity? The opportunity for what?

Loading her clothes into the tub, while her mind lingered on Blue. She shouldn't have cornered him back there at his truck. She had no right to demand details about his personal life. Not when he'd already made so many sacrifices for her benefit.

Where were her running pants? And sports bra? Lindsay lifted her duffel bag and looked underneath. She looked by the change and the soap machines. Then she remembered. They were back at the trailer, on the bathroom counter, where she left them when she went to unlock the door for Blue. They were the things she needed to wash the most.

Oh well, she could go back and get them. She owed Blue an apology anyway.

Blue tossed his ratty oil stained t-shirt in the hamper and reached for the button-up he'd worn earlier. He couldn't help but remember the expression on Lindsay's face when she'd barged into his room, the appraising way her eyes flicked across his body.

Sucking in his gut, he jabbed his fingers against his flesh. He was still in pretty good shape. Nothing like he used to be, when he and Donnie hit the circuit and practiced non-stop in between. When he made a point to lift weights in order to keep an upper hand on the steers that weighed upwards of seven hundred pounds. Blue let out the breath he didn't know he'd been holding and shook his head.

He was starting to think like a man daring to consider the possibilities. That's what got people in trouble at the poker table. A smart gambler didn't give a shit about the possibilities, only the odds—and Blue knew he was a long shot at best. The human equivalent of a gut shot straight. Lindsay deserved better.

Sliding his arms into the shirt, he buttoned it and eyed the beat-up Stetson beside the bed. Maybe no one at the tables would recognize him if he wore the battered old hat since he never wore it on television.

Lindsay came in the door just as he stepped into the living room. She looked surprised to see him. "I forgot my running stuff."

Nodding, he tried to avoid more thoughts about those sky-blue panties.

She returned to the living room a second later with the bundle of clothes tucked in the crook of her arm. Her face had softened from earlier, but part of him missed that pouty look of offended righteousness.

"I'm sorry for my attitude earlier. I have no right to be angry with you. Not with everything you've done for me."

His eyes flicked downward to the silky blue fabric peeking out. "I haven't done anything." He resisted the urge to say yet, instead concentrating on her face.

"Yes, you have." She stepped closer. "You didn't have to give me a ride. Or listen to me badger you about your past. I've taken advantage of your—"

"No, you haven't." He turned away. He was the one on the verge of taking advantage. Every word out of her mouth, every movement of her body stirred him. He hadn't felt like this since Staci, since college.

"I'm trying to apologize. Why do you have to turn away every time I speak to you?" She grabbed him by the shoulder.

"I have to." His voice came out hoarse.

"Why?" She pulled him around to face her.

Blue opened his mouth to speak, but the words died on his tongue.

Lindsay took one look at his face and grimaced. "I'm sorry. There I go again. I had no right to ask that. Don't know why I can't keep my nose to myself. You bring out the worst in me." She turned to leave. "I'm sorry. I'll go do my laundry. I just wanted to apologize, and I'll try to do better to stay focused on my own business."

He reached for her. "Wait!"

She stopped, still facing the door.

"You don't. Bring out the worst in me, I mean. The worst is already inside of me. You've just opened up my mind to things I thought were dead."

Lindsay turned around. He waited for her to ask what things, but she simply studied him in silence.

"When I first saw you back in Idaho, I thought you were a ghost. That's what I was searching for. And you appeared there on that dark road, looking like an apparition." Blue bowed his head. "I thought you were my wife. Or at least her spirit."

"Blue." She reached for his hand.

"I tried to find her in you, but then I realized it was myself I saw in you. The hurt, the painful memories. It was like looking in a mirror. By helping you, I thought I would feel better about my own failures."

"You have helped me," she said.

"I was being selfish."

"You were being human. Everyone wants to feel better about themselves. That's why people volunteer and work to help others. Without guilt and shame, the world as we know it would be gone tomorrow."

Guilt. Now there was something Blue knew about. Shame was what he hoped to avoid. "I don't want to hurt you."

She squeezed his hand. "You couldn't do anything to hurt me more than I've hurt myself." Lindsay leaned into him, resting her cheek against his chest.

Pausing, he resisted for one brief moment before wrapping his arms around her and pulling her tight against his body. They stood there for several long minutes. The warmth of her body engulfed his resistance, but Blue told himself this was as far as they could go. He could never commit to another woman, and Lindsay needed, no deserved, permanence to her life that he simply could not give.

# 22

Ruby limped down the hall, holding the soggy left side of her skirt out away from her body. Her feet throbbed from another twelve-hour day at the café, and she hated the way the damp fabric clung to her hip. She wasn't too crazy about the size of those hips either, but that was an entirely different matter.

Over the years, she'd packed the equivalent of a ten-pound sack of sugar on each thigh. Too bad she wasn't made of sugar, because if water melted her, she'd be thin as a wafer cookie. Not a night went by without her getting soaked when she sat on the edge of the tub to wash Briley's hair. The child's boundless enthusiasm had a way of spilling forth, but only during bathtime did Ruby wish the girl were a little more reserved. A little more like her father.

Briley inherited her mom's outgoing personality and sometimes that unfettered spirit was the only thing that kept Ruby afloat. Seeing the world through youthful eyes forced her to notice the tiny wonders and miracles adults often forgot all about, or simply ignored.

Entering the living room, Ruby paused to study Buster while he chewed on a toothpick. Leaned back in the recliner, he had his socked feet propped up. The cotton had nearly worn through at one of his big toes. From the television came the sounds of a Hollywood gunfight. Buster sat watching the Western with a smile glued on his face. Oblivious to both his threadbare socks and the extra pounds on her hips.

She sat and said, "Briley wants you to tell her a bedtime story. She wants to hear the one about a racehorse named Rooster and his sister Sara, who's a mule."

Buster's eyes crinkled. "That's not how it goes, but close." His knees creaked and popped when he stood. "Rooster is in love with a mule named Sister Sara. Guess that might be confusing for a three-year-old. Should've called her Katie Elder, I reckon."

Ruby smiled. "Let me guess Rooster is full of *True Grit* even when pursued by his archenemy *Pale Rider.*"

"Hey, that sounds good." He nodded.

"One of these days Briley is going to discover you're a fraud. Either that, or John Wayne and Clint Eastwood will come looking for their royalties."

He laughed. "First rule of good storytelling is tell what you know. And I know Westerns."

Reaching for the romance novel beside her chair, Ruby shook her head. Tell what you know. If she did that, her stories would be filled with nothing but worry and heartache, unless she took Buster's cue and copied the fantasy world she read in these books. Where every man, regardless of how gruff or gristled, has a tender side and is willing to act on his desire.

In the real world, she'd met very few men willing to expose their true desire, and fewer still who were willing to take action. Although in fairness, when it came to her and Buster, she was the one unwilling to act.

She read half a chapter before Buster came in and resumed his throne before the television. The toothpick still dangled between his lips.

"That was quick," Ruby said without looking up from her book.

"She fell asleep right after Rooster moved *North To Alaska* and before Sister Sara could count her *Fist Full Of Dollars.*"

Ruby returned her focus to her novel. The hero scooped up the reluctant heroine and carried her over his shoulder away from the old homestead. Despite her protests, he dumped her over the saddle of his trusty steed and rode away without bothering to inform her a band of outlaws was on the way to burn down the house.

That was the trouble with men. They expected women to do whatever they wanted without explaining the particulars.

"He still hasn't called me," Buster said.

She stopped reading, but didn't lift her eyes from the page. Now that he'd started, Buster wouldn't let up about Blue until he left for the night and went home to his own bed.

"Have you talked to him?"

Shaking her head, she squinted at the letters. Maybe just this once Buster would take the hint. Although she knew he wouldn't. Used to be, he only brought Blue up once or twice a month, but here lately Buster's tirades had become an every-night thing. If only her brother could put aside his anger and resentment long enough to call Buster.

"Somebody has to know where he is. This day and age, a man can't just disappear from the face of the earth."

"He can when he doesn't want found."

"Blue needs a damn cell. Hell, even an old saddle bum like me totes a cell phone."

"You're missing the point. Blue wants to be lost. He doesn't want found. At least not until he finds himself."

"Don't hand me that *find himself* line of crap. That's the same thing the hippies use to say when what they really wanted to do was hitchhike all over the damn country and smoke dope." Buster rubbed his chin. The toothpick danced between his lips. "You don't reckon Blue's on dope, do you?"

"No. And you better not accuse him of such when we both—"

"What about Donnie. He got a cell?"

"Yes, but—"

"Bet he knows where Blue is. Hell, they might even be together. Not even Blue can shake a tapeworm like Donnie."

"Donnie is not a tapeworm. He's Blue's friend. Maybe the only one he can still claim." She shot Buster a pointed look.

"You got his number in that book by the phone?" Ignoring her glare, Buster took off for the kitchen with his chest puffed up like a bantam rooster.

"Yes but—"

"Why the hell haven't you thought of this before now?" He acted like he'd just solved the world's greatest mystery.

Ruby let him go even though she knew he was sniffing up the wrong trail. Tracking Blue by using Donnie's scent would lead to nothing more than a pile of bullshit.

She could've told Buster that Blue was in Idaho, but the truth would've only opened an entire new line of sarcasm. Buster didn't understand the concept of grief. Of course, he was the same man that for years dutifully drove fifteen miles to spoon-feed his disabled wife dinner, and then another fifteen back to the embrace of another woman.

She'd spent many a sleepless night contemplating the

moral complexity of her love life. Then again, every detail of her entire life had been out of whack. Nothing ever came without a price to be paid as penance for some long-forgotten deed that she didn't have sense enough to remember or regret.

Giving into her feelings for Buster hadn't been easy. She fought the urges for as long as she could, but now that she was older, Ruby knew resisting the heart was as futile as plucking gray hairs to fend off middle age. One left you bald, but still feeling old. The other left nothing more than a bellyful of the what-ifs.

Now here she was staring fifty in the eye with more gray hair than black and an entirely different set of regrets. She sighed, because there wasn't a thing she could do, except maybe trade one regret for another.

Buster's voice drifted from the kitchen. So he'd gotten a hold of Donnie. Returning her attention back to the make-believe world on the page, she didn't bother to listen to the conversation. Blue wouldn't turn up until he wanted to.

Five minutes later Buster came in and said, "Donnie says he's at Crowfoot's. Or at least headed there."

Ruby marked her place with the tip of her finger. "You're not fool enough to believe that?"

"Donnie said Blue was going to get Winder in shape. Said they're going to hit the circuit together next year."

"And if a bullfrog had wings, it wouldn't bump its ass." She lifted her finger and read on. She made it to the end of the chapter until Buster started in again.

"Donnie's still in Vegas. At the National Finals. He said Blue left because he didn't want to watch. Blue said he won't watch until he qualifies."

Ruby arched a brow.

"If I called Crowfoot do you think he'd tell me if Blue was there?"

She shook her head, more out of disbelief Buster had bought into Donnie's pipe dream than to answer.

"I gotta make a run up to El Reno Monday anyway to pick up Briley's saddle," he mumbled. "Crowfoot's place can't be more than seventy or eighty miles from there."

Ruby put her book down. "What is it you need Blue for so bad that it can't wait? You know he'll be here a week or so after Christmas. He always is. What could possibly be so important that you'd want to drive three hundred miles on a wild goose chase?"

Buster sucked air in around his toothpick. "Mostly I'm going to pick up Briley's birthday present, but if there's a chance I'll find Blue, then it's high time I get done what should've been finished long ago."

# 23

Blue drummed his fingers against the green felt. Through a cloud of smoke, he stared across the table. The other player met his gaze. A slight smile tugged at the corners of the younger man's mouth. "Sorry. I know I'm holding up the game, but..." He sucked in a rush of air through the gap between his front teeth.

Blue kept his expression flat. The young guy was the second-best player at the table, but if he thought he could rattle a pro by stalling, he had a lot left to learn. Of course, the man didn't know he was playing a pro.

"Boy, this is a tough." The man shook his head.

A mask of patience, Blue waited, while underneath the placid surface he struggled not to reach across the table and choke his opponent.

"I shouldn't even call, but reckon I'll raise." The staller shoved his chips forward.

The next two bettors folded. That left only Blue to challenge for the pot. Blue knew his pair of jacks wouldn't take the hand. He would fold, but first he stared at his cards as if making a life -or-death decision. The other man's grin became a bit more noticeable. The guy thought he knew what he was doing. He thought his reluctance had tricked Blue into staying. He thought his rehearsed golly shucks speech would sucker Blue in. He thought he was playing a fool.

"I fold." Blue slid his cards toward the dealer.

The grin vanished. The staller had won, just not nearly as much as he'd hoped. No doubt his charade had worked at some frat house party or sitting around his buddy's kitchen tables. Blue knew he could take all the man's money given enough time, but he doubted his patience would hold out that long. Not when every pause in the action found him thinking about Lindsay.

As the dealer dealt the down cards for the next hand, Blue vowed to try. Otherwise, his resolve would never last, and he couldn't give in to temptation. He couldn't afford to risk his emotions, or hers, for a brief interlude of pleasure.

An hour later, Blue's chip count had tripled, but his tolerance had vanished and his jaw ached from being clenched. His resolution was crumpled as a discarded beer can. He'd come to the poker table in search of way to pass time. Not make it stand still. Along with the staller, the table now had a woman who couldn't stop talking, and a middle-aged accountant type who insisted on whistling nonstop.

Poker was supposed to flow, have a steady rhythm like a mountain stream. This game had turned stagnant as a cesspool. Not only was the pace slow, but the players predictable. With nothing to keep Blue's mind occupied, guilt and need. Heartache and desire. All that crap floated to the surface and neither the queen of hearts nor ace of spades offered help.

"So anyway, my ex calls me up and says he's getting married." The woman emitted a grating, horse-like laugh. "And then do you know what he asked me?"

No one around the table gave any indication they wanted to hear, but Chatty Cathy carried on undeterred. "He asked if

I would sing at his wedding. Can you believe that? I mean, I have a purty singing voice, but the nerve!"

Blue stared down at his pocket aces. You couldn't ask for better cards to open, yet he placed them face down on the table and stood without a word.

"Bet ya'll didn't guess that about me." The woman carried on. "That I could sing. Well I can."

Gathering his chips, he walked away from the table as the woman launched into an off-key version of *I Will Always Love You*. The theme of the Andy Griffith Show, courtesy of The Whistler, accompanied her warbling. No poker pot in the world was large enough to linger in the midst of that so Blue cashed out and left the Midnight Rose Hotel and Casino.

The cold quiet November air bolstered his spirits, though he still couldn't shake the conflictions from his gut. Walking to the corner, he lit a smoke and peered down the hill at the campground. He could see the top of his trailer under the amber glow of the facility's lights, but the angle was wrong to tell if a light shone inside.

It was almost midnight, but he felt certain Lindsay would be awake and waiting for him. Waiting for an explanation why he snuck away the second she returned to the laundry room. Waiting to know why he'd stayed away all day and half the night. Waiting to see if he would reach out to her again. Blue ground his cigarette out with the heel of his boot.

A group of tourists passed by, jarring Blue's attention back to the busy sidewalk. He looked up Bennett Street, in the direction of The Lucky Cuss.

Chris was up to something. No, it was more than that. Chris was always up to something. Blue didn't mind that he was involved. He could take care of himself, but the casino owner needed to leave Lindsay out of his plans. Whatever they were.

He gave the trailer another glance. The need to see Lindsay tugged at him, but common sense told him to go pay his buddy a visit instead.

The laminated sheets of the photo album crackled as Lindsay turned the pages. The pictures meant more to her now than when she first looked at them. Blue had become a real person and less of a mystical rodeo star riding to her rescue.

Lindsay turned to another page. The image of Blue atop his horse. Up there above the world, he struck an impressive figure. He looked much the same now as he did then, except more lines etched his tanned face. And the eyes were sadder now, whereas in the past they possessed an almost devilish gleam. Or maybe that was only the glare of the flash.

The next photo was an action shot. His heels dug into the splayed arena dirt as his arms pulled on the head of a steer. The tendons in his neck showed the strain. His biceps bulged. Blue's appeal went beyond physical appearance, but Lindsay couldn't deny the feelings he stirred in the hollow of her stomach. The very same feelings that in the past had led  to bad decisions. The same feelings that allowed Rusty Hawkins to lure her into the back of his silver Trans-Am.

But Blue was different. Over the years, for her own well-being, she'd learned how to fight off desire. Get away from the situation, occupy her mind, and concentrate on the flaws of whoever had captured her lust. None of that worked with Blue.

He'd been the one to flee the situation, although she wasn't surprised to see him drive away the second she returned to the laundry room. She'd meant to grab her clothes and rush back, but he'd had other plans.

In the effort to stave off both boredom and thoughts of him, Lindsay spent the day exploring the town. A museum in an old house that had at one time served as a brothel. Half a dozen shops. The library. Knowing he would be in one of the casinos, she avoided those places, yet all Lindsay could think of was how she felt in his embrace.

Inside The Lucky Cuss, Blue went straight to the security guard he'd talked to the night before. "Where's your boss?"

The man frowned, but pointed to the ceiling. "Upstairs." After a few seconds the man squirmed under Blue's intense gaze. "Fourth floor. In his office. Want me to call him?"

Blue shook his head as he handed the man a fifty. "I know where it's at. You stay right here. I want my visit to be a surprise."

The guard pocketed the bill. "Most likely, he already knows you're here."

Gritting his teeth, Blue took the stairs two at a time. At the top he paused a second to catch his breath. No doubt Sergio would be in there with Chris, but Blue's mission was simple. Go in, tell Chris to leave Lindsay alone, make certain the man understood, and leave. For once, Sergio could keep his mouth shut.

Blue knocked on the door once and stepped inside without waiting for an invitation. Chris stood at the window with his back to the room. Sergio was stretched out on the leather couch.

"Hello, Blue." Chris didn't bother to turn around.

"The little lost vaquero." Sergio sat up and rubbed his eyes. His smashed nose spread across his face like a deflated punching bag. Between the cocaine and years in the boxing ring, the cartilage never stood a chance. "I heard you were in town, *ese*, but I did not believe. I told Chris he cannot be here. I smell no cow shit."

Blue focused on the casino owner. "I want to talk to you. Alone."

"Ahhh. You are going to hurt my feelings. We are all old friends. What cannot be said among friends?"

Blue turned his hard stare on Sergio. "We're not friends, and I don't have a damn thing to say to you. So leave."

The Puerto Rican stood and folded his arms across his chest. "It is not your place to send me away. This is not your office."

Chris finally turned away from the window. "Wait in the hall, Sergio. We'll only be a minute."

The boxer sauntered across the room until mere inches separated his face from Blue's. "Don't think I'm leaving because of you. You do not scare me." Sergio started toward the door. With his hand on the knob, he paused. "I hear you brought your *crica* with you."

Blue took a step toward the grinning idiot. His Spanish was spotty at best, and *crica* was not a word he knew, but he knew the other man well enough to guess. "Leave." He growled through clenched jaws. "Like you were told."

"Relax. I'm only trying to help, *maricón*. She'll need a man who can stand up and perform." Sergio raised a forearm and fist. "Unless she smells like your horse, or is built like a cow. In that case, she is yours to keep." The Puerto Rican laughed.

Blue closed the gap between them in two strides. His fingers squeezed Sergio's throat choking off the man's mirth, but the boxer ripped his arms upward to break the grip. In the same instant, he ducked low and delivered a rapid left hook. Blue's ribs absorbed the punch. He grunted as the air left him, but he managed to lean forward with his upper body and pin his opponent against the wall. Aiming for the groin, Blue thrust his knee upward. The blow only glanced Sergio's hip as he turned.

Free from the heavier man's weight, Sergio danced to the right and struck with brisk left-right jab combination. The first punch snapped Blue's head back as it landed square on the cheek below his eye. The second grazed his ear.

Blue ducked his head and lunged forward wrapping his arms around Sergio's arms and torso. The two of them crashed into the wall. Paneling cracked and gave way as each struggled to get an arm free to deliver another blow. Neither inflicted any punishment before a hoard of security guards rushed into the room and yanked them apart.

Chris stood in the center of the room, shaking his head.

Blue struggled to free himself from the grip of two men. His chest heaved as he tried to catch his breath. Right then, he decided to quit smoking. He glared at Sergio.

The former boxer merely smiled. "Those cows you wrestled never hit back did they?" He did not resist his captors.

"Take Sergio down to the bar and don't let him go until Mr. Riggins has left the premises." Chris's voice took on an edge as he gave orders. "Bert, you and Tully go wait in the hall. Make certain Blue doesn't go looking for trouble when he leaves."

The Puerto Rican said, "Let him come. I told you I'm not scared."

"And I told you to go downstairs."

"You're the boss." Sergio allowed the other men to lead him into the hall. Before the door closed he looked over his shoulder, winked, and puckered his lips as if blowing Blue a kiss.

When they were alone, Chris grabbed Blue's shoulder. "Let it go. You'll get your chance."

Blue shrugged away the casino owner's hand. "Don't tell me what I can or can't do. I'm not one of your lackeys."

"I never said you were, but I can't be having a brawl in my place of business. The gambling commission—"

"Screw the commission. Tell that bastard to keep his mouth shut, and everything will be fine. The next time he says a word about Lindsay I'll—"

"You'll what?" Chris fired back. "Sergio popped you twice before you could blink."

"I've been hit harder."

"Maybe, but that knot under your eye still looks like hell."

Blue reached and felt his cheek. The swollen skin was hot and puffy. "He got lucky. Next time I'll put him on the ground, and we'll see what he can do."

"I can't have the two of you diving across the poker table at each other."

"Unless you tell me exactly what the hell's going on you won't have to worry about me being there. I'm tired of the games."

Chris strolled over to his window and stared down at the street. "What games?"

A crease formed in Blue's forehead. "You're up to something, and I don't like it."

Keeping his back to the room Chris said, "What exactly are you accusing me of?"

"I didn't come up here to make accusations. I came to tell you not to mess with Lindsay. Leave her out of it. She's not a part of any of this between me and Sergio. And don't be making bets with her."

Chris turned back around. A grin covered his face. "It was just a friendly little wager."

"You've never made a friendly wager in your life. If you make a bet it's because you want something and you know you can win. I don't want you or Sergio talking to her. Period. If you can't give me your word on that I'm leaving town."

"If you leave now, Sergio will say you got scared."

"I don't give a shit what he says. He's a used-up coke-head."

"Maybe, but you've yet to outlast him at a final table."

"There are more important things," Blue said.

"Like Lindsay?" When Blue didn't answer, Chris spoke again. "You sure are hell-bent on protecting her. Mind if I ask why?"

Blue stared at the man he had once thought of as a friend. Now he wasn't so certain. "Because she deserves better than she's had."

# 24

Like a gentle rain shower, her tears fell with soft plops on the laminated sheets. One salty drop landed squarely on the face of Blue's pregnant wife, obscuring the woman's delicate features. Wiping her eyes, Lindsay lifted her head and stared at the ceiling.

She did not want to stand before her father and wither like a petunia beneath a blistering August sun. She wanted to be strong, look him in the eye, and say what should've been said nine years ago, but even these pictures turned her into a puddle of mud. How could she face down her father and all the hurts of her past, when she couldn't even cope with a grief that wasn't her own?

Her father. Her mom. Rusty Hawkins too.

Lindsay had plenty of tough words for them all, but she carried a fear that Rusty, when told the truth, would simply shrug his shoulders and say, "Oh, well." The sorrow had always been hers to carry alone, but somehow she believed telling him the truth would lighten that load. The thought he might be unconcerned by the news scared her in ways she'd never faced head on.

Exhaling a steady stream of air, she lowered her head and again stared down at the photographs. She wiped away the salty drops with the bottom of her shirt.

*"Get tough, Parker."* She echoed one of her old track coach's favorite sentiments. Lindsay stared at the woman forcing herself to focus on the enlarged belly. Again, she pulled out the picture of Blue's child and stared. *"No pain, no gain."* Another of Coach Bacon's beloved motivational statements.

Lindsay knew pain. The gain never had materialized. "I can do this," she spoke to the little girl. "I have to do this." Blue's daughter smiled back with that incessant dimpled grin. *"How do you run a five-thousand-meter race?"* Another plagiarism of her high school coach. *"One stride at a time."* When she convinced herself, Lindsay slid the photo of Blue's child between two pages, snapped the book shut, and carried the album back to the cabinet.

"One stride at a time." Now to take that first step.

She rummaged around until she located a piece of paper and a pen to list the points to make with both her father and Rusty. Once satisfied, she would read over them silently until she could do so without breaking down. Then she would speak them aloud to herself. Maybe, if she progressed fast enough she could even practice her speech on Blue.

No, she shook her head. She had to stop thinking about Blue. He had enough troubles of his own without her unloading on him simply for practice. Not that he would linger long enough for her to tell him anyway.

*"Focus on the path ahead. Don't worry about the scenery or the other runners. They have nothing to do with how you perform."* Lindsay wrote FATHER at the top of the page and drew a number one beneath.

*"Come race day it boils down to you and the hard ground beneath your feet. One will punish the other. Decide now which it will be."* She smiled. Coach Bacon would be pleased to hear

her recite his speeches, although Lindsay wondered if she wasn't cracking up. Of course, all the runners used to wonder the same thing about Coach.

*"A pound of performance is worth a pickup load of promises."* His personal favorite. He said it at least once a day in practice, to the point her teammates mocked him for it, but Lindsay now realized he'd been right.

She'd broken countless promises to herself.

Allowing her pessimism to shrink away, Lindsay lifted her head at the rumble of an engine. The sound grew louder and then ceased.

A truck door banged.

Blue was back.

Folding the sheet of paper, she stuck it beneath the cushion on the couch to work on later. No doubt Blue would head straight for his room to avoid any prolonged human contact. She found it disconcerting that her irritation at him returned so quickly when she'd just vowed not to worry over him or his actions.

Lindsay picked up a tattered copy of *Field and Stream*. The trailer door opened, filling the room with a rush of cool air. She thumbed through the pages without looking up. Pictures of deer. An ad for Skoal Wintergeen Long Cut. Turkeys with their feathers fanned out. An ad with the image of a pickup plowing through mud.

Lindsay flicked her eyes upward for a brief second. Blue stood in the doorway. Watching her. She quickly returned her attention to the magazine.

Built Ford Tough. Waiting, she read the slogan a dozen times. She refused to speak first. Blue was the one who left. Let him explain why he ran away. Why he ran every time she reached out. Let him sort through the awkwardness. Let him wonder what to say for a change.

Turning the page, she tried to hold her gaze to the glossy print, but once again she glanced up. Their eyes met for the briefest of seconds before she regained control. But then she looked again. High on his cheek was a swollen and angry red knot.

Despite her intentions, their eyes locked. She didn't want to speak, but she couldn't stop herself. "What happened?" She pointed at the injury.

He shook his head as if to ward away her question like a pesky fly. "Nothing." He paused never letting his gaze leave hers. "Lindsay." Regret pooled in his eyes. "I never should have left. You deserved better."

His words penetrated her resolve. The magazine fell from her grip. The look on his face told her she did not want to have this conversation, even though she'd waited for it all day.

He stepped forward. Lindsay's breath quickened.

"I've tried like hell to ignore you. I can't do it anymore." He moved closer still.

"Blue—"

"Let me finish." He reached out. His rough hand caressed her face. "I'm not sure I'm capable of any of this, but I have to try."

She stood and turned her back to avoid his eyes. She couldn't say what needed said. Not with him looking at her like that. With both hurt and need lurking in the shadowy depths. It would be so easy to fall into his arms and lose herself instead of facing what lay ahead in Oklahoma, but now she had made up her mind.

"I can't." The declaration fell from her mouth like a dead bird from the sky. She stared at the orange flames dancing in the fireplace.

"What do you mean you can't? You can't what?"

"I can't have this conversation. I can't invest any of my-self in you. Not if I—"

Blue turned her—to face him. "I'm not asking you for anything. I'm simply telling you how I feel."

A lump formed in her throat. "You don't have to say a word, but..."

She didn't know how to finish. *But I just promised myself to remain focused* didn't quite quantify the myriad of emotions inside her.

"But what?" Blue reached for her hand.

The heat from his palm, the strength in his touch called to her. "But I'm afraid." The statement flew from her before she could stop it. Lindsay didn't even know why she chose those words.

"Afraid of what?" He gripped her shoulders.

"I don't know." She bowed her head. Relationships cer-tainly didn't scare her. Not anymore. She'd been in enough of them to know they were only temporary.

"Me? Do I scare you?"

Lindsay laughed despite herself. "I've never felt more secure with anyone. It's just that we don't really know each other." That wasn't the problem either. She'd been attracted to other men based on far less than she already knew about Blue. His allure wasn't in question. He'd long ago captured her interest.

"I haven't given us that chance," he said. "I haven't given us any chance."

"I just can't," she answered. "I don't have a real answer, but I can't. Yesterday I wanted you to hold me, this morning I wanted you to kiss me, but standing here now, I just can't.

Don't ask me to explain." She stepped around him to reach for the door.

He grabbed her hand and pulled her back. "You can't, or you won't?" His eyes searched for an answer.

Lindsay looked at her feet. "It's not that simple. I can't commit to anything but going back to face my father. That has to be my focus."

"I don't want to stand in your way, but I can't turn my back on how I feel."

"You've had no problem before now."

He grimaced. "I'm sorry. I've been a fool."

"And now what? What do you expect from me?"

"A chance."

Lindsay squeezed her eyes shut. She shook her head. "I've never taken a single chance in life I didn't later regret."

"Stop taking chances, and you might as well get up from the table." Blue's voice sounded raspy.

Before she could open her eyes, his lips collided with hers. His arms circled her in a tight embrace. Lindsay's resistance crumbled against the warmth of his mouth, the firmness of his body pressed to hers.

She kissed him back. Wished she hadn't. Then did it again.

Blue was the one to break contact. His eyes explored hers as if searching for a sign. She willed herself to say no, to stand firm, but her willpower caved. She did not have Blue's strength.

Cradling Blue's face in her hands, she guided him close. "I shouldn't do this," she whispered. This wasn't her first time to give in to desire. Nor was it the first time that she knew going in, she would be the one hurt in the end. Yet, she closed her eyes and dove into the unknown.

Heat from their second kiss burned away the last of her doubts and the last of her rational thoughts. Pressing her body against his, she thought only of the hardness of his body, the tenderness of his touch on her neck, the scrape of his flesh against hers as his mouth moved close to her ear.

"Should I stop before it's too late," he whispered.

"It's already too late." Her fingers slid beneath his shirt.

The muscles in his stomach tightened at her touch.

"I've thought about you all day." He nibbled her lobe as he spoke softly.

"Just today?"

"No." His lips brushed her neck. "But today I gave up trying to fight you off." His hand slid up her back.

Lindsay closed her eyes as he lifted her shirt over her shoulders. The fireplace hissed as his fingers slid across her skin. His lips moved down her neck. His tongue left a wake of heat and desire.

Consumed by hope, the flame they'd both tried so hard to extinguish now burned beyond their control. Blue's touch stoked her body. Lindsay gave in to the weakness of her flesh.

Her fingers found the button of his jeans. Then the zipper. She reached for him. Blue's lips found hers again. He pulled her tight and still she kept her hand wrapped around him, feeling the warmth, the beat of his heart in her fingertips.

# 25

Blue stared at the camper's shadowed ceiling as if he expected Staci to suddenly appear in the darkness. He'd heard it said loved ones keep watch over those left behind. If so, what would Staci think? Would she be shocked? Angered? Or just hurt?

The same thought came to him in Vegas each time he gave in to his body's demands and shared a bed with a woman. His guilt had been especially hard to escape that first time after his wife's death. But he could chalk up that one, and the others that followed, to a physical need. A hunger that meant nothing more than the rumble in his stomach.

What he'd just experienced with Lindsay was something different. Not a need, but a desire. A longing, not to quench a thirst, but to nurture a budding new shoot of life.

What he felt now wasn't regret. He hadn't meant it to happen like that. His intention was to share his feelings with Lindsay, not his body, not her body, but something happened. Something swept them up.

"What if this doesn't work?"

Blue leaned up on one elbow. He'd thought Lindsay was asleep until she spoke the very question on his mind. Unable to provide an answer, Blue reached out and stroked the silky skin on her stomach.

"What if we discover we're too different?"

He turned toward her. "What if we don't?" He kissed her.

"What if the way we feel doesn't last?"

Blue laid his head against her bare breast. Her heart thumped steady in her chest. "Shooting stars are fleeting, but I feel privileged every time I see one streak across the sky."

She kissed the top of his head. "What's going to happen tomorrow? Or when we get to Oklahoma? Where do we go from here?"

"I don't know," he said with bare honesty. "At one time, I thought I could see the future. Maybe not the details, but the basic way it would shape up. I was a fool to take life for granted. One bad decision can erase a lifetime of dreams."

The beat within Lindsay's chest sped up. In the dark, he couldn't make out the features on her face, but he could feel the tension in her body as she said, "It doesn't even have to be your decision."

# 26

Lindsay woke with the weight of Blue's arm draped across her body. A gentle rasp escaped his mouth with each breath. The minutes ticked by as she lay there, content in the dark stillness. Blue made her almost believe the shattered pieces of life could be dusted off and reassembled.

He stirred in his sleep and rolled onto his back. Lindsay took this as a sign to slip out of bed and get dressed for her daily jog. The sky outside the window had not begun to lighten yet, but the clock in her body said morning was close.

She peeked out. A few snowflakes drifted lazily to the ground in the amber glow of the campground's parking lot.

Dressed and almost ready, Lindsay laced her Nikes.

"You're up early."

She could just make out Blue's outline in the hall. "I didn't mean to wake you."

"You didn't. I reached for you and you were gone. It's not even six yet," he said. "You could come back to bed and wait until sunrise."

She stood and stretched. "I like to run early. When the world is still peaceful and quiet."

"Let me get dressed. I'll go with you."

She laughed. "I'll put in eight or ten miles. And I'm not

going to stop for smoke breaks along the way."

"I quit smoking."

"Since when."

"Since last night." Blue stepped into the trailer's living room. He pulled her close. "I worry about you out there, alone, in the dark, but I'm not stupid enough to think I could keep up."

"I like to run alone. It's my time to think and sort my thoughts."

Blue gave her a final squeeze and let her go. "You might like the road south out of town better. You'll pass a big gold mine and not much else until you hit a town called Victor in about five miles."

"Okay."

"That way you can avoid the casinos."

"Okay," she said again.

Lindsay left the trailer and took off in the direction of Victor. The snow was light and only occasionally did a flake land on her face. Her legs felt good. Resilient, strong, the way they used to when she was running out in front of the pack and headed for the finish line. A lot of years had lapsed since she felt even a shred of that confidence.

Lindsay ran on. The white flakes grew bigger but their numbers didn't increase. Buoyed by her newfound intimacy with Blue, her body and mind felt alive this morning, but she'd pinned hope on men's backs before, only to have each failed relationship dig a deeper hole.

The weight of this realization slowed her pace as she neared the town of Victor. She wanted to make the hurt go away. Find a place in the world where she could feel good about herself again. If only she knew where to look.

At the city limit sign, she turned around and headed

back to Cripple Creek, back to Blue.

Given his track record, she wondered if he would even be at the camper when she arrived. Of course, he'd surprised her this morning. He seemed reluctant for her to go, offering to come along, and then in his subtle way guiding her away from another encounter with Chris.

But the real shock had been last night. The determined way he revealed his feelings, even after she tried to turn him away. Thinking about Blue revitalized her legs. The energy began to pool back in her muscles. Her stride increased.

The memory of his words, his touch, and his fervor swept her along even though she'd vowed to remain true to her mission. But why couldn't she have both? Blue knew where she was going. He might've even guessed the root of her trouble. She'd told him her college dreams were dashed by pregnancy. Lindsay hadn't mentioned a child, but then neither had he.

The gravel crunched beneath her feet. The snow fell with more intensity now. An inch or two had accumulated along the edge of the pavement. Blue had no way of knowing what her father had done. It wasn't as if the procedure left a large A emblazoned on her forehead.

Lindsay forced herself to slow as she again passed the gold mine. Focusing on proper breathing techniques, she tried to relax. Blue would understand. A man who'd experienced the pain he had, would relate on a level none of the others had. She used to tell all of her boyfriends about her past, but none of them had truly gotten her anger, or reasons for dwelling on a past she couldn't change.

Blue would. He cared for her on a different level than anyone had since...well, since she was a little girl. For a while Lindsay confused lust for real emotion. But those boyfriends could only hide their true motivations for so long. They charmed her with false promises and false affections, but Blue's words, his emotions had been genuine. He'd wanted more than sex. She'd seen need and hunger before. Men could lie with their clothes on. They could lie when they wanted to talk a woman out of hers. They could even lie and say they loved you afterward. But Lindsay had never met a man who could hide his true motive during the act.

Blue had made love to her. As a man who wanted her. Not one simply needing a warm body beneath his.

The slow, deliberate kisses. The tender stroke of his fingers. The gentle, measured way he'd moved with her, instead of against her. A man consumed by mere hunger was reckless and rough, full of unbridled passion and exuberance. Blue had the passion, but in an unhurried, controlled way that told Lindsay he savored her.

There in the darkness they'd shared more than their bodies. An unspoken recognition passed between them. An acknowledgment that life had turned its back on them both and somehow they'd found each other. Only time would tell if they were meant to stay together, but as Lindsay rounded the bend and spied the campground, with Blue's truck still parked beside it, she made a decision. The time had come to tell him about her past.

Blue smiled when she entered. "Breakfast is ready."

The smell of grease hung in the air. "Let me jump in the shower first."

"Let's eat first." He motioned toward the table. "While the food's hot."

Lindsay sat and watched while he ladled out a thick slice of ham, at least two potatoes worth of shredded hash browns, a pile of scrambled eggs, and a couple of biscuits onto her plate. He dished himself a similiar heaping plate before filling two cups of coffee.

"How was your run?" He sliced off a chunk of the ham steak.

"Good. My legs felt great. Better than they have in years." She picked at the hash browns. Apparently, he'd forgotten her eating habits differed from his, but she didn't have the heart to dash his well-laid plans.

They ate in silence for several minutes. Blue stared out the window, and she tried to think of a proper lead in to say what she wanted.

After a while, he said, "Snow's really coming down."

She nodded and tried to disguise the irritation welling within her. After the night they'd shared and all of her good intentions, the best either of them could come up with was more stupid talk about the weather.

"I've got to ask you a favor," he said still looking outside. "But first I have to tell you something."

Lindsay put down her fork. Blue's reluctant tone told her she might not want to hear what was coming.

"I have a daughter. Her name's Briley. She turns four the seventeenth." He turned his sad, dark eyes to Lindsay.

Obviously, he expected her to respond, but she didn't know what to say. Now didn't seem like the right time to reveal she'd gone through his photo album.

"I can't be there on her birthday, but I want to send her something special. Thought maybe you could help."

"Is it because of me?"

Blue frowned. "Is what because of you?"

"That you're not going to be there. It must be hard to be away from your daughter on her birthday."

He stared down at the table. "Not as hard as being

there."

Lindsay reached for his hand. "I don't understand."

"I just want to get her something nice. I can't go back to Texas. Not this time of year. Has nothing to do with me giving you a ride, but I thought maybe you'd have a better idea what a four-year-old girl would like."

"I'm not very good with children"

"You're one up on me. Least you've been a little girl." Again, Blue stared blankly out the window. "I know I should be there. Wish I could. Ruby takes good care of her, but Briley needs a parent."

"We could leave now. You could make it in time for her birthday."

Blue closed his eyes. "I can't."

"Why?"

He didn't answer.

"I'll go with you."

"No."

The harsh tone made Lindsay straighten.

He took a deep breath. "I can't go back. Not right now. Will you help me find her a present or not?"

"Blue, I don't understand. Why not go see her?"

Shaking his head, he stood, and carried his plate over to the trash.

Lindsay watched as he scraped his half-eaten breakfast into the bag. "Talk to me."

"You wouldn't understand," he said. "No one does."

He started to walk away, but she grabbed his arm. "Don't shut me out now, not after last night."

Blue stared at her, meeting her gaze. Lindsay took a deep breath. Maybe telling him her past would make it easier for him to open up. Closing her eyes to hold back the tears she knew would come, Lindsay said, "Mine would be nine years old this year. Every child I see brings it all back. I avoid the diaper aisle in the grocery store. The smell of baby powder still brings tears to my eyes." Her shoulders shook as she wept.

Blue sat beside her. He took Lindsay in his arms.

They sat there, rocking to some unheard lullaby, holding each other for several long minutes. Finally, she said, "I didn't want to do it. My father said I was too young, had too much ahead of me to raise a baby. Nobody ever asked me what I wanted." Sobs racked her body. "He made the decision, but I signed the papers. I let them take my baby from me and I never spoke up to tell him I wanted something else." She buried her face in Blue's chest.

His strong arms held her tight until the heartbreaking quake within her soul subsided to mere tremors.

"Afterward my father expected me to just forget and move on. He couldn't understand the void I felt." Lindsay inhaled deep. Anger took the place of sorrow as she said, "So I left. I ran away. I wanted him to wonder where I was, to feel what it was like to lose a child."

"You haven't been back?"

She shook her head. "Not in nine years."

Snow drifted down outside while they sat clinging to each other. Blue's chest rose and fell against her cheek. She wanted him to say something, anything, but he remained silent. At least he still had his arms wrapped around her. At least he hadn't dismissed her past with a shrug. At least he understood what it felt like to lose someone.

"Tell me about your wife."

The movement of his chest stopped. His grip relaxed and for a brief second Lindsay thought she'd gone too far, but then Blue said, "I miss her. It doesn't seem like four years.

Not most of the time anyway. But sometimes it feels like forever."

His breathing resumed. "It wasn't Briley's fault. Staci made her choice to stop taking her blood thinner. And even if I had been there when she went to the doctor ..." Blue sighed. "I'm not sure I could've changed Staci's mind. I'm not sure I would've wanted to."

His words stacked up in Lindsay's mind like a logjam on a river. *Doesn't seem like four years. Not Briley's fault. Made her choice.*

Blue's wife died giving birth. The arrival of his child meant the end for his wife. No wonder he couldn't be there for her birthday. To him it was also a death day.

Lindsay's heart quickened. How could Blue stomach to hold her and confide his pain? His wife had made the ultimate sacrifice for her baby, and Lindsay had not even mustered the courage to tell her father no.

"You must think I'm weak. Compared to your wife."

"Giving up a child you carried inside of you has to be hard. Maybe harder than sacrificing yourself."

A second set of tears spilled down Lindsay's cheeks. The last of her doubts about Blue melted. He was right. Many times she'd wished for the ability to trade her life for the one she failed to fight hard enough for.

"Was it a boy or a girl?"

Lindsay hesitated. No one had ever bothered to ask, and she'd never told anyone out of fear they'd ridicule her for being so certain of a fact she had no way to prove. But Lindsay knew deep within her gut that the baby would've been a girl. When she closed her eyes and imagined what her child would have looked like, she saw long black hair and pink frilly dresses. Lindsay would forever think of her stolen baby that way. "A girl."

"Have you looked for her?"

"What?" Lindsay sat up. She looked at Blue.

"Do you know who adopted her? Have you tried to find her?"

Unable to speak, Lindsay stared at Blue.

"I'm sure it would be hard to see her, but maybe you'd feel better just to know she's okay."

Lindsay opened her mouth. What words could she use to tell him her baby wasn't okay? "I ... she's ..."

"Staci was adopted," he said. "We talked about adopting one day ourselves, but she wanted a child of her own first. She wanted at least one person in this world that shared the same blood she did."

Lindsay closed her mouth.

She couldn't tell Blue the truth.

Not now.

Not ever.

# 27

Staring out the camper's window, Lindsay avoided eye contact with Blue as he prepared to go search for a present. The snow had picked up, and the white flakes swirled around the campground's gravel lot. Several inches covered the ground, with more in the sheltered areas where the wind hadn't swept it away.

Stuffing his battered black cowboy hat down low onto his ears, Blue said, "Sure you're going to be okay?"

She nodded. The lie had slipped easily off her tongue. "I don't feel well."

Blue had offered to stay, to put off the search for Briley's present until Lindsay felt well enough to go along. "No, go ahead," she'd said. "It will mean more if it's something you choose anyway."

After he left, Lindsay hoped the time alone would help her come to grips with the contradictions of their past, but sitting there in the RV she wasn't alone. Not truly. Regret and guilt sat right there beside her. She'd let Blue down. She'd let herself down. All these years, she'd avoided the word abortion, refused to speak it aloud. But never before had anyone assumed she'd given her baby up for adoption. She should have set things straight, but after hearing of his wife's sacrifice, Lindsay simply lacked the courage to speak the truth.

So much for all that *One stride at a time* rhetoric. It wasn't as if Blue suggested she volunteer in the local nursery. Or baby-sit an infant. Or even so much as look at a child. He wanted help buying a present for a four-year-old. For his little girl. He'd asked Lindsay because she was female. Because he wanted to be near her. Because they'd opened their hearts and lives to one another. Not to flaunt a choice his wife made.

Crossing the room, Lindsay went to the photo album. She found Briley's picture tucked in the back. Such a pretty little girl. Those blonde curls. Her plump dimpled cheeks. The same heartrending, dark eyes as Blue.

What a thing to inherit. Sorrow. Briley was too young to know it now, but someday the full tragedy of her life would take hold. The sadness surrounding her would sink in. She would realize her mother died because of her. That her father couldn't look at her. That she was to blame. A heavy fate for a child to carry.

A special birthday present.

The girl deserved that much.

Lindsay dressed in a warm sweater and headed out in search of Blue. Bennett Street housed most of the shops so he would probably be there, somewhere among the stores tucked in between the various casinos. Despite the wind blowing in her face, a sense of virtue and merit came over Lindsay as she trudged up the hill. Finally, she was taking a stride. A stride with a dual purpose. A stride, not only to help herself, but also to bring a dash of joy to an innocent child.

Coming to the intersection, she looked first to the left and then to the right. Which direction? Most of the activity and businesses were to the right so she walked that way. Snow swirled around her feet as she passed the gambling establishments of The Midnight Rose, The Brass Ass, and Creekers. She crisscrossed the street to peer into stores with names like The Rocky Mountain Canary, Maudie's Incredible Emporium, and The Silver Mine. All without a trace of Blue.

Nearing The Lucky Cuss, she cut to the far side of Bennett to get as far away from Chris's place as possible. From the middle of the road, she spotted Blue, black cowboy hat and all, duck into a store directly opposite her least favorite casino, and its arrogant owner.

A sign above the door read The Motherlode Mercantile. Just before she entered, Lindsay gave a fleeting glance at The Lucky Cuss Casino. Her eyes drifted upward. There in the window of the fourth floor stood Chris, watching the land like an evil lord over an impoverished kingdom. She turned away when he lifted a hand and waved. At least Blue would be here if the pompous idiot decided to descend from his golden throne.

Moving deep into the store, she found Blue. "Find anything?"

He shook his head. "Nope. Apparently, a town that sells itself on gambling and a rowdy past isn't the place to find a perfect present for a four-year-old."

Her arrival hadn't surprised him. Matter of fact, he spoke as if she'd been right there beside him all along. Lindsay surveyed the room. Etched shot glasses, t-shirts, playing cards, poker chips, postcards, flakes of real Cripple Creek gold floating in little plastic vials.

Blue was right. Nothing in the place looked suitable for his daughter. She eyed the rubber band guns, train engineer hats, and a selection of paper dolls stacked in the small children's section with distaste. "Maybe the next store will have something."

He shook his head. "I've already been to most of 'em. They're all pretty much the same."

"In that case, we'll have to go somewhere else to look. There has to be a town around here with some specialty shops, or maybe a mall."

He paused and squinted his eyes. "Maybe Woodland Park. It's a good forty-five-minute drive. After that, it would be Colorado Springs and that's an hour away."

Lindsay smiled. "I don't know about you, but I have plenty of time."

"After you then." He motioned toward the front of the store with a sweeping wave.

His hand lay gently on the lower curve of her spine as they approached the exit together. She liked the fact that Blue hadn't made a big deal about her sudden recovery. His touch and easy manner confirmed she had done the right thing, not only for herself and Briley, but Blue as well.

Opening the door, he stood back to let her step through. As the cold air hit her face, Lindsay became aware of the man leaning against the No Parking sign. Actually, she didn't take full notice until the individual stepped forward to within a few feet and sized her up.

"Tell me something, *Cabron*." The man's Spanish accent filled the air as he stopped searching her body and focused on Blue. "How does a *pendajo* like you find a woman like this?" Again, his eyes feasted on Lindsay.

Blue stepped in front of her. "Turn around, and walk back across the street." His voice seeped with more venom than she would have thought possible.

Lindsay lifted her eyes skyward. As expected, Chris stood behind his glass shield taking in the scene.

"You should introduce me." The man peered around

Blue's larger frame and extended a hand her direction. "Sergio."

"She's not interested." Blue reached behind him and searched her hand out. Finding it, he pulled her forward all the while keeping his body between her and Sergio's. When she was beside him they stepped passed the offensive man, together.

"Don't turn your back on me, *maricon*."

From the corner of her eye, Lindsay saw Sergio reach out in the same instant Blue released her hand. Spun around by Sergio's grip on his shoulder, Blue brought his fist from down low and connected with a vicious blow. The punch landed flush on his opponent's nose.

Sergio staggered back and shook the mop of black hair on his head. A smile emerged on his face despite the crimson river trickling from one nostril. He raised his arms in a boxer's stance and began to bounce on the balls of his feet. "You're a fool. You can't beat me. You never have, and now you'll take a beating in front of your lover." He flicked his left fist forward and when Blue moved to block it, Sergio drove a right into his gut.

Blue's hat fell to the snow as he doubled over. Sergio delivered a jaw-rattling uppercut. Lindsay gasped when Blue sunk to his knees, but in the same instant he grabbed Sergio's legs and pulled the boxer to the ground.

The two of them rolled and grunted until they slid off the curb and landed in the gutter with Blue on top. He shoved Sergio's chin back at the end of his long left arm and threw punches with his right. At first, Sergio blocked most of the blows, but with each hit that landed, his resistance crumbled.

"Blue, stop it." Lindsay stood in awe as the strikes rained down.

Blood splattered the snow accumulated along the street. "Stop!"

Oblivious to her screams, Blue wailed on his opponent with disregard to all else. His fist collided with fleshy smacks and low heavy grunts to Sergio's face, head, and chest. Blue didn't seem to care where the blows landed as long as they connected and brought pain to the other man.

Finally, a group of security guards poured forth from The Lucky Cuss. Two of the uniformed men pulled Blue off while another kneeled next to Sergio. A fourth stood in protection of the invisible boundary between the two. Lindsay looked up, and sure enough Chris still stood there watching.

Blue's chest heaved with exertion, but he did not struggle against his captors. Instead, he glared down at Sergio.

One of the guard's radios crackled. "Let him go."

Lindsay recognized the voice as Chris's. She looked up. His form had vanished from the window.

"Make sure he makes it back to his truck. Then bring Sergio to my office."

When the men released Blue, he walked over to the sidewalk, picked up his hat, and took off down the sidewalk.

Lindsay hurried to catch up. They covered a block and a half before turning down a narrow alley-like opening between two buildings. His labored breathing provided the only sound as they stepped out into a parking lot behind the structures. Shaken by the violence she'd witnessed, Lindsay didn't say a word as they walked to Blue's truck.

They drove back to the campground before he spoke, "I'll get things ready out here if you want to start inside."

She gave him a puzzled look as he backed up to the camper. "We're leaving?"

"Should've left the day we got here." The truck door

slammed behind him as he got out.

Blue rummaged through the trailer's storage box for the tools he needed. His fist ached, and his heart still beat wildly. He wished Lindsay would get out of the truck and go inside. He didn't want to answer her questions. Not right now. Not until he calmed down.

A few minutes passed before she finally opened her door and slipped inside. He hated that she'd seen him in that light, but he did not regret giving Sergio a lesson. The man had that much, and a lot more, coming.

A pickup pulled up and parked as he continued to work. Blue gave only a fleeting glance the vehicle's direction as one of Chris's security guards got out.

"Mr. Vanderspice wants to see you."

"Tell him I'm leaving."

"He said not to leave without coming to see him first."

"I don't care what he said." Blue cranked the handle to lower the trailer into the back of his truck.

"He said no charges would be pressed if you come talk to him."

"He said," Blue spat the words as the hitch settled onto the receiver. "Tell your boss if he's got something to say he should come say it himself. Tell him I'm leaving just as soon as I'm ready. Tell him I'll be by, but not to listen to his bullshit. Tell him I'm coming to pick up what's mine, and then I'm gone." He turned his back on the man and stomped away.

Thirty minutes later, he had hitched the RV, connected the trailer lights, and double-checked the wheel hubs. Everything was ready. Lindsay, having finished the inside, sat in the passenger seat. So far, she hadn't wanted an explanation or asked questions, but he knew that would change. Blue climbed in and looked over at her. "Ready?" He touched her arm, trying to let her know nothing had changed between them.

She nodded.

"I have to make two quick stops. First at the office to settle up, and then over to Chris's place."

Her brows shot up.

"Don't worry. I just have to pick up a couple of things. I won't be but a few minutes, and I won't get in any more fights."

She rubbed her neck. Her questions would come next. "What was that all about anyway? It happened so fast."

"You have to understand, me and Sergio's problems started a long time ago. Normally, we give each other a wide berth, even when we're forced to sit at the same poker table, but for some reason he's pushed for a fight this week."

"But you threw the first punch. Couldn't we have just kept walking?"

He sighed. "No. You don't know the man. He wanted to brawl. When he grabbed my shoulder, I did what I had to. I'm sorry you had to see it." With that he started the truck and revved the motor to let Lindsay know he'd finished explaining.

Pulling up next to the office, Blue parked and went inside to pay. As he handed over cash, the man behind the counter counted the bills, ripped off a receipt, and wished him a good afternoon and happy traveling.

Back outside, the snow continued to fall as Chris pulled up behind the wheel of the same pickup the security guard had shown up in earlier. Four sets of antlers now stuck up from the battered bed.

Blue waited until the casino owner got out before saying, "Good, you saved me a trip." He reached over the side, lifted both sets of mule deer antlers and carried them over to his truck.

Chris watched without offering to help. "If you leave now, it'll cost me fifty grand." He paused as if waiting for a comment. When none came,  he added, "I made a side bet you'd beat Sergio. Given your past performances against him, I got two to one."

Lowering the tailgate, Blue lifted the heavy six-by-six rack of the bull elk he shot back in October.

"Stay. I'll make sure Sergio keeps his mouth shut."

"You haven't been too successful at it yet."

Chris stared down at his feet.

Blue stopped and shook his head. "You've been here in this low-stakes town too long. I thought you had some grand scheme, and all you had was a weak fifty G bet on something you couldn't even control. You used to be better than that."

Lifting his head, Chris smiled. "You think that's what this is about? You think I kept you around town to make that bet? That was an afterthought, made this morning as a matter of fact." He turned and stared at Blue's truck where Lindsay watched the two men from behind glass.

Blue hoisted the second bull's antlers. The one Donnie had shot. "I should've picked these up and left the next day. Like I meant to."

Chris followed from one truck to the other. "Stay. Play the game. You can beat him. You've always been better than Sergio, but you let him rattle you. I'll make certain he remains on his best behavior."

"I'm leaving. I already closed his mouth. I have nothing to prove to you, or anybody else. You shouldn't have made a bet you had no control over."

The smug look on Chris's face seemed to say he did have

control.

Blue didn't like it. "You might have power over Sergio. But don't think that carries over to me."

"You need me more than you know."

"The hell I do."

"I've already helped you, Chris said. "You're just too damned blind to see it."

Blue brushed past the casino owner and reached for his door handle. He had nothing left to add.

"Why do you think I made Lindsay sit and have breakfast with me when I knew you would be waiting on her? Why do you think Sergio pushed you so hard about your girlfriend? Who do you think sent Sergio down to the street?"

His hand on the pickup door, Blue waited.

"Oh, I never would've done it, had I known what I do now. But how could I have guessed? You arrived alone, and then Lindsay came in a few seconds later. If I'd have seen the two of you together."

Blue spun around. "What are you getting at?"

"That you finally decided to open your damn eyes and realize the world still spins. That you need her. That she wanted you." Chris shrugged. "I saw the potential the first five minutes after you showed up, but it took jealousy to make you see it. I knew if I kept you in town long enough." He displayed a toothy grin. "A man can only shack up so long in a tiny space with a woman like that and not give in to carnal lust."

Blue's fist sent Chris to the snow-covered dirt. "Got anything else to say?"

Touching his jaw tenderly, Chris nodded, "I knew you'd defend her good name. I know you. You protect those you care about. Be pissed, but you know I'm right."

"Keep talking and you can recuperate with Sergio."

Chris stared up with the same smug look.

Blue pointed down at the man still splayed in the dirt. "You can't jack with other people's lives whenever you feel like it."

"I can when they don't bother to live."

Blue opened the pickup door and sat behind the wheel.

Lindsay gave him a wide-eyed look as if she feared he might hit her next.

Chris climbed to his feet. "You two take care of each other."

Blue glowered at the other man and reached for the door to close it, but Chris caught the metal frame in his hand. "By the way, we're even," his voice took on the tone he reserved for his employees. "You saved my life once, and now," his eyes shifted to Lindsay, "I've just dealt you one hell of a river card. Don't screw up your hand."

# 28

Lindsay stared out the window as Blue motored the rig up out of the valley and the town of Cripple Creek, Colorado. She'd jogged this same path that first morning, when Chris interrupted her run. Today, the road seemed even steeper. Snow continued to come down at a steady, but sparse rate despite the fact she could see patches of sky amongst the low, gray clouds.

A mile or two went by before Blue said, "He was right, but wrong at the same time."

"Chris?"

Blue nodded. "Each time I head up to Idaho it gets worse. Used to be I could find her there. Her memory anyway. This time I couldn't."

Lindsay didn't say a word. She didn't need to ask who the her in question was.

"I went to the café that morning knowing it would be my last time," Blue said. "I planned to leave Eagle's Rest and never go back. I let you think I was doing you a favor. I let it seem like I was rescuing you. But you rescued me. Alone, I would've crawled away from Eagles Rest. Found someplace to hide. I would've started drinking again. Hell, I almost bought a twelve pack Thanksgiving morning."

"Did you tell Janine you weren't coming back?"

Blue shook his head. "Didn't have the guts."

They'd gone only a short distance when Blue slowed and turned off the highway. A sign read, *Welcome to Mueller State Park*. He pulled the rig up to a visitor center, and shut off the engine, but he didn't open his door or attempt to get out. Instead, he sat there staring ahead at nothing. Finally, he turned to face Lindsay. "Meeting you changed my plans. Kept me from folding a bad hand. Like catching the right river card. Chris was right about that, but he's wrong about the rest. Last night didn't have a damn thing to do with him. Last night wasn't something I had to be manipulated into. Last night was about me and you. No one else."

He reached over and gently caressed her cheek. "I hope you know that."

Lindsay closed her eyes at his touch. She didn't want to cry, but tears pooled behind her lids. Tears she couldn't fully explain. Emotion was not something Blue parted with easily, and she understood the significance of him doing so now. But she also understood how fragile their relationship was. How fragile they both were.

Blue had gone to Idaho in search of his wife. And that first morning he'd confused Lindsay for her ghost. Lindsay could never live up to his memories of her. She wasn't even sure she should try. There was no future in playing second fiddle to the past. "Are we camping here?" she asked with her eyes still pressed shut.

He pulled his hand away from her face. "At least for tonight. Tomorrow we can go into Woodland Park and look around for a present. Like we planned back in Cripple Creek. Unless you've changed your mind."

Lindsay opened her eyes. Blue stared back at her. His expression asking if she'd changed her mind about more than shopping. "Blue, I'm not Staci. I'm never going to be."

He nodded before looking down at his red, swollen hand. "I need to ice this." Getting out, he stood in the open door and looked back in at Lindsay. "I never asked you to be Staci. I'm sorry that's how it seems."

Blue was inside only a few minutes before he reemerged alongside a park ranger. The ranger pointed up the road. Blue smiled and said something that made both men laugh. Finally, Blue shook the man's hand, not with his damaged right, but his left, and headed back for the truck. She stared at those hands as he approached. The very hands that delivered a brutal beating only an hour ago The very hands that caressed her body last night. The contradiction stood stark in Lindsay's mind, stark as the differences between her and Staci.

Blue slid in behind the steering wheel and fired up the truck without saying a word.

"I'm sorry," Lindsay said. "I was wrong to bring up your wife. I do this. Push people away when they get close. Especially men. Life's easier that way, but I'm sick of always waiting for the bottom to drop out."

"You ever notice," Blue said, "one of us is always apologizing to the other."

Again, Lindsay thought about last night. "Not always."

"But way too often for my liking. What do you say we strike a deal?"

"What kind of deal?"

"No more apologizing," Blue said. "No more tiptoeing around the past. Let's leave the past where it is, behind us. Let's forget everything that happened more than thirty-five seconds ago and simply enjoy the now."

"Why thirty-five seconds?"

He offered up a crooked grin. "Seems as good a number as any."

Lindsay smiled back. "If I didn't know you better I'd think you just made a spontaneous decision."

He extended his sore hand. "Do we have a deal?"

She reached out.

"Be gentle," Blue said. "I already forgot what happened, but let me tell you, this sucker hurts like hell."

She laughed. And it felt good to do so.

Blue spoke little as they parked and set up the RV, but Lindsay no longer felt compelled to disrupt the silence. She was comfortable simply being near Blue, working alongside him toward a common goal. When they had the camper unhitched, level, and hooked up electrically, Blue hiked up the hill to a large patch of snow. She wondered what he was doing until came back down with a large zip lock bag packed full. She didn't say a word until he had the bag wrapped in a dish towel and pressed against his swollen hand. With mostly a straight face, she said, "You know, only a man would go to so much trouble for a few bruised knuckles."

"Oh yeah," he answered. "What would a woman do if she was injured and there wasn't a single bag of healthy ice within twenty miles?"

Lindsay leaned close to him and whispered, "This woman would find a distraction to take her mind off the pain."

Blue smiled and pulled her down on to his lap. "I like the way you think."

Later that evening, Lindsay awoke disappointed to discover she was lying alone. They'd made love right there in front of the fireplace, on a bed of hastily gathered blankets. Even now, without Blue at her side, Lindsay could taste his lips, feel the heat of his mouth moving down her body. She missed the way the muscles in his back tensed as he moved with and against her at the same time. And she wished he were here beside her, pleasing her yet again, in his slow deliberate way. Not caring that it was the middle of the afternoon, not caring about anything but her and her body.

They'd laid there most of the afternoon, holding each other and whispering about places they'd been and places they'd like to go. Blue spoke of a poker tournament down on the Gulf Coast in January. He'd asked her to come with him to Biloxi. To watch him play. To bring him luck. In February there was to be another big tournament in Italy. He'd never traveled overseas to play, but he said it might be fun to go, if she'd join him. Lindsay liked the idea. Jetting off to Europe to watch her boyfriend compete for fame and fortune.

And believing they would do just that was easy when Blue was holding her, whispering to her in his deep, slow Texas drawl. His mouth so close to her ear every word sent a shiver down her spine. Somewhere in there she'd drifted off, like a child lulled to sleep by a bedtime fairy tale.

A steady rasping noise coming from outside captured Lindsay's attention and pulled her mind away from the afternoon. Wrapping a sheet around her naked body, she stood and peered out a window. Dusk was fast dissolving into darkness, but she could see Blue out there doing something with the racks of horns Chris delivered just before they left Cripple Creek.

Lindsay slipped her clothes on and stepped outside. Blue stopped his work and placed the hacksaw he'd been gripping to the side. He slowly flexed his hand as she walked nearer his makeshift workbench on the open tailgate. The swelling had mostly gone down but the bruising along his knuckles had turned a deep, dark shade of burgundy.

She pointed. "What are you doing?"

"Cutting these elk racks in half," he explained. "They won't fit through the door otherwise."

"What's the story with them anyway? Why did Chris give them to you?"

"Me and Donnie shot 'em back in October. I left them in Cripple Creek since I was heading to Vegas. Crowfoot, the man who keeps my horse, makes stuff out of them."

"What kind of stuff?"

"Knife handles. Chandeliers. Candle holders. Whatever he can sell." Blue picked up the hacksaw and went back to work cutting through the bony plate between the elk antlers. He stopped every so often to flex his sore hand.

Lindsay stood silently by, staring at the fine white powder of sawed bone that drifted down and collected on the ground. Powder that had once been bone and skull. That had held not only the antlers together, but protected the very life of the animal. And one thin strip of metal scraped across the foundation reduced it to dust.

A reminder how fragile life really was.

29

They stayed at that same campground two nights. Without success, they searched for Briley's present in Woodland Park. They moved closer to Colorado Springs searching for three days both there, and Manitou Springs. Again without success. From there Lindsay and Blue spent a night in Lamar, Colorado, followed by stays in Garden City, Hutchison, and Wichita, Kansas. All the while searching for that perfect birthday present for his daughter. All without luck.

Many times Lindsay wanted to tell Blue the truth about her past. That her child was not out there living with another family. That she hadn't carried her baby to full term. That the papers she signed were not adoption papers. But their days were filled with the search for a birthday present for a little girl who existed because her momma had made a different choice. And their nights were filled with each other.

By day, Lindsay was afraid to offer herself up for comparison to his wife, and by night she was too selfish to risk not falling asleep in his arms.

If only they could find the right present. Until then, the birthday would remain at the forefront of Blue's focus and along with that memory, the anniversary of his wife's death. Lindsay could never reveal her truth while the shadows of his wife's sacrifice hung so close overhead.

The stack of animal horns in the corner shifted, and clicked together as the trailer rocked and swayed. Lindsay sat motionless. She'd gotten used to the bump and movement of the camper as Blue hitched it up. Tomorrow would make two weeks since she first met him, although it seemed as though they'd been together much longer. They'd traveled across Idaho, Wyoming, the corner of Utah, Colorado, and now here they were in Kansas, not even a full hour away from Oklahoma.

Having spent nearly every waking minute with him, she hoped today was not the beginning of the end. Their relationship had already moved beyond a point with which she was accustomed, but the more time they spent together, the more Lindsay became aware of their differences. She'd been with other men longer, but never had she been involved with anyone on such an emotional basis. The physical side of their relationship had grown. In the darkness of the trailer their bodies meshed and moved as one. They knew exactly how to please one another. Blue was a strong confident lover. In the bedroom, he possessed none of the guarded reluctance that dominated their first days together. And afterward, with her in his arms, he would whisper and tell her things he never would reveal in the light of day.

He told her about his drunken friendship with Sergio right after his wife's death. How he tried to drink himself to death. He told her he went to Vegas to lose it all. His grief. The insurance money. Shame for abandoning his daughter. Guilt, for the times he wished Staci had listened to her doctor's advice and made a different choice. Mention of that choice put Lindsay on edge.

Each night they spent together, touching, tasting, sharing each other's body. Afterward they would talk deep into the night, but it was always Blue that found sleep first. There in the dark of night, Lindsay would lay in his arms and try desperately to think of a way to tell him she'd made the other choice.

The trailer jolted again, and Lindsay knew this meant Blue was hooked up and ready to go. She moved over to the electrical panel near the door and pushed the button to retract the slide-ins. The room closed in on itself and shrunk. Being so close to Oklahoma, Lindsay felt as if the world was doing the same thing.

Ten minutes later, they were on the road.

Lindsay pointed to a billboard advertising a mall. "Want to stop there?"

Blue shook his head. "No. I'm not sure what I'm looking for and I'm sick of wandering around stores."

She felt bad for him. Besides the places they camped, there had been countless stops in other towns throughout Colorado and Kansas. The only positive thing to come out of their search for Briley's present so far was that it had slowed their arrival in Oklahoma, but now, the Sooner State loomed dead ahead.

The search for a birthday present made Lindsay realize how little Blue actually knew about his daughter. No doubt, the task had done the same for him. At first Lindsay asked questions. What does she like? Dolls? Playing dress up? Ballerinas? Fairy princesses?

Blue couldn't answer a single question with confidence. He'd remembered seeing a Barbie or two, and one time over the phone she told him about a horse.

Lindsay stopped asking when she realized how depressed trying to answer made Blue. And despite her loyalty to him, part of her felt disheartened, even disappointed in him for not knowing. A child needs a father. Especially one who already lost her mother.

They traveled south down the Kansas turnpike in almost total silence, but when they reached the tollbooth, Lindsay felt compelled to start a conversation. The Oklahoma border lay a mere four miles ahead.

Twisting in her seat, she looked straight at Blue's face. She wanted to be talking when they crossed the state line. "Tell me more about Crowfoot."

"Crowfoot? What about him?"

Her eyes flicked forward. No sign yet, but she knew it'd be coming. "He keeps your horse, and makes things out of horns. There has to be more to him than that. What's he like? How do you know him? What kinds of things does he make out of these horns?" She fired off questions in machine gun fashion.

Blue gave her a funny look, probably because of the quiver in her voice. She gave another glance down the highway. Not yet, but closer. She could feel it with every revolution of the truck's tires. "Well? Aren't you going to answer?"

He shook his head. "They're antlers not horns. Cows, goats, sheep have horns. Deer, elk, moose have antlers."

"What's the difference?"

"Antlers fall off every year, horns don't. Animals with antlers shed them in early spring. They regrow before fall."

"So why go hunting?" *Keep talking. About anything. Anything but Oklahoma.* "Why not follow the deer around come spring and pick up the antlers when they fall off?"

This time he scratched his head. "I don't hunt for the antlers. I enjoy the meat, but that's not even why I go. You ever heard an elk bugle from fifty yards out when it's only you and him on the side of a mountain?"

"No."

"You should. There are a million reasons why I enjoy hunting. The challenge of it. The primal satisfactions of enjoying a meal you're responsible for on every level. The quite solitude of the stalk is a feeling I can't really describe, but if you've never walked a game trail at four in the morning, under a blanket of stars, I don't think I can make you understand."

Lindsay closed her eyes at the slight bump of the truck and the change in the sound the tires made against the road surface. She knew what that meant.

They'd crossed over into Oklahoma. The state never had been known for its superior roadwork.

In a rush of air, she released the pent-up breath from her lungs and opened her eyes. What had she expected? Her family to be lined up at the boundary? A lightning bolt to strike her dead?

In truth, she hadn't known what to imagine, but she'd figured something would change. If only within herself.

"You okay?"

She nodded. "We're in Oklahoma, right?"

"Yeah."

"Nowhere left to hide now."

Blue reached over and touched her cheek. "I told you, we'll stay at Crowfoot's as long as you want." His hand slid down to the tight muscles in her neck. "He's got a nice place. The Cimarron runs right through the property. No one will bother us there."

His strong fingers massaged the tightness that had settled between her shoulders. She wished with all her might that his words would prove true. Part of her longed for the

two of them to keep hiding from the rest of the world forever. To travel wherever the wind blew them. To start over
together. But they could only bury the reality of their lives
for so long.

She'd tried to start over countless times. Now she realized to truly start over, she had to go back to the point where
her life went wrong. Back to Norman, Oklahoma. And the
same gravitational force would eventually pull Blue to Texas.
He was too good a man to go on forever ignoring his daughter.

They rode that way, with his touch reassuring her, with
his nonverbal commitment to stand beside her and soothe
the pain. He didn't utter a single word, yet she felt oddly okay.
Because they had each other.

Blue signaled and exited the interstate beneath a sign
that read Stillwater and pointed east down State Highway 51.

A few miles later, when the town came into view, he
said, "Crowfoot used to help out at the college. He tried
to teach us what to expect from the animals. How to spot
and feel what they were going to do next." Blue shook his
head. "More times than not, he could tell which direction a
bull or bronc was going to turn out of the gate, even if he'd
never seen the animal buck. And the steers. Crowfoot could
watch them load up and tell how they'd break once the chute
opened."

Lindsay smiled as they turned down a gravel road. "Why
is it that all your friends have some kind of sixth sense? Chris
read people and numbers, and now Crowfoot, the Rodeo
Whisperer."

"I'm serious, he can do it."

"I don't doubt that, but why do you have this thing for
people like that? Why are you only attracted to the clairvoy-

ant?"

"I'm not." He slowed the truck and idled through a cattle guard. "I'm attracted to you, aren't I?"

"Are you saying I have no special abilities?"

He shook his head. "You have special abilities, but ..."

An Australian shepherd bounded out from a barn to bark and jump alongside the vehicle.

"But what?"

Blue smiled and stuck the Ford in park and shut down the engine. "I just don't think reading people is your specialty." He opened his door, and the dog jumped in, sticking its head in his lap. "Maybe you'll have better luck with Takata here." He grabbed the dog under the chin and turned it to face her. "Hurry. What's he thinking?"

Lindsay looked at the pooch's different-colored eyes and fired back. "He's wondering how on earth you talked such a pretty woman into riding with you."

Blue laughed and let the shepherd go. "Damn, you're exactly right. Guess you're a dog whisperer after all." Still grinning, he stepped down onto the red dirt so common in Oklahoma.

She followed him to the barn, which was the largest structure on the place. An old house with a rusted metal roof sat off to the side, and a wooden corral butted up against the south side of stalls. The early afternoon air felt warm and inviting against her skin. More late Septemberish than what she expected for the seventh of December.

"Yo! Anybody around?"

A horse whinnied to Blue's call. The dog followed along at his heels.

"Is that your horse?"

"Doubt it. He's probably out to pasture."

Lindsay gazed across the field. Away in the distance, she saw a couple of horses, down near a tree line, which she presumed to be the Cimarron. For some reason, she had an urge to see Blue's trusty steed.

"Wonder where Crowfoot is? Truck's not out front, but I figured he might be back here unloading feed or something."

"Doesn't the man have a first name?"

"Of course he does."

"What is it?"

"You'll have to ask him." Blue grabbed a rake and a shovel hanging against the wall. He opened one of the stall doors and began raking and scooping manure as if that were the most normal thing in the world to do the second you arrived.

Lindsay watched dumbfounded.

"I knew him nearly a year before he told me," Blue said dumping a pile in the wheelbarrow perched in the aisle.

"What's the big secret?"

"No secret." Dust particles and bits of straw floated in the air above his head. "He says first names aren't important until you decide whether or not the person's a friend."

"It took him a year to decide that?"

Blue paused long enough to lean against the wooden rail and smile. "You might be surprised, but I ain't the easiest guy to get to know."

She watched him work, moving from one stall to the next until a dark band of sweat formed down the middle of his back. Each time the wheelbarrow was full, he hauled it out back and dumped the contents into a huge pile. She began to see how he'd developed his strength.

"Is this what you do here? Work?"

He shrugged. "I do what I can when I can. Crowfoot

has been good to me."

She nodded. Blue fit in here among these stalls with Takata, the Australian shepherd, at his heels. He moved about with a peaceful, almost happy expression on his face. It was clear Blue was comfortable here, that this place served as his oasis. He belonged here much more than he did in some fancy tin box on wheels out in a lonely campground.

The dog cocked its head to the side for just a moment before tearing out of the barn in a dead run. Blue leaned the rake against a post and went to stand in the doorway of the barn. A smile lifted the corner of his lips at the sight of a pickup kicking up a dust trail along the dirt drive.

Blue squinted as the vehicle parked. "Who the hell is that with him?"

The doors opened and two men got out. The smile vanished from Blue's face. "What the hell is he doing here?" He shook his head and took two steps out into the sunlight and said, "Come on. I'm not answering all the damn questions by myself."

# 30

Blue leaned against the corral's weathered gate. The morning dew seeped through his shirtsleeves as he watched Winder graze out in the field. The horse's breath, visible in the cool half-light of dawn, billowed around his head. A rooster's crow echoed from the chicken coop back behind the barn. Takata lay in the frost-covered grass at Blue's feet.

Crowfoot walked up and leaned his long slender arms over the top rail. He watched the big buckskin graze without ever looking directly at Blue. Part Cherokee and part Pawnee, the man never said much, but when he did speak his words always held meaning. At least for Blue.

Yesterday, Crowfoot had been especially quiet. Of course, Donnie's constant yammering made up for that fact. Deep into the night, he kept at it with tales of the finals in Vegas, his flight into Oklahoma City, and when he ran out of new material, he launched into stories of the past. With Lindsay being a new and eager listener, he retold all the classic stories of life on the rodeo circuit. Blue didn't have the heart to tell his friend that Lindsay had already heard most of the tales. But then again, Donnie added enough of his own details, some less true than others, to spice up the anecdotes.

Blue turned to Crowfoot. "Where's Donnie? Still

asleep?"

"Nope. I fried bacon. He's in there seeing how much he can eat. Better get some before it's gone."

"I'm good," Blue answered.

Winder pawed the earth. Shaking his head, the horse blew a cloud of hot breath from his nose.

"He feels good. Frisky. He needs ridden," Crowfoot said.

Blue ignored the not-so-subtle hint.

"Want me to saddle him up for you?"

"He's fine where he stands."

The screen door on the house banged with a pop that seemed unnaturally loud compared to stillness of the morning.

"Where's Lindsay?" Donnie's Texas drawl floated in the chilly air. Unlike Crowfoot, he started talking before he reached the fence.

"Running."

"Huh?"

"She jogs every morning. Ten miles or so."

"What the hell for?" Donnie hocked up phlegm from deep in his throat and spit over the top rail.

Blue didn't bother to answer. He'd wondered the same thing himself when he first met her, but now he understood. Her runs were his poker games. The one time she could step outside of herself and forget—concentrate on something other than what might've been. Donnie would never understand that need. He was too cocky, too self-assured to ever want to escape his own thoughts.

"Hey, let me bum a cancer stick." Donnie nudged Blue's shoulder. "I ran out of Copenhagen, and Crow wouldn't stop for a new can."

"I quit smoking."

"Since when?"

"Since I decided to." He could feel both men watching him, but Blue continued to stare at his horse.

The sun broke the horizon behind the barn, bathing the land in amber streaks of light. The building cast a long shadow across the three men.

"Damn, I sure could use a dip." Donnie spit again. "My body needs nicotine to function."

"You should quit, too," Crowfoot said.

"Hell," Donnie snorted and laughed. "I should do a lot of things, but that don't mean I'm gonna."

"How's the shoulder?" Crowfoot asked.

"Ready to rock." The youngest of the trio rotated his surgically-repaired rotator cuff for show. "Doc should clear me to ride next month. Then I'm gonna hit some of them PBR shows. Vegas stirred the itch. I shoulda been down in the dirt instead of up in the seats. That's why I left early. I'm taking after you, Blue." Donnie rubbed his hands together. "Ain't going back 'til I qualify."

Crowfoot nodded. His long black ponytail swayed each time his head bobbed. "You'll make the top fifteen this year."

"Damn right." Donnie puffed out his chest.

Crowfoot turned to Blue. "How about you? What will you do this year?"

Blue took a deep breath. "I'm retired. No more rodeos for me. The two of you need to get that through your skulls."

"Ah, hell," Donnie whined. "You gotta miss it. We had a lot of good times out on the road together."

"That's the difference between me and you." Blue stared straight at Donnie. "You only remember the good times. There are things I miss, but not the all-night drives from one event to the next. Not living on fried burritos gone stale under a heat lamp. Not waking after a six-hundred-mile trip to Cheyenne bruised and sore because some salty steer ducked at the wrong time and kept me away from the pay window."

"Shit." The corners of Donnie's lips lifted into a broad grin. "You make it sound all bad. What about that time in Mesquite when—"

"It wasn't all bad, but it wasn't all good either. Poker is easier on my body, and the money's a hell of a lot better."

Crowfoot pointed out into the field. "Why keep the horse?"

Blue stared at Winder's cream-colored coat. A dark line ran down the ridge of the gelding's spine. Its mane and tail were also black, but Blue saw more than horseflesh when he looked at the animal. He saw the past. He saw the hopes, dreams, and good times he and Staci once shared. He saw the love in her eyes when she handed him Winder's reins for their second anniversary.

Rubbing his jaw, Blue waited until the surge of emotion subsided. He nodded at Crowfoot. "You're right. Sell him. He should be out there running down steers."

"You can't sell Winder." Donnie's voice took on a dumbfounded tone. "Staci bought him for you."

Invoking his poker demeanor, Blue said, "Having him here doesn't change the fact she's gone."

"Neither will acting like nothing has changed," Crowfoot added.

"I've heard it from both of you before. Hell, I've heard it from everybody. I'm not going to ride Winder, or any other horse. I'm done with the rodeo."

Crowfoot sighed. "Your heart was never in the arena."

Blue pushed away from the fence. He was sick of people

he considered friends trying to straighten him out. At the camper steps, Blue opened the door and went inside. He was trying to accept fate. Move on. But they didn't understand he was being torn in two. Attraction for Lindsay pulled against his loyalty to Staci. And damned if he knew how to hold onto either one without abandoning his grip on the other.

Lindsay jogged up the rutted dirt drive. Donnie and Crowfoot stood over near the corral fence. She waved but neither waved back. Their words were hard to make out, but as she began her cool down stretches Lindsay sensed they were arguing. Donnie kept pointing out into the field and the volume of his voice rose with each sentence. Cutting her stretches short, she climbed up the camper's steps to go inside and give them privacy.

Blue stared when she walked in. An odd look graced his face. The photo album sat on his lap, unopened.

"Is everything okay?" She'd never seen him with the book before. Matter of fact he'd never even mentioned its existence.

He nodded. "How was your run?"

"Fine." She tried not to stare at the album, but him having the pictures out made her uneasy. Maybe it was guilt for having looked at the pictures so many times without permission. "I'm going to jump in the shower."

"Okay."

She expected him to crack open the pages, but he merely sat there with a blank expression. He didn't even seem to notice she still stood there watching.

"Are you sure nothing's wrong?"

Blue rubbed his temples. "Just sick of everyone assuming they know what's best for me." He offered a reluctant grin. "Telling someone to raise is easy when it ain't your money on the table."

Lindsay sat beside him on the arm of the couch. She laid her hand on his shoulder. "What do they want you to do?"

"Donnie wants me to rodeo again." He looked up at her. "And if I'm guessing, Crowfoot wants me to drag you to the altar, then start rodeoing."

"What do you want?" Her question was the type he routinely ducked, but for some reason Lindsay knew Blue would answer this time.

Lowering his eyes, he let out a deep breath. "What do I want?" he repeated her question. "I want so many things. Some aren't even possible, and I'm not sure I deserve the ones that are." He paused before adding. "I want my choices to be easy, but they never are."

She leaned down and kissed him on the forehead. "Just so you know, I'm a long way from wanting to walk down the aisle. And it's not up to you to decide what you deserve. That's out of all of our hands."

"You're probably right." He patted her knee and stood. "Go take your shower. I'm going to put these pictures up and fix me something to eat before I start on the barn. Want me to make you something?"

"No, I've seen what you eat for breakfast."

Under the warm spray of water, Lindsay couldn't help but think of Blue saying Crowfoot wanting him to drag her to the altar. It had been a long time since she'd thought about a relationship other than in terms of when it might end. Used to be, she daydreamed about a long-term future with all her boyfriends. Even Rusty Hawkins. Lying there in the back of his Trans-Am, she had dreamt of their wedding which seemed inevitable at the time. She could picture herself standing at the front the First Baptist Church all decked out in her flowing white dress.

Turning off the water, Lindsay felt flattered Blue's friend thought so much of her. She tried hard to imagine a future with Blue. Where would they live? Texas? Or would they travel all over the country in the camper? Mrs. Lindsay Riggins. The name sounded awkward. She shook her head. What about his daughter? She couldn't see herself taking care of a child. Any child. Though Lindsay did feel sorry for the girl.

Nope, Lindsay couldn't envision her and Blue together years from now, but neither could she visualize the day they would part ways. She felt comfortable with him. He'd finally started to open up, and his steady influence had gotten her back to Oklahoma. On her own, Lindsay would've turned back long before now. She needed Blue in more ways than one, and she wanted to believe he needed her just as much.

Dressed, she found Blue at the table eating his usual carnivore brand of breakfast. This time he had a couple of sausage patties tucked inside a single piece of white bread folded in half. She grabbed an apple off the counter and sat beside him just as a knock sounded.

"Come in!" he called out.

Crowfoot entered and stood in the space between the kitchen and the living area.

"Have a seat." Blue motioned to an empty chair.

Crowfoot stood where he was. "You serious about selling the horse?"

Lindsay looked at Blue. He only nodded.

"How much?"

"He ought to fetch ten anyway, but you'd know better

than me. I haven't kept up. Just make sure he goes to somebody that'll use him. No more standing in a field."

"Maybe you should think about it a day or two," Crowfoot said.

"No." Blue shook his head. "Four years is long enough to think about it. I'm not going to ride him. Somebody else should. Let him run again. Just sell him for what he's worth. You know what's fair and keep the money. I don't even want to know when it's done."

"He's not my horse. It's not my money."

"If it makes you feel better, I'll give you the horse first, and then you can sell him." Blue stuffed the rest of the meat and bread in his mouth.

"I don't like it, and you won't either, but it's your choice." Crowfoot turned and left without waiting for Blue's response.

Lindsay waited until they were alone again. "Is that why you were upset? Are you sure you want to get rid of Winder?"

"There isn't much I am sure about anymore, but getting rid of that horse is one of the few things I don't have a single doubt over. Another is that the barn roof has a leak, so let me up so I can get my boots and hat and get to work."

She stood, although she could almost feel the tension swelling within him. When he rose to his feet, she wrapped her arms around his broad frame. He would balk if she spoke her sympathy aloud, but she wanted him to know she understood and was here for him. To her surprise, he squeezed her back and kissed her on top of the head before breaking free from her embrace and disappearing to the bedroom.

Alone in the kitchen, Lindsay worried about Blue. He'd always been withdrawn, and she'd known from the start a terrible hurt lurked in his past, but he'd always seemed like a rock perched out in an ocean of pain. Strong. Sturdy. Rigid enough to absorb the relentless waves.

Now every wave seemed to erode a layer from his hard-shelled resistance. His inability to find Briley a present. The impending anniversary of his wife's death. The decision to sell his horse.

And Lindsay felt powerless to deflect so much as a single drop of the building storm.

# 31

For the last half hour, Blue had focused his energy, his muscles, and his mind on repairing the barn's roof. Everywhere he looked, he spotted decaying wood, water damage, and enough work to last several days. Plywood, support beams, tarpaper. Damn near every bit of it needed ripped off and replaced. The heft of the hammer felt good in his hand as he climbed the ladder. Swinging, he made impact. Splinters and years of dust rained down, but Blue barely noticed as he assaulted the structure. After a few blows, he put the hammer down and reached for a long crowbar. Wedging the shaft of steel between a sheet of plywood and the main support beam, he used his strength and body weight until the nails groaned and wood cracked. Sunlight spilled into the gap.

"I'd have done that," Crowfoot said, "but I'm getting too old to be going up and down ladders."

Satisfied with his progress, but slightly irritated by the interruption, Blue stepped down. "I don't mind. Gives me something to do." He repositioned the ladder and climbed back up. Hoping to be left alone, he again reached for the hammer. Physical work he could handle. Give him good sturdy tools and the solid feel of wood and steel over unstable human emotions any day of the week. Or unwanted advice, which he feared would come next.

Another board gave to his incessant blows. Blue continued to work steady. Reposition the ladder. Beat and bang until the wood gave way to steel and determination. Move and set up again. Through it all, Crowfoot stood in silence and watched. Ignoring his audience, Blue made good progress, although this was the easy part. Demolition required no real skill or forethought, simply brute force and action.

Fixing the damage was another matter. Over the years the structure had settled. New four-by-fours wouldn't simply fit in place like the old ones. Nor would the sheets of plywood. Blue would have to cut and sand and make the new pieces fit and even then, there would be slight differences.

Nothing ever remained the same. Not fifty-year-old barns. Not life. Not his own mind.

Blue knew his friend had a purpose for lingering, but damned if he was going to stop working to ask.

Crowfoot finally stepped forward and gazed up at the gaping hole in the roof. "Donnie been in here?"

"Nope."

"He will be." Crowfoot turned and started out of the barn before stopping. "Do me a favor. Toss that hammer outta reach when he does."

Lindsay looked up when Blue walked in. She'd expected him to quit over an hour ago. But no, he stayed up on that roof working well past dark, even when the temperature dropped along with the sun. "You looked tired," she said.

He sat at the kitchen table. "Feels good to do more than sit at some felt table, or behind a steering wheel."

"Crowfoot cooked supper. Said for us to come on over when you finally climbed down."

Blue nodded. "I'll take a shower first. Why don't you head on over?"

"I'll wait."

"No. Go ahead."

She frowned at his tone. Blue had been as distant today as the first days they spent together. He'd barely managed a word, even when she climbed the ladder to take him something to drink. He seemed hellbent to pull back and hide from what they'd built all those days on the road.

Neither Crowfoot nor Donnie seemed surprised or concerned over Blue's absence, but as the three of them sat down to eat, Lindsay couldn't shake her unease. She'd never been the kind of woman to hold on too long, clinging to false optimism instead of facing reality and moving on, but Blue's attitude made her wonder where their relationship stood.

Donnie dipped a ladle into the huge pot in the middle of the table. Until now, Lindsay hadn't considered what Crowfoot might serve for dinner, but as Donnie dipped out the contents, she began to worry. She'd seen the stuff Blue ate, and could only presume his friend's palates were similar.

"Crow makes the best stew and cornbread anywhere." Donnie lifted the dish towel off a steaming pan.

"He does at that." Blue walked in and sat beside her.

She hadn't heard him come in the front door, so she was both surprised and pleased to see him. In truth, she hadn't counted on him to show at all, and certainly not so soon. On top of that, she could handle stew. Judging from Donnie's portion, there were plenty of vegetables, and the pieces of meat were small, easily avoidable.

Crowfoot waited while everyone else filled their bowls.

"How's that roof?"

"Got over half tore off, but it all needs to go."

The three men at the table crumbled their cornbread over the stew and dug right in. Despite the hearty aroma, Lindsay dipped her spoon and took the smallest of sips of the broth. Tasty.

Talk around the table centered on the barn, horse feed, and other matters of which she knew nothing, but she enjoyed listening just the same. Blue was more personable than he'd been all day, and the meal was excellent, filled with carrots, onions, mushrooms, and celery. Not what she expected from a lifelong bachelor.

Donnie looked at his watch. "Finals will be on in a bit."

Crowfoot looked at Blue as if he expected a reaction, but the latter said nothing.

Last night Donnie had talked about the rodeo finals, but Lindsay hadn't realized they were still going on, or that they were televised. Growing up in Oklahoma, she wasn't a total stranger to the sport, but she'd never paid much attention to it either. Now she wanted to watch, if for no other reason than to know more about Blue and his past.

"Sounds interesting, count me in," she said.

"Not me." Blue pushed away from the table.

"Come on, Blue." Donnie urged. "Stay and watch. We'll teach Lindsay the ins and outs."

"I only know about the outs." Blue turned to Lindsay. "Don't believe everything he tells you. It's not all glamor and gold buckles."

Blue left when she and Donnie went to living room. Crowfoot put away the dishes while Donnie plopped down on the couch with the remote.

"How'd that stew grab you?"

"It was great."

"Ever ate elk meat before?"

She shook her head, refusing to look at Donnie, but she could tell by his tone that he was grinning from ear to ear.

"Pretty good, huh?"

She nodded, not bothering to tell him she never tasted the meat. He was the type of guy who liked to feel as if he'd pulled one over on her, and she liked him well enough not to disappoint, but Blue could've warned her.

Crowfoot joined them just as the broadcast came on. The first event was bareback riding. Lindsay watched in silence while the two men discussed the riders and horses as if they knew them all. All but two of the riders stayed on, but according to Donnie the scores were low. He and Crowfoot used terms foreign to her, such as rake, marking out, and pickup man. Next came the steer wrestling. Lindsay leaned forward, studying the screen as if the secrets of Blue's past would materialize right there in the dirt floor of the arena. The competitors were all big men. She marveled at the ease and grace with which they slid off their speeding horse and onto steers with huge horns.

"Blue was as good as any of them," Crowfoot said.

"Better," Donnie added.

"I would've liked to watch." And she meant it. Because despite their assurances, and the photos in his album, she had a tough time picturing him charging hard down the arena. Everything Blue did was so calculated, guarded. He was certainly as big and strong as the men on TV, but that reckless daring abandonment had apparently left him long ago.

Team roping and saddle bronc came next. Listening to Donnie and Crowfoot gave Lindsay a new appreciation for the sport and everything that went into it. Barrel racing followed.

Donnie leaned forward as the camera focused on a woman with shoulder-length blonde hair. "Here she comes."

Lindsay read the information on the screen, Kacy Jo Dement from Tonkawa, Oklahoma. Her horse's name was Desert Wind. "Her horse looks just like Winder."

"They came from the same stud," Crowfoot said.

"Kacy Jo and Staci bought 'em at the same time," Donnie chimed in.

The woman took off. Rounding the barrels in quick order, she posted a time just shy of fourteen seconds. The first of the night to break that barrier.

"Yes." Donnie pumped his fist. "That's gonna put her right there for tomorrow."

"Right where?"

"For the title. Championship is decided by yearly earnings. Going in, Kacy Jo was third, but she's already earned enough day money in Vegas to move up to second. With that time, she'll gain more ground. A win tomorrow and she should be world champ."

"I take it she's a friend of yours."

"Mine, Blue's, Crowfoot's. We all went to college together. She was Staci's best friend."

Bull riding came next, and Lindsay could see the event fired Donnie up. She tried to picture him on a bull, and while it was an easier image to conjure than seeing Blue compete, it still seemed unbelievable that any sane person would crawl on top of animal that large and mean. But then again, based on the stories Blue had shared, it was debatable Donnie could be classified as sane.

"I can't believe you ride those. They're huge." Lindsay voiced her disbelief aloud.

"Big, small, wild or tame. I'll ride anything with hair on it." Donnie winked at her. "And a few things without."

Crowfoot sighed. "Leave your love life out of this."

The telecast ended after the bull riding. Lindsay stood. "Thanks for letting me watch."

"Tomorrow night is the finale," Donnie said. "Talk Blue into watching. Kacy Jo will be upset if he misses her win."

"I'll try, but you know how he can get."

Donnie rolled his eyes. "Trust me, I know his moods better than anyone."

Crowfoot cleared his throat and said, "And you'll know them again. Soon as you tell him about that horse."

"What horse?" Lindsay asked.

Donnie disregarded Crowfoot's statement with a wave of his hand. "Nothing. Crow just likes to worry."

Lindsay was sleepy, but the cool night air revived her on the way out to the trailer.

"How was the rodeo?" Blue asked when she entered. "Did you get the play by play, Donnie style?"

"It was fun. Interesting. I'm impressed y'all could do those things."

"Don't be fooled. It's not rocket science."

Lindsay folded her arms over her chest and studied Blue. "What?" he asked.

"Why can't you take a compliment or admit you have talent?"

"Where did that come from?"

"You have these amazing abilities. Everyone looks up to you, but you downplay your skills. Why?"

He shifted in his chair at the kitchen table before saying, "I'm just trying to get along. I'm not trying to earn anyone's appreciation. Nor do I deserve it."

"Why didn't you tell me the stew come from a wild animal?"

"I knew you wouldn't eat the meat."

"What if I had?"

Blue raised one brow. "Did you?"

"No."

"So, what's your point?"

"I wish you would talk to me. Tell me what's going on in your mind, but you've barely spoken a word to me all day."

"I'm trying to get that roof fixed. I appreciated the tea, but I had work to do."

"What about supper?"

"What about it? Elk meat is good. It won't kill you."

"You could have stayed and been sociable. Donnie and Crowfoot wanted you to."

Blue shook his head. "I thought you wanted to talk? Seems to me you want to argue."

"Tell me about Kacy Jo."

His eyes narrowed. "What about her?"

"She's in second place. She might win tomorrow. Donnie said she would be upset if you don't watch."

"He's probably right."

"Will you?"

"Will I what?" Blue wanted to know.

Their eyes remained locked.

"Watch?"

"Doubt it."

"Why?"

"Because, she's part of my past. And I'd rather look to the future."

<h1 style="text-align:center">32</h1>

Their third day in Oklahoma mirrored the second. Lindsay whiled away time talking with Crowfoot and Donnie, and meandering around the acreage, while Blue toiled on the roof and avoided all things resembling human contact. Crowfoot cooked the men huge T-bones for dinner, but he grilled a chicken breast just for Lindsay's salad. After supper, Blue abandoned them once again, while they sat down to view the last night of the rodeo.

Lindsay was tired and almost opted out of watching herself. For the first time in years, she'd ran in the morning and then again right before dinner, putting in over twenty miles for the day. In the back of her mind, she was entertaining the idea of finding a half-marathon somewhere to enter, but she had a ways to go before she'd be ready for that. A long time had gone by since she ran for anything but herself, and even longer since she set goals. But watching the rodeo and listening to Donnie had rekindled her competitive juices.

Maybe those same competitive juices were what made her join Donnie and Crowfoot in the living room. Through the entire broadcast, Lindsay kept thinking back to last night.

*She is part of my past.* My past. Blue refused to say more, but Lindsay couldn't help wondering if Kacy Jo had ever been more than just Staci's best friend. Maybe it bothered her more because last night, for the first time since Cripple Creek she and Blue had simply gone to sleep. Without making love.

As usual, Lindsay had laid awake long after Blue drifted off trying to decide what it all meant. Was his back really hurting from working all day? Was he mad at her for asking about Kacy Jo? Or was he simply losing interest?

Lindsay paid little attention to the rodeo until the barrel racing came on near the end. Finally, the announcer brought up Kacy Jo and the other two women who still had a shot at winning the overall championship. One competitor was in her fifties and had won twice before, another was only twenty-three and on her first visit to the finals. But the focus of the segment was on Kacy Jo. She was the prettiest, and judging from the interviews, the least humble of the three. Five years in a row she'd qualified, never finishing higher than fourth. Already, she was guaranteed third, a personal best, but Kacy Jo looked straight in the camera and said in her sugary-sweet Oklahoma accent, "The folks back home expect me to do my best, but I expect more. Anything less than the championship will be a disappointment."

The youngest rider came up first and turned in a time of fourteen flat.

Donnie spit a stream of tobacco juice into an empty Dr. Pepper can and scooted to the edge of his seat.

Crowfoot shook his head. "Solid time."

The camera showed Kacy Jo and Desert Wind. The horse's feet pranced with eagerness.

"Settle him," Crowfoot whispered.

Kacy Jo took off fast. The horse kicked up dirt.

"Too hard," Crowfoot said and sure enough Kacy Jo took an extra wide loop around the first barrel.

"That's going to hurt her time," one announcer said.

At the end of the ride, fourteen point five-four flashed in the corner of the screen.

"That's why they call it the money barrel." The other commentator added. "The first turn sets up the whole ride. You can run the rest of the cloverleaf clean, but if you miss on that first turn you're in real trouble as Kacy Jo just found out. That time will drop her out of the day money, and dash her hopes for the overall."

Lindsay leaned back. Normally she wasn't a jealous person, and she had no logical reason to dislike Kacy Jo, but she couldn't deny her satisfaction in seeing the other woman fail.

<h1 style="text-align:center">33</h1>

Blue stared at the hole up above. Two more sheets of plywood and he would finish the roof. He would've finished yesterday, but the lumberyard closed early on Sundays.

"Looks good."

Blue turned at the sound of Donnie's voice.

"Gonna get her finished today?"

"Not until I go buy some lumber." Blue hoped to finish by lunch. The project had become bigger than he ever intended, but it had given him the opportunity to think.

"Lindsay will be glad."

Blue let that remark go. He knew she was upset he'd been hiding on the roof, and he wasn't stubborn enough to deny that's exactly what he'd been doing, but he'd needed time alone, away from Lindsay. Not because he didn't want to be near her, but because that's all he wanted. Lindsay didn't realize he spent every second on that roof tearing down more than an old wood and decking.

Blue didn't like the look on Donnie's face, or the way he shuffled from one foot to the other, but he'd known something was brewing. Might as well get it over with. Crowfoot warned him a couple of days ago, but Blue had hoped Donnie might come to his senses for once and abandon whatever crazy notion filled his head. Tension lined the younger man's face. They stared at each other a few seconds before Donnie walked to the tack room. He emerged after few minutes carrying a heavy saddle. A braided lead rope and wool blanket hung over his shoulder. Slinging them onto the top rail of a stall Donnie said, "I'm taking Winder out for a ride."

"Leave him where he's at."

Donnie nudged a dried clump of horse shit with the toe of his boot. "He needs ridden. You ain't gonna want to hear this, but you need to know." He paused.

"Know what?" Blue stepped closer to his friend.

Donnie lifted his head to stare at Blue. "I bought Winder."

"The hell you did." Blue headed for the barn door. "Where's Crowfoot?"

"Leave him out of it. You told him to take care of the sale. Like I told Crow, I'm buying that horse. Whether I buy Winder from him, you, or whoever you decide should have him. One way or another I'll end up with that horse."

Blue whirled around. "Why? Can't you see I'm trying to move on? You think it helps to be reminded of everything I've lost?"

"Maybe you should take a look at what you still have."

"I can't hang onto every single thing Staci ever gave me. I'm sick of trying to live on memories."

When Donnie didn't answer, Blue said, "You don't bulldog. Why do you want Winder? Just to torture me?"

Seconds ticked by. A streak of light poured inside from the hole in the roof. Dust motes floated in the air. Crowfoot's mare whinnied from the far stall.

"You're not the only one who misses her around here." Donnie's Adam's apple bobbed. "You don't own the sole right to grieve. You think this has been easy on the rest of us. Hell, Blue, we're not even supposed to whisper her name." He shook his head and lowered his voice as he said, "Damn it, Blue, I lost her and you both. I loved Staci, too. No, not the way you did, but I still think about her sometimes. She meant a lot to me. One of these days I hope to find a woman half as good."

"I hope you're so lucky, and if you are, I hope to hell you never lose her. But that doesn't change my opinion. When Winder leaves this ranch, I don't ever want to see him again."

"That's bullshit. You can't hide from what you've lost anymore than you can chase it down, but if that's what it takes to own him, I'll make damn certain you never lay eyes on Winder again. And I'll take care of him. Like Staci would want."

"You don't know what Staci would want."

"I know she wouldn't want to see you like this," Donnie fired back.

"Tell me one thing. What are you going to do with Winder?"

"I'll haul him with me since my old traveling partner up and quit on me. There are plenty of bulldoggers who need a ride, and even when I don't cash, you can bet your ass Winder's share will make enough to fill our tank and get us to the next show."

"Screw it. Buy him." Blue spit in the dirt.

"I already did."

Lindsay heard the truck drive away just as she turned off the shower. She peeked out the trailer window in time to see

Blue's taillights disappear. Apparently, he hadn't heard her say she wanted to ride to town with him.

The uncertainty, worry, and anxiousness built within her as she dried her hair and dressed. She couldn't help but feel Blue was trying to tell her something. His aloofness. Refusal to spend time with her. Failure to hear a word she said. Maybe Donnie could give her a clue. At least he would talk to her.

Outside, it was the kind of bright clear morning that made you feel good to be alive. The air held enough crispness to make every breath refreshing. Monday, the eleventh of December. Exactly two weeks shy of Christmas and here she was in Oklahoma. She never would've thought that possible only a few weeks back. If only Blue would let her know what he was thinking.

She found Donnie in the barn. "Is that Winder?"

"Yep." He grunted and tugged on the leather strap around the horse's belly. "Damn, he's gotten fat."

"Blue go to the lumberyard?"

"He left. Can't say to where. He wasn't exactly in a talkative mood."

"Oh." Maybe she wasn't the only one Blue was ducking. She realized the barn needed repair, but didn't he understand she needed him as well? Not twenty-four hours a day. She recognized he was a man that required room. She didn't want, or expect a constant, cloying type of relationship, but Lindsay did want reassurance that what she felt, what they had shared, was real—and had a chance to continue.

Donnie slid his hand up the horse's neck. "Let's shake off the dust, ol' boy?" He spoke in calm, even tones.

Even he seemed oblivious to her presence, so Lindsay stepped closer to reach out and touch Winder's flank. "He's beautiful."

"Don't get behind him. He ain't been saddled lately so he's gonna have a few kinks to kick out."

"Sounds like his owner."

Donnie looked her in the eye. "I'm his owner. I bought 'im. Hate to say it, but Winder here has more fight than Blue these days."

Until now, she'd never heard Donnie utter anything but respect and awe for Blue. Now she detected sadness, maybe even a tinge of anger. She understood Donnie's position. She'd been there herself, but at the same time she felt the urge to defend Blue. "He's got a lot on his mind. And he's really focused on that roof."

Donnie raised one brow. "Trust me, that roof is the last thing he's thinking about. The harder Blue works, the more you can be sure his brain is wrapped around something, but he's too damn stubborn to admit that. Thinks the world is a poker table. Always bluffing, trying to hide what's on his mind. Even when he holds a winning hand."

Lindsay got the feeling Donnie was talking to himself as much as to her. "I was supposed to go to town with him, but I guess he forgot."

"He wasn't thinking when he left. He was too mad at—" Donnie stopped at the sound of an approaching vehicle.

Takata barked from somewhere out front.

"Maybe he did remember." Lindsay started for the barn door.

"Nope. That dog wouldn't be barking like that at Blue."

Blue pulled out of the lumberyard with his mind made up. He'd finish the barn and leave. He and Lindsay were better off on their own, where everyone wasn't intent to keep throwing his failures in his face. Out there on the road, when it was just the two of them, that's what he wanted to get back to. He would take her to see her parents. However long she wanted to stay was fine. He could set up his camper out at Lake Thunderbird. There wouldn't be much of anybody around the lake this time of year, and it was only a few miles out of Norman. And there were two casinos right down the road. He'd never played poker in either of them, and the stakes would be low, but it would keep him busy while she straightened out things with her family.

The second Blue turned down Crowfoot's long dirt drive, he knew his plans were doomed. He kicked himself for not seeing this coming, but then again, he hadn't been thinking too clearly about anything other than Lindsay.

Pulling his truck up next to the long, sleek black and chrome trailer, he got out. A shriek pierced the air and before he could prepare himself, or do anything to stop it, Kacy Jo Dement had her arms wrapped around his neck and her lips pressed to his.

Breaking free from her affection, he stole a glance behind Kacy Jo. There, next to the pasture fence, stood Lindsay taking the scene in. Farther out in the field, he could see Donnie making wide circles atop Winder.

"God, Blue," Kacy Jo said. "You are a sight for sore eyes. It's been too long."

He smiled back and stepped around her. He tried to keep his focus on Lindsay. *What is she thinking?* But the sight of his longtime friend beyond her, riding around on that horse, made it hard to concentrate.

Kacy Jo hurried alongside as he approached the fence. She hooked her arm through his and said, "Donnie told me he bought Winder."

Blue pulled his arm away.

She kept talking. "I knew he was full of B.S. in Vegas when he said you were training again, but I can't believe you'd—"

"Believe it. I'm done with it all." He reached out and laid a hand on Lindsay's shoulder. "Have you met Lindsay?"

"Yeah, we met." Kacy Jo did a poor job disguising her jealousy.

"We traveled here together. From Idaho." He smiled at Lindsay, but she didn't return the gesture. "She means a lot to me."

"Have y'all stopped in to see Briley?" Kacy Jo flashed her fake television smile and leaned in close to Lindsay. "Briley is his daughter. She'll be four next week."

"I know," Lindsay said in tone he hadn't heard her use before. "I've been helping Blue search for the perfect birthday present."

He was proud of Lindsay for standing up to Kacy Jo, but he knew the barrel racer well enough to know she would never relent when challenged, and Lindsay deserved better than to be roped into a battle based on some misguided loyalty Kacy Jo had for Staci's memory.

"Excuse us a second." He put his hand on the small of Lindsay's back and guided her towards the trailer, away from Kacy Jo. Opening the door, he waited as she climbed the stairs and went inside. He followed.

"What? Why did you push me in here?" Lindsay looked and sounded miffed.

Blue ran his fingers through his hair. The words had come easy in the truck, but now he didn't know where to start. The sight of Donnie riding around on Winder and then

Kacy Jo being here. It all had him flustered the way he never got in a card game. He took a deep breath, and told himself to look at the facts, the numbers, the way he'd judge a hand and decide what to wager. Of course, this wasn't just a game. He was dealing with life here. "Lindsay ... I." Shit—he wished she wouldn't look at him like that. Worried, scared, eager, angry.

The sound of a diesel motor disrupted his attention. Blue went to the window and lifted the curtain. "Son-of-a ..." He gritted his teeth at the sight of the white crew-cab dually. "How much worse can this day get?" He spoke more to himself than to Lindsay, although she'd joined him at the window.

"Who is that?"

"Wait here," he growled.

Lindsay watched Blue stomp out to the road up to the house. He took a defensive stance between the tire ruts, folding his powerful arms across his chest as if shielding everything behind him from the occupant of the vehicle.

She slid the camper's window open.

"What do you want?" Blue spoke the moment the stranger's feet touched the dirt.

The man, ignored the statement as he got out. Stuffing a black cowboy hat onto his head, he extended his hand. "How are you Blue? Is that Kacy Jo's rig?"

"Cut the shit, Buster. What are you doing here?"

The man lowered his offered handshake. "You refused to call me, so I came to find you. I had to pick up Briley's saddle in El Reno, and since Donnie told me you were here—"

"Donnie told you?" Blue looked over his shoulder in the direction of the pasture. The wrinkles on Blue's forehead deepened as he returned his focus to the unwanted guest. "I don't appreciate being tracked down like some rabid coyote."

"Get over it." A toothpick dangled from Buster's lips. "I need to talk to you."

"I don't have anything to say."

Buster hooked his thumbs in his belt loop. Lindsay judged him to be in his mid-to-late fifties. His black hair was peppered with gray and the curve of his legs told of years spent horseback. A pot-belly hung over his Wranglers.

"Good, because I didn't come to listen. I came to talk, and by God you're going to hear me whether you like it or not."

Lindsay had never heard anyone dare use such a tone with Blue.

"When you coming home?"

"That's none—"

"It damn sure is my business." Buster pointed a finger. "I'm tired of pussyfooting around. I've wasted too many years as is. You don't deserve the courtesy, but I'm giving it just the same. You object to me marrying your sister?"

The front door of the house banged as Crowfoot came outside. Donnie and Kacy Jo walked up behind Blue.

A raven called and took flight from the tree behind the house as Blue laughed. "You came all the way here to get my blessing? Since when did you give a rat's ass about my say? Besides, that's between the two of you. You and Ruby's love life is none of my concern."

"The hell it's not. Long as we're raising your daughter it's your concern."

Blue's eyes narrowed. "Careful."

"Don't act offended. You don't have that right." Buster dug in his shirt pocket and held up a small box. "I'm giving this to Ruby soon as I get back. With or without your permission."

"Then why bother asking for it?"

Lindsay felt torn. Her loyalty for Blue made it hard to side against him, but she didn't care for the way he talked or treated Buster. The man seemed to be trying to mend fences.

"Two reasons." The older man held up one finger. "Because, unlike some people, I still believe in doing what's right. And second, I need to know if you'll be back to stay with Briley when we leave for the honeymoon. I'll take her with us if need be, but I need to know."

"What makes you so certain Ruby will say yes?"

"I'm not giving her a choice. She's made excuses for years, but I'm not going to let you stand in the way anymore."

"Don't pretend it's all my fault." Blue shook his head. "I wasn't the one who was married, ducking out on my wife to go screw somebody else in an empty hotel room."

Buster punched him as the last word hit the air. Lindsay gasped. She scrambled for the door. Blue was bigger, stronger, and at least twenty years younger, and she'd seen what he did to Sergio. Blue might kill an older guy like Buster. But when she got outside, Donnie, Crowfoot, and of course Kacy Jo, were already there.

Donnie held Blue's arm, but Lindsay knew he could shake loose if he really wanted to. Crowfoot stood between the two combatants as they stared each other down. Buster's chest heaved. He spat the toothpick into the dust. Not one said a word as she walked up behind Blue.

"Don't ever ..." Buster started to speak, but stopped when he noticed Lindsay.

In the instant before Blue turned around, she wished she'd stayed in the camper, but not even that regret prepared her for words he spoke through clenched teeth, "Lindsay, go back inside."

His command slapped her in the face. She lowered her head and turned without a word.

"Who the hell was that?" Buster's voiced boomed behind her.

"Her name's Lindsay, but she's no concern to you."

"You have the gall to mention my wife, while you're out cavorting around, while your sister is busy raising your kid."

"Come on, Buster," Donnie spoke up as she reached the trailer. "Blue's not exactly cavorting around. He picked her up in Idaho. He's just giving her a ride."

*Just giving her a ride.* Is that what Blue told his friends? Lindsay shook her head. Their voices carried through the RV's open window.

"Shut up, Donnie," Blue said.

"I'm just trying to help."

"I don't need your help. I don't need anything from any of you."

Standing at the window, Lindsay couldn't believe Blue's tone. She understood he didn't like Buster, but Donnie was his friend. Tears streamed down her cheeks. The men outside continued to argue, but no longer caring to listen, she went to the window eager to close out the voices.

"Now Buster, you know Blue's not like that. That woman is just some hitchhiker he picked up. She don't mean a thang to him."

"Be quiet, Kacy Jo. This isn't your concern either," Blue said.

*Just giving her a ride.* Just some hitchhiker. Lindsay pulled the window down and slumped on the couch feeling as if she had indeed been taken on a very long ride.

# 34

The shouting continued as Lindsay stuffed her belongings in duffel bags, but she could only decipher a few words from inside the camper. My daughter! ... Stubborn jackass! ... Responsibility! ... She didn't want to hear their argument, but just as their voices rose to a level she couldn't shut out, the noise broke off. She quickened her pace to be ready when Blue came in. He might try some feeble attempt to explain, or he might sulk off to his bedroom, or to the top of the barn. Either way, she didn't plan to stick around.

A vehicle started and rumbled away.

A few seconds later, a second motor cranked, and this time she looked out the window in time to see Blue's taillights. Kacy Jo jogged up the path after him, like some kind of faithful dog.

Lindsay shook her head. So, he was going somewhere else to pout. At least she had time to get her things in order before leaving.

Blue turned right out of Crowfoot's and drove a mile or so following the dust cloud behind Buster's pickup. To avoid catching the other vehicle, Blue lifted his foot from the gas pedal and coasted down the rutted dirt road. No reason to hurry, now that he'd escaped the concerned expressions of his friends. He didn't want to answer their questions, or listen to their attempts to calm him. And he damn sure didn't want to hear anymore advice. The solution was always so much easier when the problem belonged to someone else.

Swallowing the bad taste in his mouth, he pulled to a stop when he came to the paved crossroad. Stillwater lay to the left, farm and ranchland laid both straight ahead and to the right. Minutes ticked by, yet he remained motionless.

The right thing would be to throw a U-turn. Go back to Crowfoot's. Face the music. Apologize to both Donnie and Lindsay. They'd only tried to help, and Donnie was right about Winder. Given the circumstances, Staci would want him to have the horse. Hell, even Kacy Jo deserved better than he'd given her.

Blue turned left toward town.

Apologies never had been his strong suit, and if he rushed back now, with raw emotions, he would only say or do the wrong thing. Later, once he calmed down and had a chance to think before he spoke, that's when he would go back. Right now, he needed to be alone.

Ruby yawned as she reached for the phone. "Riggins Restway."

"Hey, good lookin', whatcha' got—"

"Ray does the cooking, not me." Interrupting Buster's performance of Hank Williams, she made no attempt to disguise the irritation in her voice. "Where are you?" She could use Buster here with her, instead of off gallivanting in Oklahoma on some wild goose chase.

"Still in Stillwater."

"You called me in the middle of the lunch rush to tell me that?" She cradled the receiver between her cheek and neck as a customer stepped up to the counter to pay. "Hang on." She counted back the change, gave the man a phony smile, and said, "Thanks for stopping in."

The bell on the front door clanged as the traveler pushed his way outside. Ruby returned her attention to Buster. "What's so important you had to call me at twelve-thirty? You know this is my busiest time." To punctuate her statement Ray set three plates on the counter that needed delivered to hungry customers. But of course Buster couldn't see them. He couldn't see anything. Not when he was off chasing rumors.

"You're in a fine mood."

"What do you want? I don't have time for this."

"I wanted to hear your voice, let you know I'm headed home."

"Briley ran a fever all night. It finally broke about four this morning."

"Is she all right? Did you call the doctor?"

"She'll be fine." Ruby cast a glance at the child curled up on a makeshift pallet behind the counter. "Right now she's asleep and I have orders to get out, glasses to refill, matters to tend."

"I picked up her saddle and got a good lead on a gentle pony from Oran Pratt. He gave me a number for an ol' boy in Sayre. I'll stop and check it out on the way home. Wish I'd a brought my trailer, but I can run over there and back in a day if need be. Still got a week before Briley's birthday."

"That's good, but I'm hanging up now."

"You're about as sociable today as that worthless brother of yours. Now I know where he gets it."

"Don't tell me you found Blue." She frowned and held up a finger to let the men know she would be with them in a second.

"Yep, for once Donnie wasn't full of shit. Blue was right there at Crowfoot's."

"What's he doing there?" The conversation now held meaning. She would've bet her life Blue was still holed up in Idaho.

"Go take care of your customers. I'll tell you everything when I get back later this evening. But you ain't going to believe me when I do."

Lindsay stared at the worn duffel bags lined up at her feet. The same bags she'd left Janine's with. A knock echoed in the silent trailer. She hadn't heard Blue drive back, not that he would knock if he had, so it was either Donnie, or Crowfoot, or God forbid, Kacy Jo.

"Come in."

Cowboy hat in hand, Donnie pushed open the door. He stood there silhouetted for several seconds, then cleared his throat. "You okay?"

Not trusting her voice, she merely nodded.

"Mind if I come in?"

When she didn't answer, he took a seat on the couch. Lindsay remained standing in the middle of the room.

Donnie's eyes roamed around until his gaze settled on the bags. "Blue didn't mean nothing by the way he acted."

She shrugged.

"Like you said, he's got a lot on his mind. Never has done a bang-up job when it comes to emotions." Donnie plunged on in behalf of his friend. "I've taken three-hundred-mile road trips where he didn't say a word. Then when he did speak, he just pissed me off. But I always get over it. He's a hell of a guy but in the heat of the moment, he don't always say or do the right thing."

"And he's never going to change." She whirled around to face Donnie.

He sighed and nodded. "Probably not enough to suit either of us, but he's some better. You've brought him partway around. You're like Staci in that. He always seemed to function better with her at his side, but get him off on a long road trip, and he'd get touchy as a sore-assed bear. Once we got back, she'd have him righted out in a day or two."

"I'm not Staci, and I don't want to be. Nor do I want to fix Blue or wait for him to get 'righted out.'"

"Blue's not all bad. He's loyal as hell. Steady. Dependable. He doesn't always make the right choice. Hell, none of us do, but he's never let me down when I really needed him."

"He let me down." Lindsay bit her lip and turned away from Donnie's searching eyes.

"That's my fault. I had him riled up before Buster got here. The two of them always go at it. And Kacy Jo being here didn't help. Blue wasn't in his right mind. You can't pay too much attention to what he says when he's like that."

Lindsay shook her head. "It had more to do with the look on his face than what he said. It's the way he sees me. I won't stay here trying to live up to the memories of his wife. I'm sorry for him and for Briley and all of you who knew her. But I'm my own woman. I need a man who sees me for who I am."

Donnie stood. "Blue sees more than you think. He does see you for who you are. And the fact he sees you at all is a miracle."

Anger surged through her. "I don't want to be anybody's therapy. I have needs of my own. And feelings."

"That's not what I meant." Donnie stood and put his hand on her shoulder. "I'm just asking you to give Blue some time. He's trying to work things out in his mind."

She shook her head. "Time won't change a thing. He's ashamed of me. I saw it in his eyes. I heard it in his voice. Even you said I was just a hitchhiker he picked up." She folded her arms across her chest and stared straight at Donnie. "I was fine to cozy up with on the road, but he doesn't want to be seen with me when his family or friends are around."

"I wouldn't let him hear you refer to Buster as family."

"Blue Riggins won't hear anything else from me. I don't plan to be here when he gets back." She picked up her bags.

"I didn't say you were a hitchhiker. That was Kacy Jo. I did say he was giving you a ride, but I was just trying to calm everybody down. And Blue never would've brought you here if he was ashamed of you. Hell, he brought you here to show off. I guaran-damn-t that much."

"What about Kacy Jo? He didn't send her away."

Donnie stuck the black Stetson down on his head. "Kacy Jo, she doesn't mean anything to him. Hell, they never got along when Staci was alive. Kacy Jo is a bit intense and self-centered, but she and Staci grew up together. Trust me, Blue doesn't give a damn what she or Buster thinks. And I'll bet my last dollar Blue has already figured out he screwed up. He'll show up after while with his tail between his legs and make it all up to you."

"No. He'll show up and act like nothing is wrong. At best he'll come back and say how stupid he was, but he'll never admit why he was stupid."

Donnie pulled a small round can from his back pocket. "That's just the way Blue is." He stuffed a pinch of snuff between his lip and gum.

"And that's why I have to leave."

"Stay until he comes back. Give him a chance. He might surprise you."

She shook her head. "If I stay, he'll look at me with his bottomless black eyes. He'll reach for me with those strong hands. He'll convince me to stay."

"Is that a bad thing?" Donnie looked at her through his baby blues. As innocent as a child, desperation hung from his every feature.

For the first time, she understood Blue's lack of patience with his friend. Donnie had never truly been hurt. Maybe physically, but never emotionally. He had no idea about the kind of pain that no pill, or time, could heal. He couldn't fathom the concept that life doesn't always work out the way it should. Lindsay hoped he never would.

"Yes, because now that I've glimpsed the end, it's all I'll ever see. Endings are what I'm good at."

# 35

From his vantage point across the street, Blue studied the small wood-frame house. Back when he and Staci rented the place, it had been white with beige trim. Now it was some sort of yellow. The paint company probably dubbed the stuff lemon drop, sun-kissed, or some other fanciful name, but yellow is yellow, no matter the name on the can. The trim remained brown, though a darker shade. The tiny two-bedroom had been their first place together. He carried her across that very threshold. Lacking the money for a proper wedding or honeymoon, they stood before the justice of the peace and then drove straight back to this rent house where they spent their first night together as man and wife. And nearly two years of their lives after.

Blue had never been back. Until now. He supposed this had been his destination ever since he fled Crowfoot's, although he hadn't realized where he was headed until he got here. He did that a lot these days. Hurry, rush off into something or someplace, without any idea what or why.

A young couple emerged from the house. Early twenties, Blue guessed. About the same age he and Staci had been when they occupied the place. The man carried an infant car seat with a pale blue blanket draped over it. He cast a glance towards Blue's rumbling truck before leaning inside the car to secure the child. The young woman, a pretty blonde, carried a large diaper bag and a fold-up stroller. In no time, they had the car loaded and backed out of the driveway headed for some family outing. The taillights flashed red as the man slowed at the end of the block and turned.

For a long time, Blue stared at the spot where they disappeared. He waited for the anger, the resentment, the jealousy that normally reared within him at the sight of such couples. He expected those feelings to come. He wanted them to come. They never did.

Instead, a drowsy weariness settled over him.

The same type of feeling he'd felt the last months out on the rodeo circuit. The sense his life wasn't his anymore. The same numbness he'd felt in the first hours and days after Staci died. Before any of it seemed real.

He returned his focus back to the house. He tried to picture her the way she'd been then. He tried to remember what their days here were like. He tried and failed.

A tear ran from the corner of his eye. Others followed. He didn't fight the flood of emotion. He hadn't shed a single tear for Staci since the day they lowered her casket into the cold hard ground, but now they flowed hot and wet.

This is what he'd always feared—the day he could no longer close his eyes and remember how her skin felt against his—the day the scent of her golden hair faded from his mind—the day she was lost to him for good.

"I don't like just letting you off at a place like this. How about I wait out here and when you're ready to leave, I'll give you a ride home?"

Lindsay shook her head. "I don't know how long I'll be. Go back to Crowfoot's. He might need his truck, and I can walk to my parents' from here. It's not far." She flashed Donnie a false look of confidence she did not even begin to possess.

"Blue ain't gonna like me just dumping you off like this."

"What he doesn't know won't hurt him. You're a better friend than he deserves."

Donnie shook his head. Not once had he spoken a serious word in the hour and a half drive from Crowfoot's, but now Donnie's boyish features meshed together in obvious concern. "Blue is my best friend. I wish I could talk you into coming back with me, but I know I can't. Still, don't be fooled into thinking he's a bad guy. He's made his share of mistakes, but he'll come around in the end. He always does."

Touched by Donnie's loyalty, she could only smile. "You're probably right. If only we had met in a different time and place. Goodbye, Donnie." She leaned across the truck's seat, kissed him on the cheek and opened her door.

Reaching into the bed for her bags, she said, "Thanks for the ride. You're pretty damned good yourself when it comes to being a friend. Don't let Blue forget that." And with that statement she shut the door and turned away from the truck before Donnie could see the tears pooling in her eyes.

Walking up the cracked, evergreen-lined sidewalk, she didn't dare look back for fear Donnie would see the tears streaming down her cheeks. Instead, she focused on the sign that read *Amberwood Manor*, and on moving her feet forward toward the entrance and the long-awaited confrontation with her father.

The door barely shut behind the last customer before Ruby turned the sign to *Closed* and began pulling the blinds. Normally, she stayed open until six, and it was only a quarter to four, but she owned the place and she could lock up any damn time she felt like.

Briley had gotten up over an hour ago. No sign of her fever, but now she complained of a sore throat. There'd been no pleasing the child, so Ruby finally gave up and asked Ray to take her back to the house. She was grateful to have Ray. He could calm Briley when no one could, and he was the only one who understood her position when it came to Blue. Once upon a time, the two of them had been just as close as Ray and Briley were now.

The last mini-blind down, she gathered the empty plates left on a table. Scraping them in the trash, she continued to think about her baby brother. Never in a million years would she have guessed he'd be in Oklahoma. Maybe Donnie was right about him training Winder.

She shook her head. If Blue was going back on the rodeo circuit, Buster would've sounded excited instead of arrogant and condescending. No, he at least thought he'd accomplished something by going to Oklahoma, and now he thought he'd get the chance to gloat and tell her "I told you so."

Well, she wasn't about to give him the satisfaction. She reached for the telephone. He might tell her the same things over the phone, but at least she wouldn't have to see him flash that shit-eating grin and use his tongue to waggle the toothpick between his lips while he told her. Besides, the longer Buster had to rehearse his speech, the more obnoxious he'd be. Ruby loved him, but he could prove tiresome when he got on one of his rants. Buster loved to be right and his voice had sounded like a man bloated with veracity.

She dialed his cell.

"Hello, Darlin'," he answered in his best imitation of Conway Twitty.

Ruby gritted her teeth. Outside of being opinionated from time to time, Buster's most annoying habit was his need to start every phone conversation with a poor rendition of some worn out country and western song. "Where are you?"

"Just pulled out of Yukon."

"Over three hours ago you were in Stillwater and that's as far as you've gotten?"

"I stopped for lunch. Dialed up that ol' boy with the pony. Told him I'd be in Sayre in couple of hours, and he said he'd be there. Sounds like a good deal. Briley might just have her a horse and saddle for her birthday."

"Well, she isn't going to be riding anytime soon. I'm pretty sure she has strep throat again."

"You best get her to the doc first thing tomorrow," Buster said.

"I was hoping you could do that. I already closed early today, and you've seen Dr. McDougal's office this time of year. I'll never get out in time for the lunch crowd."

"The vet is coming early tomorrow. We've got cattle to doctor, and I don't like the way that scratch on Melody is healing. With her nursing that foal, I can't take any chances."

"I'll figure out something." She could hear the sounds of traffic on the highway all around Buster. The doctor business hadn't been her real reason to call, but she'd hoped it would provide lead-in to discuss Blue. It hadn't, so she plowed ahead on her own. "Tell me about Blue."

"What about him?"

"What was he doing at Crowfoot's?"

"Hiding."

"You don't tell people where you're going when you want to hide. Nor do you go the first place everyone will look."

"Don't ask me. I never said he was right in the head, and after what I saw I'm not about to start now."

"What did you see?"

"We'll talk about it tomorrow. It'll be too late by the time I get in tonight."

"I want to hear it now. Briley is in the house with Ray, and tomorrow she'll be right there listening."

For several seconds all she heard were the sounds of the road. Her heart accelerated. What on earth had Blue gotten himself into?

"He had a woman with him."

"A *what?*"

Buster cleared his throat. "You heard me. Some gal he picked up on the side of the road. While you're home taking care of his sick daughter, he's been out on the road ruttin' like bull elk with some damn hitchhiker."

"That's ridiculous."

"I saw it with my own eyes. Blue was more worried about the fact I bought Briley a saddle than her well-being."

"Blue loves his daughter."

"That's bullshit, and you know it."

"No, it's not. He just doesn't—"

"Stop right there. I'm tired of you defending your innocent little brother. You weren't there. You don't know what I saw or what was said. It's time we cut our losses and move on." Buster's voice took on that all-knowing tone again.

"Cut our losses? What are you saying?"

"Briley doesn't need him bouncing in and out of her life.

She needs stability. We're her family. Me and you. It's time we find a lawyer and file for custody."

# 36

Blue pulled away from the little rent house, the place where many of his dreams had first taken root. If a man truly had to hit rock bottom before he could climb back to the top, Blue was passed ready to hit that bottom.

Sinking, sinking, sinking.

He'd been falling for such a long time. That first year he'd tried to drown himself with whiskey. Lose his money gambling. Turn the world against him. None of it worked. He simply became a troubled drunk with fewer friends.

In the beginning, he tossed away money at the poker tables. Played like a fool, and lost better than half the insurance money. Then something clicked inside him. A bit of his old competitive nature reared within him. He got tired of people whispering. Saying he'd lost his mind. They couldn't have been more wrong. He still had his mind. The memories, the longings, the same goals. All he'd lost was self-respect.

Oddly enough, Sergio made him see that.

Not a single drop of alcohol had passed between his lips since the night Sergio, riding cocaine high, mouthed off during a tournament at the Horseshoe. Five security guards and a slew of other tournament players kept the two men apart, but the adrenaline rush was all Blue needed to overcome the whiskey and become the feared poker player he was today.

One thing didn't change. The pain.

No matter how many winner's checks he cashed, the pain remained. No matter how many miles he traveled, the memories still filled his head. No matter how many days, weeks and years slid by, Staci never left him. All he had to do was close his eyes and she would be there. The vanilla scent of her shampoo. The soft smoothness of her tanned skin. The light in her green eyes. The faint freckles of her cheeks. It had always felt as if she'd just walked out of the room. Until now. No one understood, but this was the very day he had always run from. What he'd always feared. He'd hid from family, chased away most of his friends, refused to get to know his daughter.

All for one reason. To keep his mind, his emotions, and his heart centered on Staci.

That's why he went to Idaho every year. To visit a place where every bend in the stream, every tree, every rock held a memory. To renew what he lost. To keep from losing her a second time.

Now, he'd even failed to hold on to her memory.

The smell assaulted Lindsay's nose the moment she stepped through the front door. The foul aroma of bleach combined with the inside of a dirty, truck stop restroom.

A hoard of wheelchair-bound seniors studied her as she tiptoed by. Hope faded from each wrinkled and liver spotted face as they realized she was not there to see them. The patients obviously longed for a visitor. They had little else to look forward to. Her father could not be as bad off as these people. They were old. He wouldn't even be retirement age until after the first of the year.

He'd always planned to retire from the post office the day he turned fifty-five. He always said he wished his birthday was the week before Thanksgiving, instead of January, so he wouldn't have to spend that one last Christmas staring at all those red and green envelopes. Decorations in those same colors hung from the ceiling and wall. A small plastic tree twinkled in the corner. White flocking spelled out seasonal greetings on every glass surface.

Walking past sprayed messages of *MERRY CHRIST-MAS, JOY TO THE WORLD,* and *PEACE TO ALL,* Lindsay supposed her father would trade all the Christmas cards in the world just to escape this place. She nodded with a shred of satisfaction that his plans had not worked out.

Nine years and thousands of miles had slipped away and finally, Lindsay was on the verge of confronting her past. For years, the mere thought of this moment sent her to tears, but as she approached the nurse's station, a calm steady resolve settled over her. For the first time, Lindsay believed she could carry out the mission. The feeling almost felt like hope.

"May I help you?" A pair of reading glasses dangled from a chain around the plump nurse's neck.

"Can you tell me which room Edward Parker is in, please?"

The woman dropped her gaze down to the bags in Lindsay's hand. "Are you a friend of the family?"

"I'm his daughter."

The nurse frowned. "Daughter?"

"That's right." She stuck her hand out. "Lindsay Parker. Nice to meet you."

"Oh." The scowl remained even when the woman offered an obligatory smile. "4C. Around the corner, on the left."

Lindsay walked away to avoid more questions. Not wishing to appear weak, she took a single deep breath and marched straight into the room. The false bravado was wasted. The man slumped sideways in the wheelchair was ill-prepared to seize upon anybody's weaknesses. He owned far too many of his own.

The only sound in the room was that of the irregular puffs of his breath and the ranting of a sportscaster on television.

Even with both eyes closed, she could tell the left was useless. Everything on that side of his body slumped and drooped like a mound of clay left in the hot sun.

His cheek. His shoulder. Even his head listed to the left. His once full head of black hair had been reduced to a ring of dingy pearl with a pale, lumpy bald spot in the middle. Her father looked like all the other old men in the place. Or worse.

She shook her head at the gaping mouth and depleted man piled in the chair. The once proud muscles now told of flaccid weakness. The sharp features that used to make him so intense and fearsome had eroded and relaxed, leaving behind a subdued, defeated appearance. She did not fear this man. In a way, Lindsay did not even feel as if she knew the sleeping figure. She looked around for reassurance she was indeed in the right place.

There on the wall was a wedding picture of her parents that she recognized. And there were several of Clay, but none of her. A football game played on the television. He'd always been a devout follower of the sport. She squinted at the screen. Oklahoma trailed Kansas State by ten. No wonder he'd chosen sleep. Of course, in the old days, he would be up ranting and throwing things at the television. Or cussing the refs.

Lindsay picked the remote up off his lap and clicked off the game. He raised his head just slightly and opened the one good eye. She stared down at his dull pewter-gray eyes.

Her father squinted, blinked his thin, blue-veined lid, and then reached up with his usable hand and wiped at his face.

"I'm not a dream." She said in the face of an intense need to speak first, though she wasn't certain he could say anything at all. "I came to see you."

He nodded and tried to sit straighter in the chair.

"Clay told me you had a stroke."

The old man's pale pink tongue licked his cracked lips. "Lll ... Lll ... Lin ... " His voice croaked out the first syllable of her name as he reached for her with his right hand.

She backed out of reach.

"Lin ... Lin ... " Tears dampened his lashes. White spittle gathered at the corners of his mouth.

Surprised by her lack of anger, Lindsay met his gaze. "I have dreams about her. She would have been a girl, you know. Sometimes I hear her crying at night. Has that ever happened to you? Have you ever sat straight up in bed and for one brief second thought it was all a dream? That your granddaughter lay safe and sound in her crib in the other room? Have you ever had that dream?"

His chin dipped down to his chest. He moved a shaking hand to his face.

"Look away all you want, but you can't run from it. I know. I've tried." She shook her head. "It didn't have to be this way."

Biting her lip to fight back tears she said, "I could have had her. My life might not have been perfect or even easy, but it would've been better than it has been. You shoved me away. You turned your back when I needed you. You and mom, all y'all cared about was hiding my mistake."

Lindsay felt confident now. She felt strong as she said, "Life isn't a mistake. We live it the best we can and make do with what happens. You can't fucking hide the truth of life. You can't erase who you are because somebody might judge you. That makes you no better than them." Poking herself in the chest she said with conviction, "And I will not let you erase who I am any damn more."

"Lin ... Lin ... " Again he reached for her. This time she allowed his fingertips to touch her wrist. "I ... I ... I ... " He shook his head.

Raspy sounds emitted from low down in his throat, but she couldn't understand.

"Tell me one thing." Her voice now sounded flat, even to her own ears.

He looked up suddenly. His fastest and most decisive movement yet. Lindsay could almost see the eagerness on his face. He wanted to give her something, but nothing he could say would be enough.

"Do you regret that trip? If you had it to do over again, would you still wake me up before sunrise and whisk me away to Dallas? Or would you take the time to sit and listen to what I wanted?"

He grimaced with pain as if she had slapped him. He blinked until the tear on his bottom lash fell and ran down his pasty cheek. His lips quivered, and again he tried to speak without any real words coming out.

"Thhh ... Thhh ... " He struck himself in the side of the

head. Once, twice, three times.

Lindsay backed away, running her fingers through her hair.

Again he tried to speak. "Th ... Th ... Th ..." His jaws tensed and his neck thrashed from side to side like a beheaded snake.

Unable to speak she watched the scene unfold. His furious movements made him look more like the father she remembered.

"What's going on in here?"

Lindsay turned at the sound of harsh words and stared straight into the scowling face of her mother. She'd expected her mom to show surprise, maybe even a bit of affection at the sight of her daughter. Instead, Bonnie Parker gave Lindsay a single, cold appraising glare before turning her attention to her husband, whose wild gesticulations and garbled moans continued.

Wordlessly, Lindsay watched her mother try to soothe her father. Bending low near his face, she whispered and patted his still left hand. All the while, his grunts strengthened and his other hand flailed in erratic jerks.

"Go wait in the hall," Bonnie Parker said with the same tone one would use with a stranger.

Lindsay obeyed in silence. Relieved to be free of the scene, she moved away from the open door and stood at the corner of the hall where it intersected with the main concourse. Looking up, she caught the eye of the same nurse who'd given her directions earlier. The woman quickly looked away.

The minutes ticked by, and yet Lindsay could still hear her father raising an uproar.

His agitation had been clear, but Lindsay sensed his

frantic movements had more to do with his inability to communicate than anger at the words she'd spoken. Did he regret his actions? He'd tried to answer, but failed.

That wasn't all he'd failed at, but Lindsay felt a sort of relief to have that first conversation over with, to have her thoughts and feelings out in the open. Now the tension lay with her mother. Lindsay never considered what it would be like to face the rest of the family. Her father had always been the great hurdle to clear. She had no way of knowing that he would be no more formidable of an obstacle than a crack in the pavement.

A few minutes later her mother appeared. "Wait out here," she said as she walked by. Approaching the nurse, her mom said, "He's upset. Maybe if you gave him something to calm him down we can get him back in bed."

The nurse cast a disapproving frown Lindsay's way.

Neither the words or cold looks drifting down the hall had a real effect on Lindsay. Maybe she should feel guilty for her actions, but she didn't. Actually, the whole thing had been anticlimactic. The entire scene seemed more like a movie, or a chapter in a book, than a real part of her life. As if she were an actress waiting to speak her next lines. These people had not been there for her when she needed them, and now, when they obviously needed help themselves, she could not conjure the desire to intervene.

Staring down at the tops of her shoes, she didn't lift her head when the nurse and her mother rushed passed and into her father's room.

"No!" His voice rang out loud and clear amongst the hushed and soothing tones of the two women. "Lll ... Lll ... Lin."

She moved to the open doorway at the recognition of

her name.

His one eye widened at the sight of her. "I ... di ... di ... did ..." He tried to say more, but his mouth merely opened and closed.

"You need to wait in the car."

Lindsay looked at her mother. The tension around her eyes. The slump of her frail shoulders. The deep lines of worry above her brow. Their eyes met and for the flash of second a threat emitted from the depths. Turning without a word, Lindsay walked away.

"No!" Again her dad called out. It seemed to be the one word he'd completely remastered.

Outside, in the early afternoon sunshine, Lindsay surveyed the cars in the lot without knowing which belonged to her mother. Once upon a time, she drove a minivan. No doubt that vehicle was long gone, along with all other public acts meant to portray maternal aptitude.

Lindsay stared down the street in the direction of I-35. A surge of indignation pushed at her. How was it she'd mustered the courage to boldly face her father, but wilted and shrank away with one look from her mother?

The big trucks rumbled down the highway. She couldn't actually see the interstate, but the sound of the eighteen-wheelers was unmistakable. They were always out there moving, headed for somewhere new. In a matter of minutes, she could be gone with the semis.

Someone would give her a ride. It didn't even matter to where. There was no absolution to be found here, there, or anywhere.

She'd been off base about coming home. It hadn't been nearly as hard as she had envisioned, but then again, being here had failed to stir her the way she imagined. She'd never bothered to look beyond the great speech she planned for her father. To the after. To what she hoped to accomplish. To what came next.

This day had hung over her like a storm cloud, but after all the threat and promise of foul weather, she hadn't even needed an umbrella.

The drone of traffic on the interstate called to her, yet the promise she'd made Clay held her in place. She couldn't leave without at least seeing him. And then there was Rusty Hawkins. Nine years was a long time, but he deserved an explanation. He deserved to know what happened. He deserved to know about their child that wasn't.

"You ready?"

Lindsay looked up to find her mother studying her through narrowed eyes. "Where's Clay?"

"Home. Where most people would expect to find their family." The iciness in her mom's voice was apparent.

Swallowing the lump in her throat, Lindsay kept her chin up and met the hard stare of her mother. "I left because of him," she pointed to the nursing home entrance. "So I wanted to see him first."

"Your father is a not as strong as he used to be. He's very vulnerable." She ducked her head and started across the parking lot. Much of the starch in her voice had vanished.

Lindsay followed, proud she'd stood her ground this time.

Her mom opened the trunk of a beige Buick sedan and waited while she placed her bags inside. They exchanged no words until they were both in the car.

"How did you know where to find him?"

Not about to get her brother in trouble, Lindsay said nothing. They pulled out of the parking lot and made a left.

"Someone had to have told you."

Her mother could've asked a lot things. Where she had been? If she'd been okay all these years? Was she married? Kids? Clay had wanted to know these things, but no, her mother's only concern was how she'd uncovered the family secret. Some things never changed.

"I suppose it was that Myra Lynn you went to school with. She works the night shift, but I'm sure you already know that. I'm sure you know all about her and how she broke the heart of her poor husband."

Lindsay turned and stared out the window. She didn't care to hear gossip about some girl she once went to school with.

"It troubles me you kept in touch with your so-called friends, but never once called to let us know where you'd run off to. Or why you felt the need in the first place."

She spun around. "Why? Don't sit there and act like you don't know why. You know exactly why I left."

They turned again and Lindsay found herself back on the street where she grew up. The tears she'd been holding in now ran freely down her cheeks.

"Calm down, Lindsay. The past is the past. None of us can change it. What matters is the present."

Her childhood home came into view.

"Please stop crying. You're going to upset your brother. He always believed you would come back." She handed Lindsay a tissue. "You don't want to ruin his dream, do you?"

Lindsay dabbed her moist eyes and shook her head. "No, we wouldn't want to do that. God forbid anyone's dreams get ruined."

37

Eyes wide-open in an unfocused gaze, Lindsay stared out the window. Multi-colored lights twinkled from the eaves of the Wylies' house next door. The Wylies had always lived there, and years ago their daughter Erika had been Lindsay's best friend. By shifting her position on the futon, she could make out the shadowy shape of Santa's sleigh and reindeer perched atop the elderly couple's roof, but tonight she had no desire to see the jolly old fat man, or Rudolph's shiny red nose. Her Christmas spirit had taken a beating with her less-than-joyous return and now lay buried somewhere deep, under the same pile of regret that had made her think coming home would be a good idea.

In recent years, she hadn't found much to celebrate, but as a young girl, she cherished the holidays. Their block had always been festively decorated. Her dad took pride in having lights strung the weekend before Thanksgiving, although he never turned them on until Thursday night.

"Only a fool, or a show-off, turns their lights on before Thanksgiving." Her father said every year when she begged him to turn them on early. Tradition and appearance dictated the rules, not the whims of a little girl.

There were no twinkling lights on this house anymore,

and only Mr. Wylie seemed to uphold the block's long-standing custom. Along with the yard ornaments and lights, of the past he'd added a real working miniature train that made a circle through the front yard while curious red-stockinged elves peeked out from behind bushes and trees. Once upon a time, she would've sat at the windowsill of her room and watched the engine circle for hours, counted the elves' shy faces and marveled at every glowing bulb. Now, it hardly seemed worth lifting her head off the pillow.

Lindsay laid there for a while thinking about her old friend Erika Wylie. Wherever she was, Lindsay hoped Erika had her own finely decorated house with enough stockings hanging on the fireplace to make her happy. Eventually, Lindsay was forced to reflect on her own situation. The satisfying ending she'd hoped for her return was gone. Her father would never be able to give her the answers she needed, and her own mother didn't want her here. To top off the dismal homecoming, she still had not seen Clay. His note had said he'd gone to Bricktown with friends. At the bottom he'd added, *Be back late. Don't wait up.*

Lindsay felt slighted somehow that he hadn't mentioned her in the scribblings, until she reminded herself the note was for their mother; he had no way of knowing she was back. Her only promise was to be here before Christmas so here she lay on the dark side of midnight, in her old room, feeling like a lost and lonely traveler in a faraway place.

Over dinner, amid anxious stares and worried, pinched-brow expressions, her mother finally got around to asking about Lindsay's well-being the last decade. However, her concern seemed to stem more from the awkward silence that had festered between them, than from the heart. Regardless of the reason, Lindsay did not feel compelled to supply answers.

Instead, she retreated to her old room.

Hours had slipped by. Dusk gave way to night and yet Lindsay did not move from her position on the uncomfortable futon. Not when her mother knocked to see if Lindsay needed anything, not when she stopped by later to say goodnight, and not now, when she fought the urge with every breath to go out in the cold and jog until the pain in her legs replaced the ache in her chest.

If she took off now, she might never stop running.

The glare of headlights washed across the room's bare shelves that once housed her trophies. No one could guess this had once been her room. The bed was gone, replaced by this ridiculous futon. The corner, where her dresser once stood was filled with a desk and a computer, the screen as dark and blank as Lindsay's life.

A car door slammed outside.

Her entire existence here had been erased. She'd always believed, secretly hoped, her family missed her. That they looked forward to her return. Instead, they'd moved on without regard to her memory.

Until she heard the scrape of the key in the lock, Lindsay hadn't realized what the headlights and car door meant. Clay was home. Her stomach gave a lurch. She sat up. Facing her brother suddenly seemed scarier than anything she'd done thus far.

But he sounded so eager on the phone. Surely, he wouldn't react how their mother had. But what if he expected more than she could, or was willing, to give? The door closed. His muffled cough reached her ears.

In reality, they didn't even know one another. He was twelve when she left. They'd both experienced so much since they last saw each other.

Lindsay stood. She reached for the bedroom doorknob, but stopped with her fingers curled around the cold metal. She didn't want to just burst from the room and say, 'Here I am. Your long-lost, and forgotten sister.' She wanted their reunion to mean something. She wanted him to understand. She wanted one person in the world to call family. One person to believe in and love, without strings or justification. One person to turn to when bricks began falling from the sky.

Clay was her last hope to find that person. He'd been pulling her here to Oklahoma ever since she talked to him from Idaho. The bond they forged in two brief phone conversations had been enough to bring her back, but now she feared that link would sever and forever be lost unless she reinforced the connection. She had to make him understand why she ran away. Why she left him alone to face their hard, volatile father and unemotional mother. And most importantly, why she had come back.

Tiptoeing down the dark hall, she passed her parent's closed door. Lindsay breathed a sigh of relief no light seeped beneath. She wanted her first conversation with Clay to be just the two of them.

The refrigerator door opened and closed, and there he was crossing the den, tall and handsome, just like she pictured. His easy gait carried him into the living room with a bowl and spoon in one hand, and gallon of milk in the other. Tucked under his arm was a box of Cheerios. She guessed him to be two or three inches above six foot. Just a few inches shorter than Blue. Clay plopped down on the couch and turned on the TV without noticing her there in the shadows.

He flipped through the channels before stopping to pour the cereal and milk. His shoulders were broad. Nearly as wide as Blue's. Matter of fact, if you lined the two of them up side by side, you would guess they were related. Of course, Clay favored their father even more, but Lindsay would rather think about Blue. Tall, strong, and athletic. Blue was built more like a workhorse, but one look at Clay conjured thoughts of an athlete.

Her brother lifted the dripping spoon to his mouth and then paused as their eyes met.

Lindsay bit her lip.

"You came." His deep voice still did not seem right even now with his muscular frame right before her eyes.

She nodded. "I told you I would."

He dropped the spoon in the bowl and stood.

Eyes brimming with eagerness and joy, he said, "I always knew you'd come back, but it's still kind of a shock. You know?" He offered a crooked smile.

Lindsay nodded. She didn't trust herself to speak. Tears flooded her eyes, and for once they were not sparked by sorrow, but hope. She stepped out of the shadows and into the light, trusting Clay would not hold her long absence against her.

"When did you get here?"

"This afternoon."

"Sorry. Didn't know, or I'd have stuck around." He stepped around the coffee table and grinned again.

"That's okay. You had no way—"

He wrapped his arms around her and squeezed off her words. "Man, I'm glad you're back." He held her that way for several long seconds. "I was getting worried."

She gathered strength from his stout embrace. He smelled like cigarettes, smoke, and beer. Probably from hanging out at some club with his friends, but she didn't care. To know her brother cared, and had missed her, and was thrilled with her return was enough to erase all the smells, and all the regrets, and all the disappointments from her mind.

Finally, he released his grip and held her at arm's length. "You look great. Exactly how I remember. Nothing's changed."

How she wished that were true.

"Sit and tell me what's going on."

She smiled, finding his excitement contagious.

"Unless you're wiped out," he said. "You can clue me in in the morning if you need to catch some z's."

"No. I never sleep very much."

"Want me to grab you a bowl and spoon?" He pointed to the coffee table.

"No, you go ahead." She took a seat on the couch a few feet away.

"Why didn't Mom call my cell? I checked my messages twice from the club."

"Let's just say she wasn't as happy to see me as you."

"Like you can tell when Mom's happy." He shoveled a spoonful of Cheerios into his smiling mouth. "Your friend Janine called. You should call her. She's worried about you."

Lindsay suddenly felt bad. All this feeling sorry for herself and she'd forgotten about Janine. "How did she know the number?"

"Beats me, but I gave her my cell after the first call. I didn't want her to call and ask for you in case Mom answered."

"I'm glad you did. Mom was upset because I went to see him first."

Clay lowered the spoon. "You saw Dad?" He ran his fingers through his hair. "Wow. Bet that set him off." He shook his head. "Wait. That's why his nurse called. When I answered, she said it was urgent she talk to Bonnie Parker. Mom looked worried when she hung up, but said they needed some authorization to give dad some new medicine. Why didn't she tell me you were back? I could've gone with her."

Lindsay shrugged. She had no way to explain their mother's actions.

"Hey, Mom what are you doing awake?"

Lindsay looked up. Expecting to see the same uptight and agitated face. Instead, she was surprised to see uncertainty, almost fear in her mother's expression. Minus her makeup and wrapped in a threadbare cream-colored terrycloth robe, Bonnie Parker looked years older than she had only hours before.

"I heard voices. I ..." She rubbed her temples. "I didn't know if you'd remember." Her voice sounded tired, almost defeated.

"Remember what? Lindsay? You think I could forget my sister? Just because you never let us mention her name doesn't mean I forgot."

"Clayton Andrew how dare ..." Her voice faltered. She pressed the back of her wrist to her forehead and leaned against the wall. "The lights are so bright in here, and my head."

"Go to bed," Clay said with authority. "You won't get rid of your migraine unless you do."

"I can't just leave the two of—"

"We're fine, Mom. Stop worrying. I'm not going to pack up and split town just because Lindsay came back for a visit. Take your pills and go to bed."

Lindsay held her breath in anticipation of conflict, but her mom merely nodded and shuffled back down the hall. With newfound appreciation for her brother, Lindsay waited until she heard the bedroom door close before saying, "I remember when she used to get migraines and we'd all have to walk on tiptoes. Dad grounded me for a week one time for waking her up during one of her spells. I missed somebody's slumber party because of it. The next week he bought me my first pair of cross-country shoes. I think he felt bad. Funny how you forget something like that."

"Yeah, I got grounded a few times myself. Every time something traumatic happens around here she takes to the bed with migraines." He continued to munch cereal.

"Is it all an act?"

"Who knows, but Dad was right. It's easier to humor her and be quiet until she gets over it than it is to try and get her to see reason. Seems like I have to come home every other week to deal with some so-called tragedy."

"I'm sorry you've had to put up with so much. I feel bad for leaving you behind to deal with them."

Clay shook his head. "Dad took care of everything until the stroke. Baseball was already over, and I only had one final left so everything worked out all right. Took a month for her to be functional again, but I was home for the summer. Once the season starts, she's gonna have to find some strength."

Lindsay didn't know what to say. Clay took such strife matter-of-factly, as if he expected bad things to happen. But why wouldn't he? A runaway sister. A mother who hid beneath sheets when trouble came. A father that reacted with anger and mindless action to every problem. It was a wonder Clay wasn't an emotional basket case. Kind of like herself.

For the next hour, they talked back and forth, asking questions of one another. He told her tales of playing ball at Baylor. This, his redshirt junior year, he was penciled in to be the Bears starting first baseman. No, he didn't have a serious girlfriend or a good grip on what he wanted to do after college. His major was physical therapy, but lately he'd started to think more along the line of education. He claimed his chances of making the pros were slim at best, but he might make a switch to education in hopes of getting a coaching job to stay around the game.

For her part, Lindsay gave Clay a rundown of the places she'd traveled. He took a keen interest when she mentioned Park City, Utah, asking her who she'd lived with and for how long. She was surprised to learn their dad took Clay there on a trip his senior year of high school. Twice, he asked if she'd ever been married. Both times she said no, and both times he frowned. The only other time she recognized disappointment was when he asked her if she still ran competitively.

"I run every day to clear my mind," she explained hoping to erase the dissatisfaction from his face. "At least five or ten miles. Sometimes more. Lately I've thought about racing again."

"I always thought you'd make the Olympics. I watched the highlights from all the marathons to see if I could spot you. Boston, New York, even the triathlon from Hawaii."

She reached across the couch and patted his hand. "I should've contacted you. So you'd know I was okay."

"I always knew you were. Dad made sure of that, but I should be mad at you."

Her heart skipped a beat. Here it came. He was going to let her know how selfish and wrong she'd been to run away.

But instead of tearing into her, Clay again flashed his crooked grin. "Doubt I ever would've dated the psycho-chick-from hell if she wasn't a runner like you."

"Psycho?"

"Yeah. Bridget Hibbs. We dated almost a year. She was

on the cross-country team at Baylor. She graduated in May, but I still have to screen my calls because she calls every other week to let me know she's getting married. I never met anybody so eager to walk down the aisle. That's why we broke up. She kept hounding me for a ring. Even acted pregnant for a couple of weeks once."

Again, Lindsay held her breath in anticipation of Clay bringing up the past, but he simply leaned back on the couch and shook his head.

"There must've been something you liked about her." For some reason, she felt sympathetic to her brother's ex-girlfriend.

"Yeah, there were things I liked about her, but they're probably not suitable to discuss with my sister."

Lindsay laughed at the serious tone of his voice, despite feeling sorry for his jilted lover.

"Bridget talked me into running this 10K with her last spring. Five minutes in, I was dying. I tried to explain to her I was a power-hitter. A shot over the wall, followed by a slow jog is my preferred exercise. At worse, I smack a line drive and have to go hard ninety feet to first."

"You sound like Blue."

"Blue what?"

"The guy that gave me a ride down here from Idaho. He used to be a rodeo star. His idea of running was from the horse to the calf and he claimed, even that was painful. He preferred steer wrestling."

"Is he your boyfriend?"

Lindsay shook her head. "Blue is about as far away from relationship material as you can get, but we had some good times on the trip. You'd like him. He's a man's man."

"That's something Dad would say," Clay answered.

"I know."

They both fell quiet. Only the chatter of the television covered the silence. Lindsay's thoughts turned to her father and something told her that's where Clay's mind went as well. A commercial came on for electric wheelchairs. The Rosco scooter promised mobility for all. Even those weakened by stroke.

"What's the prognosis? Will he ever be able to talk again? Stand up on his own?"

Clay shrugged. "He made progress for a while, but lately he just sleeps. Maybe he'll try again now that you're back."

"Clay." She waited until her brother looked at her. "I'm not staying. There's nothing for me here."

"We're here."

"There is no we, there's only you. Mom would just as soon see me gone, and I can't just forget what he did. Stroke or no stroke. And you have your own life. I'll keep in touch, but once I leave I won't come back. Not to see them anyway."

"What did he say when he saw you?"

"He tried to say my name, but I did most of the talking. He tried to answer but I couldn't understand. He didn't really get any words out. Just noises, and then he got upset, and Mom showed up and told me to leave the room."

"Her idea of dealing with a problem is to ignore it. She couldn't do that with you in the room."

"If I stay I'll always be the problem."

"No." He shook his head. "You're not a problem now. You took her by surprise is all. Watch, tomorrow morning she'll wake up and act like you never left."

"That's not what I want either. You can't run away from the truth, or simply ignore reality. I've tried. Sooner or later, it eats you up. That's what drove me away, and that's what kept me moving all these years."

"It hasn't done Dad any good either."

Lindsay met her brother's dark solemn gaze. A day ago, she would've found satisfaction in the knowledge her father suffered, but sitting here, staring at Clay's slumped shoulders and frank face, none of those feelings materialized. Not a hint of accusation tainted his words, but she felt the weight of his statement just the same.

Their father's swift and heartless actions had ruined her life. Nothing would ever convince her otherwise. If Lindsay had been wrong about anything, it was that she never put any of the blame on her mother, when in fact her parents had probably arrived at the coldhearted decision together. Even now, nearly a decade later, Lindsay could recall every detail of that evening and night.

Her mother, after drawing a confession out of Lindsay, locked herself in her room, whereas her father sat in his recliner, bearing a pained expression. Clay had been away, spending the night at a friend's. Her father hadn't blown up the way she anticipated. Instead, he remained motionless in his chair, staring at a black television screen. The only time she remembered him sitting with the set turned off.

Dusk faded into darkness and yet her dad just sat there. She tried to talk to him. Tried to tell him it would be okay. She had it all worked out in her mind, but he didn't hear a word of her plans. Finally, she gave up and went to her room to cry. No doubt, her parents made the decision together in the black of the night. The next morning, her father woke her before daylight, and herded her off to Dallas.

He never told her where they were going. He didn't need to.

Lindsay shook her head to clear away the images of that

horrible morning. She'd given in to their ambush then, but she refused to make concessions now. She cleared her throat. "Do you know why I left?"

"I know what Dad told me, and that's enough for me."

Clay's words sawed through the cord of trust that had developed between them. He'd chosen a side. He didn't care what she had to say. He believed whatever lies their father had implanted. Her eyes welled with tears.

"Lindsay, don't." Fear flashed across his face. "I'm not saying Dad was right. He won't even tell you that."

"What are you saying?" She suddenly felt like a goldfish ripped from the safety of its bowl. Foolishly, she thought her brother would be the one person to never judge her. To whom she would be able to talk to without prejudice or fear. The one person who would not abandon her.  And yet, here she was gasping for air.

"Lindsay." He grasped her cold clammy hand. "You're my sister, and always will be. You don't know what hearing your voice was like. I've missed you."

The foreboding, unspoken "but" hung over her head. *But you ran away ... But you turned your back on the family ... But you are wrong.*

She feared his next words even as he said them.

"But you have to understand, he's still my dad. I have a good idea what happened. He's tried to tell me. More than once, but I always stopped him. No, he's not perfect. Never has been. Never will be. But good and bad, he's my dad."

Clay stood and paced the room. "Right there." He pointed to a place by the fireplace. "I challenged him one day. I stood right there and called him an old man. Told him he couldn't control my life forever. I was seventeen. He gave me every chance to back down. I wouldn't. We stood toe-to-

toe. He told me to take my best shot." Clay shook his head. "I did."

Lindsay waited to hear more. She tried to picture the scene. Clay ready to fight their father. The blue veins bulging in his young neck. The hard stare of the older man's eyes.

"He never moved. I didn't have the guts to hit him in the face, so I drove my fist into his stomach with all I had. He never even grunted. Just looked me straight in the eyes, shook his head, and sat back down. I stood right there like an idiot until he told me to go take out the trash."

Staring up at the ceiling, Clay's Adam's apple bobbed with emotion. "He never mentioned my stupidity again until the day he dropped me off at Baylor. Said he wished it would've been that easy with you. And then for the only time in my life I saw him cry. He tried to tell me why you left. He tried to tell me why he could never make up for it. I wouldn't listen. I stopped him, but not before he said he'd give anything to have the chance to stand toe-to-toe with you and let you have your go. Said he wouldn't be able to bluff his way with you the way he did me, but it would be worth it to see you again."

Lindsay said nothing. Take out the trash—take out a baby. The two were hardly the same. If Clay wanted to believe their father was such an honorable man, let him. She knew otherwise. An honorable man would've listened to her. If not before, at least afterward. An honorable man would have reached through her pain and consoled her. An honorable man would have ... would've tracked her down, looked her in the eye, and begged for forgiveness instead of waiting and hoping.

Now, he'd cheated her again. Her father was gone. She couldn't stand toe-to-toe with the man she hated. He couldn't stand, period. He couldn't even talk. Couldn't offer apologies, or an explanation. He'd vanished and left behind the broken shell of a man to absorb her hatred.

"I know you don't want to see him, and I promised not to ask," Clay said. "But—"

"There's no chance of forgiveness."

"He doesn't expect any."

"What does he expect?"

Clay shook his head. "I can't answer that. Except to say like me, he always expected you to come back. He never lost hope. Even when that private investigator swindled him."

"Private investigator?"

"Dad hired this idiot to find you. A few months later, the guy comes up with an address in Park City. That's why we went there. Dad told Mom he was taking me and one of my friends for spring break. We drove all the way out there."

Lindsay did the math in her head. Clay was a redshirt junior in college. So that would've put them in Utah four years ago next March. She'd left the week after Valentine's Day. Sven had sold one of his snowboards and bought her an engagement ring, so she picked a fight and caught a bus back to California.

"And what happened?"

"Dad went by himself to the address. He wouldn't let me go. He came back and said nobody there ever heard of you. Dad threatened to sue the private investigator.

"You were there, weren't you?" Clay sounded hurt. "I wanted to ask earlier when you mentioned Park City, but—"

"No. I left that February."

"We were that close." Clay held up two fingers only an inch apart. "I've never seen Dad take anything that hard. Not even when you first left, but it didn't seem real then. They both tried to hide it from me, but I heard them whispering, and that boyfriend of yours kept coming by until Dad pulled a twelve gauge on him."

"Rusty?"

"Yeah, his dad came over then, and I thought there was going to be bloodshed. They yelled at each other on the front lawn. Dad about Rusty needing to keep his pecker in his pants, and the other man said our whole damn family was crazy. The police came and everything.

"When Dad came in, Mom said he'd let the cat out of the bag. That the whole block would know. Until then they always told me you'd gone away to a private school. That's what they told Rusty and the high school, too, but when you didn't come back for the summer, the rumor got started they sent you to the convent to become a nun."

"We're not even Catholic."

"Mom might still convert if she thought everyone would buy that story."

Despite everything, Lindsay laughed. Clay did, too.

He sat back down on the couch beside her. "Just between the two of us," he lowered his voice to a whisper, "Mom is a little bit crazy."

They laughed again until Clay slung an arm over her shoulder and gave a gentle squeeze.

# 38

After hours of talking, Clay dozed off watching some rerun. Knowing she would never sleep herself, Lindsay laced up her Nikes and slipped outside. Predawn darkness now consumed the block. The Wylie's twinkling lights had long been turned off for the night. In the distance, a lone dog barked, disturbing the Sunday morning silence as Lindsay took off on her run.

Her mind and legs automatically took the same route she once covered twice a day. Even after the long absence, a sense of familiarity came over her as she set out. In a way, it felt as if she'd never left. The first mile fell behind at a brisk pace, and in a matter of minutes she rounded the corner of Lindsey Street.

She'd been named for the thoroughfare, the place where her parents first met, but when she was born, someone at the hospital accidentally changed the E to an A.

Accidentally.

Her entire life was built around accidents.

Had her Mom never driven her car smack dab into the back of her Dad's truck that day on Lindsey Street, she wouldn't even be alive. A simple fender bender at the corner of Elm and Lindsey led to both her and Clay's existence.

Who could predict when the next fate-altering event would occur, when it took so little to create lives? And even less to destroy them.

Pushing her muscles harder than normal, harder than she should without a proper warm-up, Lindsay covered the three miles to the OU campus in just over fifteen minutes. She would never be able to keep this pace. Not if she intended to put in her usual distance. Yet something pushed her on, faster and faster.

The Seedsower statue still stood at the south end of the oval and the tall red-bricked dorms still loomed over lush green lawns, yet the campus didn't hold the allure it once possessed. Used to be, she could almost sense the promise in the air, smell the hope and eagerness, see the future of those who sought an education and a better tomorrow. The call of college life. Even though her true dream had been to attend State over becoming a Sooner, the spirit was the same, and every trip through the institute's grounds had bolstered her eagerness to savor university life.

At Elm, she turned north. Working her muscles with a furious vigor, she passed the university's familiar buildings. Robertson—Hester—and Ellison Halls. By focusing her energy on how fast she could reach the next structure, Lindsay managed to hold off the ghosts of yesteryear.

Across Boyd Street, past the president's house, away from the entire OU campus, she ran. Following the route of old, she would've already turned back for home. Instead, she continued straight ahead.

Her lungs burned, her legs throbbed, her sides ached, yet nine years of running fueled her flight. She couldn't stop. Not now, not here. The hounds of the past nipped at her heels.

Her breath came in ragged, visible bursts as she struggled to maintain her pace in the cold morning air. The truth now seemed so clear. She didn't leave home to escape the memory of her pain or the hurt of her loss.

Lindsay's stride broke into an uneven gait.

She stumbled, almost falling, yet continued to push herself even as her muscles threatened to break down.

Crossing Main, she staggered forward.

Her vision blurred, from tears of both physical pain and mental fatigue. Her body wanted to shut down, yet her mind urged her on. Her legs were no longer a part of her as she struggled onward.

Sophomore year of high school, she'd felt like this at a race in Tulsa. Sick, and cramping from dehydration, the last five or six hundred yards were torture. Down all week with the flu, she never should've competed that day, but Lindsay refused to give in. To admit she didn't belong on the team. That she didn't have the strength to battle adversity. That she couldn't fight through the pain and finish.

That she was like her mother.

Lindsay zombie-walked that last fifty yards of the race, but she made it to the finish. The very earth beneath her feet had been spinning, but before she could fall to the ground, he was there to catch her.

He'd always been there to catch her. Until he wasn't.

Lindsay stopped running and clutched a street lamp for support. Her body heaved. The muscles in her legs twitched uncontrollably. Like that long-ago race day, she no longer had the strength to hold up even her head. Yet she could now see what she'd never allowed herself to admit. He was always there at the finish line. Win or lose. He was there to cheer her on, or hold her up if necessary, but he was always there.

Sweat dripped from her brow and fell to the cold concrete at her feet. Her father had always been the one thing she could count on, yet the one time she most needed his support, he let her collapse. And collapse she had. When it truly mattered, she hadn't had the strength.

She failed, and he let her.

In her mind, she could still see the fear in his eyes that day. Had she recognized a glimmer of hope, a shred of affirmation, a reason to put up a fight, things might've turned out different, but one look at the defeated slump to her father's shoulders, and she allowed herself to be led like a lamb to the slaughterhouse. Like a weak dishrag of a woman. Like her mother.

That's what she'd fled all these years. Not the pure evil incarnation of her father that she tried so hard to believe in, but the mere fact she herself never fought hard enough. She should have fought for herself. For her future. For her child.

Lifting her head, Lindsay surveyed her surroundings. There, at the end of the block, sat the building that now housed her father. Her legs had carried her to the place where her mind refused to travel—her father's bedside.

# 39

Another round of pounding rattled the hinges as Ruby gathered her robes around her middle, hurried down the hall, and turned on the light in the front room. "Hold your horses! I'm coming."

She squinted at the dark shape beyond the oval window in the door. "Buster?"

"Yeah, it's me. Open up. It's mighty damn cold out here."

Twisting the lock, she turned and frowned at the clock as a rush of frosty morning air seeped in.

Worry suddenly gripped her. "What's going on? Is something wrong? What are you doing here this time of day?"

"Nothing's wrong." Buster hung his cowboy hat on the hook, his good hat without the battered crown and sweat stains. And he'd ironed his shirt, combed his thin hair up over the bald spot.

She touched his cheek. It was smooth. Sniffing the air she asked, "Is that aftershave?"

"Might be." He looked away, but not before she caught the slightest tinge of color in his cheeks.

"Are you going to tell me why you're all gussied up and banging on my door at five-thirty in the morning?"

"I wanted to see you before you opened up."

Ruby frowned. "You see me every morning. You forget about all those gallons of coffee you've drank at my table?"

"You ain't gonna make this easy are you?" He reached up as if to straighten his hat, but dropped his hands suddenly when he realized there was nothing on top of his head, but his slicked down hair.

"Make what easy?"

He patted his shirt pocket and then pulled out a small velvet box. "I can't get down. This cold front has got my knees stiffer than a ... Well hell, Ruby. You know I'm no good at talking but what I'm trying to say is ... Will you marry me?" He opened the lid and thrust the box forward.

"Buster, I—"

"Before you say a word, let me do some talking." He handed her the ring and folded his arms across his chest.

With the nature of his business out in the open, he seemed more like the confidant the man she knew. More than ready to share his viewpoint and let his opinion be known, but she had no intention of letting him gather a head of steam. "I thought you were no good at talking."

"I'm not. But that's never stopped me before."

"Buster, you know I love you, but—"

"Then hear me out."

Determined to gain control, she pressed on, "Nothing has changed."

"Damn right it hasn't, and I'm tired of it."

"Don't do this Buster. It's not fair."

"Fair to who?" The volume of his voice rose.

Briley coughed. They both turned and stared down the dimly lit hall toward her bedroom.

Seconds passed in silence until Ruby made certain she didn't hear the telltale creak of bed springs, followed by the patter of little feet. "You're going to wake her up."

"Ruby." The tips of his rough fingers caressed her neck. He traced the tender area just below her jaw line. "I want you to be my wife," he whispered.

She closed her eyes to avoid looking at him. "We've talked about this before."

"Talk." He spit the word out as if it were poison. "My craw is stuffed full of talk. We're like a couple of hayseed kids dreaming about big city life. It started out with, 'We can't. What would people say? Cold-hearted Buster cheating on his crippled wife.' Or, 'Look at that Ruby Riggins? Can you believe she would allow a married man in her bed?' We ran from that talk for years and you know what? They said it anyway. Would've been better to get it over with, instead of letting it fester. Nothing will ever change the way I feel about you."

"Not for me either, but—"

"And then when she passed away, you said let's wait six months, but then Briley came along, and Staci died, and it turned into 'Let Blue have some time.'"

"It's about more than Blue. Don't make him the villain."

"You're right. It's about me and you." Buster cradled her face in his weathered hands. "I'm on the downhill side of fifty, and every day that goes by is another day I don't have what I want. No, what I *need*. I want to be more than a part of your life. I need you."

"Briley needs me, too."

"I know she does. We both do, but she also needs stability in her life. Me and you," he pointed at his chest and then at Ruby, "We're her family. We need to be together."

"We are together."

He shook his head. "Not officially. The sooner we face the facts and realize our roles, the sooner we can stop living for a tomorrow that's never going to arrive."

She bristled and pulled away. "What are our roles?"

"Face it, Ruby. We're all she has. Blue might float in once or twice a year, but he won't be here when she needs him the most. We will."

"He takes care of her. He sends money."

"That's bullshit. Money is no replacement for a father. If you'd let me take care of you like I want, he could keep his money. You work like a dog, and you don't have to. I want you and Briley to move out to the ranch."

"I can't abandon this place."

"Tell me one reason why not? What is there here for you?"

"Ray depends on me."

"I'll hire him. The food they cook out in the bunkhouse is barely edible anyway."

"You have three men. You're going to hire a full-time cook for three guys who think Jack and Coke is a two-course meal?

Buster smiled. "If that's what it takes."

She bowed her head. Guilt welled inside her. Buster was right, and she did love him, but the truth was, she was afraid. Not of being his wife, she'd wanted that for so long, but of what saying yes ultimately meant for everybody concerned.

Without a home base, Blue would become more nomadic, more lost. Pride would never let him set foot in Buster's house, even if she lived there. He might already be gone forever, but she hated to cut the cord and alienate him all the more.

And then there was Briley. Ruby loved the little girl as much as any mother, and without a doubt Buster did too, but nothing could replace the bond between a parent and a child.

She'd tried her best, but growing up, Blue never knew what it felt like to be loved unconditionally and without blame. He might not even realize it, but even though Ruby's love for him had always been absolute and unconditional, it had not been without a longing for freedom, without resignation, or without the black cloud of what-if looming overhead.

Regret never entered the picture, but there were times she felt trapped. Maybe Blue sensed that. As a small boy, he used to sit on the edge of her bed and ask questions. *Why she never left like her older sisters? Didn't she want to travel and see something besides the cars that passed in front of the restaurant? Was she ever going to get married and have a family?*

He tried to mask the worry, but concern always churned behind Blue's dark eyes. She always answered the same. He was family enough. Countless times, she explained to him the love of a single person was all anybody needed. She said it to soothe him, never knowing how fully he would take her words to heart.

"Ruby?"

She blamed herself for Blue's restlessness and inability to cope with Staci's death. As a boy, the maternalistic love of his sister had sufficed, but boys turn into men, and Staci became the one he needed. The one he clung to. Nobody else realized it, but underneath all of Blue's accomplishments, under that tall muscular frame, beneath that stoic shell, he was that same needy little boy who used to sit on her bed and seek assurance.

"Ruby?"

She looked at Buster.

"For once, ask yourself what you want. What would make you happy? Don't worry about anybody else."

She never begrudged Staci for the power she held over

Blue. Knowing he'd found happiness was enough—then he lost her. Without the beacon her love provided, Blue became lost. If only Ruby could make him truly see Briley. If only she could keep him near enough to take in and feel the light that shone within his daughter. If only she could make him see into those same dark eyes that used to stare up at her, that underneath that radiant head of blonde hair was a little girl eager to adore him, and in the middle of that tiny chest beat a heart, that he, along with Staci, created. Blue needed to discover that the last, and best part of his wife, lived in the spirit of his daughter.

"Are you listening to me?"

She nodded without speaking. To deny Blue that opportunity would not only deny him the chance to live again, but also lead Briley down the same path Blue traveled. Without a chance to know her father, she'd never know who she really was, or what her mother gave up to bring her into the world. Briley, like Blue, would always have that thread of insecurity.

"I can't take her from him." She hoped Buster would understand what this statement meant and not make her say no in exact terms.

"You can't take what she doesn't have."

"I can steal her hope, and I won't do that."

Buster nodded and turned around. He grabbed his hat and reached for the door before turning back around. "Instead, you've stolen mine."

# 40

The cigarette glowed like the eye of an evil serpent as he inhaled the nicotine deep into his lungs. Blue held the smoke inside for several long seconds, before letting the gray wisps escape through his nostrils.

Yesterday morning, she was here lying beside him. Now, she was gone.

Yesterday morning, he hadn't smoked in over a week. Now, it seemed as if he never quit.

Yesterday morning, he awoke with two women on his mind. Now, he'd lost them both.

They were still here, filling the crevices of his brain, their presence lingering, yet they were no longer tangible. Another cloud of smoke rolled toward the dark ceiling as Crowfoot's rooster sang out. The crow served as his warning. Soon, the sun would flood the world with harsh light, and he would no longer own the cover of darkness. The shadows, where he inspected his sorrows, would be erased and he would be forced to interact, defend his actions, act as if tomorrow mattered.

If only the sun would stay below the horizon for one day, but no, it would be up there shining this morning like it had the day after Staci died. And Donnie would be there in his face asking him questions, wanting to know what Blue was going to do next. And Crowfoot would keep watching him. Not saying a word, just watching, his expression saying more than those who never shut their mouth.

Blue took another drag. He could lay right here in bed, ignore his friends, and smoke the day away—if only the sun would do its part. But the outside world didn't care what he wanted. In the cold and darkness, he could justify his beliefs. By day, they burned away like mist. Others welcomed the light, the warmth of company. Why couldn't he be like them? Like Lindsay?

She would be out running right now.

Closing his eyes, he could almost see her. Her hair, pulled back in a ponytail, bouncing with each stride. The strawberry tinge to her cheeks. The winded motion of her chest as she paced and stretched to cool her muscles. The faint sweet scent of her sweat after she ran, or when they made love.

And her skin. He missed the smooth contours of her body. The way she shivered at his touch. The aggressive, almost hungry way she accelerated their passion in bed, even as he tried to pull back and savor those moments.

He swung his feet to the floor and crushed the cigarette in the ashtray sitting on the night stand. Rubbing his eyes, he forced himself to stand. The last thing he needed was to lie here and think about Lindsay. They shared this bed for a mere two weeks. Somehow it felt longer.

To make losing Lindsay easier, Blue tried to blame her for stealing Staci. He wanted to believe she chased his wife from his memory. He'd attempted to pinpoint the exact time he could no longer close his eyes and feel Staci there beside him. He used to think she would simply walk into the room one day and kiss him on the check the way she used to after a quick trip to the store.

When did he stop believing it was all just a bad dream? That was the question that kept him up all night, propelled him to drive back into Stillwater for a carton of Marlboros. He still couldn't answer with any certainty, except that it happened before Lindsay entered his life.

His heart still ached for Staci, but not in the same desperate way it once had. He still missed her every day, but not with every breath, and he still loved her, but no longer could he say he loved only her.

Only the last part of that knowledge could be traced to Lindsay.

He'd left Vegas chasing something he'd feared was already gone. In Idaho, those fears became reality.

Blue limped down the hall. Yesterday, he'd flung himself into finishing the barn. No one followed him up onto the roof, and he'd stayed up there long after he'd finished, after darkness set in. Even though Donnie tried on two separate occasions to get him to come inside and eat.

Splashing cold water onto his face, Blue stared back at the pair of dark eyes in the mirror. They belonged to a stranger, but damned if Blue knew how to find the man he once knew.

By the time he'd showered, enough light drifted in through the windows that Blue didn't need to turn on the bedroom light to get dressed. His knee ached from climbing up and down the ladder, but he didn't bother to search out his pills. Maybe the knee would hurt like hell and he could think about something other than the pain no medication could touch. The knee had rescued him before. Surgery freed him from the rodeo and the memories that way of life stirred.

Limping to the trailer door, he lit another cigarette and stepped down into the frost-covered dirt unsurprised to see

Crowfoot already leaning against the pasture gate.

"Was beginning to think you were gonna sleep all day," Crowfoot took a sip of coffee as his rooster let loose yet again.

"I might've," Blue took his spot on the fence, "But who the hell can get any shuteye with that damn rooster going off."

Crowfoot's stare lingered on the Marlboro pinched between Blue's fingers.

"I finished the roof," Blue said before the conversation took a direction he didn't want to travel.

Crowfoot merely nodded before transferring his gaze to the horses out in the field.

"That oughta take care of your leak."

Crowfoot took another sip of the steaming black liquid, but said nothing.

"Got anything else needs fixed up?"

"Few things."

The seconds ticked by.

A horse whinnied.

Blue waited.

"You gonna tell me what, or do I have to guess?"

Crowfoot pushed away from the fence and took several strides toward his house before he turned back around. "You don't need me to tell you what needs fixed."

# 41

Her steps echoed down the dimly lit hall. Most of the doors were closed, or at least pulled nearly to. Either way, they were all dark, but as Lindsay rounded the corner she saw the glow emitting from her father's room. Despite the early hour, she'd expected him to be awake, waiting for her.

The right side of his mouth lifted in a smile when she stepped inside.

"L ... Lind ... say." He closed his eyes in obvious concentration. "I hoped you'd come back." His breath came out in short gasps.

Unlike her previous visit, she had nothing prepared, no words that fought to get out. Her anger and resentment replaced by weariness, both physical and mental. There was so much she still wanted to say and ask, yet she simply sat on the edge of the bed. The run, along with all the revelations that came with it, combined with a lack of sleep had siphoned away both her energy and bitter fury.

Using his foot, her father turned the wheelchair until he faced her. "You." Again, he had to close his eyes in order to finish his thought. "You still run?"

She nodded even though she sensed his comment was more of a statement of observance, of her disheveled and sweaty appearance, than a genuine question.

"Good."

They stared at one another for a while. The slightest effort, such as talking or moving the wheelchair, left him spent and she could see him gathering strength to go on.

Lowering her gaze, she said, "I've never stopped running."

"I never ... want ... wanted to ..."

The grief in his voice drew her chin up. She stared into the face of the man she'd spent the last nine years despising.

"Hurt you," he finally got out. Reaching down beside his useless left leg, he produced a sheet of paper. "I'm sorry." The words were clear and precise, and this time he kept his eyes open and focused on her.

She looked away again as he handed her the awkwardly folded note. Her hand trembled as she reached for the letter.

Her father's eyes brimmed with emotion. Lindsay could see eagerness on his face. He wanted her to read his message, yet she clutched the paper in her sweaty palm without unfolding it. She didn't trust herself to stay composed, and she wasn't ready to let him see her breakdown.

Not wanting to concede to his guilt, she stood. "I'll read it on my way home."

Disappointment flashed across his face. The flaccid muscles on his left side made it hard to read his expression, but no doubt this was his apology for all that had transpired. Abandoning the very emotions that had dogged her for so long was not something she could do at the mere hint of atonement so Lindsay stood and made her way outside without looking back.

Her hair and forehead were still damp from sweat and the icy breeze scraped across her skin. She shivered.

Common sense told her to go inside, call a cab or even Clay. Instead she sat on the edge of a cold concrete planter. There were no flowers, only the remnants of a barren, dying patch of Pampas grass. Cigarette butts and lumps of chewed gum littered the piles of sun-bleached mulch.

Unfolding her father's words, she read,

Lindsay,

There's so much I have wanted to say to you, but now that you're back I don't know where to start. It is unfair to say, but seeing you again has brought me more joy than I deserve. I only wish I could stand and hold you or at least speak my feelings directly to you instead of this letter, but if uselessness is my only punishment, I am lucky. I deserve worse.

Please believe I never meant to hurt you or drive you away. Me and your mother only wanted the best for you. We misjudged what the best was, and I have regretted that every day. Even as I write this I wish that somehow I could turn back the clock. Not for myself or for the ability to walk and talk again, but to give you the life you once wanted. My greatest hope is that one day you can still find happiness.

You asked me about my dreams. Yes, I have sat up in bed and for one brief joyous moment thought it was all a nightmare. Then the truth would hit me. I wish I could say that I have dreamt of my grandchild. It hurts now to write that word, but I only thought of the child I lost. You.

Love Dad

His handwriting became smaller and harder to read at the bottom of the page. The line below his signature almost unreadable, but she reread the words three times. Waiting, expecting, yet the rush of emotion she anticipated never materialized. Not long ago she had dreamed of hearing these very words. Of shaming her father and forcing him to see the wrong he committed, but this apology did not conjure the sense of victory she once imagined.

What did she feel?

Anger? Not on the same scale, or with the same determination she once possessed, but a single letter could not erase years of heartache.

Sadness? Maybe, for now it was clear that no matter how many sorrowful admissions of guilt she heard, nothing could replace the life she lost.

Cheated? That one word summed it up more than any other. Fate had cheated her from hearing her father's words. Her stubbornness had cheated her from facing the facts before now. Blind resentment cheated her of her true memory. All this time it had been easier to hate her father and blame him than to accept the fact, that yes, they let her down, but even more she'd let herself down.

When he rousted her out of bed that morning, she could have said no. In the car, on the way to Dallas, she could have said stop. At the clinic, while he'd gone inside to sign the documents and take care of the paperwork, she could have gotten out of the car and disappeared. Yet she did nothing.

Her dad wasn't without fault. Lindsay never would have made the trip to Texas on her own. He could have stayed with her instead of coming back outside and sending her in to fend for herself. And in the days and weeks afterwards, before she left, he could have consoled her, or let her mention the whole ordeal without frowning and casting a worried look her mom's direction.

Lindsay couldn't say who deserved more blame, but ultimately she was the one who had to live with her inaction. Tomorrow, the next day, or next year, she would be the one to come to terms with the past, on her own and without the crutch of blaming someone else.

Wednesday and Thursday mornings passed in similar fashion. Lindsay set out before dark for her run, and just as the sun came up, she would find herself in front of her father's nursing home. However, unlike the first trip, she now went of her own volition, not at the insistence of her rebellious legs, and she took a more direct route at a slower pace.

Each visit followed the pattern set the first day. He would smile and speak a few lines, which she guessed were well practiced and rehearsed because at a certain point he gave up and handed her a letter that answered, or at least addressed, questions she asked the previous morning. By Friday, Lindsay found herself looking forward to the daily meeting.

Clay had gone back to Baylor to finish out the semester. Fortunately, he was due back today. Conversations with her mom were difficult without him. They didn't fight, but only because each and every word spoken was guarded and bland, unlike her father where they continually plunged into the scars of the past.

Lindsay's only real outlet were the visits to see her dad. No one here knew anything about Blue, but still she thought about him often. At she could talk herself into believing what they shared out there on the road was nothing more than a diversion. A way to not think about her destination, but then out of nowhere she would miss him with such intensity it left her nauseous and itching to pick up the phone and call to see if he was still camped at Crowfoot's. But what would she say if he was? He'd hurt her. With his words, his actions and his aloofness. And if she let him, chances were he'd do so again.

Still, each talk with her father brought her closer to some unseen finish line. She didn't have the foresight to know if the path was a 10K or a full-blown marathon, but for the first time in years she believed maybe she was on the right course.

At the sight of Amberwood Nursing Home, she slowed and began her cool-down routine. By now, she'd identified her father's window and could see the soft pale glow within. No doubt, he watched for her, and for the first time she wondered if he'd seen her coming that first morning.

She made her way inside and down the quiet hall. The nurse at the desk looked up as she passed, but no more than a fleeting glance.

Each time she saw her father, she recognized a bit more of the man she once loved and clung to for support. Physically, he didn't look as tired, though that could be because she'd gotten used to the sight of him. Nevertheless, he seemed to get stronger each day, saying a bit more and perhaps even moving with less effort. Mentally, they both had become stronger.

Yesterday, she stayed and read his note while he watched. Neither of them broke down, although there were times his eyes flooded, and she had to look away to remain in control of her emotions.

"How's my girl?" he asked when she entered the room.

"Cold. I thought the tip of my nose was going to fall off." Taking her usual seat on the edge of the bed, she bent down to peer out the window at the clouds. "Feels like it could snow."

"You ... you." He paused and took a deep breath. "You used ... to ... luh ... love ..."

She nodded. "I still love the snow." She'd already learned he got all the more frustrated if she finished his sentences for him, but he didn't seem to notice when she pressed on as if he had finished his thought.

"I knew you did."

"Some things never change."

Her father shook his head. "Everything changes."

A nurse poked her head in. "You okay, Mr. Parker? Anything I can get you before I leave?"

He lifted his right hand and waved her off. When they were alone again, he said, "I knew, because of your choices."

Lindsay frowned. Partly because his words were difficult to understand and partly because she was unsure where the conversation was headed. "My choices?"

"To live." After a few seconds he continued, "Santa Fe, Taos, Durango, Big Bear, Park City."

Her eyes widened. Clay told her about him tracking her to Utah, but she had no idea her dad knew more than that.

"I lost you after Utah."

A lump formed in her throat.

"Your friend. The foreigner. In Utah," he added at her confused look.

"Sven?"

"He told me you hated me. Said you never wanted to come home." Her father didn't look at her as he spoke. "Until then ... I thought ... you ... were ... just afraid."

"I was afraid." She lowered her voice. "I hated everyone. You, me, the whole world."

For several minutes, the only sound in the room was her father's labored gasps.

Finally she said, "Sven wanted to marry me. I ran away from him, too."

"Did you love him?"

The question, like the entire direction of the conversation, made her wary. She didn't know how to answer. There'd been times in her life when she thought she loved someone only to discover she loved something about them, but not the entire package.

"Not the way I needed to," she finally answered.

"Did you love that Hawkins boy?"

"No ... but I thought I did." Yesterday, she'd asked her father about Rusty, if he knew what became of her old boyfriend, but the mention of his name shook her father, and she hadn't been able to understand his reply. Even though their talks had been candid, she was surprised to hear him bring Rusty up on his own.

"He loved you."

"How do you know?"

"He told me."

"When? Does he still live in Norman?"

"Read." He handed her the piece of paper.

She started to unfold the slip until her dad put a hand in her wrist. "Not now," he said as he leaned his head back. "I'm tired." With his eyes closed, he asked, "Is Clay back?"

"He'll be home this afternoon."

"Send him ... to ... see me."

"Hey! Whoa!" Donnie jumped out in front of the truck.

Blue rolled down the window.

"Hang on a second. Don't leave. I got something for you."

Donnie set his Stetson down on the hood and took off for Crowfoot's house. The screen door barely banged before he was back out on the porch again. Blue didn't like the grin on his buddy's face.

Stuffing his hat back down on his unruly hair, Donnie said, "This is the address of the place I dropped her off."

"Who?"

"Lindsay, dumbass."

"I don't want that." He started to roll up the window, but Donnie grabbed hold of the glass.

"Crow said you were headed down to the city."

"To get Briley something for her birthday. If I don't get it in the mail today she'll never get it in time. Might not anyway."

"Stillwater's closer." Donnie spit a wad of snuff juice into the dirt. "They got stores, and a post office. Supposed to snow later. Why go all the way to Oke City when the roads could get slick? Unless you got other ideas."

"Wipe that smile of your face. I don't have to explain a damn thing to you or anybody else, but I'll tell you just to shut you up. I can't get her present in Stillwater because I've already looked there and they don't have what I want. Besides, Lindsay's in Norman, not Oklahoma City."

"Ain't a shittin' difference. They're right there together. And why'd you shave, and put on that nice shirt. Don't be so damn stubborn. Take the address."

Blue gritted his teeth. "You really think I'd need your help to find her? We rode halfway across the country together. I know more about her than you'll ever know."

"Whatcha gettin' Briley?"

"It's a surprise." And with that he put the truck in gear and punched the gas.

Donnie let go of the window and jumped back as Blue fishtailed down the rutted drive.

Crowfoot walked up. He waved his hand to clear the air of the dust Blue had kicked up with his hasty departure. "Kind of testy, ain't he?"

"Yeah." Donnie scratched his head. "He wouldn't take the address. Said he didn't need it. Claimed he was only going shopping for Briley."

"You believe him?"

The two men watched as Blue turned out onto the pavement without slowing down the least bit. They heard the powerful motor accelerate as he gave it gas.

"Shit, I don't know." Donnie stuffed another pinch of Copenhagen between his lip and gum. "Blue's moods and notions are harder to figure than some hormonal woman's."

"Or a love-struck fool." Crowfoot smiled.

"You think he's going to find her?"

"Does horse shit stink?"

# 42

Store after store. Row after row of pink boxes. Shelf after shelf of dolls that cried, crawled, walked, talked, smiled, winked, slept, and pissed themselves. About the only thing Blue hadn't spotted was one that shit itself, and at this point, not even that would surprise him. What he hadn't found was a present for Briley. Here he was at yet another mega toy store with nothing to show for it.

A damn saddle. Buster had gotten her a saddle, promised her a horse, and who knew what else. Blue couldn't top that.

The whole thing pissed him off. The idea of his daughter being under the influence of the man, forcing horses and all that crap down her throat. Before long Buster would have a barrel course set up in his corral, and he'd want to start hauling her all over the country.

He'd taken dozens of trips with the man. Buster expecting—no counting, on Blue to win. And when he did, everything was fine. Buster would be all smiles and hang his arm over Blue's shoulder while somebody snapped a picture. People would stop by the horse trailer to offer congratulations, and Buster would say things like, "Hardest-working cowboy I know," or "Blue's got enough talent even I can't screw him up," or "Better than any son I could have."

Lose, and it was an entirely different story. Ten minutes after the rodeo, they'd be loaded and on the road. Buster never yelled or screamed like some of the other competitors' dads. He simply said nothing. Least not for the first hour or so. There were only a handful of junior rodeos near the house, so most of their trips were long. A hundred miles or so in he would start in, saying things like, "What a waste," "Don't know why I bother," and "Never shoulda' expected anything else."

That was Buster's problem. He never had. Never had a son of his own, so he tried to make Blue it. Never had to work for the ranch he inherited, so he thought the world should always give him what he wanted. Never had competed for a damn thing, so he fed off Blue's glory.

Then when the scholarship offers came in, Buster crowed like a bantam rooster. He strutted around the College National Finals as if he'd invented the sport.

Not that it was all bad. Blue conceded they had a lot of good times, visited a ton of places. He owed Buster for giving him a start in life. He hated to guess where he'd be without the man, but he'd repaid his debt, whether the old bastard admitted it or not.

"Excuse me." Blue addressed a woman with two young kids and a swollen belly which announced a third not far off. She barely looked old enough to be out of high school, yet she had a basket piled high with diapers and formula. "Excuse me, Miss," he tried again when she kept walking.

"Me?" She stopped. The smallest child, a boy, sat in the basket his tiny feet kicking like a swimmer's.

"How old is your daughter?" Blue pointed to the oldest hiding behind her momma's leg.

The woman cast him a worried look.

"My daughter turns four this Friday," he explained. "And I don't know what to buy her. I've been away so I don't have a clue what little girls her age like."

The mother's face relaxed. She pulled the child out from behind her. "She's five."

"Great. That's close." Blue knelt down. "Hi."

The girl buried her face, so Blue stood and again stared expectantly at the woman.

"She's shy."

He nodded. "If money was no object, what would you buy her?"

The woman laughed. "Money's always an object, but I'd love to build her a playhouse. With real windows and curtains and stuff."

"Do they sell those here?"

"No, they just carry the plastic ones. You have to build the nice ones yourself."

"Oh."

"I like Barbies," the little girl announced.

Blue smiled, but the sound of her tiny voice stirred his sadness. Briley deserved better than this. Him begging for answers from complete strangers. Maybe he should call his daughter and ask what she wanted.

He thanked the woman and the little girl and set off determined to go call Briley, but his enthusiasm died once he left the store. An icy drizzle had started to fall, but more than the weather dampened his mood. Ruby would answer and he'd have to hear a speech about the way he'd treated Buster, and how he should come home, and how money couldn't make up for him being gone. In the end, he'd get mad and hang up without ever talking to Briley.

Pulling out of the strip mall, he paused to let a jogger pass by. What made people want run in weather like this? Lindsay had gotten up to jog in colder temperatures and at least once in the snow. He watched this woman until she disappeared down the street. Even though the two looked nothing alike, she made him think of Lindsay. Shopping for Briley had been so much easier with her by his side.

Hell, breathing had been easier.

Enjoying the solitude of the afternoon, Lindsay leaned back on the couch, flipping through the channels. She needed to get up and change clothes, but she couldn't get motivated. Clay wanted to take her up to Bricktown tonight, to celebrate her homecoming, but the idea held little interest to her. Not only did she not have anything to celebrate, but it seemed crazy they'd transformed a rundown area of downtown Oklahoma City into a touristy hot spot.

However, Clay and their mother would be back from their visit to the nursing home soon, so she really needed to get moving to avoid disappointing him. Lindsay had tried to match her brother's enthusiasm, and she was glad he was home from college, but her dad's letter this morning left her with a heavy heart.

Almost the entire page had been dedicated to Rusty. The fact her father hadn't liked him and for years blamed the boy for costing him his daughter, but then a few years back he decided to track Rusty down.

Her old boyfriend lived an hour and a half west of Oklahoma City in Clinton, Oklahoma, or at least he did when her dad found him. He worked as a loan officer in a bank, and the two of them had gone to lunch. According to her father, Rusty broke down in tears when told the real reason Lindsay left. He told her dad that a part of him would always love her so now her dad wanted her to call him or go for a visit in the hopes they could pick up where they left off.

But Lindsay knew that would never be possible. She couldn't simply turn back the clock and pretend nothing went wrong. Nonetheless, the revelation made her sad, as it no doubt had her father.

In the note, her dad admitted to hoping the worst for Rusty. That he would be broke and worthless, living out of some rundown mobile home in a seedy trailer park. At least then, he could've held onto some sense of accomplishment that he'd prevented her from a bad life, but Rusty had proven him wrong, by making something of himself. And now, sitting on the couch, a part of her wished her father had been right. Rusty had moved on, her mother had certainly moved on. It seemed as if only she and her father bore the scars of yesteryear.

Lindsay stopped her restless clicking of the remote and stared at the screen. A group of men were huddled around a poker table. Her heart quickened. One of the players had a black cowboy hat and for one brief second she thought it was Blue, but when the camera focused on the man, he had long black hair and a beard and the announcer said his nickname was Jesus.

Except for the hat, he looked nothing like Blue. Iceman, that's what that fan called Blue at the filling station. It suited him more now than she realized at the time. Her pulse ebbed. It irritated her that she'd gotten so excited at the prospect of seeing him on television. She reached for the remote, but then there he was. Not Blue, but Sergio. With that cocksure grin, and smart-aleck expression. She found herself wishing Blue was there, to wipe that condescending smugness off the man's face. The way he had in the streets of Cripple Creek.

This had to be old footage, because she was willing to bet Sergio still bore bruises from that altercation. Turning off the television, she stood to go get ready, but her Mom burst into the living room, stomped across the carpet, down the hall to her room, and slammed the door.

Clay came in a few seconds later. He shook his head and dusted snowflakes off his shoulders.

"What's going on?"

"Dad sent her out of the room so he could talk to me alone. Mom went manic on the way home because I wouldn't tell her what he said." Clay walked through the front room and into the den before turning around. "Come on, he wants me to give you something."

She followed her brother to the old shed in the backyard where an inch of white powder now covered the grass. Clay unlocked the door and began unstacking boxes from the top shelf.

"Hope you're not looking for the sleds. I don't think there's enough—"

"Here they are." Clay sneezed as dust filtered down into his face. "You want me to carry the boxes up to your room?"

"What's in them?"

Cobwebs hung from his hair and he had a gray smudge across one cheek, but Clay smiled anyway. "Your stuff." He pulled off first one lid, then the other.

There were her trophies, plaques, and medals, along with other relics of the past.

Clay reached down and held up a gold metal. "About a year after you left, Mom went nuts one day and made me help her load this stuff in the car. We drove down to the 7-11 and threw it all in the dumpster."

Lindsay shook her head.

"I called Dad at work and told him, so he left the post office, climbed inside the can, and rescued it all. It's been hidden out here under the Christmas decorations ever since."

They each carried a container to Lindsay's room in the house. Clay sat his down and looked around the sparsely decorated bedroom. "Maybe it'll seem more like home now."

Lindsay tried to picture her dad crawling in a dumpster, but the only real image she could conjure of him was in a wheelchair.

"I have one more errand to run for Dad. Soon as I get back I'll change, and we can head out."

"Does it have anything to do with me?"

"Of course, but don't worry," he added at her expression. "It's even better than the trophies."

Each item she pulled out of the box took Lindsay back in time. Her cross-country accomplishments, her high school annuals, a homecoming mum. Some of the things dated all the way back to junior high and elementary. Spirit ribbons, the stuffed Pound Puppy she used to sleep with every night. An honorable mention certificate for a fifth-grade spelling bee, although it bore a large stain probably from being in tossed in the garbage. She couldn't believe her dad salvaged all of this.

"Where did you get that?"

Lindsay looked up at her mother.

"I can't believe this," her mom picked up a plastic rose somebody once gave Lindsay for Valentine's Day. "Is what I was sent out of the room for? This junk." She dropped the flower.

"It's not junk to me."

"Maybe you shouldn't have left if you cared so much."

Lindsay just stared. She could see the anger, the pure hatred on her mother's face. "I can't believe you threw all my stuff away without a thought."

"You think you can just waltz in here like nothing happened. Your father might not remember the hurt, but I do. I threw away your things, but you threw away your life, and my future. You might as well have killed your father."

"If you'd have tried to understand, or listened to me, instead of hiding in your room, maybe none of this would've happened."

"Don't blame your mistakes on me."

Lindsay stood and stared at her mother. "What mistakes?"

"Sleeping around, getting pregnant, and all the rest." Her mom vaguely waved one hand.

"The rest of what?"

"Crying, carrying on, moping around the house, and all that other business." Her mom folded her arms across her chest.

*Business?* How dare her mother diminish the act with such an abstract word. Lindsay stepped toward her mother. "Business? Business? You can't even say the word can you?"

Her mom backed up several steps.

"Come on. Let me hear it. Say it."

The doorbell rang.

"Say what?"

"Abortion."

Her mom closed her eyes. She put a hand to her forehead.

The bell rang again.

"You better answer the door," her mother said in sort of a whiny moan.

"No. Not until you have the courage to say it." Tears streamed down Lindsay's cheeks. She challenged her mother to say abortion even though for years, she'd stricken the word from her own vocabulary.

"Come on let me hear you say it. Abortion."

"How dare you try to take the high road and hold it over my head. I did it for you. I thought it would be easier. I thought we could all move on afterwards."

"You thought I would just forget. You thought I wouldn't want someone to cry with me. To hold me and—"

"I did cry."

"Where? Locked away in your bedroom?"

Her mom lowered her head as the bell rang again, followed by a flurry of knocks. This time Lindsay pushed past and hurried to the front door. She flung it open and stared straight up into the dark bottomless abyss of Blue Riggins' soulful eyes.

# 43

Lindsay stepped outside and pulled the door shut behind her. "What are you doing here?"

Blue's fingertip caressed her cheek. "Are you okay?"

She turned away. "I'm fine."

"Were you crying?" He cradled her chin and gently forced her to look at him.

Determined to stay angry, she twisted away. "Is that how you thought you'd find me? Crying? Bawling my eyes out for you?"

"No, I ..." he shook his head. "I'm sorry for the way things went at Crowfoot's. I truly am. I wanted to see you again. To try and explain."

She blinked to buy time. Blue seemed genuine, but then again he was just like her mother. Things at Crowfoot's. Neither could say what needed to be said. Did he even know what he had done, or did Donnie have to tell him?

Blue watched, waited, studied her face. He'd played enough poker to gauge her frame of mind, and clearly she didn't want him here. Nor did she show any desire to discuss why she was so upset. Not with him anyway. He turned to walk away.

"Wait."

He stopped.

"Why are you here?" A hint of forgiveness laced her words.

"To see you," he replied without turning around.

"But why?"

He faced her with his hands up in the air in gesture of surrender. "What do you mean why?"

"I mean what happens next? Where are we supposed to go from here?"

"I don't know, Lindsay. Nothing happens the way I think it should. I quit trying to predict the future a long time ago. I can't say what next month holds, or next week. Hell, I don't even know about tomorrow, but right now I'm here and you're here, and that's all that matters to me. I screwed up. There's nothing else to say except I miss you. If you want me to leave, I will, but I had to come see you. To say I'm sorry for being a jackass."

She lowered her head. Again, Blue waited. This time he couldn't see her face, or read her eyes, and for a few seconds he feared she would send him away. Only when her shoulders quivered did he realize she was crying. A sob escaped her lips as he wrapped his arms around her.

They stood there under the gray clouds of winter with a light snow falling. Blue held her, savoring the beat of her heart against his chest. The smell of her hair. The warmth of her skin. He closed his eyes as her tears dampened his shirt.

Nothing felt so right as her in his arms. The cold meant nothing. "I was never ashamed of you," he whispered. "Finding you has been the only good in my life—"

"Lindsay?"

At the sound of the woman's voice, she broke free of his grip and turned toward the door. "Go back in the house."

Lindsay spoke harshly.

"What's going on? Who is he?" Scorn dripped from the woman's words. "As your mother I have the right to know."

Blue tensed. Part of him wanted to step between the two and shelter Lindsay, yet he held back. She was more than capable of taking care of herself.

"Don't act like you suddenly care. Go hide in your room."

"I do care. I've always cared."

Lindsay shook her head. "You sure as hell never showed it."

"That's not fair." Tears welled in the older woman's eyes. "You were always your father's girl. I never had a chance."

"Go ahead. Twist this around until you're the victim. Poor Mom. Nobody loves her. Nobody cares about your feelings. Nobody understands. Everyone is sick of the routine. Clay, Dad. Me. It was always about you. Be quiet, you don't want to upset Mom." Lindsay adopted a mocking tone. "Think of your mother, you don't want to bring on another spell, another migraine."

"I never dreamed I'd have to stand here listening to my own daughter run me down."

"I'm not running you down. I'm telling the truth. The truth everyone else is too scared to say for fear you will launch into hysterics. No wonder Dad had a stroke."

"How dare you." The woman pushed open the door and raised a hand as if to slap Lindsay. "You blame me! You blame me!" A cold fury laced her tone. "We both know who destroyed him. You're the one who ran away. You're the one who left us here to deal with the problems you created. You want me to say it. I'll say it. Abortion. Abortion! Abortion!"

Leaning her head back the older woman screamed yet

again, "Abortion! Are you happy? Now the whole neighborhood knows the truth."

A new batch of tears streamed down Lindsay's cheeks,
and from somewhere deep down inside, she made a sound
that reminded Blue of a wounded animal.

"I'm not going to let you stand on your high horse and
preach to me like I'm the villain. That might work on your
father, but I still remember what happened. You spout about
the truth. Well, the truth is you slept with that boy. You got
pregnant. You ran away. Those were your decisions. Live with
them." Her mother turned on her heels and stomped inside
the house. Pausing in the doorway, with her back to them she
added, "You ruined this family. Not me."

Blue waited. He expected Lindsay to burst into tears, but
as her mother disappeared back inside the house, she instead
faced him and smiled. A timid, disillusioned smile of disbelief, but a smile nonetheless.

Her brows arched. "Sorry you tracked me down?"

Despite the charade, he recognized the hurt on her face.
Blue met her gaze to make certain she knew he understood,
and stood with her. "No. I'm only sorry I drove you away."

She looked at her feet. "Don't blame yourself. My
mother was right. Leaving, hurting people is what I do best.
I would've found a reason to leave sooner or later, whether
you gave me one or not."

Lindsay lifted her head. "She was right about everything
else, too. I lied to you."

Her scarlet cheeks glistened, and her black lashes were
damp. She looked so vulnerable, yet he'd never considered
her more beautiful. He wanted to hold her again, but she
backed away when he stepped forward.

"I never meant to lie," she whispered. "I wanted to tell

you the truth about my past, about why I ran away from home, but then you told me about your wife and how she died. And the one time I tried to explain you thought I meant adoption. And—"

"Don't do this," Blue said. "You don't have to explain."

"Yes, I do. You deserve that much. I needed you, and I couldn't bear to think how you'd view me after the choice your wife made. I feared you'd see me as weak if I told you about the ... the abortion." The word still felt foreign on her tongue, but she was determined not to hold anything back. "Without you, I never would've come back to face my family. I might've gotten on a bus bound for Oklahoma, but I never would have ridden the entire way. You gave me the ability, the strength, and the motivation to come home again."

"Someone would've given you a ride."

"The ride was the least of it. By falling for you, I didn't have to think about the past with every breath. I knew you were hurting, too, and I was selfish. I prodded and exposed your scars, just so mine wouldn't ache. I went through your photo album. Late at night, I sat and stared at Briley. I looked at the pictures of your wife's swollen belly. I saw the smiles on both your faces. I thought about the love y'all had and lost because your wife chose to take a risk. Meanwhile my family turned their back on me and simply shuffled me off without any real chance to make a choice. They were ashamed of me, and I let their shame settle in my mind and fill the marrow of my bones."

Blue sighed. Shame. He knew the gut-wrenching feeling well. Shame. It had dogged him longer than he cared to admit. Shame. The one thing he never found an escape from. Not at the poker table. Not out there on the road these past years. Not here on Lindsay's doorstep.

He cleared his throat. "That's what brought me back to you. I was ashamed when you left, but I was too stubborn to do anything about it. I wanted to blame you for losing Staci. When she died it hurt, but it didn't seem real. I always felt she was still close, just outside of my reach. I knew she was gone." He shook his head. "I thought somehow I could find her again. Over time, I lost that hope. That happened before we ever met, but it took finding you for me to admit it."

"Oh, Blue." This time she reached for him. "Why do we have to be so screwed up?"

"Maybe that's why we found each other."

She laughed. A sad, dejected laugh. "Two train wrecks meeting in the night."

They held each other for several minutes, surrounded by the utter silence of a gentle snowfall. Neither spoke, for fear they would have to let go and face what came next.

A car pulled into the drive, but Blue ignored the distraction. "I'll go back to Crowfoot's and pick up the trailer. I can park out by the lake. We can—"

"What's going on? Is everything okay?"

Lindsay let go and smiled. "Clay meet Blue."

"Nice to meet you." He extended a hand.

"Same here." The boy had a stiff grip.

"Hey, you're that poker guy."

She threw her hands in the air. "The world-famous Iceman," she teased. "The whole world knew you before me."

"We play at school. I've seen you on TV. You're the man, when it comes to bluffing."

"Thanks."

"I'll run in and change," Clay said. "You gonna come with us, Blue?"

Blue looked to Lindsay.

"Clay's taking me out to eat."

"To celebrate her being back. We're going to run up to Bricktown. You're more than welcome to join us."

"Thanks, but I have a few things I need to take care of."

"You should come," she said once her brother went inside. "Clay won't mind."

Blue cleared his throat and gazed off down the block. "I still have to find Briley something for her birthday. I'm not even sure I can get it there in time."

"So deliver it yourself. Or forget the present altogether and just be there for her party. Having her daddy would mean more than anything you can buy."

"I can't," he whispered.

"Why?"

Blue didn't want to answer. "What about a playhouse? With real curtains and cabinets? Not those cheap plastic ones, but the kind you build. Think she'd like that?"

"I'm sure she would. And she would like it even more if you built it with her, and sat inside afterwards sipping imaginary tea."

"I can't do that."

"Yes, you can. You need to."

"Don't you understand? Everyone else sees it as her birthday. They stand around celebrating, while all I can think is this is the anniversary of Staci's death."

Lindsay grabbed his shoulders. "Think about Staci. Think about what she would want you to do."

Blue's face turned hard. The muscles in his jaws tensed. His brows formed an angry V and his lips drew into a thin line before he said, "Drop it. I can't go back. Not now."

A voice inside her head told her to stop, but determined to break through, she ignored the intuition. "I know it's tough, but I came back to face my past and—"

"Yeah, and what did it get you. A face streaked with tears, and a fight with your mom. Maybe you should worry about your own problems and stay out of mine."

"Blue—"

"No, let me finish. Just because you looked at some pictures doesn't mean you have the answers. You don't know a thing about Staci, or how it feels to lose your whole life."

"I lost my child."

"You made a choice."

Their eyes locked. He could see the hurt his words inflicted, and for a second he thought Lindsay would turn away.

Instead, she surprised him. "Yeah, I had choice and I didn't take it. I let myself be led to what I can't help but feel was the wrong decision for me. And you're right, I don't know Staci, but I know she made a choice, too. You might think it was wrong, but your wife did what she thought was best. Show respect for her decision. Nothing will bring her back, but she lives in Briley. Even I can see that from the pictures. Staci's gone. You've already lost her. Go home, before you lose your daughter too."

He turned, and walked to his truck. Here in the street, along the curb, the snow was more of a dirty sludge. Lindsay called his name as he trudged through the slush.

"Blue! Blue! Blue!"

He opened the door and slid into the driver's seat, but she was there beside him before he could shut it.

"Don't do this," She urged. "Don't go away mad. For once I'm not trying to drive you away."

"You give me a speech I've heard a thousand times from a dozen different people, but you don't want to drive me away? What do you want?"

"I want to see you happy."

"Forget about me. What do you want for yourself?"

She nodded and stared at him with conviction. "I want to look at myself in the mirror and not cringe. I want to think about the past without being consumed by anger and regret. I want to love and be loved without thinking I don't deserve it."

"I don't know how to give you those things."

"I'm not asking you to. I have to find them on my own."

Blue nodded, not because he fully understood, but because he accepted the fact she was lost to him. He started the truck.

"Where are you going?"

"Back to Crowfoot's."

Disappointment crossed her face. "Please, Blue, just—"

"Don't say it. I can't. Maybe later, but not now."

She kissed him on the cheek. "Call me," she said, but he only nodded and put the truck in gear. He drove away, without looking her direction.

# 44

Lindsay watched until Blue's truck rounded the corner. An increasingly common sight in their relationship.

*Relationship?*

She shook her head. Why she'd even have such a thought was a mystery. They had shared a few things—a trip—a pain filled past. And a few weeks of passion, yet so many things divided them. Lindsay wondered if she'd ever even see him again as she trudged back to the house.

"Where's Blue?" Clay asked when she entered the house.

"Gone." She flopped on the couch. At least her mom was nowhere to be seen. Probably sequestered in her room under the guise of another spell.

Her brother sat beside her. "Janine just called again." He laid a hand on Lindsay's shoulder. "I told her you're fine, but she's really worried. You need to call her."

"I will."

Lindsay couldn't say why she'd put off dialing her friend, but somehow she wasn't ready to go into all her problems just yet. Especially those involving Blue. Janine idolized him so, thought he was the perfect man, and Lindsay didn't want to hear a speech about how stupid she was to let him go.

"I promised her you would call before we left," Clay

said, handing her his cell.

"Okay, okay." She grabbed the phone. The last thing Lindsay wanted was to make a liar out of her brother.

Blue lit a cigarette as he pulled away from Lindsay's. Of the dozen or so scenarios that had ran through his mind beforehand, none of them fit the actual scene. She hadn't outright rejected him, or blasted him for his behavior at Crowfoot's. No, she'd done worse. Lectured him.

He took a long drag on the Marlboro and rolled down the window. The cold air hit his flushed face. A few flakes were still coming down, but it wasn't snowing hard enough to make him roll up the glass. He should've known not to expect too much. His hopes and dreams never had stood up to reality.

Interstate 35 sat a good deal lower than the main thoroughfares of Norman. To reduce the grade, some of the on-ramps made sweeping three-hundred-degree turns that created grassy bowls. These pockets had collected more snow than other areas.

Blue might not have noticed any of this if not for the hordes of people that had flocked to these spots to sled down the embankments. Some had actual plastic sleds, but most seemed content to hurl themselves downward on big pieces of cardboard. There were several piles of crumpled brown mush where the flattened boxes had become too wet to sit on and slide.

Blue shook his head as he made the circle and picked up speed to merge with traffic. There were so many things wrong with the picture. It was one thing for reckless teenagers to do something stupid, but a good percentage of those around the inclines were young kids, and Blue spotted more than one parent assisting a child up the hill. These people seemed unaware that only fifteen or twenty yards away there was an interstate. With icy pavement. Where cars, pickups, and semi's blew past at speeds of sixty miles an hour.

None of them seemed to care. They ran up the hills, tossed snowballs through the air, slid down to the bottom. All with smiles on their faces.

Janine answered on the third ring with, "It's about damn time."

"Is that anyway to greet an old friend?"

"It is when she leaves on the spur of a moment and doesn't call so much as once in over two weeks. Tell me about Blue."

"There's nothing to tell."

"A woman doesn't travel halfway across the country with a good-looking lumberjack of a man and have nothing to tell."

"How do you know he brought me back?"

"I know Blue, and I know you. He's too good a man to make a damsel in distress ride a filthy bus and you're too ..."

"Too what?"

Janine cleared her throat. "Well, I figured either he would take you all the way, or you'd be back in a few days, or somebody would call asking for a reference because you got halfway home and decided that was close enough."

Lindsay wanted to take offense or get mad, but she knew her friend's assessment was the truth.

"Besides, Clay told me you were out front talking to Blue."

"And you conjured up the rest of that baloney in the ten minutes since."

Janine laughed. "Pretty much. So what's going on between the two of you?"

"It's complicated."

"Of course it is. Anything with testicles or tires is complicated. Start with how you ended up with him instead of on a bus."

Taking a deep breath, Lindsay launched into the story: Idaho, Wyoming, Colorado, Kansas. She laid out their slow crawl back to Oklahoma. Janine asked a few questions, but for the most part simply listened. Chris, Sergio, Donnie, Crowfoot and Kacy Jo. Lindsay covered them all, but she only mentioned Blue in regard to how he related to these other people. For some reason, she was reluctant to divulge the more intimate details of her travels.

Janine saw right through her. "Yada, yada, yada. Tell me about Blue."

"I did."

"No, tell me how the two of you ended up in bed together."

"Who said we did?" Despite the line of questioning, Lindsay realized just how much she'd missed Janine's voice.

"You forget. I know you. The less you talk about something, the more it means to you."

"It's over now, so there's no reason to dwell on him."

"Over? How could it be over if he's still there?"

"He's not. I just sent him away." Lindsay wanted to sound unaffected, unconcerned, but even she could hear the sadness in her tone.

"Why?" Janine wondered. "You're leaving something out. What's going on? Don't make me come down there."

This time Lindsay told the complete story. She gave her friend every last detail, right down the photo album, the way Blue's wife had died, the way she lied to him in Colorado, and her reasons for leaving Crowfoot's. She ended with her and Blue's last confrontation just a little while ago.

"I still don't see why you wanted him to leave."

"I already have all I can handle here."

"Don't let the past get in the way of the future. You can't change what's already happened."

The closer Blue got to Crowfoot's, the easier it became to see the other side. The danger of playing in the snow-filled bowls didn't seem as real without the hum of the busy highway so near. The joy etched on the kids' faces dulled the sense of idiocy he'd first labeled the participants with. Maybe it wasn't the best place to sled, but chances were nothing would happen. People had probably used those embankments for years, and at least the children would have a memory of an afternoon shared with their parents. For the rest of their lives they would smile each time they drove that section on interstate.

Lighting another cigarette, Blue stared ahead at the pavement. What would make up Briley's childhood memories? His infrequent calls? Did she look forward to them? How could she? It wasn't as if they occurred often enough to expect. His visits? Not likely when he hadn't been back in almost a year.

He took a long drag. What were his own memories?

Snatches of conversation with his dad, but no real fondness for the man. Same with his mom, even though she lived a good deal longer. They'd both seemed so old, so tired, so busy trying to run the motel and restaurant.

Ruby was the one who nurtured him, read to him. Whispered stories at bedtime. Then there was Buster. Much as Blue hated to admit it, the man shaped his life far more than either of his parents. Buster introduced Blue to a way of life that enabled him to forge his place in the world, to define his existence.

Blue Riggins—Rodeo Cowboy.

For a time that had been enough. Then Staci came along. She would've always been enough if ...

If what? That had always been the question.

If he'd been there the day the doctor discussed the dangers of Staci halting her blood thinners during the pregnancy? But no, he'd been off at that rodeo in Arizona and only knew what Staci shared with him.

If he didn't blame her death on his desire to make the national finals? But he'd missed most of her appointments while traveling.

If she'd never become pregnant in the first place? But she'd wanted a child so badly. And so had he.

The thought had always been there, surfacing only at times like now when he was at his worst. Used to be, he drank to cover the cancer that threatened to spread beyond the dark folds of his brain. Then he learned to shove the vile notion to the back of his mind while sober.

Blue looked at himself in the rearview mirror. He wanted to say it. To finally speak the words aloud and get them out in the open. He would be the only one to hear. He parted his mouth. The Marlboro dangled from the corner of his lip.

He stared at the desperate eyes looking back for as long as he could, but then he dropped his gaze back to the road.

How could he? How could he speak aloud the most self-ish thought he'd ever had? How could he say part of him wished Briley had never been born—when it wasn't true?

Rolling down the window he snatched the cigarette from his mouth and threw it out into the cold. The rest of the pack followed.

His friends were right. If Staci saw him today, she would break down and cry at the sight of him. She would hate who he'd become. Blue could feel her disappointment. He could never justify the despicable thoughts that sometimes infected his soul. How many nights had he and Staci lain in bed to-gether and talked about the future? Trying out the sound of baby names. Micah Blue Riggins ... Lacey Ann Riggins ... Ella ... Kaden ... Briley Nichole Riggins.

Lindsay was right. He had turned his back on Staci's de-cision. And if he really admitted it, his decision as well. Not that he ever could have changed her mind. Staci wanted to be a mother. Heart valve be damned. She never would have chosen a different path.

So determined to be a mom that Staci lied to him. Kept the truth of the doctors warnings to herself. Until it was too late.

Damn it, she lied to him.

Staci lied to him. Didn't trust him with the truth. Maybe that's what hurt most of all.

Blue got off at the next exit, turned underneath the overpass, and headed back the way he'd just come. Some-how, he would play a part in Briley's memories. Somehow, he would find a shred of the dream he once shared with Staci. Somehow, Blue would find a new truth he could live with.

## 45

The bedsprings creaked beneath Ruby as she rolled over and opened one eye. She didn't need the clock on the bedside stand to know she'd overslept. The lavender patch of sky visible through the curtains told her enough. The last few nights had been worry-filled exercises of frustration, so it said something that her body had finally given in. Not exactly a soothing, peaceful sleep, but a night full of crazy dreams beat one with no rest at all, and Ruby had to start somewhere. They weren't nightmares in the true sense, but simply strange.

Cinching her robe, she slid on her slippers and made her way down the hall to start a pot of coffee. Buster wasn't likely to come for breakfast, but she'd have something ready in case. The hairs on the back of her neck stood on end as she crossed the living room. Stopping, she looked around. Nothing seemed out of place. She tried the doorknob. Still locked. Yet something still felt out of whack as she headed to the kitchen.

While the Folgers percolated, Ruby thought about the strange dreams. One thing was clear. She watched too many Westerns and read far too many romance novels set in the same time period. In one dream, Buster rode his horse right inside the café, grabbed her arm, and attempted to pull her

up into the saddle. The harder she tried to climb on, the taller
the horse and rider became. In another, she got lost amidst a
sea of cattle with Briley perched on her shoulders. No matter
where they turned, a side of beef blocked the way. Briley just
giggled, but Ruby had worried a stampede would take them
both down.

There'd been others of similar theme. A stagecoach
pulled up to the café, but instead of people getting off, snakes
slithered out. Ray threw down his apron and headed for the
door. Ruby had clung to his legs and begged him not to quit
on her too, but Ray said, "Ain't no man going to stick around
here with you and them snakes."

That's what it all boiled down to. Her greatest fear. That
no man, in any capacity, would love her forever. The worry-filled sleepless nights. The crazy dreams. The reason she
couldn't just say yes to Buster's proposal.

Ruby had a problem and she knew it. If only Buster
wasn't so stubborn. He could give her more time or leave
their relationship the way it had always been. The debate continued in her mind as she mixed biscuit dough. A yes meant
pledging forever. A yes meant giving all of herself. A yes
meant losing her independence, her security. Buster could
provide for them with ease, but she and Briley might prove
to be more than he bargained for. Ruby had taken care of
herself for so long.

What if she closed the restaurant, sold the place, married, moved out to the ranch, and then he changed his mind?
Where would that leave her and Briley?

It was easy to claim nothing would change, but look at
all that changed since she said no. She'd barely seen Buster
since. He'd stopped by twice, but only for a few minutes,
more to see Briley than anything else. Claimed his cows need-

ed doctoring, but Ruby knew better. No doubt the herd did have the scours, he'd just turned them out on winter wheat, but he had cowboys to take care of that. Buster was punishing her for rejecting him. She could only pray this pouting was temporary.

Biscuits in the oven, Ruby showered and dressed. All the while, she tried to convince herself she'd made the right decision. What was the point of them getting married? They already had each other. Surely, Buster didn't doubt her devotion, her faithfulness. He stayed the night anytime he felt like it. She never pressured him to stay or go. Most men would like that kind of freedom.

Marriage worked for some, but Ruby knew plenty of others that had been destroyed by the institution. After her father died, her mother became a shell of the lady she'd once been. And her sister Opal in California. Her husband's infidelity and abandonment changed her. The whole family knew about Wanda, even if Opal refused to admit the woman was more than a roommate. Then there was Blue. Look how Staci's death affected him.

Tying her shoes, Ruby nodded to herself. She'd heard the old phrase, "Better to have loved and lost, than never loved at all," but love is one thing, marriage another, and she'd yet to meet a person forever scarred because they'd never married. It was like those romance novels she read. Love came easy, it was the business side of things and the outside world that complicated matters. Even Romeo and Juliet would have lived if they hadn't argued against society. Ask for too much and you might just get more than you wanted.

She couldn't smell the biscuits yet, so on her way down the hall she peaked inside Briley's door. Nothing said innocence like the sleeping face of a child, and sometimes Ruby needed the tranquil sight to remind her of the things still right in life. Standing in the doorway, she stared at the wayward blonde curls. The flawless rosy cheeks. The gentle rise and fall of her tiny chest.

"She's beautiful, isn't she?"

Ruby jumped and gasped. Blue leaned forward without taking his eyes off his daughter. Until then, she hadn't seen him leaned back in the corner of the room.

"Didn't mean to scare you," he whispered, still watching Briley.

"What are you doing here?" Her voice sounded harsh, almost accusatory, so she quickly added. "I mean when did you get in?"

"Last night." He sounded tired. "She looks like Staci."

"She always has."

Without a single look Ruby's direction, he nodded.

"Coffee is on. Biscuits will be ready soon. I'll start the gravy and sausage."

"I'll eat later."

"You sound tired. Have you gotten any sleep?" She grimaced. He didn't like being mothered and she knew it, but she couldn't stop worrying about him just because he didn't like it.

Her fears that he'd take offense were unwarranted as Blue simply said, "I want to be here beside her when she wakes up."

Briley looked so cute, perched up in her booster seat. Blue sat beside her, behind the wheel of his big truck. Ruby could see the pride in the little girl's smile as they backed away, so even though the snakes from her dream had set up shop inside her stomach, she grinned and waved until they were out of sight. Ruby couldn't remember ever being this nervous.

*Briley, you be a good girl for your daddy.*

*Briley, don't whine and carry on, show your daddy that you're a big girl.*

*Briley, remember your manners.*

Blue had been the one to finally say, "Leave her alone. We'll get along just fine."

And they seemed to be. They had polished off breakfast and now were headed to Amarillo in search of a lumberyard. A playhouse? Where on earth did Blue come up with such an idea? No doubt, Briley would love the present, but it didn't seem like the kind of thing that would ever cross her brother's mind. Shaking her head, she headed inside the café to help Ray get ready for the lunch crowd. That woman Buster met in Oklahoma had to be behind this new side of Blue.

All through lunch, Ruby debated how best to break the news to Buster. If she called him and said, "Blue was back," it would come across as, "I told you so." But if she made no attempt to tell Buster, he would eventually show up and who knew what would happen. No doubt the two would argue. Blue would get mad and leave. Buster would chastise her for not warning him, and once again, Briley would be the one to suffer.

The lunch crowd kept her busy for several hours. She barely had time to take and deliver orders, refill glasses, and collect money, much less ponder Buster and Blue, but a little after one, the place thinned. With only two tables occupied, both by locals who'd already been served, neither of which she particularly liked, Ruby reached for the phone and dialed

Buster's cell.

"Hello." A cow bawled in the background.

Maybe he'd told her the truth. "Can you hear me?" She still didn't trust those tiny little phones. She never expected anyone to hear a thing on them, but Buster swore by his.

"I'm kinda busy here, Ruby. What do you need?"

"Come for supper tonight." She'd already decided it would be better to get the two stubborn men together before Briley's party tomorrow. That way they could get their initial quarrel over with and not spoil the celebration.

"I'll try to make it, but it'll be late. I'm up to my elbows in cow shit, so I'll have to change first. Hang on."

She listened while he called out orders to one of his cowboys. Back on the line he said, "That dumbass Jimmy couldn't pour piss out of a boot."

"Blue came back for the party."

Another cow bellowed, drowning out Buster's reply.

"What did you say?" Ruby asked.

"Said I'll pass on supper. I'll be too damn tired to deal with his bullshit."

Ruby sighed, even though she'd expected him to bow out when he learned of her brother's return. "I hope you're not going to make some excuse to miss tomorrow night."

"I'll be at the damn party. You should know that. I'm not the one with a history of disappointing Briley, but I ain't got time for this now." He hung up without a goodbye.

"Hey Rube! A customer called out. "What kinda pie you got!"

"Lemon meringue and coconut cream." She never had liked Royce McEwen, and she damn sure didn't like him calling her Rube, so for the benefit of this week's female companion she added, "I might have a slice of that pecan your wife likes so much. You want me to check?"

"Give 'im hell, Ruby." Jim Sampson laughed from the other table. He was alone today, but he too had been known to show up with a woman other than his spouse.

Royce shot the other adulterer a look. Both lived just outside the small community of Grand. Jim farmed and ranched, while Royce strictly ran cattle. Neither had ever measured up to their daddy's reputation, and both considered themselves God's gift to women. Surprisingly, they'd married well, but the mere eighteen miles between here and Grand didn't stop them from flaunting their conquests on a regular basis. Ruby supposed they came here since she'd once been the other woman herself.

An hour later, Blue and Briley showed backed up. Through the front window, Ruby could see long boards jutting from the back of the pickup. "Did y'all find a playhouse?" she asked when they walked inside even though the answer was clear.

Briley shook her head. "I don't want a dollhouse."

Ruby frowned. "That's not very nice. Your daddy—"

Blue cut her off with a laugh. "She didn't like the ones with lace curtains and real windows. She settled on a fort."

"A fort?"

"For when the Indians come." Briley jumped into Ruby's arms.

She staggered from the weight of the child. "What Indians?"

"They won't scalp us if we have a fort."

Ruby gave Blue an apologetic look. "We watch a lot of Westerns."

He nodded. A sly grin lifted the corner of his mouth. "That's what Briley said. Except for the nights you make her go to bed early so you and Buster can kiss."

"We do not ..." Ruby stopped. The warmth of her cheeks told her they'd already turned red. She would only dig herself deeper by explaining. "Little girls are supposed to go to bed early."

"I'm not little. I'll be four tomorrow, and Blue says I can stay up late as I want." Her tiny head jutted forward as she pursed her tiny lips into a pout.

"Don't get sassy with me or you'll go to bed right now. And you should call him Daddy."

"I told her she could call me by my name if that's what she wanted."

"You think that's wise?"

Blue nodded. "I haven't earned the right to be called anything else."

# 46

"I'd cramp your style." Lindsay guided Clay toward the hall. "The two of you go. Have fun. You can't pick up girls with your sister tagging along."

"Come with us," Brandon, her brother's friend, said, "And Clay will be the only one looking."

Lindsay laughed. Not at Brandon's feeble attempt to woo her, but at Clay's gaping mouth. Brandon had given her the once over when they were first introduced, and for the last ten minutes he'd gone out of his way to make direct eye-contact.

"Are you hitting on my sister?"

Brandon shrugged and winked at Lindsay.

"That's sick, dude."

"What's sick is you never telling me you had a sister, much less a beautiful, sexy—"

"Save it for the club." Clay pushed his friend into the hall.

Brandon looked back over his shoulder. "At least come eat with us. We'll bring you back after if you want."

"No, thanks."

"My treat."

She gave the guy points for persistence.

"Dude, she's got a boyfriend," Clay said as they ducked into his room. "And I'm going to tell him to kick your ass if you don't cut it ..."

Their voices faded. Did Clay really think of Blue as her boyfriend? If not, what was Blue, and why couldn't she shake him from her head? She'd lived with other men for months on end, and they never infiltrated her mind the way he had. There were times when this had been a good thing. Without the distraction, she never would've made it back to Oklahoma, but now she needed to concentrate on matters at hand.

Like how to give back the money her dad had given her without inciting another round of arguing. This morning, he'd been adamant the funds belonged to her.

The front door closed with a bang. Seconds later Lindsay heard the roar of an engine as the boys took off for their Saturday night on the town. A tinge of regret hit her as she went to the window and watched them drive away. She should've gone. Life was going to go on whether she jumped on board or not, but something held her back, and there was more to it than she didn't want to encourage Brandon. After all, she could handle the affections of a wannabe Romeo much easier than another long, lonely night by herself.

Framed pictures dotted the hall's dark paneling. Most of the photos had been here as long as Blue could remember. Faces of people long dead. Grandparents, aunts, uncles he never knew. Others he recognized. His older sisters. The ones who moved away and never looked back. Ruby as a young girl and woman. And of course, there were those of himself. Alone, and with Staci. He turned away, not wanting to travel down that road.

In the living room, Ruby read in her recliner. Asleep and curled into a tiny ball, Briley nestled against his sister's hip. An old black and white movie filled the television screen.

His footsteps echoed on the hardwood floor. He stared out the front window at the darkness beyond the elms that partially shielded the house from the highway. Tonight, headlights were visible through the bare limbs. As a boy, he'd spent many a long night in his room listening to the world drive by and dreaming of a different life. That room now belonged to Briley.

Walking away from the window, he circled around behind Ruby's recliner and the empty chair he knew belonged to Buster.

"I wish you'd sit." Ruby turned her book face down on the arm beside her. "You're pacing like a lion in a cage."

"She always fall asleep this early?" He reached over his sister's shoulder to touch his daughter's cheek.

Ruby shook her head. "No, but today was a big day for her." She stared up at her brother. "For all of us."

He turned away from the hope in her voice and the joy on her face. Blue recognized his sister wanted to ask questions, pin him down on how long he planned to stay, but he wasn't ready for all that. He wanted to stay. Do the right thing. Be the father he should be, but it wasn't that easy.

That's what Ruby couldn't understand. Or Buster. Or Donnie. Or any of the others who liked to dispense advice. They acted like he was stupid. Unable to see what he should do. Blue knew damned good and well what he should do. He'd always known. That didn't mean doing the right thing came easy. A fat man knows he shouldn't go back for that second helping. An alcoholic knows he shouldn't have just that one to take the edge off, but doing the wrong thing was always easier. Eating that extra slice of pie, doing that shot—leaving.

Ruby loved him and understood the pain he felt was real. She wanted to help, to understand, but she'd always stayed. That's just what she did. She couldn't see the other side, so for Blue to sit down and talk to her the way she wanted, to try and explain the other side, was pointless.

Only one person knew how painful it was to come home again.

Lindsay hurried down the hall to answer the phone. Janine had already placed her nightly call so it was probably one of Clay's friends. Or a telemarketer, though it was late for that.

For one brief moment, Lindsay hoped the caller might be Blue, but like glitter in the wind, the fanciful notion dissipated. By the third ring she felt ridiculous. Like a school girl waiting on her latest crush to call. Or Cinderella, waiting to try on that shoe. Blue was a lot of things, but no one would mistake him for fairytale prince.

"Parker residence." She answered the way her father taught her so long ago.

"Lindsay?"

She smiled. "You're no telemarketer."

"Sorry to disappoint," Blue said. "But that's a career I've never considered. I couldn't sell a ceiling fan to the devil."

Unable to contain her happiness, she giggled. "Wanna bet? Just by calling, you've sold me on the idea you're a fairy prince."

This time he laughed. "Once a kid in grade school called me a fairy, but no one has ever confused me for a prince."

Lindsay hopped up on the kitchen counter. She kicked her bare feet. "I can't believe you actually called. You didn't even ask for the number."

"I memorized the number when you had me call your brother and the last thing you said to me before I left was to call."

"Since when did you ever do anything I suggested?" She cringed. Not wanting to think another lecture was on the way she quickly added, "I felt so bad when you left yesterday. I'm sorry for the things I said."

"Don't be. You were right. How was Bricktown?"

"Crazy. We got there late. After you left, I talked to Janine for almost two hours. She was quite put out at me for the way I treated you."

"I doubt that. How are she and Missy getting along?"

"Still butting heads, but Missy finally told her she was pregnant. She's due sometime in May, but Janine said she might go crazy before then. Said she might pack up and join me in Oklahoma. Just to get away."

"Janine will never leave the Talon behind. She might kill Missy, but she'll never leave Idaho."

"I couldn't imagine her anywhere else," Lindsay said. "Besides, I like knowing she's there. That way I know there's always one place I can go and be welcome."

Blue didn't like the sad, defeated tone of Lindsay's voice. He'd hoped she could talk him through his own doubts and anxiety, but she obviously had enough of her own. "Things still rough with your mom?"

"Not rough exactly. She's locked inside her room with a supposed migraine. With any luck, it'll be the weekend before she comes out and accuses me of blackmail and extortion."

"It'll get better."

Lindsay sighed. "I wouldn't bet on it. All this time I've been angry with my dad, blamed him for everything. The funny thing is I never stopped to think about her, but she did the same thing even back then."

Blue waited. He sensed Lindsay needed to talk.

"My father used to mean everything to me. I depended on him. Mom was always flaky, but growing up I never knew how crazy she really was. When I got pregnant, I didn't expect her to help. To give me a shoulder to lean on. To brush back my hair and tell me everything would be all right. I expected my father to do those things. That's why I blamed only him. Why I hated him. He let me down. My mom had been letting me down for years. And the worst thing, I let him just take care of everything his way when I got pregnant. Just like my mother always let him take care of everything. In the biggest moment of my life, I turned into my mother. My weak dishrag mother. I couldn't forgive myself for that." Her voice quivered.

Blue's heart broke for Lindsay. Hearing her cry made him ache for her, but he had no idea how to make Lindsay feel better.

"My dad wants to give me money," she said after a few silent seconds. "Nearly thirty-thousand dollars. He cried and pleaded with me when I tried to refuse, but there's no way I can keep it." She sounded stronger now, more composed.

"Why?"

"There are a thousand reasons not to, and only one why I should."

"Does the one outweigh the others?"

"Not for me. I can't put a price on my grief. I don't want

to be beholden to him just because I'm broke."

"I thought you said he wasn't to blame."

"He's not. Not entirely anyway, but if I take his money I'm saying a lot of things I don't want to. And then there's my mom. I'd prove her right all over again."

"Maybe you shouldn't worry about proving her right or wrong. Do what's right for you."

"I wish I knew. Last night at the restaurant, when Clay handed me the ATM card and savings book, I thought I knew. There was no way in hell I wanted that money, but then Clay explained the account started as our college fund. Clay wants me to keep it. Dad gave him half the account when he got a scholarship."

"So take it."

"It's not that simple. Dad kept the papers hidden in a safe-deposit box. Mom knew nothing about the account until now. Why would he keep something like that from her all these years?"

"Who knows, but he told her now. What reason would he have to lie to both of you?"

"Guilt," Lindsay said with conviction. "Clay said she lost her mind as soon as she heard. Started screaming about years of overtime my dad worked, how he never took her to see her family in Iowa, never let her buy a new car. Basically, she said the money should've been spent on something useful instead of a pathetic attempt to buy back the loyalty of someone who obviously didn't give a damn about anyone but herself."

"And you think that's what he's doing?"

"Maybe. I'm not really sure. He can only say so much and passing notes only goes so far." Lindsay sighed.

"Do what's right for you. Take the money. Don't take

it. But make the decision on your own. Once you start doing things to prove someone wrong or right, or to get even,
you've given them control. Don't worry about your finances.
If you need money, I can—"

"I'm not taking your money either. That's my whole
point. I want independence. Financially, and emotionally."

Blue paused. Judging by her absolute tone, she wanted
to overcome her problems on her own so he simply said, "I
have faith in you, but if you need—"

"Thanks, just your voice lifts my spirits, but let's change
the subject. You didn't call to listen to me whine. What's going on up there? Crowfoot and Donnie keeping you in line?
Let me guess, y'all ate possum innards and pork rinds for
supper."

He ignored her attempt at humor. He'd called to hear
her voice, to reach out to her for support, but now didn't
seem like the time to unload his troubles. She had enough to
deal with.

"Blue?"

He shook his head and answered. "Yeah."

"You okay?"

"I'm fine." He took a deep breath. He was supposed to
be the strong one. Here to support Lindsay in her battles. So
why did he feel such a need to tell her about the restlessness
gnawing at his bones—that while Briley slumbered and Ruby
calmly read, his heart wanted to explode. The walls. The ceiling. The very Texas sky was shrinking, pressing down on him.
He just wanted to unload the thoughts in his head on someone who might understand the pressure, the fear, the doubt.
He wanted to hear her say it would all be okay.

"I'm not at Crowfoot's. I came back ... To be with Briley."

"That's great." Her voice bubbled with enthusiasm. "I knew you could do it."

"I'm not sure I can."

"You're a good man Blue. Briley needs a father. You know that, or you wouldn't be there."

He stared out the kitchen window.  Nothing but blackness as far as he could see. The last few years his life had been just like the view. Dark, devoid of color or light. Only recently had the idea of dawn seemed real. Lindsay had provided him that warmth, that spark of golden promise. He had to trust her now and speak aloud the doubts he couldn't chase away on his own. "I wish you were here. By my side."

Before Lindsay could respond, he whispered, "I keep going back to the night Briley was born. It was so cold. A storm blew in that morning. I should've known Staci would go into labor, but Buster needed my help. All afternoon we worked to get his cattle squared away. I should've stayed with Staci. By the time I got home, she'd already started. The pain in her eyes scared me, but she said it wasn't time. The doctor had given her instructions when to head for the hospital."

Blue kept his eyes shut as he spoke. He could picture everything as if it were happening now.

"I tried to tell her the roads were slick. That we should go." He'd replayed the events of that night a thousand times in his head, but this was the first time he'd ever spoken them aloud. "Supper was already on the table so I sat. Pork chops. I didn't eat three bites. I couldn't. I was worried about her. About the baby."

He paused and opened his eyes before the memory became too real. Already, he could smell the grease in the air. See the blue veins in Staci's neck each time a contraction hit. Here he sat in Ruby's kitchen, but for all the world, it felt like the one he and Staci shared. He stared hard at the crayon drawings tacked to the refrigerator in an attempt to dislodge the all-too-familiar guilt and worry from his chest—to remind himself of his place in the present—to escape the past. But the memories bubbled to the surface

"The roads were slick from sleet. Ice pellets bounced off the windshield, but still I drove too fast. We had to go all the way to Amarillo. Almost forty miles. When I got off the highway, I slid right through the intersection. The streets were deserted, but I hit the far curb hard. Hard enough to make Staci gasp. That could've caused it. The doctor didn't think so. He said blood clots were always a concern with Staci's heart valve. She stopped taking the meds that were supposed to prevent her from clotting because she feared they would cause a miscarriage." Again, Blue stopped in an effort to gain control.

He was grateful to Lindsay for giving him this time. For waiting, listening, without asking questions.

"Maybe if I'd gotten her to the hospital quicker. I should've told Buster to take his cattle and go to hell. Or I could've insisted we leave right when I got home. Or I could have gotten us a motel room in Amarillo. I knew she was close." His words spilled out in rapid fire.

"Blue."

"Her doctor had already said it could come anytime."

"Blue."

"Or I could've made sure she took her medicine. Or—"

"Blue!"

He stopped when Lindsay shouted.

"Listen to yourself. Life isn't something you can second guess."

"Life," he sighed. "Who's talking about life? I'm talking

about death."

"Talk about it then," she said. "But you can't change the past, and you can't bring her back. It wasn't your fault. Believe the doctors, and don't pick through your memories for the bad. Find a few good things to hold onto. Let the rest go."

"I can't. I can't see her anymore. Not the way she was. I can see the way she looked on that cold table. I can see the way she looked in the casket. I can't see her smile, hear her laugh, remember all the things we planned to do." He gritted his teeth to hold back the tears that threatened to fall. "I keep looking at my watch and thinking right now I was staring at a plate full of pork chops, or right now is when we should have left." When Lindsay didn't say anything, he added in a dejected tone, "Maybe I'll feel better once tomorrow comes and goes."

"You won't."

Far from sympathetic, her words hit him hard.

"Not until you stop looking backward and deal with your emotions head-on."

"I am dealing with them," he growled. "I came back. Do you think I wanted to? Do you think this is easy?"

"Going back is not a miracle cure. I thought it would be for me, but it hasn't been. Getting here was hard, but staying has been even harder. I will get through. The next time I leave, it will be because I want to. Not because I have to."

He lowered his head. Lindsay was right. He had no reason to be angry with her. It was himself he was angry at, and this wasn't the first time.

"That first year I drank whiskey to forget. Each day I'd wake up feeling like shit, and I'd tell myself, don't do it. Don't break the seal on another bottle. My head would pound. My hands would shake. I'd get mad at something, or somebody.

I'd tell myself just one, to calm my nerves and chase away the hangover. After I gave in, there was no reason not to have a second, a third."

He heard Ruby get up from her chair. He followed the sound of her footsteps down the hall to Briley's room.

"That's where I'm at now. I know I should stay. I should've stayed all along, but now, because I've been gone so long, I don't know where to start. There's a voice in my head saying, go ahead, leave while everyone is asleep. They've gotten along fine without you. You've screwed up too many things to start over."

"Death you can't change," Lindsay said. "Your screw-ups you can. I'm trying. You're trying. Don't give up. Don't give in. I still believe in us. I still believe in our future. You have to ask yourself what it is you believe in."

"It's been a long time since I believed in anything."

"Me too."

They sat in silence for several long seconds. Connected by miles of wire. Connected by pain. Connected by hope.

"You're the only reason I came back," he finally said.

"No. I might have pushed you, but you went back because your heart told you to."

"People have been pushing me since Staci died. You opened my eyes. You led me back."

"I can say the same, but like I said, coming back was the easy part." Lindsay sighed. "It's figuring out what to do next that has me confused. I'm going to be lost when Clay goes back to school. I can't stay here in this house with my mother."

"You could come here. Stay with me. Or I could still park my trailer there."

"No. You have enough to worry about."

"Damn it, Lindsay, quit pushing me away. Don't you get it? I need you more than you'll ever need me. Let me come get you tonight. I can be there by morning."

"You need to be there for your daughter's birthday."

"I will be. We will be. We can drive straight back. You would give me strength to make it through tomorrow."

Lindsay heard the pain in his voice. He was struggling. Tomorrow would be even harder, but instead of offering support, she said, "Someday you'll look up, and I'll be on your porch, the way you were on mine, but right now I need time."

Blue cleared his throat. "You're forgetting. I have front steps. Not a porch and who knows where they'll be parked any given day."

"I have faith," Lindsay said. "That those steps will be parked where they need to be."

They talked a while longer but steered clear of dredging up more pain. Finally, Lindsay hung up and leaned against the kitchen wall feeling like a coward.

*Wait*, she'd said. *Give me time.*

For what? She had no idea. He'd laid his heart out, told her his every fear, his every regret, his every desire, and she'd pulled away. Done the very thing she accused him of back at Crowfoot's. Sure, he'd run away, but he came back. Tracked her down at her parents. Called her on the phone.

And now, when he needed her most, she wouldn't be there.

# 47

Ruby had long since gotten used to the bangs and creaks of the house's old pipes. Anymore she rarely noticed, but this morning her heart lurched with each and every rattle. As long as the noise continued she was safe, but she feared what would happen once the clatter stopped.

Lying in the dark, she tried to conjure levelheaded reasons for Blue to be up and in the shower already. After all, even as a child he'd been an early riser, up at dawn. But then again, he had to be bone-tired. Midnight had come and gone before she heard him go to bed last night, and he spent the night before driving in from Oklahoma and watching Briley sleep. Now here he was up at quarter till five.

Why?

Like an anvil on her chest, the question sat there. Heavy, steady, unyielding pressure.

He was leaving. He wanted to be gone before Briley awoke. He wouldn't come back. Not this time. Like blows from a hammer, Ruby's fears struck the shield of calm she so desperately tried to construct. There was no way to rationalize his behavior.

Tossing back the covers, she got out of bed and wrapped her robe around her, cinching the belt tight. She couldn't let him do it. Not on Briley's birthday. Blue might be her brother, but no way in hell she would allow him to dash in, build the hopes of an innocent child, only to sneak away in the night.

Pacing at the foot of her bed, she rehearsed her speech until she heard him leave the bathroom and make his way down the hall to the spare bedroom. She found him sitting on the edge of the bed, bent over pulling on his boots.

"What is it this time?" she demanded.

"Huh." He grunted and tugged at the leather finger pulls.

"Let me hear your reason this time. What's your excuse for breaking her heart?"

"What are you talking about?"

"The least you can do is stick around and tell her yourself. Don't leave your dirty work for me. I'm tired of defending you. Buster is one matter, but Briley deserves more."

"I'm not leaving."

"You're not?" she asked, suddenly feeling foolish.

"Well, I am, but I'll be back later," he added. "Soon as I take care of a few things."

Ruby narrowed her eyes. "At five in the morning?" She'd never known Blue to out and out lie to her.

"I want to catch Buster alone."

"You're going to his house?" she asked in disbelief.

He nodded. "Unless something has changed, he never goes anywhere until he drinks a pot of coffee. Without his hired hands around, I might have a chance to get a few things squared away. Buster's not quite the ass without an audience."

Hands on her hips she said, "I'm going to tell you just like I tell him. Just because the two of you want to act like a couple of puffed up bullfrogs doesn't mean I want to hear you croak about the other." When he didn't respond, she asked, "Want me to fix you breakfast?"

Blue shook his head and started to step around her. She caught his arm. "Promise me you'll be back for the party."

He looked her in the eye. "I'll be here."

Ruby turned away to hide tears she couldn't really explain. She made it halfway down the hall before he called her name. Without turning, she stopped.

"Why have you always stayed?" he asked.

"Stayed where?"

"Here. With me. The restaurant. With Briley. All your life, the whole world has gone to hell around you, and you've stayed. How do you do it?" There was a sadness, a resignation to his voice she'd never heard.

Turning to face him she said, "It's nothing to be proud of. I haven't stayed because I'm strong, or at a great sacrifice, I've stayed ... I stayed out of fear." Her eyes welled again and this time she hurried away knowing she would not be able to contain the tears.

Safe, inside the kitchen, she chastised herself for being silly. Even as the salty drops continued to flow, Ruby asked herself why. Her measly problems paled in comparison to most. She had no reason to bawl like a baby, yet here she was doing that very thing.

"What is it, Ruby? Tell me what's wrong."

"Nothing." She kept her back to her brother. Blue had more important matters to deal with than her flaky notions.

"What are you scared of?" He placed a hand on her shoulder.

She shook her head and tried to rein in her emotions, but the tears refused to stop their incessant flow. "Everything, nothing. I'm just crazy. I shouldn't have said anything. I don't even know what I'm talking about." She pulled away from his grasp and opened the refrigerator.

He stood there while she kept her head stuck inside. To cover her irrational actions, she pulled out a carton of eggs and turned around, this time with a brave face. "Sure I can't make you breakfast?"

Blue studied her for several long seconds. She nearly wilted under his worried gaze, but then he said, "I'm not going to pressure you, but you don't have to deal with everything alone. Not anymore. I'll be here when you need me."

"You have any idea what time it is?"

"Almost six," Lindsay answered.

"Not here," Janine groaned. "It's half past four, and in case you've forgotten, you're the one who likes to get up at the ass crack of dawn."

"I know it's early, but I couldn't sleep."

"Tell me something I didn't know." Janine sounded awful.

"I'm sorry. I'll let you go."

"Talk," Janine croaked. "I'm just tired and grouchy. I had a long night with Missy."

"No. You're tired. I'll call later, when—"

"Talk. Before I fall asleep."

"Okay, but remember, you asked for it." Lindsay took a deep breath and launched in. She relayed her latest conversation with Blue. Finally, she said, "I don't know what to do. I've been up all night thinking about him."

Janine said, "Let me get this straight. You don't want him to come to Oklahoma."

"No, he has obligations in Texas."

"Right. So go see him. It's obvious you want to."

"I can't."

Lindsay waited for Janine to ask why not. Or to say anything. The seconds ticked by. Nothing. "Are you asleep?"

"No. Thinking with my eyes closed."

Lindsay rubbed her temples. "Why is this so hard?"

"Because you're scared."

"Scared of what?"

Janine sighed. "His daughter. You're afraid of her. The way you always are with kids."

"I am not afraid of ... Wait, how did you know that? I never told you that."

"You didn't have to. I saw you leave the room anytime a baby or small child came on television. I saw you tremble every time Billy and Trish brought their baby in the café. I saw your reaction when I told you Missy was pregnant."

Lindsay shook her head. "All of that's true, but Briley doesn't affect me that way. Between staring at the girl's picture and searching for her present, it feels like I already know her. I'm not worried about meeting her. I want to."

"What about that hoochie-momma barrel slut. Maybe you're scared Blue is in love with her."

"Kacy Jo? She's not Blue's type."

"Thought you said they had some kind of past."

"I did, but I read too much into that. I was looking for a reason to be mad at him when I left Crowfoot's."

Janine yawned. "Maybe it's Blue. You're afraid he's not the man you think."

"No. I know what kind of man he is, and so do you."

"So, go."

"It's not that easy," Lindsay said.

"It's not that hard, either."

"Give me one reason why I should."

"He asked. He wants you to. You want to. I don't see the problem. You can't expect to find happiness if you're too afraid to look for it." Janine yawned again. "Go jog, do whatever it is you do, and call me back when you decide I'm right."

Lindsay hung up. She wasn't afraid to look for happiness. She'd already found it. The problem was convincing herself she deserved it.

Blue hadn't been there in a good while, but the habits of men like Buster never change. The codger would be at the kitchen table, coffee mug in hand, plotting his day. Just as Blue's senses told him when to attack another poker player and raise, he knew this was the time to seek out the surly bastard. A mangy blue heeler barked and danced around the pickup as Blue pulled up to the house. With each yelp, the dog emitted a white cloud of breath. Buster would know he had company. Most likely he'd peg the visitor as one of his worthless two-bit cowboys. Blue walked around to the back and knocked on the kitchen door. In times past, he would've just opened it and gone in, but the days of him being that welcome were long gone.

"Yeah!"

He stepped inside.

The old man looked up. Steam arose from the mug in his hand. His eyes showed no sign of surprise, but he'd always been a hell of a poker player in his own right. Blue spent more than one night in a hotel room losing to him. The lessons would've proved costly had they played for more than toothpicks.

"What do you want?"

"We need to talk."

Buster took a sip of coffee. "You might. I don't."

Blue gritted his teeth. He'd known this would be hard, nevertheless he pressed on, determined not to lose focus or show the least sign of anger. "What's the story on my house?"

"Your house?" Buster chuckled. Not with any sense of cheerfulness, but with sardonic disdain. "My mind must be slipping. Last I knew you didn't have a house."

"Save the sarcasm. How much do you want for it?"

Buster closed one eye, set the chipped mug down, and said, "I don't give a damn about the house. Should've torn it down before now, but my land is another story. That piece of ground has been in my family since Texas was its own country. I gave you ten acres for your wedding. Your choice. Remember?" When Blue didn't reply Buster added, "'Course you do. You had that house built right on the rim of the canyon. You and Staci could see forever."

"I screwed up. Is that what you want me to say?"

"Most people would give their left nut for a place like that." The old man blazed on. "Especially starting out. But not the great Blue Riggins. Oh, that Riggins' pride. You took everything as a birthright. Like God bestowed you with all that talent, with a pretty wife. You couldn't handle reality. Life. Ain't no such thing as a birthright. Ain't nothing free in this world."

The muscles in Blue's stomach contracted. His fists clinched. "You know all about birthrights, don't you? You never had to work for any of this." He spread his arms out wide to encompass the house, land, everything.

Buster slammed his fist down on the table. The coffee sloshed over the rim, forming a dark pool on the scarred

Formica top. "I've damn sure worked to keep it. Don't you think I wanted to give up after my wife's accident? You think it was easy to see her like that? To spoon-feed her? To know I'd never have a child of my own?"

"If you loved her so much, what were you doing with my sister?"

"That wasn't something I planned." Buster folded his arms across his chest and smiled. This time a hint of happiness slipped into the expression. "I found Ruby by accident. I was looking for companionship. There were times I had to get away and talk to someone who could talk back. I wasn't looking for someone to love. But I sure as hell found her."

Buster heaved himself up and found a rag to clean his mess. "I could've stuck my head in the sand. Ignored the world. But to what good? You lost Staci. I know it hurt like hell, but she gave you something in return. Be thankful you didn't have to sit by and watch her go an inch at a time. We shoot horses and cattle to put them down, but when it comes to folks we love, we force applesauce down their throats and pat them on the hand while they wither and die."

The truth of the speech sobered Blue. One visit to the nursing home with Buster had been more than he could handle. Blue couldn't condemn the other man's behavior after years of witnessing his wife's decline.

"Now the same thing is happening with Ruby."

Blue's heart lurched. Was his sister dying? Is that what she was scared of, why she'd started crying? "What's wrong with Ruby?"

"I'm losing her. I don't know why, but I can sense it. The day after I got back from Oklahoma I asked her to marry me. Hell, I practically demanded it and still she said no."

"Is she sick?"

"That woman is healthy as they come. I just can't reach her anymore." Buster shook his head before giving Blue a good long look. "Tell me the whole story. What's going on in your head? What are you going to do with that house?"

"Live."

"Alone?"

"No, with Briley."

Buster narrowed his eyes. "What about that tramp I found you with?"

Blue raised his hand and pointed a finger straight at the other man's face. "Lindsay is no tramp."

"What is she?"

"What she is, is none of your business, but I wouldn't be here if not for her. I can't say what will happen, but long as I have a say, she'll be a part of my life."

"So." Buster nodded with the smugness of a man who thinks he knows it all. "Your world crumbles and you leave us to pick up the pieces. Now you find some new gal that smiles and tells you how great you are and suddenly we're supposed to throw our arms open and welcome you back.  All because you got your willy wet."

Blue swallowed his pride. He refused to argue, not that he could if he wanted. "I just want my house. You gave me the land. I built the place. I abandoned it. There's no excuse for the way I handled it. So name your price."

"I don't want or need your money. You turned your back on all of us when you signed that place over to me and walked away. You shit on me, on Ruby, on Briley, and on yourself. Money doesn't erase that kind of stench. Only way to get out of a cesspool is start digging." Buster folded his arms across his chest. "Grab a shovel and prove a few things. Then we'll talk."

"What do you want me to prove? I'm back. I'm not going anywhere. That house is a part of me, a part of Briley."

"A part of Briley? She's never lived there. You made sure of that when you ran."

"That place was her mother's dream. I want Briley to know that."

"Don't pin your guilt on me. This ain't the poker table. You can't bluff me."

"Bluff?" Blue shook his head. "I told you. Name a price. You want every cent I got, it's yours. I have nothing else to offer."

Buster scratched his head. Slowly, he began to nod. "Tell you what. Hit the circuit again, qualify for the finals, and the place is yours. I'll sign the—"

"No. That's part of me is gone. I couldn't do it even if I wanted. And I've already spent too much time away from Briley."

"So, what are you going to do? Hang around here? Get a job at the feedlot? A man has to make a living."

"I have enough to take care of Briley and me."

"Not if you give it all to me."

"I can make more. I can play a tournament here and there. Fly in and out and only be gone a few days a month."

"Not without a stake," Buster countered.

"Someone will stake me for a share of what I win."

"You're mighty damn confident. What if you don't win?"

"Damn it, Buster!" Blue raised his voice despite his best efforts to take the abuse. "I'm not you. I don't claim to have all the answers. I'm trying to sort things out—to find a routine, a place to start over. If I have to work at the feedlot, so be it. I'll shovel shit in your barn if that's what you want, but I won't abandon Briley again."

"Hmmm." The old man folded his arms, obviously proud of himself for rattling Blue. "You already quit once. I'm not sure you got enough sand to stick in the saddle."

"Maybe you're afraid I do?" Blue took the opposite seat at the table. "You want to call me out. Let's do it right. Get out those toothpicks you love so much and divvy them up. We can play hold'em for a couple of hours and see who comes out the better man."

"You'd like that." Buster smiled. "A man with nothing to lose is always willing to gamble, but what's in it for me?"

"What do you want?"

"I already told you."

"Pick again. I'm not going back to the rodeo."

The cagey rancher didn't respond for several long seconds. He used the time to study Blue through narrowed eyes. Finally, he said, "What's Ruby think of all this?"

"She doesn't know why I came out here."

Buster eased forward in his seat. "She mention me?"

"Yeah." Blue nodded and leaned forward, knowing he was setting Buster up.

"What did she say?"

The eagerness on the old timer's face made it hard for Blue to keep a straight face. "She wanted to know why I was coming out here so early."

"And?"

Blue leaned back and smiled. "I told her you wouldn't be half the asshole you normally are without an audience."

Several seconds passed before the rancher's expression changed and then it was slight, but disappointment, not anger, darkened Buster's face. Blue had expected and hoped for anger. Instead, for the second time, he almost felt sorry for the bastard. Not wanting to ruin things for his sister, he added, "She defended you. Told me she wasn't going to put up with me croaking about you."

"She tells me the same thing. Wish I had a dollar for every time she called me a puffed-up old bullfrog for saying you were worthless. Lazy. A weak-minded quitter. A—"

"I get the idea."

Buster took another drink of coffee. Grimacing as he swallowed, he pushed back his chair and stood. "Never could stomach this stuff lukewarm." He poured the contents in the sink and reached up to the cabinet. "Want a cup?"

"Yeah." Blue didn't look forward to the notoriously bad coffee, but he realized this was as close to a peace offering as he would ever get.

"This hasn't been easy on Ruby you know." Buster kept his back turned as he poured. "She's smack in the middle. Between me and you. Between wanting you to come back, and not wanting to lose Briley. She'd never admit it, but she worries you'll show up and take Briley away. She loves that girl."

"I'm not fool enough to think I can do this alone. Briley. Me. We both need Ruby."

Setting the mugs down, Buster resumed his position at the table. "What about this new gal? What if she don't take to raising someone else's daughter?"

"Lindsay has her own troubles, but she knows all about Briley. She's the one who convinced me to come back." Blue tried not to shudder as he drank the bitter brew.

"What's her secret? How'd she do what no one else could?"

"She made me feel ashamed." Even now, Blue could taste the acrid flavor of guilt at the back of his throat.

"Hell, we all tried that."

Blue stared at the old and beaten down tabletop. "Everybody else told me to be ashamed, she made me feel it."

He would never reveal the secrets of her past to anyone just to make them understand, but Lindsay knew the other side of the coin. She put Staci's sacrifice into perspective. The rawness with which Lindsay told him of her past had finally broken through his grief. She left no doubt, that given the chance, she would give her life to bring her child back.

Without ever saying it, she forced him to see life overshadowed death. Staci knew that when she made her choice. She knew a part of her would live on forever in Briley, and it scared Blue to think he'd almost missed that.

Briley had never known her mother, yet Staci's spirit, the very spirit he'd chased all the way to Idaho, struck him the instant he walked into her room. That's why he sat up all night watching her.

Now it was everywhere. Her smile, her expressions, even her walk bespoke of her mother. Yet there was that little extra something that made Briley stand on her own. That's what would keep him home. His heart ached when he thought about not seeing who his daughter would become, the person she would grow into, the true value of Staci's gift.

When Blue finally lifted his head, he was surprised to see Buster had moved to the window above the sink. Staring out at pink-tinged horizon, the man simply waited.

"Wish I could explain how she made me come to understand, but I can't." Blue spoke to let Buster know he appreciated the time and solitude the perceptive codger had allowed him. "I'll just say fate dealt us the same hand of cards."

"Life's not a damn poker game, Blue. You can't fold just because you got shitty cards."

"I know that, now. And yeah, I should've known it all along, but meeting Lindsay was my river card. I was down to my last chance, when she showed up. She saved me."

The minutes ticked by. Buster stood, staring out into the gathering light. Finally he said, "Screw up again and you'll only think I was an asshole before."

He glanced over his shoulder and gave Blue a look. "You might as well move back in that place. Been nothing but trouble. Tried to rent it for a while but the idiots charred half a section. Burning trash on the windiest day of the year. Least you got more sense than that. Kids got in last Halloween. Broke a couple of windows and painted up one wall."

"I stopped out there the night I drove in. I'll get the place cleaned up. This time, I'll carry my end."

Buster nodded. "I do have one favor."

Blue waited. Things had gone better than he'd ever expected. As long as the request had nothing to do with the rodeo, he'd try to accommodate.

"That sister of yours is as mule-headed as you. Tell her she doesn't need to kill herself at that damn fool café. Tell her I need her worse than any hungry traveler. Tell her I know I'm a hard-headed old bastard, but I'll wait forever as long as I still have a chance. Maybe she'll listen to you. I've told her a thousand times, but it never does any good."

He said all of this as the sun broke over the horizon and bathed the kitchen in a pale orange glow. Blue knew how hard it was to put your heart out on the line, so he walked over and stood beside the other man. The three women in his life, Lindsay, Briley and Ruby all came to mind. The lessons they had taught him. He patted Buster on the shoulder. "How about we don't tell Ruby anything? Let's figure out a way to show her."

# 48

Nervous anticipation danced in Lindsay's stomach as she pulled away from the café. The directions were easy to follow. After a whirlwind day, she was close.

Chalk-like dust billowed behind the car. The big black cows grazing out in the fields never lifted their heads as she sped along the rough caliche dirt road. The flat terrain allowed her to spot the house at least half a mile before she turned down the narrow drive.

Lindsay opened the car door and stood there as the dry Texas dust settled around her feet. She could taste the powder on her tongue as she looked the place over. A board covered the house's big front window. Spindly weeds and pale yellow tumbleweeds filled the flowerbeds along the porch. Paint hung off the eaves in withered strips.

"It's a pretty little place. You can't miss it," Ruby had said when she gave Lindsay directions. Buster had replied, "Ain't all that pretty anymore, but it's the last house on that road. You can't miss it."

They were both right. Lindsay could see what once had been. She could imagine the wood scraped clean and freshly painted, she could imagine bright tulips and pansies pushing up through the brown soil, and the view of the sunset out the front window would be spectacular.

"Nice car."

She jumped. Caught up in her gawking, she hadn't noticed Blue, but looking around she still couldn't find him.

"Up here."

There he was on the roof, his broad shoulders and face silhouetted against the fading sky. In the waning light of pre-dusk, she couldn't make out his features, but still she detected a hint of a smile in his voice.

"You got a thing for roofs don't you," she said.

"Kind of like you got a thing for changing your mind. Don't move." Blue disappeared to the other side of the roof.

Curious, Lindsay leaned against the fender of the car she'd bought this morning with part of the money from her dad. She'd said goodbye to her mom through the bedroom door without so much as a response, but in the miles between Oklahoma and here that no longer seemed important Some things simply never changed.

The nursing home had been her last stop before leaving. She'd feared taking the money would feel like a settlement for her grief, but the joy in her father's eyes made her see he simply wanted one last chance to give her something. Without strings. She'd told her dad she'd come back to visit when she could. He'd squeezed her hand and said he hoped so.

Lindsay would keep that promise as well as the one she made her brother. Clay wanted her to attend at least one of his baseball games, and she could hardly wait for spring and the chance to see him power a homer over the fence. But for now, this is where she needed to be. No, wanted to be.

Blue reappeared. This time with a ladder. Lowering it to the ground, he said, "Climb up, I want to show you something."

Her steps rang like a tin bell as she made her way up the aluminum rungs. Blue held out his hand when she reached the top. "Close your eyes."

This eagerness was a side of him she'd never seen. The idea of walking around blind on a roof scared her just a bit, but she trusted Blue. Eyelids closed, she reached for his hand. He led her to the peak of the roof line before he said, "Okay, open them."

Lindsay gasped. Only a rock's throw from the back of the house the ground split open and dropped into a huge crevice. Driving along the flat ranch land Lindsay had never expected to find such a huge and spectacular canyon. She stared dumbfounded. The setting sun cast the jagged landscape in shadows, yet its rugged beauty was unmistakable.

"You should see the sunrise over that ridge," Blue said, as if he'd been reading her mind.

"It's beautiful."

Blue gave her hand a gentle squeeze. "This is an off-shoot of Palo Duro Canyon, second in size only to the Grand Canyon."

The pitch of the roof, combined with the fact she was staring down into a huge opening in the ground, made her a bit dizzy. Or it could be that she had been going non-stop like a crazed woman since early this morning. "Can we sit?"

He let go of her hand and held her arm just above the elbow. Every third shingle was either missing or sticking straight up so Blue made a place for them by flattening a couple of wayward shingles with the toe of his boot. A coyote yapped from somewhere down in the canyon.

Blue turned to her. "I'm glad you're here, but hope I didn't make you feel like you had to come."

"I didn't come because I had to," she answered. "I came

because I wanted to."

After a few minutes of silence, Blue said, "When the clouds are right, those rocks down there turn pink just before it gets too dark to see."

"I'd like to see that."

"I want you to. Briley has never seen it either. She might not even care."

"She will if you do."

A second coyote, farther off, answered the other. Two lonely hunters calling to one another.

"She's even more beautiful than her picture," Lindsay said. "I met her at the café. You should've seen her smile when I told her I came special, just for her birthday. She said her daddy was coming to her party too."

Blue's eyes widened. "Did she actually say Daddy, or did she call me by my name?"

"She said Daddy."

He leaned closer and kissed Lindsay on the cheek. "I needed to hear that." He pulled her closer. "And I needed to see you. Thanks for being here."

"This is where I want to be," she answered.

Blue turned those dark eyes toward her and in them Lindsay saw a tenderness in the depths as he said, "Lindsay, I love you."

She bit her lip to keep from crying until she trusted her own voice to say, "I love you too."

They sat for a few minutes in the fading light until Lindsay said, "Your sister is worried you won't be there for the party. She asked me to bring you back."

Blue pressed his lips to Lindsay's before saying, "You already have."

# Questions and Topics for Discussion

1. Some people believe the first sentence of a novel sets the tone. Would you agree or disagree, based on this book?

2. This novel examines various relationships between men and women. Lovers, siblings, and father/daughter with Blue and Ruby's roles blurring the lines between the latter two. How do you think Blue's approach to life and love was shaped by Ruby's dual roles?

3. How did running away transform Lindsay's life? Do you think she would've found happiness sooner had she stayed and faced her pain, rather than hiding from it as she moved in and out of relationships and towns?

4. The novel implies Staci took a known risk to better the odds of birthing a healthy baby. Do you think it was this "gamble" that pushed Blue to become a professional gambler, or is his latest occupation more attuned to who he truly is as a person?

6. Which character in the book did you like best? Why?

7. Which character did you like least? Why?

8. Ruby and Buster's relationship was complicated from the beginning. How did the facts about his bedridden wife shape your opinions of Buster, and did that opinion change by the end of the novel? If so, how?

# <u>Questions and Topics for Discussion</u>

9. Idaho, Cripple Creek, Oklahoma, Texas and the roads between. How did the author use setting to help tell this story?

10. Lindsay grew up in a conventional family setting with two parents and one sibling. Blue on the other hand was a late in life baby with mostly distant siblings, an elderly mother, and no father present. How do you think this formed Blue and Lindsay's ideals in regards to family and relationships?

11. Which character do you feel grew more by the end of the novel, Blue or Lindsay? In what way did they most change?

12. In Blue's poker game of choice, Texas Hold 'Em, the River card is the last chance to make or break a hand. Do you beleive Blue and Lindsay were each other's river card? Or would one or both of them have found resolution and happiness either way?

13. What do you think the author's purpose was in writing this book? What ideas was he trying to get across?

# Acknowledgments

I could not have written this novel without the help of my writing brethren, Ryan McSwain, Jonathan Baker, Mike Akins, and Monica Pinion. Y'all were the critique partners, cheerleaders, and friends that oversaw the final push and I can't thank each of you enough.

Through many revisions these people weighed in and helped me dial in the characters and story. Hilary Sares, Vicki Schoen, Jennifer Archer, Val Conrad, Caron Guillo, Andrea Huskey, Kathy Thoms, Brenda Linsky, Kimberly Lynne, Kathy Lundburg, Tony Hill, and Merry Monteleone. Thank you for reading and commenting. Danielle Lincoln Hanna is a great editor any writer would be lucky to call upon and I am grateful for her work spent honing this narrative as I closed in on the final draft.

As I worked to bring out that final draft I realized I was close, but still needed the sharp eye of a shrewd editor I could trust to deliver the truth without trampling upon my writing voice. That person was Erica Orloff, and there is not an editor alive that does it better. Thanks Erica.

I believed in this book for many years, but it was the faith these backers put behind both me and the story that finally brought it from manuscript form to the completed novel. Thank you so much Alex Keto, Ryan McSwain, Kathy Lundburg, Jere Tooley, Jarrod Johnson, John Wilsterman, Stephen Parish, Jennifer Archer, Keith Bartlett, Sandy Carlile, Crystal Phares, Dan Johnson, Aaron Sage, Betty Grubb, Oral Morgan, Charlotte Rush, Eric Stallsworth, Janet Morgan,  Kim Francis, Drew Kennedy, James Beasley, Steve Tunnel, Vicky Schoen, Marcy McKay, Kathy Martinez, Wes Reeves, Melanie Swiftney, Lorraine Broertjes, Kimberly Black, Jon Lovitt, Lisa Pawlowski, Isayah Henry, 22collectiv, PJ Pronger, Larry Smith, Jeff Dennis, Adam Gonzales, Manan Kacheria, Beth Smith, Misty Manasco, Ray Ashton Jan Bruckner, Beth Moore, Marcus Briscoe, Michelle Cwiertney, Connie Erwin, JR Harris, Deborah Ellitt-Upton, Colleen Gareau, Criss Roberts, Brad McBride, Julie Page, Michael Stephens, Tony Hill, Mark Terry, Rebecca Vinson, Jason Adams, Catharine Brandes, Mike Akins, Debra Hathaway, Shirley Cameron, Patrick & Kayla Parsons, Andrea Huskey, Mark Ferry, Scott & Angie Lessard, Reid Kerr, Shauna Roberts, Liz Davidson, Karin Huddleston, Jeff Hibbetts, Andrea Hostetler, Sarah Laurenson, Jenny Ursini, Monica Reha, Mica Stone, and Lee Richardson.

Both this novel and Barbadum Books would not exist without the kindness and faith from the above individuals.

Thank y'all so much.

# About the Author

A native Texan, Travis now lives in the Southern California with his wife, a slew of kids, and a horde of critters. He writes both Women's Fiction and Humor. Travis is best known for his comedic coming-of-age memoir, THE FEEDSTORE CHRONICLES, and his long running blog where he pontificates, about both writing and life -- which for him means bacon, beer, and books.

# Other Works Available

The Feedstore Chronicles in print, ebook, and audio.
Twisted Roads in print and ebook
Whispers available now exclusively on Kindle
Hemingway w/Dan Johnson in Audio and Print